Red House

Joss Stirling

One More Chapter
a division of HarperCollins*Publishers*
The News Building
1 London Bridge Street
London SE1 9GF

www.harpercollins.co.uk

HarperCollins*Publishers*
1st Floor, Watermarque Building, Ringsend Road
Dublin 4, Ireland

This paperback edition 2021

First published in Great Britain in ebook format by
HarperCollins*Publishers* 2020

A catalogue record for this book
is available from the British Library

ISBN: 9780008422646

This novel is entirely a work of fiction.
The names, characters and incidents portrayed in it are
the work of the author's imagination. Any resemblance to
actual persons, living or dead, events or localities is
entirely coincidental.

Set in Birka by Palimpsest Book Production Ltd, Falkirk
Stirlingshire

Printed and bound in Great Britain by CPI Group (UK) Ltd,
Croydon CR0 4YY

*In loving memory of Ann, who loved Oxford,
children's books, gardens, and thrillers.*

'When the holly bears a berry, as blood it is red'

Sans Day Carol

Chapter 1

Leo

The gardener got more than she bargained for when she spread bark chips around the holly tree. She'd intended to keep down weeds; instead she'd unearthed a body.

DI Leo George stood over the human remains that the forensic team had carefully excavated. The upmarket houses of Central North Oxford were seldom on his radar; reports from this area were on the occasional break-in, very rarely a violent crime. It was an area of millionaires, educational institutes and private school boarding houses: quiet, well-run, and careful not to attract the attention of the authorities.

'Ugly bugger, isn't he?' said DS Harry Boston, stomping up to join Leo. He looked like a polar bear rearing on hind legs, thanks to his huge white coveralls. They were not kind to those who carried extra weight around their middles.

'So would anyone who has been mulch for a year,' said Leo.

'I bow to your gardening expertise, Inspector.'

'Oddly, I don't use bodies to fertilise mine.' Leo's voice was distant as he moved around to get another angle and make way for the photographer.

'Then who did here? Some Monty Don wannabe turned murderous?' asked Harry. 'I'd say it's taking green burial way too far.'

Leo didn't respond, though Harry's question was exactly the one they would have to investigate. He watched the forensic team gently ease free an arm, bone clad in a tight brown gauntlet that had once been skin. He was reminded of the peat bog man from Tollund, ancient witness to the old violence of human sacrifice. What sins had this corpse been made to bear? There were the remains of a watch and rings – they should help with identification. If you told yourself this was an archaeological dig, then the sight of the radius peeking through leathery flesh became less grisly. The body certainly wasn't fresh. It would take the pathologist a while to work out age but from the decomposition that had already taken place, Leo was guessing at least a year. Yet neither was it a really ancient burial like Tollund. Last time he'd checked, Iron Age people hadn't worn jeans with a leather belt and eagle buckle. The size and clothing suggested male, but with the face skeletal, collapsed nose and a grinning row of teeth, they would need confirmation on that too. The hair was long and wispy black so that gave scant clue.

He turned away, having seen enough. 'Where's the gardener who found the body, Harry?'

'I've a constable sitting with her in the kitchen. Her name's Marigold Green. Talk about names deciding your career choice.' Harry followed Leo up the path towards the detached house. Made of golden brick with red accents, steeply gabled roofs, and tall chimneys, it was one of the biggest houses in central Oxford still in private ownership. From the front you couldn't tell that it had a large garden to the rear stretching over half an acre to back on to the garden of the house in the next road. This plot had been landscaped to within an inch of its life: immaculate lawns, tidy gravel paths, clipped and sculpted trees. Even the holly had been shaped into a form like a Victorian lady's crinoline skirt, which, Leo supposed, suited the age in which the house was built. The berries formed a red pattern against the green reminding him of a William Morris print. To his eyes, however, this house didn't so much have a garden as a showroom. It was barren of wildlife, blasted into extinction by the frequent application of weedkillers. That was the only way to stop the encroachment of daisies and dandelions that would arrive in their droves from the nearby park and meadows. He preferred a messier, healthier garden himself. The only odd note was the fallen fence panel at the end of the garden, like a rotten tooth in a Hollywood star's smile. He'd have to find out how long that had been like that as it potentially gave another point of access.

Stripping off their coveralls on the terrace, Leo and Harry entered through French doors into the kitchen. This too had been renovated so that all period detail had long since disappeared: the surfaces were grey granite, the floor white marble, the fittings space-age.

'Miss Green?' Leo approached the woman sitting at the glass-topped kitchen table. She was the only thing out of place in this house with her muddy corduroys and dirt-encrusted hands. Bundled up in a fleece, she had a solid, strong frame, which went with her profession, and a crop of greying auburn hair held back in a scarf. This was no landscape designer who gardened only on software; this was the person who got the job done.

'It's *Mrs* Green actually,' the lady replied, cradling the mug of tea that had been made for her.

'My apologies, Mrs Green. I'm Inspector George of Thames Valley CID. I know you've already spoken to my officers, but would you mind telling me again exactly what happened here this morning?'

The lady sighed. 'Well, Inspector, I came in for my usual visit. I come once a week in the summer months, once a fortnight in winter. To be honest, there's not much to do here as the owner keeps the garden very low-maintenance – no flowers or fruit and veg to speak of.'

'I noticed.'

She grimaced. 'Not my choice, but I'm only the contractor. The customer is always right.' She let the ironic tone do the arguing for her. 'Anyway, I decided to put bark down around the holly tree and the bay on the left side of the garden, keep it tidy-looking. He likes his sculpted trees, does Mr Chernov.'

'Is Mr Chernov in residence?'

She shrugged. 'I've never met him. I get my instructions through an agent who finds all of us.'

'Us?'

'The staff – cleaning crew, gardeners, household maintenance people.'

'What's the name of the agent?'

'Glass Tower Services. They've an office in Summertown, but I think their headquarters is in London somewhere. They arrange for the purchase of properties for overseas clients like this one, and then run them for them. I usually deal with a

4

lady called Heather, but we've also never met, only spoken on the phone. I imagine they come to check we're doing the job but I really don't know.'

Leo nodded to Harry, who went out to contact the agent. 'Thank you. Please, carry on with what happened.'

'I decided to turn the soil before putting down the bark, take up a few stray bits of self-seeded couch grass and herb Robert – there's not much in a garden like this so I don't have to do it very often. I worked my way towards the holly tree – in fact, I almost stopped before reaching it but there were some holes that made me keep going. Something had been digging up the border.'

'Any idea what?'

'A dog maybe, or fox. I think we can guess why now. I was just going to even it out. It only took a couple of spadefuls and I came across a shoe. It struck me as odd, as this garden was completely scraped clean and new topsoil laid after the building work was done, so it couldn't be a discard from years back.'

'Do you know when that was?'

'About eight years ago? It was bought by developers from one of the theological colleges. It used to house students but Luther Hall sold it to sort out problems with their pension pot – a little goldmine it turned out to be. Anyway, the developers renovated it from multiple occupancy back to a single family residence and that was when Mr Chernov bought it. He had kids at a private school near here so used it when he visited them.'

Leo looked around the many-roomed house with its exclusive furnishings and fittings. 'In effect, it was an occasional weekend place?'

Mrs Green cradled her mug. 'I know. Crazy, isn't it? One has to wonder where the money came from.' She gave a cough in which Leo thought he heard the word 'Putin'. He had to smile. 'Still,' she continued, 'I'd prefer to be me with my little cottage in Eynsham rather than an oligarch with so much money they know the price of everything and the value of nothing.'

Leo agreed with that. What was the point of owning a big plot of land like this that you didn't even keep as a garden? 'You found a shoe?'

Closing her eyes briefly, she swallowed against bile. 'Yes. I knelt down to pull it out and realised it was still attached. That was when I called 999.'

'And you did no more digging?'

'I didn't disturb the body any further, Inspector, I promise. I watch the TV. I know that the best thing a member of the public can do when they find something is stop and report it.'

'You did exactly the right thing. I think that's all we need from you now but if you'd leave me with your details in case we have follow-up questions?'

She felt in the pocket of her corduroys and pulled out a card with a marigold logo. 'Here you go.'

'Thank you, Mrs Green. Before you go, do you know any of the neighbours?'

'Round here?' She gave him an incredulous look. 'They're not very friendly and hardly my type. I think next door is a study centre for artificial intelligence, Lord knows what that really means, and beyond that there's a family – Asian of some sort. Hong Kong Chinese maybe? There's a little man in a big college-owned house who says hello – not sure of his name.

Paul Something. The house is in flats and he keeps the graduate tenants in check. Then there're the Prices at fourteen
opposite – formidable couple, influential locally. They run the
North Oxford Protection Society. They don't talk to my kind.'

'Your kind?'

'Non-resident staff. They think houses like this take away
the distinctive character of the area. They see me as the enemy.
Oh, there is one exception in the red house that shares the
boundary at the back. There's a really sweet girl who's just
started house-sitting, taken over from the last one. He rarely
said a thing beyond hello even when I offered him cuttings.
Anyway, this nice one always says hi and stops for a chat when
she sees me, unlike everyone else round here.' Mrs Green
smiled. 'Well, she would, wouldn't she, because she's normal.'

'Normal?'

'Not stinking rich. It insulates people, money. Makes them
feel better than the rest of us.'

'And yet you took the job?'

'Do I look stupid? Ridiculous amounts of money for
keeping the lawn like a bowling green – it's a good gig.' She
got up and put the mug in the sink. She gave it a quick rinse
and turned it upside down on the drainer – possibly the first
time it had been used, from the look of the sparkling surface.
'But money can't buy you everything. Doesn't stop there being
a body buried at the bottom of the garden, does it?'

As a final word, it was a good one, thought Leo, watching
her drive off in her flower-decorated van.

Chapter 2

Jess

I was in the middle of unwrapping the crib scene from the tissue paper when the realisation struck me.

'I'm officially single. Consciously uncoupled – or decoupled, like a railway carriage. In the sidings.' I stared down at the baby in the manger and wrapped him back up again. Too soon. He wasn't due for four weeks.

'What's that, dear?' My colleague, Jennifer, grappled a rope of Christmas lights, like a little tweed-clad Tarzan wrestling a skinny python. The snake was winning.

'I'm thirty-one, but for the first time, I'll be alone at Christmas.' I placed Mary in the stable behind the empty crib. The pieces were an exquisite hand-carved set from Switzerland, gift of some Victorian benefactor. Anything more modern or plastic wouldn't fit in these surroundings so it was brought out from storage every year and I had been given the responsibility of arranging it. This was what my life had become: temp job holder of lowly positions, aspiring private investigator, relationship disaster area – all wrapped up untidily like the Secret Santa no one claims.

'Oh, Jess, but what about your mother – and your sister?' asked Jennifer. 'Can't you spend it with them?'

'You mean tag along on someone else's Christmas? Sorry, but that's a kind of torture for me. They don't mean to but they treat me like the family failure.'

'I'm sure they don't see you like that.' Jennifer didn't know my relatives. My silence must've tipped her off that her optimism was misplaced. 'What did you do last year?'

'Last year I had a guy, Drew, and we did the cute couple Christmas thing – his-and-her stockings, breakfast in bed – it was lovely, but then it all became very George Michael.' Drew was now in a relationship with his yoga instructor and spending his Christmas in the Austrian alps. I wasn't bitter and jealous, no, not at all.

Jennifer wriggled free of the electric cord. With her spiked white hair, she looked like she had been electrocuted, but fortunately the tree lights weren't plugged in yet. 'Oh, Jess, I remember exactly how you feel. When I was in my twenties I lost the man who I thought was the one for me, and I struggled for a few Christmases. But then Neil came along, and the twins, and now the grandkids. George Michael was right – save it for someone special.'

She didn't really know, did she? I thought darkly. When she'd been alone there'd been no Instagram, no Snapchat, no Facebook telling her every other second how fabulous everyone else's life was.

Jennifer gave up on the knot and plugged in the lights to check they were worth the bother. LED bulbs flashed in a frantic twinkle. 'Jesus! Sorry, Lord.' Jennifer bobbed a head at the cross that hung over the altar of the college chapel.

'That's not very St Nicks, more Ibiza nightclub.' I found

the control and switched to constant. Why was that the seventh setting? So easy to overshoot and go back to the disco beat. Did the makers do that on purpose to annoy, a kind of passive-aggressive payback for having to sell Christmas stuff all year round? 'I think this one, or the slow fade setting, is better.' Bothered by loose strands as I stooped, I plaited my hair away from my face, securing the end with an elastic tie I kept on my wrist. Thanks to my blonde colouring, I'd always been one of the angels in my primary school nativity – a bit of serious miscasting. 'Explain again why we do this and not the students? I mean, it's for their benefit we decorate the college so early, isn't it?'

'Thanks to our eight-week terms, they'll all be home before Christmas really arrives. I think of it as our Advent decorations.' Jennifer turned off power to the lights and began the painstaking task of sorting out the snarls. 'I don't put up my own decorations at home until mid-December. What about you?'

'Not sure I'll bother this year. It's not exactly my house, is it?' I pulled a face at the glum-looking shepherd. Life must've been tough out on the hillsides to make him look quite so stressed. Silly sheep, predatory wolves and then an angelic choir: it must've been a strain to keep track of everything.

'Oh, but you must!' Jennifer sounded scandalised. Over the month we had worked together, I knew that Jennifer saw the holiday season as one treat after another.

'Why? Who'll even know? It's just me, Flossie and a Tesco turkey-meal-for-one.'

Jennifer gave a humph of disapproval. 'You'll know, that's

who. And I said that you were welcome to join us. And what about your friend Cory?'

And feel like the fifth wheel? 'No one will want me barging into the midst of things. And Cory is trying it with her ex-husband there, for the sake of the kids. I'd just complicate things. It's a family day. I'll be fine.'

'I don't like to think about you like that! You, alone with that scruffy mutt of yours.'

'I'm in the most fabulous house in Oxford, so don't pity me. And Flossie's not a mutt.' She totally was but someone had to fight Flossie's corner. A cocker spaniel, with the biggest brown eyes ever, Flossie had had the misfortune to belong to a killer. I'd adopted her, then left her temporarily with my ex-boyfriend's parents, and finally bitten the bullet to find a housing situation that would allow me to resume my responsibilities as her owner. Cory said taking a house-sitting job from a concierge agency so I could keep Flossie with me in Oxford, had been a blatant attempt to fill the yawning void left by my lack of significant other. She knew me so well, but so what? I could no longer bear my own company and thought I could at least give the dog a lucky break. It was a bit of a lucky break for me too, being paid to do little more than occupy a mansion. There was money in that – who knew?

A twist of old newspaper unravelled to reveal the innkeeper and his wife, both with the wide-eyed surprise of people shocked out of their humdrum lives by events beyond their control. Something about their united stance reminded me of my sister and her husband, who looked on my harum-scarum life with similar horror. They loved their quiet existence on their Cotswold farm and there was no more devoted couple in England. They looked after their kids and our mother too – quite the little family support network.

Next I unwrapped Joseph, the poor neglected hero of the piece, putting up with so many shenanigans. 'And I don't know about the self-partnering thing the celebs are doing. I can't stand myself most of the time so to be stuck with me? That sounds a really bad idea.'

Jennifer frowned at a particularly challenging tangle of wire. 'Self-partnering? What's that?'

'It's the way to describe yourself that isn't as negative as single.' Joseph wouldn't stand straight so I wedged him against the wall. Age catching up with him, I decided.

'In my day we used to say young, free and single – not self-partnered. Ah-ha!' With one last pull the lights became a single strand. 'Behold: my untwisting genius!'

'Well done. You're amazing.' However 'free', as Jennifer suggested, that felt to me a little too much like the freedom to be lonely.

'Ladies!' The chaplain flapped into chapel in his white surplice, approaching like a heron landing on the stretch of river that flowed through the college grounds. The Reverend Sanyu Masane, originally from Uganda but for the last twenty years a popular fixture of the Oxford scene, lit up the place with his warm smile and overflow of generous spirits. He had large ears and a broad face – an indomitable presence. 'Thank you, thank you!'

The shy figure of the college organist accompanied him, Sanyu's slender shadow. Errol, a state school boy from Hackney, had found his way, much to his surprise, to an Oxford organ scholarship at St Nicholas' College, thanks to his musical brilliance and sponsorship by a generous rapper. I had befriended him since we had both arrived at the college in October and had felt equally at sea in the St Nick's culture. He was still finding it hard to fit in; not very surprising, perhaps, as the majority of his peers were white, middle-class and confident, the kind that did well in the rigorous selection interviews. These young students, no matter how well meaning, would find it hard to imagine what Errol had overcome to get here. Some of his stories had shocked me, which was a surprise as I'd spent some of my teens living on the streets and thought I'd seen it all.

'I don't know what I'd do without you two angels helping me get ready for the carol service,' continued Sanyu. 'Most wonderful time of the year? Busiest time of the year, I would say.' He went into a peal of laughter, richer than the chimes of the bells in the college tower. 'Do you want help with the lights, Jennifer?' Sanyu dived for the end that Jennifer had just wrestled free, getting it caught up in the skirts of his robe.

'Actually I don't need . . . well, if you want to reach to the top and fasten it there?' Jennifer evidently gave up her brief flirtation with the idea of keeping accident-prone Sanyu far from the electrics and decided he could be made useful by reaching the top of the tree without the stepladder.

'Of course, dear lady, of course!' He promptly stood on some of the bulbs in his eagerness. There was a crunch.

'Never mind, Sanyu, we've more,' said Jennifer in a resigned tone. She turned back to the boxes the porters had brought out of storage for them. 'Somewhere in here.'

Knowing when to steer clear of Sanyu's chaos, Errol gave me a little nod and disappeared into the organ loft. I chuckled softly and started unpacking the crib animals. Soon our decorating was accompanied by the flow of silver and gold tones from the famous instrument. The notes glided up to the filigree stonework on the ceiling, a gorgeous display of carving that reminded me of palm trees. The chapel was a gem of Tudor craftsmanship and I told myself never to take any of this for granted, no matter how familiar it became as a place of work.

Errol ran through a complicated organ voluntary, the sort of piece that accompanied the arrival of Dracula in a horror flick. It was always a puzzle to work out how such powerful music could come from the hands and feet of such a small bespectacled guy. Poor Errol: he still had the looks of a much younger lad, not having yet hit on the growth spurt. He must be worried, having reached eighteen. Where was an 'Eat Me' cake when you needed it? Or was it 'Drink Me' that made Alice grow? I couldn't quite remember, though it had been one of my favourite children's stories. That was fitting as I was now living in my very own kind of Wonderland.

'Sanyu, I think you should know that Jess is threatening not to celebrate Christmas,' said Jennifer, the rat.

'I did not say that!' I protested. Sanyu would never stand for it. 'I just said I might not decorate the house this year.' My latest attempt to make the finances for my private investigations business stack up involved being the live-in caretaker of a large detached house in north Oxford. These were the tree-lined streets where old academics mouldered in properties too big for them, and new Russian oligarchs prowled, looking to buy up the houses to put in their double basement garages and swimming pools. My employer fell in the latter category, though I'd never met him, everything having been arranged through an agent. It was quite a change, I can tell you, from the attic room in my friend Cory's family home in Summertown.

'Come and help at the homeless shelter on Christmas Day. That's where I'll be,' said Sanyu. 'All my children and my wife will be there. It is great fun.' He put a tinsel crown on his head.

I had a brief image of the church hall in the centre of town populated by the fragile blanket-wrapped souls who found their way to the city streets and the robust Masane clan. 'Thanks, I'll think about it.' I knew I'd be a better person if I did sacrifice a sofa and telly day for something less selfish but the problem was I just didn't want to be around people, more specifically the happily married sort and their offspring.

'There's no need to be alone for Christmas,' continued Sanyu. 'Everyone is welcome.'

But what if you wanted to be alone? 'I know. Thank you.' I avoided a commitment by showing him Jesus in his wrappings. 'Where do you want the baby?'

'Hide him round the back of the stable. I'll only lose him if I take him.' Sanyu knew himself well. He was a man whose family brought him a whistling car key as he was forever misplacing things.

'OK. There you are, Jesus.' I put the little wooden baby under a pile of straw. It felt wrong, like I was leaving a child in a shoebox on an orphanage doorstep. I felt a sentimental tear well but I could blame the supermarket adverts for that as they had started with their *A Christmas Carol/Oliver Twist* vibe of Victorian orphans and Dickensian feasts and I had been feeling guiltily that I might be a Scrooge ever since.

'Jess, I wanted to ask you,' said Sanyu, reaching up to loop the new strand of lights over the top of the Christmas tree. 'Would you read the sixth lesson in the Nine Lessons and Carols Service? It's the one traditionally read by a member of the college staff. The head porter did it last year.'

'Me?' I had only been a member of the college admin staff for a month or so, having taken the job to cover someone's maternity leave. I'd just finished a stint in a wacky commune so needed some nine-to-five work to steady my somewhat erratic life. So far so good but realistically I expected my impulse-driven nature would see me out of the door before my term was up.

'It's your office's turn and you'll help the gender balance. The BBC will be there and we don't want to come across as an old-fashioned institution stuck back in the past.'

But that's exactly what we are! I wanted to protest. 'What about Jennifer?'

'I did it in 2004 and 2015.' Jennifer's voice came from deep inside the Christmas tree. Was she actually under it?

'Third time lucky?' I suggested.

Jennifer wasn't to be moved. 'Do it for the team, Jess. We can't ask Paul; he's the wrong gender.'

And the office manager combined high-maintenance with being an insufferable bore. I would bet that his demands before he was prepared to perform would make a Hollywood A-lister blush.

'Please, Jess, I would take it as a personal favour,' said Sanyu.

At this moment, with impeccable timing, Errol moved on

to play 'In the Bleak Midwinter' with its heart-wrenching lyric. 'What would I give him, poor as I am?' I knew my goose was cooked. Try as I might, I still was a sucker for the Christmas spirit.

'Oh, well. OK.'

'Excellent.' Sanyu clapped his hands together and shook them overhead in victory. 'Rehearsals start once we get rid of the students – I mean, wave a fond farewell to the undergraduates. It's a ticketed event for alumni and locals. I imagine we will get a good turnout this year with the BBC deciding to feature us as part of their Christmas programming.'

I finally woke up to that part of the deal. I'd never heard of that happening before. 'Why are they coming? Did King's College Cambridge go offline for a year?'

'Oh, hadn't you heard? I thought it was all over the college.' Sanyu draped a tree frond with a strand but it was too weak to hold the weight, so it bent and the lights tumbled to the next level where they looked perfect. He hummed happily at this fortunate accident. 'The documentary makers are shadowing Errol, doing a series about how scholarship students sponsored by the rapper Fresh are faring at college. Errol is their Christmas episode, because of the music.'

'No, I did not know that.' Errol hadn't told me. I wondered why? 'So, not radio?'

'No, television. To be broadcast on Christmas Eve.'

'Really?' My voice was a squeak.

'Live.' Sanyu beamed at me in his position as a super-large angel on top of the tree. Jennifer switched on the lights so the tree sparkled. 'Isn't that splendid?'

Chapter 3

Leo

The body had been removed for autopsy but there was still work to be done in the garden looking for traces of victim and killer. Leo divided the garden into sections, asking the search team in particular to look out for any tool that could've been used to dig the shallow grave. The gardener had said she always brought her own equipment so there was a chance some DNA or fingerprint evidence could be lifted from any tool used even after all this time. The householder hadn't visited for over a year, nor had any guests used the property, so the only people in and out of the house had been staff, who could be identified as soon as the agency responded to their attempts to contact it. If the staff could be eliminated as suspects, then any other trace might well lead to the killer.

That was his theory. Life rarely proved so cooperative.

Leo had set up temporary headquarters in the kitchen. Mrs Green had access to the house to tend the indoor plants so at least there had been no delay in gaining entry.

'Still no joy from Glass Tower?' he asked Suyin.

The sergeant shook her head, neat bob of black hair

swinging. Leo knew he could trust her to get the job done, and thoroughly. She was a very impressive officer, fast-tracking through the system. He tried not to think of it as breathing down his neck. He knew how unpleasant it was to have a colleague resent you.

'The Oxford office appears to have closed up shop, sir,' she said, eyes on her screen. 'I'm just trying the London office now, but looking at their online presence, I can't see any recent activity. The website is still up but there're no updates to any of their social media feeds for several weeks, not since early November.'

'Do you think they've gone out of business?'

'That's possible. If I don't get any response from the London number, I'll do a search and see if they've gone into administration.'

Leo moved away to allow her to get on with that. But maybe there was a quicker way to find out? Going to the window that looked out on the front garden, he dialled Marigold Green.

'Mrs Green? Sorry to disturb you again. It's Inspector George. Just a quick question: have you been paid by the agency recently?'

'Inspector, funny you should ask – I was just wondering the same thing.' He could hear the sound of birds in the background; she must already be at her next job. 'I tried phoning them to tell them what happened and couldn't get through. That's not normal; Heather is always very responsive. I then checked my internet bank account and saw that they're late with my November payment. That's not like them either; I'd say that they were my most prompt customer.'

Glass Tower's teetering status was looking increasingly fragile. 'Right. That's helpful.'

'You'll let me know if you find out what's going on?'

'I will. Thank you.'

Ending the call, Leo tapped his phone thoughtfully. 'Harry?'

His sergeant came in with a mug of tea. 'Inspector?' Reluctant to give him respect, the older sergeant was still avoiding calling him 'sir'.

'We need to find out everything we can about Chernov, in particular where he is now. Maybe he can tell us who's been to the house in the last eighteen months.'

'Yeah, I can see the Russian mafia boss really being open with us about who he decided to plant under his roses.'

Sarcasm aside, Leo could see that Harry might have a point but it was dangerous to assume anything so soon in an enquiry. 'We still need to find him. He has to be informed what's going on here.' They had a warrant to search the premises but it was usually executed in the presence of the owner or their representative. 'See what you can find out about him from the house – any other addresses or information about his businesses. While you're doing that, I'll look him up online.'

Leo sat down opposite Suyin and pulled one of the laptops towards him. Anatoly Chernov. Fifty-five. Two marriages, both ending in divorce, three children from the first, now in their late teens and early twenties. From the social media profiles of the two youngest, both daughters with that overgroomed look many girls had these days, thick eyebrows, long fair hair, lots of mascara. Girls attempting to be Barbies, which seemed a retrograde step for equality. The oldest child, a son, kept a low profile online. From his sisters' posts, Leo was able to learn that Alexei appeared to be very much a chip off the old block, a younger, fitter-looking version of his father with a penchant for thick gold jewellery. His business listings involved some Russian power companies and he seemed remarkably senior for such a young man. Of his father, there was no mention in any of the family postings. He hadn't been on the Swiss skiing holiday the girls had bragged about, but then the senior Chernov's ex-wife had been there so that wasn't surprising. Going further back, there had been no sign of him on the yacht around the Greek islands in the summer or at the villa in Northern Cyprus. Leo began to wonder. Buying a house near the children's school suggested an involved father; absence from any family events would indicate either a policy of not being pictured online or . . . something else.

Putting the computer to sleep, he walked around the house, examining the family photos that did show Anatoly. The man always seemed to stand a little apart from the others, either in a seat in the middle like a king on his throne or to one side like a director guiding his actors. The children would have their arms around each other or be goofing around while Dad would look on with a perplexed expression. Maybe he just didn't like cameras but Leo got the distinct impression the man wasn't socially at ease in these relaxed situations. From the pictures Leo had seen of him in the press or at formal events among business colleagues, Chernov found that his natural milieu.

Upstairs in what looked like one of the girls' rooms, thanks to the proliferation of sparkles, Leo found what he'd been hunting for. It was a photo of Anatoly at a school barbecue, trying to look as though he enjoyed the slightly drizzly weather that accompanied the summer celebration. But more importantly, he was wearing jeans held up with an eagle buckled belt, the Chernov off-duty look.

Taking the photo with him, Leo went down to the kitchen.

'I think we may have just identified our victim.' He placed the picture where Suyin and Harry could see it.

'Is this . . .?' asked Suyin.

'Anatoly Chernov, oligarch, friend of the Russian President.'

'Christ! Who would take out the big boss?' said Harry, looking spooked. 'If this was a political hit, do we have to worry about radioactive substances?'

Leo went cold, his mind suddenly sharply focused. They would have to entertain that possibility, wouldn't they? After Salisbury, it would be stupid not to check, no matter how unlikely. 'We'd better warn the pathologist and the gardener and get ourselves checked out. Call the team in from the garden. No more digging until we're sure what we're dealing with.'

Harry went out to summon the scene of crime officers inside.

'What do we do, sir?' asked Suyin. She looked very pale.

'Let's keep our heads about this. It's just a precaution. The chance that this is a Russian secret service hit is slight. Until we know either way, we minimise exposure and keep working.'

By the time he'd called it in and set the wheels turning with his superintendent, a rather chastened team had gathered in the kitchen. Leo decided that the advice of keep calm and carry on would work here.

'OK, everyone. I have to stress that there is no evidence yet that we're facing anything other than an ordinary crime of violence. We are taking sensible precautions due to recent events but there is absolutely no need to be concerned at this point. Let's keep the enquiry moving along. Did you find anything that could've been used to dig the grave?' he asked Trevor Kent, the seasoned uniform he'd put in charge of the search.

Trevor had the hangdog look of a man who had done too much overtime in wind and rain over his long career, the sort of face that in olden times would've suited a shepherd out on exposed hillsides. 'No, sir. The place doesn't have any tools lying about. The shed has a leaf blower but that's it. That looks brand new and never used. We didn't find a spade.'

'So the killer took it away with him?'

'And maybe didn't get it from here, not unless he cleared the place of all gardening tools.'

'Another thing we'll need to follow up. Thank you, Trevor.'

'God, I'm starving,' said Harry, dumping a pile of household correspondence on the counter. 'If it's gonna be my last meal, I could do with more than a bag of crisps and a digestive biscuit.' He caught Suyin's expression. 'I thought I'd be able to nip down to the pub, didn't I? Not enter quarantine.'

Again, in his own blunt way, Harry was right: the team could do with a break. And wasn't there something about an army marching on their stomach? Marching might not apply here, but police officers certainly worked better if hunger was kept at bay. 'I realise it's extraordinary circumstances,' said Leo. 'I'll order some pizza, but get it left outside so we don't come into contact with anyone.'

24

The atmosphere in the kitchen immediately improved.

'The inspector's getting out the old credit card. He must really think we're done for,' said Harry sardonically.

The best way to handle Harry was not to rise to his jabs. 'Harry, could you get an order together? I'll check in with the superintendent, see when the hazardous material team will be with us.'

Pizza arrived before the terrorist unit. Good to know that come the apocalypse, there would still be time for a margarita slice before dying, thought Leo. He was halfway through his second piece, when he glanced out the window and noticed a dog nosing around the grave site. A spaniel, clearly a pet rather than a stray as it looked well cared for and had a collar. It must've come in through the fence at the bottom of the garden. At least that answered the question as to what had been digging holes in the flower bed.

'Team, we've been invaded,' called Leo, dumping his slice.

They had a fun few minutes trying to catch the playful creature. It was only when one of the SOCOs tried the lure of pizza crust that it trotted happily into the house.

Leo knelt down and rubbed its chest. He liked dogs though his job meant he couldn't keep one. 'Sorry, dog, but you'll need to stay with us and get checked out. Then we'll see about getting you back to your owner.' If they weren't all in quarantine.

This was not how he'd thought this day would go.

Chapter 4

Jess

Paul Cook, Head of the Development Office at St Nicholas' College, was not pleased.

'Reverend Masane asked Jess to do the staff reading?' he asked in that calm, quiet tone that was a cover for quivering anger. Now in his late middle age, sweep of greying fair hair brushed back from a high forehead, and always dressed in a three-piece suit, Paul gave the impression of a man who never relaxed. He also used his hobby of photography to provide photos for our college publications, which explained the camera he carried as his accessory.

'That's right, Paul,' said Jennifer sweetly, ferrying the empty boxes that had held the tree decorations to the chapel door for collection by the porters. I kept silent, busying myself sweeping up the straw and pine needles we had scattered on the floor. I couldn't afford to annoy Paul, not only because he was my boss, but also he lived in a flat not far from me and was a big presence in the neighbourhood association. He could make life difficult for me both at home and at work.

Paul stood in the centre of the nave and gazed up at the

lectern, doubtless imagining himself there and delivering a reading in his plumy tones. 'I believe it is my turn this year.'

'Didn't you do it in 2010?' asked Jennifer.

'You've done it twice.'

'And Jess never. Besides, Sanyu is concerned about gender balance, Paul,' said Jennifer reasonably. 'With the Master, chaplain, head chorister and senior fellow all being men, he's hunting for spaces for women on the programme. It's the best look for St Nick's.'

Crouching with the dustpan and brush, I was very tempted to say I didn't want to do it and that I was happy to bow out and let Paul read, but something held me back. Dislike of Paul probably. The college Development Office was a fancy name for fundraising. My job was to milk the past students by appealing to their nostalgia for the best days of their life. I also helped Jennifer out with the admissions of new students at the busy times of year. Paul had a way of undermining his staff as if their success came at his expense. When he could put them down in some way, he felt he was winning.

'Jess has no experience – and the BBC will be here.' He lined up a shot of the crib, then lowered the camera. With a sniff of disapproval, Paul tried to adjust Joseph in the stable to a more prominent position and the figurine promptly fell over.

'It's not really our decision, is it? The chaplain organises the service.' Jennifer buttoned up her cardigan, signal she was on her way out. 'Is there anything else today, Paul?'

Our manager held up the camera to take a shot of the nave, then lowered it. 'I'm not happy.'

Of course he wasn't.

'The decorations in here – they aren't enough.'

'It's how we've always decorated the chapel,' said Jennifer patiently. 'You know that. We've used all we have.'

'There seem to be fewer lights than in previous years.'

That actually was true. The tree looked a little underpowered, thanks to Sanyu's misstep.

'And everything appears so tired. Look at the crib: the figures barely stand up straight. What will the BBC make of that?'

I gazed up at the amazing ceiling, multicoloured stained-glass with its flights of angels, the ranks of tall white candles and brass fittings. Anything that came out of a cardboard box from storage was hardly going to compete with what was always here.

Paul rounded on me. 'Jess, you've not shown much initiative since you arrived. The Master is already on at me to look again at our office, restructure some jobs to make us more efficient. It's time you stepped up. I'm giving you this project as a chance to prove yourself.'

'What?' I'd only been here a few weeks and he was threatening my job? I wasn't worried for me but I was covering a woman who was planning to return in six months. 'Sorry? I don't understand.'

Paul rocked up on his toes, an oddly gleeful gesture. 'I'm putting you in charge of making sure the chapel looks perfect for Christmas Eve. I want something really impressive – something to blow the socks off the BBC producers and make them want to come here every year.'

'But Paul . . .' began Jennifer.

'No, I've made up my mind. Seeing how Jess is taking such a big part in the service, she will have a vested interest in making sure the backdrop is suitable. Won't you, Jess?'

This was payback. Did he expect me to say I couldn't do it? Was he hoping I'd back out so he could step in?

A rebellious spirit sparked in my chest. I hated bullies. 'Fine.' I emptied the dustpan into the black sack.

'Fine?' Paul was surprised by my easy acceptance.

'What's the budget?'

'Budget?'

'You heard Jennifer say we've already used all the decorations we have in storage. If I'm going to do this, I'll need some money as I'm guessing homemade decorations aren't what you had in mind?'

Paul had become used to me shying away from him, keeping quiet during meetings, so to discover that I actually had opinions and a challenge for him was clearly a shock. 'Budget,' he repeated. 'Of course, there'll be a budget. I'll discuss it with the Master tomorrow in our weekly meeting.' Obviously, he hadn't even thought of any of this before two minutes ago.

'Do you want me to get some quotes before you do that?' I asked. He looked at me blankly. 'From events companies? They're the only people who'll have the resources to make the impact you have in mind.' One benefit of my peripatetic life temping was I had a fair idea about lots of unusual things, such as how much it cost to stage an event.

'The college is not made of money.' Paul was now fuming and said it as if this had all been my idea in the first place.

'Of course it's not.' I was enjoying seeing him squirm.

'I'll tell you how much you have to play with and you'll then work with that. No blank cheques.' With that, he marched from the room. If he could have slammed the ten-foot chapel doors, he would've done so, but they were too heavy and bound with iron.

'What a . . .' said Jennifer, biting her tongue in deference to the holy place. 'Sorry, Jess. Neither Sanyu nor I meant to drop you in it.'

'Paul is such an ass.' I stood Joseph back up and leant him against the donkey and gave Jennifer a brilliant smile. 'Don't worry. I wasn't planning on doing my house so I can do the chapel instead. How hard will it be to add a few more lights? This place is a Christmas card even without that.'

Jennifer wrapped herself in a homemade scarf, a striped one-of-a-kind piece from her fashion designer son. 'Let's hope that doesn't fall into the category of famous last words.'

Cycling home through dark streets, trying not to slide on the slick of leaves heaped in the gutters, I told myself there was nothing to worry about. Paul was just working off his anger at being passed over for a role he wanted. I made a bet with myself that he had complained at primary school if he were made a shepherd rather than a king. Habits formed in childhood were remarkably persistent.

Turning into my dark drive and using the bike light to work the combination on the gate, I stacked the bike against the garage. I was supposed to keep the passageway clear, but what the owner didn't see, wouldn't bother him. I'd been placed here by an agency who looked after houses for overseas clients, reference provided by Cory. My mansion was owned by an absentee billionaire from Central Asia. Putting the key in the lock, I opened the side door.

'Hey, Flossie, I'm home.'

There was no reply of frantic barking and eager tail wagging.

'Flossie? Flossie!' I wandered through to the kitchen, switching on lights and trying not to worry. The bed by the Aga was empty.

Then I saw the note on the counter from the contract cleaner, Mrs Pettifer, who was my sworn enemy. *Let dog out into the garden but she wouldn't come back inside. She needs training.*

Thank you, Mrs Pettifer, for stating the obvious. So what had she done? From the evidence, she'd given up and gone on to her next client.

I opened the backdoor and peered into the dark garden. There were many places for a dog to hide, due to the flower beds and vegetable patches the householder had proudly maintained. The place was stuffed with Victorian whimsy as they had gone for an *Alice in Wonderland* theme, dotting statues of the characters in different parts. The Cheshire Cat, for example, sat on the wall and smiled scarily at me as I checked by the outhouse. The caterpillar curled on a bird bath in the shape of a toadstool in the middle of the vegetable patch. It was my job to maintain the gardens but winter was letting me off easily. I'd merely had to harvest what others had planted. The last house-sitter had even made jam. Were they expecting me to do that too? The potential for disaster was huge.

'Flossie?'

There was no answering woof.

Taking a torch from a drawer, I made a quick circuit of the garden and paused by the drunken panel in the wooden fence at the bottom. It had blown down in a storm some time ago and needed mending. I'd been meaning to mention it to the nice gardener of that property so she could pass on a message to the owner as I was told by my predecessor that it was their fence, not ours. I'd have to find a diplomatic way of saying that the householder really had to do something about it if he didn't want my dog getting into his immaculate garden. She liked to bury bones; the owner of that house liked lawns like Centre Court on the first day of Wimbledon. You see the problem?

Lights were on in the house which was unusual as it was normally empty. If I were going to go hunting for Flossie in the neighbour's garden, I'd better get permission. My predecessor had warned me that the owner sometimes had formidable-looking security people in tow. Russians. Possibly with guns. It sounded very exciting but not if I became target practice.

Going back through my house, I grabbed the keys and a leash and went out onto the street to walk the long way round. My house was a late Victorian gothic castle of a place built from red brick, complete with turret and arched windows. If Hollywood was looking for a location for a live-action *Scooby Doo* haunted house, they need look no further. The one we shared a boundary with, in the next road, was more classically North Oxford, built from the golden bricks that were common round here. I pulled on the metal bell which, rather pleasingly, rang a three note chime.

After a short wait, the door opened. Detective Inspector Leo George stood in the doorway.

There was a very long pause as we took in the fact that we were unexpectedly thrown together after over a month of radio silence. I thought we had been heading for a date after the White Horse cult killings, but he'd stood me up at the last moment and not been in contact since. I'd been so hopeful but that too had died a death, like a cutting planted out too early and caught in a late frost. I'd not chased him as I couldn't stand the idea of being in a relationship that blew hot and cold.

'Jess? What are you doing here?' he asked, finally finding his voice.

'Same question back at you.' But then I noticed he wasn't alone. Other officers were searching inside the property. The penny dropped. 'Don't tell me: someone's dead?'

He nodded. 'And you?'

'I'm living at number thirty-seven, Howell Street. House-sitting actually. It backs on to this place.'

Realisation dawned for him too. 'You're the nice house-sitter.'

'Glad my Yelp reviews are positive.'

'The gardener here told me about you – not you specifically but she said she chatted to the friendly house-sitter.'

Alarm spiked. 'Marigold? Is she OK?'

'Yes, she's fine. She just found – something.'

'A body. Don't worry, I won't tell anyone.' I then worked out where it must've been. 'Oh yuck.'

Leo now noticed the leash and the door opened wider. 'Come in. I think we've kidnapped your dog.'

'Flossie?'

'Is that her name? I didn't even know you had a dog.'

He wouldn't, would he, not having taken his chance to get to know me?

He closed the entrance behind me. 'She got in the way this afternoon so we took her inside, not knowing where she'd come from. She's with the team in the kitchen. We had a scare about possible hazardous waste but we've been given the all-clear, so she's free to go.'

'Hazardous waste? What, like asbestos?'

'Not quite.'

I didn't get a chance to ask him what he meant as he'd already led me into a huge kitchen-dining room. The house might've been built by nineteenth-century architects but it was definitely someone from the twenty-first century who had been let loose in here. The steel grey units and marble counters were spotless. An elegant single orchid sat on the windowsill, white blossoms trembling. Flossie leapt up from the blanket under the table and came over to greet me, abandoning the police officer who had been looking through paperwork at the counter.

'You might remember DS Suyin Wong,' said Leo.

The sergeant looked up, then quickly at her boss.

I held up both hands. 'The body had nothing to do with me. I'm here for the living.' I knelt down and clipped on the leash to Flossie's collar.

The other sergeant I had also met before, Harry Boston, ambled in from another room, a box of computer gear in his arms.

'Gawd almighty, if it isn't Miss Trouble herself! How've you got yourself involved in this one?'

I think I amused and annoyed Harry Boston in equal parts, but as he'd once bought me a drink when I most needed it, I was trying to think charitable thoughts about him. 'Not involved. My dog got through the fence at the end of the garden. I'm just rescuing her.'

'Blame the forensic guys. They fed her pizza,' said Suyin.

'I was wanting to ask about the fence. It's the only part of the garden that isn't smart. How long has the panel been down?' asked Leo.

I felt oddly annoyed he'd gone straight into questioning mode without stopping to explain why he stood me up. It was like we were strangers again.

'No idea.' I kept my tone clipped. 'I've only had the job since the end of October. You'll have to ask my predecessor. I was told the fence belonged to this house so wasn't my employer's responsibility to mend.'

'And who is your employer?'

'A Mr Akmal Gulom. He's from Uzbekistan. I had to look it up on a map. It's a big place. The Silk Road. Samarkand.'

'But you haven't met him?'

'No.'

'So how . . .?'

'An agency.'

'Let me guess: Glass Tower Services?'

'Been checking up on me, have you, Inspector?'

He had the grace to look a little flustered by that accusation. 'No, Jess, they manage this property too, so it was an educated guess. Who do you deal with at the agency?'

'A woman called Heather. I met her once when she interviewed me. That's all I know, apart from the fact they pay well.' Flossie was pulling on the leash. 'Can I go now?'

'Yes. I'll see you out.' Leo guided me to the door.

'Bye, guys,' I said cheerily to the sergeants. That was my philosophy: pretend like everything is fine and one day it will be.

'Bye, Jess,' said Suyin. 'If you hear from Heather, will you let us know?'

'Sure.'

'And try to keep your clothes on this time,' called Harry, chuckling at my expense. Just because I ended up naked at two crime scenes, some people would never let me forget!

Leo stood at the front door. I noticed how his smart lace-up shoes sank deep into the white pile carpet.

'Who puts white carpet in a hallway?' I asked.

'Someone with more money than sense.' He glanced over his shoulder towards the kitchen. 'Jess, I want to apologise. For what happened in October.'

'Oh? For what exactly? For standing me up or for not getting in contact to explain?'

He looked down, a hank of black hair falling forward. It was tempting to push it back but we didn't have that kind of relationship, not Mr Gorgeous Unattainable Policeman and me. 'Both, I suppose.'

'It's OK. You're a busy guy. Work takes over, I expect.'

Flossie was sniffing the leg of a side table with rather too much interest. I'd have to get her out of here.

'It wasn't work. It was a family emergency.' He met my gaze. 'Ongoing emergency. I don't have a social life at the moment.'

'Ri-ight.' I suppose as excuses went, it wasn't bad. 'Don't beat yourself up, Leo. It probably wouldn't have worked, would it? Us, dating? I'm all over the place and you're the straight arrow. I'd've driven you crazy after a few weeks.'

He shook his head in denial. 'Jess, I really am sorry. I'd like to make it up to you.'

'Sir!' One of his officers was calling from upstairs. We looked at each other.

'Work calls,' I prompted.

'Can I ring you? So I can make a proper apology?'

I wasn't sure that I wanted that. There was a danger I'd like him too much and, when he decided he'd had enough of me, it would hurt like hell. I'd decided the near-miss had been the best thing that could've happened for my emotional survival. 'Leo . . .'

'You're still on the same number?'

I nodded.

'OK. I'll call – arrange something.' He opened the door so Flossie and I could exit. 'It's good seeing you again.'

I opened my mouth to say, 'And you,' but fortunately he'd closed it quickly. Idiot. I shook myself, much to Flossie's bemusement, who wasn't used to her human exhibiting such doglike characteristics.

'OK, hound, let's go for a quick walk then supper. How does that sound?'

That sounded fine to her so she led me off around her favourite circuit.

38

Chapter 5

Michael

Michael Harrison checked his tie in the mirror. It had been a while since he'd done this. After the accident that robbed him of his ease of mobility, Michael had shied away from the dating scene. The last year had been a slow but steady finding of his new identity: differently abled than he had been in the past.

Not content, he redid the knot. The easiest had been, in retrospect, his media image: the wheelchair psychologist, invited to comment on criminal cases involving psychopathic or particularly extreme behaviours, such as terrorism. Professionally, he'd had a successful book and a promotion to an academic job in Oxford. Icing to that cake had been when Inspector George in Thames Valley had brought him back into consulting with the police, which, to be honest, was the part of his job he enjoyed the most. That was when he felt most needed.

Now the tie looked right.

But his cufflinks were wrong. He'd better change them. He searched through his collection, looking for a pair his wife, now deceased, hadn't given him. He couldn't take memories of Emma on this outing. People – notably his ex, Jessica, his old friend Charles – had told him he'd got stuck in his grief, with few friends and a limited social life. They'd told him to chance a relationship again.

And so the bold move into dating. He backed away from the mirror to check his wallet had both cash and cards. He'd made himself fill out an application and pay the fee for one of those sites that matched university-educated professionals with each other. It had come as a surprise, but perhaps fore-seeable in hindsight, that one of the local matches the website suggested was someone he already knew a little: Cory Reynolds, Jessica's landlady until very recently, before Jessica moved to house-sit that incredible redbrick pile near the park. When Cory's home had been invaded by a disturbed young woman, he had hosted Cory and her two children in the middle of the night, a safe place for them to go while the police (and Jessica as it turned out) dealt with the matter. That meant Cory had already met him and, if she agreed to date him, they could skip the whole 'how did you end up in a wheelchair?' conversation. She'd be seeing him because she was interested.

He arrived early at the restaurant in the Ashmolean Museum. The modern extension at the back of the old building had opened up new areas of the museum, including the roof, and this relatively new restaurant was one of the best in Oxford. With so much college dining every evening, the city was surprisingly short of decent places to eat – and college meals could be pretty dreadful sometimes. You had to pick your college carefully or you might end up with cold beans and wilted salmon. He'd asked for his table to be near the window so they could look out over the Randolph Hotel and the skyline of the city centre. Christmas trees twinkled on the restaurant terrace and in the windows of the five-star hotel across the road, reminding him he'd better decide what he was going to do this year for the holidays.

He ordered a cocktail and pondered his choices. Last year, he'd gone to his parents' retirement place in France but had found the travel and moving around there a chore. He wondered what Jessica was doing. Would it be odd to ask his friend to spend the day with him? She might take it as meaning that he was angling for more than simple friendship. Christmas seemed so fraught with significance. Perhaps it was safer to spend the day alone?

Cory hurried in only a few minutes late and was steered to his table by a discreet waiter.

'Michael, sorry to keep you waiting. The children were playing up, knowing I had to get out.' She hovered, evidently wondering what was the correct greeting, then decided on a quick kiss to the cheek. 'I've been so looking forward to this all day.'

That made Michael relax. 'Me too.' He smiled up at her, appreciating that she had put a great deal of effort to polishing up her usual mumsy vibe to smart thirty-something who looked like her photo on the website. Attractive rather than ravishing, she had styled her hair, put on more make-up than usual, and was wearing a pretty matching earring and necklace, little blue chips of some semi-precious stone. Ah, something neutral he could pick on. 'I like your jewellery.'

She touched her necklace self-consciously. 'Oh, thank you. I got them in a market in Beirut on my last visit to the Lebanon. I can't remember if I told you, but I assess development projects for DfID, specialising in refugee access to education.'

He'd known she worked in the aid sector but had assumed that meant a desk job at one of the big charities, not going abroad for the Department for International Development. 'That sounds very interesting. You must tell me more, but what about ordering a cocktail first? I can recommend the Ashmolean Gin Fizz.' He toasted her with the drink he'd already ordered.

She gave him a teasing frown. 'You started without me?'

'I was worried you might stand me up, so I decided to look as though I was meaning to dine alone.'

She shook her head, smiling. 'I'd never do that to a date. One of those sounds lovely.' She leaned forward a little. 'The advantage of travelling by bike, I don't need to worry.'

He gave her a conspiratorial smile. 'And I was planning on taking a taxi home. So tell me about Beirut.'

By the end of the meal, Michael was feeling a little drunk. Not because he'd had more than was good for him, but because he'd forgotten what it was like to enjoy a meal in a clever woman's company. Cory reminded him of a toned-down version of Jessica: a little reckless at times, wanting to live life at full throttle, but she took more care with herself as she had her children to consider. He had been missing . . . what was it? Liveliness? Yes, that was a good word. All his colleagues at Magdalen seemed so serious and staid. It was a gift to laugh with someone and relax.

'You mean the computer geeks think that you can help them achieve near-human intelligence in AI?' she asked on hearing at his newest role in the artificial intelligence institute that had just opened in Hay Road.

'I'm not a numbers man myself, but apparently one of the approaches to programming is algorithms that mimic the synapses in the brain, and there I can help with my under-standing of psychology. At least that's the theory. I'm coming in under a big grant from the Chernov foundation, so I won't be the only one. It's all very cutting edge.' In fact, he now put it first on his CV as it was where so many academic disciplines were moving.

'That sounds . . . scary,' said Cory, pushing her empty coffee cup away. 'I've just watched *Blade Runner*.'

'Ah. We're a long way off androids who can pass for human. At the moment robots have even more trouble negotiating stairs than I do.'

At the end of the meal, they split the bill.

'I really enjoyed myself,' he said. 'Thank you.'

'I did as well.' She looked down a little shyly. 'Would you like to do this again? It's really freeing seeing someone who already knows I come with baggage.'

'Baggage?'

'Two children.'

Michael had managed to forget about them during the meal. Not that he disliked children, but he wasn't at ease with them usually. Cory's two had been sweet, though, when they'd stayed, enjoying riding on his motorised armchair and pretending to blast into space. Maybe he could learn to cope?

'I don't see them as baggage, but as assets.' He hoped he was telling her the truth. He wanted to mean it.

She beamed. 'That's so sweet of you.'

'And yes, I'd very much like to do this again. It's been a while for me, a bruising few years you could say, but tonight was the first time in a long while I've felt really off-duty.'

'Excellent.' She reached out and took his hand. 'Just one thing: I didn't tell Jess we were meeting. Did you?'

'No. I didn't want to land you in an awkward situation with her. I know you're friends.'

'Maybe we could keep this to ourselves, just for the moment, see how things pan out? No point having a big heart-to-heart with her if we only go on a couple of dates.'

Did she not like him? 'I'm hoping it might be more than that.'

She smiled reassuringly. 'So am I, Michael.'

'But you're right. Jessica would find it odd maybe. I'd find it awkward explaining us to her. Let's wait until we know where we're going with this.' The secret felt a little thrilling, bringing them closer.

Cory looked relieved. 'Yes, let's wait. Knowing her, she'd probably just be pleased for us.'

'Yes, knowing her.' The waiter signalled that his taxi was waiting downstairs. Michael pushed back from the table. 'I'm heading down in the lift.'

'I'll ride with you.'

They left the restaurant together, her hand resting on his shoulder.

Chapter 6

Leo

Closing down the temporary incident room he'd created at the house, Leo was acutely aware that he hadn't said even half of what he'd wanted to Jess. He was still cursing himself for that. Why didn't life come with a rewind button? Maybe the strange rollercoaster day of considering radioactive poisoning then being given the all-clear was some excuse, but he knew it was more likely due to his inability to communicate with those he cared about. Given a do-over, would he manage any better?

Leaving an officer to guard the murder scene overnight, he called it a day at 10pm and ordered everyone to reconvene at Kidlington, Thames Valley Police HQ, at eight the next day. They had made some progress despite everything, tracking down the family solicitor and putting in a request for DNA samples from a blood relative or dental records. These were needed so they could confirm the theory that it was the householder himself who had ended up in the garden. Either that or Mr Chernov himself might turn up alive and well as a result of the outreach. The lawyer had been decid-

45

edly cagey though, refusing to say when he'd last had contact with the Russian.

Though it was not on the most direct route, Leo drove past the house where Jess was living. Suyin was fairly certain Glass Tower had shattered into a million pieces, so he'd also have to deliver the bad news to Jess that she might not get paid. But not tonight. He'd let her sleep undisturbed in that Victorian castle house she was inhabiting. There were no lights on, apart from one up in the turret room. Was she sleeping up there? He could see that appealing to her.

He turned the car for home, deeply dissatisfied with himself. Had it been a lie to say he'd stood her up for a family emergency? His mother was a walking, talking crisis, but couldn't he have slipped away, kept some of his own life going even while she settled in his house like a plague of locusts? His problem was that he felt emotionally eaten clean away, leaving but a stick of a man going about his business. Maybe he wouldn't feel like that if he'd had someone like Jess in his life to help share the load?

He slowed for a group of students weaving in front of him on their bikes, Father Christmas hats and tinsel giving them an early festive feel. At least they had bike lights, if not helmets; one out of the two was better than many students managed. He could tell them from experience at road traffic accidents that being brainy did not protect you from your own stupidity. But they wouldn't want to listen: at twenty, they felt immortal.

They managed to peel off safely to their chosen destination, The Cape of Good Hope pub, so named because it formed a wedge between the two traffic currents of the Cowley and

Iffley Road. At their age, he'd never had the illusion of invulnerability, thanks to his mother's emotional vampirism. He'd wanted to die at eighteen; at twenty, he was only just recovering the will to live. His own university life at Durham had been a slow awakening from a bad dream.

Which had returned and was occupying his spare room.

No, it was better to make sure anyone he had feelings for stayed away from his mother. He mustn't regret keeping Jess at arm's length. Experience surely had taught him that. His mother would kill everything in her path, his own invasive species of ground elder.

He took the turn by the Peugeot garage into Iffley village where he had his little cottage with its big garden. The street narrowed and took on a village air. All the lights were on at his own house. This habit of his mother's drove him crazy. Why had she even been in his bedroom to switch on the light in the first place? He sat in the drive, listening to the car clicking and settling into dormancy after the short ride across town. She would still be up, wouldn't she? Having spent the day alone, she'd be waiting for him to tell him about her latest minor dramas and emotional crises. Leo wished he had siblings to help dilute his mother's focus but she'd never had another child after him. Now she was getting too old to attract her preferred style of man to play the nurturing partner so was latching on to her son as her Plan B. This was the longest she'd ever stayed with him. A more ruthless person would've turned her out, Leo knew that, but he'd tried this a few years ago and it had backfired spectacularly. She'd started turning up at work and when he was out on dates, basically stalking him. No counter action on his part, from ignoring her to demanding she leave, had dented her confidence that she had every right to be there. He'd tried so many strategies that he felt like he was in the middle of his very own Groundhog Day where he hadn't found the combination that broke the spell.

This time he was attempting the minimal interaction policy, which seemed a decent holding pattern. Work had become his refuge and as long as he returned each night, she hadn't yet had the gall to follow him there again. How long could this go on? On other occasions, he'd known that it would be temporary; that once she'd regrouped or found a new boyfriend she would move on. Alarmingly this time she showed no signs of shifting. She'd told him she'd got in trouble with the wrong sort and was worried for her safety. Her policeman son felt a safe haven for Haven Keene.

His grandparents hadn't been aware of the irony when they gave her that name. Like Mrs Green the gardener, his mother had fashioned her life in the image of her name so she was eager to find one safe spot after another, never creating her own.

The front door opened. A slight, almost girlish dark-haired figure stood in the entrance. From a distance she looked young enough to be his girlfriend. Only close to could you see the lines life had etched around her eyes and the thickening of the face towards the neck. 'Aren't you coming in?' she asked, not bothering to keep her voice down.

Mindful of the sleeping neighbours, Leo got out, picked up his messenger bag and went inside. The house even smelt strange with her in occupation. She liked a brand of essential oils that she burned obsessively in the kitchen and small living room. Leo suspected she did it to hide the smell of what she preferred to smoke. Officially she was a non-smoker, but Leo had found stubs of enough hand-rolled cigarettes to give the lie to that claim.

'Hello, Mother.' He didn't put his bag down, knowing she'd go through it when his back was turned.

'Have you eaten? I made you supper but you didn't call.' She'd left her long hair loose and her big eyes were outlined in kohl. He thought of it as her waif look, meant to be appealing, except she'd picked her audience poorly.

'I had something at work. And I told you not to make anything for me.'

'But it seems silly to cook for just myself, with you working so hard and no one looking after you.'

Was that what she told herself she was doing? Looking after him?

'Made any progress on finding somewhere else to live?' He knew the answer, of course.

'But it's not safe for me! I told you that.' She put a cover over the plate of risotto she'd reserved for him.

How much this was the case and how much a figment of her imagination, he didn't know. 'It's not sustainable, you living here. I need my space.'

'But you're barely here – and I'm your mother!' She shoved the plate in the fridge and let the door slam, glass jars clanking.

Leo walked out into the garden. Solar lights dimly lit the path to his pond.

'Leo, it's pitch dark out there! You'll trip!'

49

He tuned her out and found his favourite bench by his pond with no difficulty. It was screened by bushes from the house. His mother didn't venture out here, thank God. He could walk this blindfolded, having laid out every inch of the landscaping himself. Putting his bag down, he rested his arms on his knees and let his head drop. Could he change the locks? She'd probably just break a window. Not come home until she was gone? But she'd probably never leave, living rent free. Forcibly eject her? She'd just charge him with assault and that would be the end of his career. Get a restraining order? It might come to that. If he took that route he'd have to make it clear he asked her to leave and gave her a deadline. This just letting things drift was not good.

But was she really in trouble?

Who knew? Surely it wasn't his responsibility to sort out the tangles that the woman who ruined his childhood got herself into? That was unfair in the extreme.

A faint plop came from the pond, possibly a droplet rolling off one of the overhanging twigs of the weeping willow at the far end. Deep in the water, hiding from sight, was his giant koi carp Goldemort and his remaining followers. How many would be left by spring? Leo wondered. Leo suspected his fish, like his mother, of vampiric tendencies.

It was chill and damp in the garden. Even in winter Leo found it beautiful, a sylvan palace of intricate interwoven branches shot through with the dark gloss of the evergreens. Sprays of red berries from holly and tiny apples on the crab decorated the borders – not that he could see these now but he knew they were there. The yellow explosion of the mahonia bush enlivened one corner, the spiky leaves looking like frozen fireworks shooting out from the main stem. *For all this nature is never spent* . . . it was a line from an Oxford poet that Leo often revolved in his mind like a lucky penny in his pocket. It brought him hope at his lowest, prevented him even from slitting his wrists at the very worst. Things come back even when all seems utterly hopeless. He just had to have faith.

Perhaps it was time he told someone about this. He'd spent thirty-six years alone; did he really want to spend the rest of his life like that? The burden of his past was crushing him slowly but surely.

'Leo, when you've finished sulking, lock up! I'm going to bed!' his mother called, acting as if the place were hers.

He sat in silence for a little longer, waiting until her words became true. She sometimes said things like that just to lure him inside. It gave him the chance to appreciate the dark smell of winter, the drifts that he left to moulder to encourage wild-life. They would be turning dark brown and black as the leaves returned to the earth. It was not good for a garden to strip it bare as Chernov had done. Over time, the soil lost its natural structure and required more and more artificial fertiliser to struggle through the growing season. Mess had a purpose.

He looked back to the house. One light had gone out – the one in the spare room. It was safe to go inside.

Chapter 7

Jess

I stood at the window cradling a mug of coffee. My office had one of the best views in the world as it looked out on the main quad. This famous landmark, featured on many a postcard, had four rectangles of manicured lawn divided by flagstone paths, and a fountain with a statue of St Nicholas carrying a child on his back in the centre. You could fit four tennis courts in here easily. The buildings themselves were a soft apricot colour, recently cleaned to get rid of their twentieth-century grime, and in the winter sunlight they glowed, seeming to belong to another, nicer world. That was until you spotted the gargoyles leering at you from the guttering, adding a little demonic to the heavenly. Something was always happening out there: porters strutting in their magpie uniform of bowler hat and black suit; students landing briefly in flocks then flying off to mysterious destinations; academics speeding by in their raven-black gowns, late for a lecture or tutorial.

Errol came into view, dressed as usual in his battered green Parka and college scarf. The difference today was that he was trailed by a cameraman, sound guy and two others on the documentary team. He had been probably told to cross the quad as he would any other day but it was hard to act natural on order. Instead he looked hunted, like they were a team in a BBC nature documentary.

Then the cameraman made the cardinal error of stepping on the grass. Mr Newton shot out of the porter's lodge like a rocket on fireworks night.

'Get off the grass! Only fellows of the college are allowed on the grass!'

The cameraman ignored him. He was probably used to location filming in war zones and jungles, and an irate porter did not scare him. He actually had the temerity to lie down to get a better angle, inflaming the situation. Mr Newton seized the camera by the lens and started pulling. This wasn't going to end well.

'Hard at work, I see?' said Paul, appearing in the doorway to look down on the two desks of his junior staff. Jennifer didn't work Fridays so I was alone.

I didn't waste time on defending myself. I was due a coffee break as he no doubt knew. 'I think you might need to do something about that,' I said instead, pointing to the confrontation on the lawn.

He glanced down at the altercation. 'Oh Lord. I told Mr Newton they had the Master's permission to film.' Turning on his heel, he sped downstairs and by the next sip I saw him join the fray. Errol, standing on the sidelines unregarded, looked up and saw me watching the fracas. I waved and beckoned him to join me. It was plain there was no more filming going to get done for the moment. He sidled away without anyone noticing and bolted up the stairs to my sanctuary.

'Bit much?' I asked as he came into the office. 'Need a coffee? Or tea? I have some herbal ones.'

'Coffee. Milky. Thanks.' He unwrapped his scarf and slid out of his Parka, halving in size.

I poured him one from the vacuum jug the kitchens supplied me with each day for visitors, added a generous quantity of milk and handed it to him. 'Does this call for biscuits?'

'Yeah. I think it does. Thanks, Jess.'

Rummaging in my desk drawer, I came up with a packet of chocolate cookies. It was Friday after all. 'Save me from eating them all myself.'

He took five. One of the oddities about Errol's metabolism was that he could eat huge amounts with no apparent effect on his body.

The dispute down in the quad appeared to be ending. 'How long do you have to go around with those guys following you?'

'They want to film me on four days over December – today and then they'll be back for the rehearsals and return with a bigger team for the live service. Fresh is coming to that.'

'A world-famous rapper is coming to our Christmas Eve service?' My rash agreement to decorate the chapel returned to me with full force. How could I impress with my Christmas display someone used to touring with sound and light shows?

'Yeah. He's a good guy. He says he likes traditions and stuff.' A second biscuit followed the first in short order.

'Are you trying to tell me he's just a regular guy, this man with a private jet and more money than God?'

Errol shrugged. 'Don't think God bothers with a bank account, but basically yeah. Sanyu's very excited.'

'That's all we need – an excited Sanyu.' We shared a smile.

'He's invited the choir from my Pentecostal church back home to join the service.'

I wondered how that would work: the white-robed choristers and a gospel choir from Hackney. Sounded like a Christmas version of Harry and Meghan's wedding. 'Sanyu or Fresh?'

'Sanyu, of course. My mum's thrilled.'

'Your mum's in the choir?'

'Yeah, and my sisters and my youngest brother. That's where I learned to play the organ. Can't sing a note. I'm the family disgrace.'

I gave him a soft punch on the arm. 'You're hardly that, organ scholar.'

'I suppose they might think different now I'm here. Mum loves this place. She'd be here every weekend if I let her.' Errol put the mug by the kettle. 'I think they're looking for me. I'd better go.'

'You're welcome to hide up here whenever you need.'

'Thanks, Jess. Oh, and how's Flossie?' Errol and Flossie were pals as he'd taken the dog for a walk when I had 'flu last month.

'She's made new friends. Snuck into next-door and charmed the police.'

'Police?'

'Yeah, they found a body in the garden.'

'What? For real?'

'Yes. I saw the news this morning that they think it's fairly recent and are appealing for information.'

'That's . . . horrible.'

'I know. Most people hope for fairies at the bottom of the garden and Flossie and I get a corpse.'

From his glum expression, I could tell he didn't share my gallows humour.

'Sorry, Errol. I got kinda used to bodies in my old job.'

He looped the scarf around his neck. 'How could anyone get used to bodies? What were you?'

'Undertaker's assistant.'

He looked very hard at me. 'Are you joking again?'

'Nope.'

'I thought you looked for missing people?'

'I do – that's what I hope to make my main line of work. All this? The undertaking, temping and so on – that's just to pay the bills.'

'You're weird, do you know that?'

'Oh yes.'

He went to the door. 'But you're interesting. I'm telling my film crew to include you.'

'Don't you dare, Errol!'

With a passable devilish chuckle, he went back down to the quad where the film crew were seeking him.

I sat back in front of the computer and returned to the winter newsletter I was compiling for past students. Errol was so relaxed with me, it was just a shame he struggled to show this side to others of his age. He probably got on with me because he had older sisters so he was used to teasing and being teased.

Back to the report from the First Eleven.

* * *

At one a message from Leo popped up on my screen. It started so well.

I need to see you.

But then it went downhill.

And if possible search your garden. Would you be able to return early and show my officers where the tools are kept?

So it was about the case.

I knocked on Paul's door. 'Is it OK if I leave now? The police need to search the grounds of the house I'm staying in and I have to be there.'

Paul sniffed as if the police search was my fault. 'I suppose you can go.'

'I'll carry on working on the display at home and will be contactable by phone should you need me. On the subject of which, how much have I to spend?'

'The Master is considering it. He did express the wish that you get sponsorship from local firms so it wouldn't come out of college funds.'

'With only a few weeks to go? That's hardly likely, Paul. You need to cultivate those kind of relationships months in advance. Does he have any suggestions for me?'

'The Master is too busy to do your job for you.'

The unfairness was breathtaking. 'Excuse me, this isn't in my job description, none of this is.'

'Then you want nothing to do with the service, I suppose? It isn't in your job description to do the reading either.'

The man was shameless. 'I'll need a budget, Paul, and I think it is definitely in your job description to provide me with one.'

He tapped a few keys on his computer with the pecking movements of the typing challenged. 'I don't like your tone.'

'And I don't like being promised a budget to do a job and then having that vanish on me.'

'I might be able to squeeze something out of the outreach fund. Five hundred pounds maximum.'

Which would probably mean some inner city school wouldn't get their widening access visit.

'Five hundred pounds won't make much of an impact.'

'Then seek sponsors. I've got a meeting.' He flounced out. There was no meeting but he did like to have the last word in any argument.

Chapter 8

Leo

The initial report on the body had revealed the cause of death. Gunshot to the back of the head. Well, that would do it. The bullet was a 9mm which suggested a handgun, but as it was the most popular brand, that did not narrow it down very much. If Chernov had personal security, they might well have handguns using that caliber, or he might own one himself. It would be worth checking who had access to the house that had a license for firearms. That was if it were legally owned, of course, and there were records.

Unravelling the business relationships of Anatoly Chernov had taken all morning and still there was little clarity as to what exactly he provided the world. He appeared to have a lot of money and no clear way of generating it. Privatised state assets and sheltering of the ill-gotten gains of the men in power seemed to be the front-runners. His capital holdings were huge. In the UK alone, he had several other houses, a share in a business park, and a stake in a football club. Then there was the yacht, the plane, the villa in North Cyprus, property in the West Indies, Turkey, Georgia . . . too many to itemise. Leo doubted the man himself would've known every-thing he owned without consulting a list. If this murder turned out to be related to Chernov's money dealings, then the suspects would be legion. When reached by phone, none of the UK holdings had heard from him, but apparently that was not unusual. He did his business through intermediaries.

And the oddest thing? That a man seemingly this big in his own world had not been reported missing by his loved ones. Most families would've been turning Oxford upside down if he'd last been seen here. Even the most impoverished family would've at least made a police report and done a public appeal on Facebook and in the media, but these cash-rich Russians had done nothing. How to account for that? That they wanted him dead or that they knew it wasn't him. This was one more reason why Leo wasn't going to sign off on it being Chernov until irrefutable proof was obtained, just in case. It seemed the territory of spy thriller, but perhaps it was a decoy in the garden, some poor guy used so that Chernov could conveniently declare himself dead to avoid some political heat back home?

'I've got a match on the rings and watch,' said Suyin, putting up on screen a photo taken from further back in the archive of images.

Anatoly was on a Black Sea beach, arm draped around wife number one. The signet ring and Rolex matched the ones now sitting in an evidence tray in forensics. There were words in Cyrillic that could help identify them as Chernov's. They were getting those translated.

Leo checked his emails. Chernov's lawyer was stalling, refusing to release dental records or ask family members to offer up DNA. He didn't believe it was his client so came close to accusing Leo of police harassment with his repeated requests. It was unbelievable: they shouldn't be seen as enemies over a simple identification. Leo's superintendent had warned him to tread carefully. The Chernovs were reportedly great anglophiles and friends of highly placed people in government. That was all Leo needed: politics.

What he did need was some way into this slippery man's life.

'Suyin, can you send that hairbrush we found in the master bedroom to the lab? It's not ideal but, if we assume it belongs to the owner, then we might get somewhere with identification.'

'Will do, sir.'

'Any news where wife number one lives?' Leo asked. 'Perhaps she'll help us if she's aggrieved enough at being dumped for wife number two.'

'Good idea.' Suyin did some more searches. 'We're in luck. She's in the UK. I've got an address for her in London. Do you want me to reach out?'

'Let's go to her. Ask for an appointment tomorrow, if she'll agree to see us.'

'It's Saturday tomorrow,' Suyin said plaintively.

Leo just raised a brow.

'OK, tomorrow.'

'I'll go on my own if you've plans.'

'It's OK, sir. Hopefully it won't take all day.'

He, by contrast, would be very happy to be away the whole weekend. 'I'll leave you to sort that out while I drive into Oxford and see how the door-to-doors are going.'

* * *

He caught up with Trevor Kent and Constable Tina Sharp, as they turned the corner into Crick Road. Stopping the car, he got out.

'Any progress?'

Trevor showed him the list they'd been working through on their door-to-door enquiries. 'We've had replies at about seventy per cent of the addresses, which is pretty good. Everyone is very helpful but nobody saw anything. Nothing was heard last year that suggested gunfire and most people repeated that it was quiet around here and they would expect to have noticed something like that. The AI Institute next door was a bust as it's new and none of the staff were here before July. None of them knew who was in that building earlier, though they think probably builders, refitting the place, so that might be worth checking.'

Could the builders have been involved somehow? wondered Leo. Some dispute that got out of hand? They would certainly have the tools for a burial.

'The Hong Kong couple two doors away,' continued Trevor, 'didn't speak much English, at least she didn't. He spoke some but was very reserved. He's a professor in the Mathematics department. Their children go to the same school as Chernov's went to, but they're much younger and so never mixed socially. They've never been inside the Chernov house.'

'Where are the net curtain twitchers when you need them?' said Leo.

'There are some, sir,' said Tina, taking over. She was a stocky woman with a lovely fruity laugh, generally popular in the squad as she always remembered everyone's birthdays and made cakes. She'd even managed to discover Leo's, which said much for her detective skills as he liked to keep these details to himself. 'The Prices across the road. They keep an eye on everyone for that society they run and were able to tell us that Chernov has definitely not been seen at the property since autumn last year.'

'Thanks. It sounds like I should go and have a word with them. Is Sergeant Boston around?'

'He's just popped over to a takeaway place in North Parade.'

'Tell him to join me when he's finished his break, would you?'

Leo decided to leave his car where it was and walk to the Prices' house. It was similar in style to the Chernov property, the same brick and architectural flourishes, but they had a well-stocked garden, bird table and wellington boots in the porch. Lived in and orientated towards relaxed living, he immediately liked it.

The door was answered by a smart-looking man in later middle age. He had his greying hair slicked back from his forehead and striking pale blue eyes, reminiscent of Ralph Fiennes as James Bond's M to Leo's mind. His gaze was currently fixed on Leo with a wary but not unfriendly expression.

Leo held up his warrant card. 'Mr Price? I know you spoke to some of my colleagues earlier. I have a few follow-up questions, if you don't mind?'

Mr Price stood aside. 'I take it you're the big gun? They warned me you might come.'

'I'd put myself at medium-sized howitzer. But I am in charge of the inquiry, for my sins.'

'Come through to the kitchen. Meredith, another visitor!'

Leo noticed the RAF insignia on the photos that decorated the wall and deduced he was talking to a retired airman. Other pictures were of Oxford colleges and the iconic skyline of towers and spires, mixed in with some images of African wildlife. A large ebony mask with crossed spears hung over the entrance to the kitchen. He'd lay money on the man having spent some time stationed abroad.

'I understand you and your wife are in charge of the North Oxford Protection Society?'

'For *our* sins,' echoed Mr Price. 'Meredith, this is Inspector George. Meredith also works part-time at St Bede's as – what do they call you, darling?'

Entering the kitchen, they found Mrs Price at the sink. She was a bit of a surprise; Leo had been expecting a female version of the husband, some pallid ash blonde in a twin set and pearls, the cliché of the senior officer's wife. Instead, she had a sunny smile and vibrant print dress and head wrap that suggested to Leo she was from West Africa rather than the Caribbean. Her diamond engagement and wedding rings were of striking contemporary designs that slotted together. Matching gems twinkled in her ears.

'Reading champion,' she said, smiling.

'Sounds fun,' Leo said politely.

'It is. I think that's another name for assistant librarian. I also travel a couple of times a year to promote the school in Africa – a little perk I appreciate as it gets me back to see my family. International students are big business. Would you like coffee, or are you a tea person, Inspector?' asked Meredith.

'Coffee, thank you.'

She placed a bone china mug in front of him, leaving the sugar bowl and a little jug of milk for him to decide how he'd drink it.

'I apologise for intruding again but my team reported that you were the most observant of the locals they've had a chance to meet,' said Leo.

'Unfortunately, I'm not sure that we were much help.' Mr Price sat opposite Leo, his wife beside him. Sunshine fell across the table from the picture windows; these overlooked a beautiful garden to the rear with some jasmine in flower on a trellis screening the shed. 'As I said to them, we've not seen Anatoly for months, possibly over a year. Isn't that right, darling?'

'We saw him a few times about fourteen months ago. You remember, Al, when he was trying to get us to agree to his ridiculous extension?'

'Oh yes, I remember that – could hardly forget that planning hell he put us through. He wanted to excavate a garage underneath that lovely house of his – with a turntable for his Porsches or whatever.' Mr Price shook his head in disgust. 'He had no idea.'

Leo stirred some milk into his coffee. 'No idea of what?'

'The history of the area, of course!' Mr Price got up and fetched a book from the dresser. It was a slim paperback account of the area, the sort privately published and sold in the local shops. Leo had seen them around the area but only now did he notice that 'Alfred Price' was named as the author of the volume that covered the streets from the University

Parks to Summertown. 'Anatoly's house – Number Thirteen – was once lived in by one of the team that unravelled DNA,' continued Mr Price, turning to the relevant page. 'Just up the road was the house of one of the Oxford Movement – you know, the religious revival under Cardinal Newman? And the physicist Schrödinger, and writers Iris Murdoch and Tolkien, all lived only a few streets away. This place has an extraordinary history – and Chernov wanted to undermine it with a motor pool to show off overpriced vehicles as if this was Las Vegas or some such place with more money than taste! Well, at least we were able to block his first application. We just have to hope we scared him off!'

Leo didn't comment that their neighbour might well be in no state to take on another planning dispute.

'The news said you found a body in the garden,' said Mrs Price, offering him a biscuit from a Christmas selection box. 'Is it anything we should be worried about?'

He took a foil-wrapped one. 'You mean, do I think there are any more victims, and that locals are in danger? It is hard to say anything at this early stage, but I think it highly unlikely. My team hasn't found any others in the garden and this one has been there a while. The danger was probably over a year ago, if it existed at all for anyone else.'

'Thank you.' Mrs Price graced him with a smile. 'I'll sleep more easy tonight.'

'And do you know who it is?' asked Mr Price. 'Do you think someone took advantage of the fact that the house stands empty most of the time? I can't imagine it involving Anatoly. He was always such a friendly chap, despite his lamentable taste in home alterations. We always got on well when we chanced to meet. It had to be either before his time, or in his absence.'

That was interesting. This was the first person Leo had met who had nice words to say about his likely victim.

'You got on well?'

'You sound surprised, Inspector. But we shared a lot, considering how different our backgrounds were. He was ex-service, like me, which meant we found we had a fair amount in common. We saw the Cold War from the opposite sides of the Iron Curtain, me as a raw recruit, he as a teenage soldier.' Price gestured to a picture on the dresser of some shiny-faced young officers lined up for their graduating class photo. 'Lord, don't we look young.'

'Far more handsome than was good for you,' teased Mrs Price.

'Thank you, darling. We coincided, Anatoly and I. We discovered that he was stationed in Berlin in the Russian zone, when I was on the other side in the British – that was just as things fell apart for the Soviet system. He certainly benefited from that.'

'Do you know how he managed that?' asked Leo, finding this information very helpful to understand the enigma that was his possible victim.

'As I understood it, well-placed father who grabbed the money for the family. Definitely not an ideologue, unless the power of money counts as a belief.'

'Can you think of anyone who you know who would have cause to harm him?'

Price looked distressed for the first time during the interview.

'Hang on, you mean . . . you don't mean that you think it is him in the garden? I thought it was some stranger you'd unearthed?'

'It's a possibility.'

'Good grief.' He took his wife's hand. 'Sorry, I hadn't picked up on that. I assumed it was someone not from around here.'

'I can't confirm that the body is Mr Chernov,' Leo said carefully, 'but it is something I'm having to consider. I can't find anyone who has had contact with him for over a year. Have you?'

Mr Price looked surprised to be asked. 'Me? No, we weren't on those terms. Just friendly neighbourly kind of chat when we bumped into each other.'

'And how did he take your opposition to his basement alterations?'

Mr Price chuckled grimly. 'Oh, he knew all right that he faced a battle royal to get those through, but he was determined that money would talk. He hadn't met our kind before. Oxford is run very differently to Russia.'

'His daughters were such pretty girls,' added Mrs Price. 'I do hope it isn't him, for their sake.'

'And what about the son?' asked Leo.

'Alex? A different sort, that one. Hard. I didn't like him,' said Mrs Price.

Mr Price patted her hand. 'He was fearfully rude to Meredith. Racially abusive about our marriage. I won't stand for that and let him know it. Reported him to the school too. Anatoly was very apologetic, brought Alex round here to say sorry. You could see the boy hated it, very grudging with his apology. He gave me the chills. I almost regretted telling the school about it and I warned Meredith never to be alone with him.'

'But we never saw the boy again once he left St Bede's. He went off to America for university,' she said.

Mr Price shook his head in disapproval. 'Things came too easily to that boy. Spoiled him. Place bought by his father, no doubt.'

'I don't think having all that money did him any favours,' agreed Mrs Price.

Leo was getting a good picture of the family dynamics. His best bet, if the ex-wife didn't work out, would be to approach one of the daughters. They sounded easier nuts to crack than Alexei. 'And can you tell me anything else about Mr Chernov that might help us with our enquiries, something that you haven't yet mentioned?'

The two exchanged a look. There was something. Leo waited.

'It's probably nothing but it's about that fence between his garden and the next. You can see it from our attic window,' said Mr Price.

'The broken panel?'

'Yes. It's been like that for years and it bothered me. I raised it with the agent who runs the property and she said there was a dispute with the neighbour on the other side as to who owned it. Normally, she would just get it fixed – a man of Chernov's wealth would hardly notice the cost – but it was a point of principle for him.'

'How can it be? He barely lived here by all accounts.'

Mr Price pointed a shortbread finger at him. 'My thoughts exactly. So I asked.' He took a bite and washed it down with some coffee. 'Apparently Anatoly and the man from the house in Howell Street were longstanding rivals from back home. By this she must've meant Russia, I suppose. The Howell Street man is from those parts.'

'Uzbekistan actually,' corrected Leo.

He nodded. 'That's what I meant. Former Soviet Union. They're all tied up together still, believe me. You can't shake off nearly a century of central control so easily. In any case, Anatoly and that Uzbek, what's his name?'

'Akmal Gulom,' said Leo.

'Maybe I did know that?' Mr Price looked to his wife.

'Planning consent,' she said. 'Swimming pool.'

'Oh lord, yes, that awful extension. Anyway, according to Anatoly, he and Gulom had had dealings that went sour much more recently and were sworn enemies. The irony was they ended up living side by side, probably unaware they would share a boundary, all because they both had children at St Bede's. It's very popular with the Russian elite and there's more than a little politics going on among the parents.'

'Better than any soap,' supplied Mrs Price. 'I help out in the library and the tales the staff tell would make your hair curl. Bodyguards at parents' evening!'

'He probably had no idea how small this part of Oxford is – how likely it would be he'd be forced into proximity with his rival. I mean, you don't give much thought to who lives at the end of your garden, do you? It's the next-door neighbours who seem to matter most and they would've seemed innocuous.'

'Did you ever see Mr Chernov in the company of Mr Gulom?'

Mrs Price hissed between her teeth, like she'd touched something cold. 'Only once recently at the school. At the St Bede's summer barbecue a few years back. I told you I could feel the tension, didn't I, Al?'

'You did. No love lost between those two.'

'There was some Romeo and Juliet element too. All very tragic. Their children were friendly and the fathers disapproved.'

So a personal as well as business rivalry. There were plenty of motives there for murder. Leo stood up as the front door bell went. 'Thank you. That will be my sergeant. I won't take up any more of your time.'

He collected Harry on his way out. His sergeant was finishing his deli sandwich on the doorstep and was still wiping his hands on a napkin. He smelt strongly of fried onions.

'New lead,' Leo said briskly as he began a text to Jess. 'Chernov's enemy lived at the bottom of the garden.'

'You mean the house where the naked chick lives?' Harry brushed crumbs from his tie.

'I mean the house where Miss Bridges is house-sitting, yes.'

'Good-oh. She's always game for a laugh, that one.'

'You'll be respectful.'

'With her? She don't need that. She's got my number, just as I have hers.'

It took Leo a little longer than he cared to admit to realise that Harry was talking figuratively. 'I regard her as a friend.'

Harry just huffed at that.

'And if she lets us in to search, we can avoid the complications of a warrant.' Chernov's lawyer was already questioning their right to be inside the house yesterday, despite the presence of a warrant and, oh yes, a dead body in the garden. 'Let's see if we can find the tools that dug that grave next door.'

Chapter 9

Jess

'When shall we three meet again,' I said dramatically as I opened the door to Leo and Harry.

'Hello, Jess. Thanks for making time for us,' said Leo. 'I hope it didn't cause any trouble at work?'

'No, my boss is a peach.'

The two policemen came inside. Flossie came to greet them, nether regions doing a full shake of pleasure. A tail wag was not enough for my spaniel.

'Is it OK for the rest of the team to look through the garden and outbuildings?' Leo asked.

'I'll open the side gate for them.' I took a keyring from the hook inside the pantry. 'They'll need this to get into the shed.' I waved at the three-person team waiting in the drive. 'Hi, guys.'

'Has anyone else used these tools?' asked a silver-haired man in a boiler suit.

'Just the old house-sitter and me.' That last was a little bit of a lie. Sure, I'd looked at them but I'd not taken them out for a spin.

'What's the name of the previous house-sitter?' asked Leo.

'Ben Major. He's gone back to New Zealand to raise vines and make wine. He liked gardening.'

'Got a contact for him?'

'Yeah, somewhere. I'll give it to you.'

Leaving the team to get on with their search, we returned to the kitchen.

'So you have a dead guy?' I asked bluntly.

'We always have dead guys,' said Harry. 'Can't get enough of them. Would you show me where the home office is, love?'

'Oh, I'm not sure I should . . .' What was the right thing here? Could I be jeopardising my job if Mr Gulom discovered I let the police into his private papers? But then, as far as I knew (and I had looked), he didn't keep much here, this being more of a weekend retreat kind of place.

'We can get a warrant if you prefer?' asked Leo.

'No, no, it's fine. Just try not to land me in trouble, please?'

'If we find anything, it won't be you in trouble, Jess,' said Harry.

I showed him the study that looked out over the garden. 'Make yourself at home. The household papers are in that filing cabinet. It's not locked. I don't think there's much else here – just the plans of the building work they did, school newsletters, that kind of thing.' I'd had a good look myself, being insatiably curious.

'Any firearms kept on the premises?' asked Leo.

'None that I've seen but maybe there's a hidden safe or something?'

'Will you give me the tour?' Leo was checking all of the family photos as we moved around the house. 'This one is Gulom?'

'Yep. There's a really cheesy one of him over the fireplace in the drawing room if you want the full splendour of my employer.' I took him into the oak panelled room in which I had great fun reading Victorian novels in front of a crackling fire. Over the mantlepiece was what I thought a terrible oil painting of Akmal in desert robes, a sub Lawrence of Arabia look. He had heavy brows and a hawkish nose. A bird of prey sat on his gauntlet. 'You'd think he was a Bedouin or Arab prince, wouldn't you, but he's a diamond trader.'

Leo stood contemplating the portrait. 'Is he married?'

'Turn around.'

On the other wall was the wife as sultana. She was pictured reclining on a couch with a leopard stretched at her feet. She was draped in diamonds, including a yellow one in her naval.

'Words fail.'

I had to laugh at his expression. 'I think they're fun. Maybe this is like their sexual fantasy life?'

'I now dread to ask: children?'

'There were two, according to Ben, the house-sitter before me. He had to move out sometimes during the school terms when the parents came to visit their kids at St Bede's. That was until the girl died in a car accident on the A34 – real shock to everyone – and they took the son out of school. They've not been back since. Sad, isn't it?' I picked up a school photo of Fatima, smiling out of the frame with that heart-breaking expectation of a full life. I guessed she was about fourteen in this one. There were none of her in the house after her eighteenth birthday.

'Pretty girl.' Leo took it from me.

'Beautiful.'

'I think I remember the case.' He replaced it exactly in the spot I'd taken it from. 'She wasn't the only casualty but the driver survived. Another passenger was badly injured. Fatima and another girl sitting in the back were killed. A lorry driver was jailed for causing it. He was proved to have been using his mobile and ploughed into their vehicle which was waiting in a queue to leave at the Botley interchange.'

'I don't blame them for not coming back here. I'd sell up and try to put it behind me if I were them.'

'So why haven't they?'

I shrugged. 'Maybe waiting for an uplift in the market? Things have been pretty stagnant for the multi-million pound home since Brexit. Or so I'm told by the neighbours. Let me show you around.'

I led him through the upper floors with the multiplicity of en suite bedrooms. 'I've actually worked out that there are more bathrooms than bedrooms. Don't you find that weird? I mean, how many do you have?'

'Just one. I wish I had more.' He poked his head into one that had gold fittings and quickly withdrew.

'You should borrow one of these. They wouldn't notice.' I opened the door to show them the lost child's bedroom, a princess chamber of canopied bed, sugar-pink walls and white furniture. A calendar from the year she died still hung on the wall. 'This one is Fatima's. It's exactly as she left it, clothes still hanging in the wardrobe. I find it sad.' I led him up a winding stair and threw open the door onto my chaos. 'Ta-dah, the Jessica bower. Also known as the house-sitter hovel.' I leant a little closer. 'It isn't en suite, but as I'm the only person here I can have a bath in a different one each day of the week.'

Leo's eyes snagged on my lingerie which was currently draped over the radiator.

'Oops. Maybe I should've tidied up?'

He just smiled and shook his head.

'If you really want to understand this house though, you've got to come down to the basement with me.' I reversed course and took him down two flights of stairs. 'Looking at this house with the spooky mansion vibe, I bet you're thinking that it'll be cobwebs and the mouldering remains in coffins, but . . .' I switched on the light to reveal the still, blue expanse of the underground swimming pool. 'I have to admit this is the best perk of the job. Technically, I'm not really supposed to swim here alone – something about insurance – but I confess I take no notice of that.'

'How could you resist?' He knelt and felt the water.

'Is that a glint of envy in your eyes, Inspector? I've been told this is Gulom's precious.' I waited for him to get my joke. 'Gulom? Gollum? Oh, never mind. What I mean is the last house-sitter said Mr Gulom had a huge battle with planners to get this built. The locals were up in arms. But it's done now and you can't see it from the outside so all that's subsided. He's been forgiven a lot for having a decent garden, unlike the one you dug up.'

'Not personally.' He let his fingers play in the water. 'I didn't take the spade to it myself.'

I glanced over my shoulder to the stairs back up. 'Wanna strip off and dive in? I won't tell anyone.' In fact, I'd probably join him.

'Sorry. Another time, maybe, I'll come for a swim. After all,

I can't have you invalidating your insurance by leaving you to swim alone. Jess . . .' He looked down. There were some cracked tiles that moved a little under his feet.

'That wasn't me. Shoddy craftsmanship – or my predecessor had a really wild party. I've reported it to the agency but they've not responded.'

'Ah. About that. We think Glass Tower might've gone out of business.'

'What? Couldn't you have led with that? Jesus, I'm owed a month's salary.' I raced upstairs to find my phone to dial Heather. It rang out.

Leo joined me in the kitchen. 'I'm sorry. We can't find anyone still working for the agency and the listing at Companies House is also out of date. But, on the bright side, they didn't own this house; it belongs to Mr Gulom. If you can contact him, then maybe he'll pay you directly?'

'Or maybe the agency has done a midnight flit with my pay?'

'Do you know how to contact him?'

I dug my fingers into my hair and squeezed. 'No, but there has to be a way.'

'I'm looking for him too.'

'Why?'

'He and Chernov were business rivals apparently.'

'And you're wondering who hated Chernov enough to plant him in his garden?'

'If the victim is him. I've still not got an ID on the body.'

'But you believe it is?'

'Signs are pointing that way.'

I looked for missing people for a living. How difficult would it be to find a stupendously rich guy who was also possibly on the run if he was responsible for a dead man next door? Probably more than for the ordinary runaway who didn't have bottomless coffers to fund their escape.

'Let me know if you find him, won't you?' I asked.

'Same here. That's one of the tasks I've set Harry, to see if there are other addresses on the correspondence.'

I perched on the edge of the kitchen table and tapped the phone against my mouth. 'You know who would have another number?'

'No, who?'

'The school. If the Guloms weren't in residence full-time, they had to have left an emergency contact number.'

'Jess, you're brilliant! The same would apply to the Chernovs too.' He glanced at his watch. 'It's four already.'

'It's a private school. Longer hours. If you go now, I bet you'll still find people there.'

He moved closer to say goodbye. I made the move into a hug and was pleased when he held it for a second and squeezed me tighter. All my old attraction to him came zinging back. To be honest, it hadn't gone very far. 'Thank you, Jess. We still need that talk.'

'Yes, we do. But go. You don't have long.'

'I'll leave Harry and the team with you. Will you still be here when I get back?'

'Not going anywhere, Inspector. I live here, remember?'

With a nod, he was out of the door and driving away.

I should've told him that on a Friday evening around school pick-up time, it would be quicker to walk.

Chapter 10

Leo

Leo cursed as yet another SUV pulled in front of him. Spits of rain mixed with sleet smeared his windscreen. Christmas lights danced on the trees and bushes on the edge of the school grounds, seemingly anxious for the students to go home. There appeared to be some informal one-way route past St Bede's for the pick-up of day pupils, which he was driving against. Giving up, and not having a child who would shudder to walk more than a few metres to the car, he pulled over and parked. He would've done better to have walked from Howell Street. Making swifter progress on foot, he could see there was a certain pattern to the vehicles: usually the driver was an attractive woman, of motherly rather than au pair age, though he spotted a few dads and a couple of men who looked more like chauffeurs. She would open the door, a child would scurry out and jump in the front, slinging backpack behind. The door would slam and the vehicle head off to the leafy villages that surrounded Oxford to a life of pony clubs and Labradors, or so Leo imagined. Quite a few of the children were staying put, though, because they were

83

boarders. Some of these were playing on the hard courts, fields being too wet at the moment, or milling about in sheltered areas holding piles of books for their evening prep. They barely looked at him, their attention all on their intricate social life among their peers, all ages from eleven to eighteen, though there were few of the older ones outside. It seemed a happy, diverse cohort, affluence disguised by the uniform of grey trousers, yellow shirt and blazer. Even the girls wore trousers these days, further eroding gender divisions. The sixth form wore casual clothes, a perk probably longed for by the juniors.

Following the signs to the reception in what was a converted house, he found an administrator still on duty. She was a grandmotherly sort of woman, a reassuring presence for parents leaving their kids there for months. He identified himself and asked to speak to the headmaster.

'Do you have an appointment?' she asked, 'because I'm afraid he's very busy today. We're holding an open evening for prospective overseas pupils.'

'No, I don't have an appointment, but I'm afraid murder rarely waits for one. Please tell him I'm here.' He wasn't going to waste time arguing.

'Murder?' The woman cast an uneasy look behind her to the parents waiting on the sofas in the reception lounge.

Leo realised how he was going to get his way. 'Yes, murder. A killing. Near here,' he said more loudly, angling his body so the nearest parents could hear.

The woman quickly rang through to the headmaster's office. 'Deirdre, I've a gentleman from Thames Valley CID to see Lawrence. Yes, I know, but I really think he should make time.'

She waited. 'Good. I'll have someone escort him over.' She put the phone down. 'He'll see you now. You need to sign in.' She turned the visitors' book towards him, with its innocuous list of educational reps, sports teachers and music tutors. 'Perhaps I'll just take a copy of your ID'

Formalities completed, the receptionist summoned a passing pupil. 'Nell, please show our visitor to Mr Buckingham's office.'

The young teenager, who had a lapel covered with badges declaring her a librarian and lower school prefect, performed her duties flawlessly. She clearly mistook him for a prospective parent.

'Welcome to St Bede's. We're a co-educational school with a happy family atmosphere. Most of our pupils go on to Russell Group universities and we got twelve into Oxbridge last year.' She reported this like sports results, which, Leo supposed, it was, between the private schools and their league tables. 'Here's Mr Buckingham's office. Enjoy your visit.'

'Thank you, Nell.' He watched her go, detecting a skip in her step as she wove her way through boys playing keepie-uppie with a tennis ball. He contrasted her behaviour with the sullen welcome he got when he went into some of the rougher Oxfordshire schools. Part of him preferred the honesty of the hostile looks and muttered insults. Wasn't that what teenagers were supposed to be like? Too much cheerfulness seemed worrying.

Leo found an Asian couple waiting outside the headmaster's office, a scared-looking boy in tow. Mr Buckingham emerged, held up a staying hand to Leo, and turned to his guests. He was a well-dressed man in his fifties, with a hearty, almost boyish air that seemed to fit the atmosphere of the school.

'Mr and Mrs Chan, and Li of course, I apologise for keeping you waiting but I have to see our local policeman first about a small matter of some urgency. I hope you don't mind waiting another ten minutes?' He managed to make Leo sound like he'd been summoned to the headmaster rather than the other way round. Kudos to Mr Buckingham for turning the tables.

Of course, the Chans didn't object so Leo followed Buckingham into his comfortable study and the door was firmly shut. The headmaster gestured to a chair and took his place behind the desk. Leo wondered how many trouble-makers made it this far. He imagined that this school rarely had any behaviour rising to Lawrence Buckingham's level.

'How can I help you, Mr . . .?'

'Detective Inspector George. It's about the body found in Number Fourteen, Hay Road.'

'Ah yes, I saw something about that on the news. What's it got to do with St Bede's?'

'The house belongs to the Chernov family. The children were pupils here at one time.'

'They were: Alexei, Harvard; Natasha, Warwick; and Anastasia, Durham.' He gave their university destinations as if that was all that was needed to be known about them. 'Anastasia left us last year – that's two academic years ago now. I assumed the family had moved away?'

'Not quite. I'm trying to identify the body that was found in the garden of their house. I have reason to believe it might be' – he had to choose his words carefully – 'someone connected to the family but I'm struggling to track them down. The school would have other contact numbers for them so I would be grateful if you would give them to me.'

From his doubtful expression, the headmaster was quickly thinking through the implications.

'It is murder, Mr Buckingham,' Leo said softly. 'They have the right to know what's going on at their own house.'

'Putting it like that, then yes. I'll ask my PA to dig those out. Are there any more questions for me? I'm very busy today, as you saw.'

'Yes, I do. In the course of my enquiries, it came up that Anatoly Chernov had a particularly fractious relationship with a neighbour, one Akmal Gulom. Mr Gulom also had children at the school?'

Mr Buckingham's attentive but impatient expression saddened. 'Ah, yes, Rashid and poor Fatima.'

'People have reported that the bad atmosphere between the two fathers even carried over to school events for parents?'

Mr Buckingham got up and went to his sideboard to pour himself some water. 'Would you like some?'

'No, thank you.'

He stood there for a moment, apparently lost in memories. 'It was a very sad chapter for the school, soon after I became head. Fatima was out with friends. They'd all just celebrated their eighteenth birthdays and it was just before A levels.' He turned, as if he needed to justify the school's behaviour to Leo. 'The older pupils can pretty much come and go as they like. They are adults, after all. Tragically, the car was rammed on the A34 and Fatima and Paulina died. To lose two such bright girls was terrible for the school, as you might imagine.'

'Yes, I remember the case. All four young people in the car were from your school, weren't they?'

'Yes. We were devastated. James spent a year in hospital with a serious spinal injury, but I'm pleased to say he's recovering thanks to intensive physiotherapy. He even managed to go to university, two years late but that was a miracle considering what he'd had to battle. Only the driver got away without injury, which I think was almost as hard for him as if he'd been injured like James. I wasn't surprised that he gave up the idea of Cambridge and chose to leave the country afterwards.'

'And who was the driver?' Leo thought he could guess.

'Alexei Chernov. We tried to keep his name out of the press as much as possible. It really wasn't his fault, as the confession of the lorry driver proved. He pleaded guilty so it never went to trial. Alexei hadn't been drinking, or driven recklessly; he was simply in a queue of traffic on the approach to the slip road.'

'But the Guloms . . .?'

'That was . . . complicated. Mr Gulom had forbidden his daughter to go out with Alexei so blamed the young man for her presence in the car. He blamed the school too for allowing them to fraternise but how we can police friendships? I'm not sure we'd want to. Mr Gulom should have moved his daughter if he felt so strongly about her dating Alexei Chernov, but apparently she begged to stay where she was happy and he gave in.' He sipped his water, composing himself. The emotion still suffused this memory. 'I think Mr Gulom's bitterness against others was really because he blamed himself. As a father myself, I can imagine that all too well.'

'Do you have a contact for the Guloms?'

'They did leave rather abruptly soon after the accident. That would be about four or five years ago. The information will doubtless be out of date.'

'But it would be very helpful, all the same. I have some questions for them about their house in Howell Street.'

'That amazing castle place? They still own it? I have wondered every time I jogged past it if they'd sold up. I went inside once, when we were on good terms, of course. Did they complete the pool they wanted?'

'Yes, they did.'

'Not sure it's quite in character with the area but the plans did look splendid. We had quite a struggle to get permission to build our own sports centre here, thanks to local opposition to infilling the land between here and the river. We managed to get it and have built a state-of-the-art facility.' He was slipping back into headmaster speak. 'You're welcome to visit it. We have regular open evenings for locals to use it as part of community engagement. We also make it available to local state schools and worthy causes for galas and such. Perhaps Thames Valley Police would be interested?'

Leo got to his feet. 'Thank you. I'll mention it to my superior. If you could direct me to your PA, I'll get out of your way.'

Mr Buckingham showed him to the door. 'It was so sad. You never forget the children you lose – the ones that die before their time. Fatima and Paulina were my first loss as a headmaster. I hope to God they are the last.'

Waiting by Deirdre's desk for her to summon up the contact information, Leo watched Mr Buckingham shift gear and go back to affable public school headmaster whose sky never had a dark cloud.

'Mr and Mrs Chan, do come through. Li, tell me a little about yourself. I hear you're fond of chess?' And the door closed.

Chapter 11

Jess

The police loaded up the tools they found in the garden shed to take away for analysis. I had to sign for the whole lot – and there was quite a collection.

'You know I won't be able to do any gardening until you bring those back?' I told Harry as we went through the paperwork at the scrubbed pine kitchen table. 'What a blow.'

'You don't sound too upset about it.'

'Oh, I am. Completely devastated.' I grinned at him.

Harry chuckled. 'Cushy number you've got here.'

'Yeah, I had no idea this kind of job even existed.' I handed back the clipboard. 'It was my friend Cory who told me about it. She met someone who knew someone . . . You know how it goes around here.'

'Bound to be dodgy money that paid for a place like this.' He rolled his shoulders, seams of his shirt straining. He could do with losing a few pounds.

'Or maybe my employer is just a very good businessman who knows his gems.' I just had to hope they weren't conflict diamonds; Cory had already given me the lecture when I took the job with a diamond merchant. 'So, do you think he did it?'

'The inspector believes there's something in it – the proximity, the rivalry. I have to agree: normal Oxford folk don't go around topping each other over fence panels. It has to run deeper than that and Russian organised crime isn't known for its gentle ways.'

I rubbed my upper arms, shivering slightly. 'And I just thought they were a flashy kind of nouveau riche family. I never considered they might be the Uzbek Sopranos.'

'Where do the new riches come from, Miss Bridges? Have you asked yourself that? Thanks for this.' He waggled the clipboard at me. 'Ah, there's the boss back. I'll make tracks and get this lot to the lab. Won't be processed until Monday now, but I take it you're in no hurry?'

'Keep them as long as you need!' I called after him.

He tapped his forehead in response.

Having parked on the drive, Leo got out of his car and had a quick word with Harry before heading towards me.

'Was the school helpful?' I asked.

'I have some new addresses to try. Thank you for that idea. I also found out something very interesting.'

Flossie came for her greeting, interrupting him at this cliff-hanger of a moment.

'Sorry, she's a bit boisterous. She needs her walk.'

'In that case, shall we go together? I can fill you in on what I learned.' And the unspoken part was that we'd get a chance to talk undisturbed by police searches and ill-timed interruptions.

'OK. Let me grab her lead.' I slipped on my coat and wellies and clipped the lead on to Flossie's collar. She was almost hysterical with excitement by this point, which didn't say much for my obedience training. 'She'll settle down, I promise.' Her sharp barks were making it hard to hear anything he said. 'Let's go before she perforates our eardrums.'

Flossie did indeed settle by the time we took the path through Wolfson College to the river meadows. I let her off the leash at South Mead and she rocketed away in the vain hope of catching a flock of seagulls. They rose from the ground and screeched their derision at her.

'Yep, I know how that feels,' I said in sympathy for my poor embarrassed dog.

'Where does she come from? Is she a rescue animal?' asked Leo.

'You could call her that, but she belonged to an old neighbour in London who turned out to be psycho-killer. Yay!' Leo smiled at my sardonic tone. 'She got taken away and I rescued Flossie from ending up at the shelter.'

'What happened to the owner? Did she go on trial?' He held back a bramble for me.

'Thanks. Judged insane and not fit to stand. It was all a con in my book. She wasn't insane. Your lot protected her.' I threw a stick which Flossie just watched as if to ask what on earth was I doing. My turn for humiliation.

'My lot?' Leo looked puzzled.

'She'd been an undercover policewoman way back. She knew too much. I think the people at the top didn't want all that aired in public court.'

'How on earth did she end up in your life?

'Thanks to Michael's wife. She was an old friend of hers. They'd been colleagues.' My ex, Michael Harrison, now an academic at Magdalen, had paid dearly for this old life of his wife, Emma, when it caught up with him after her death.

Leo was quiet for a few moments, thinking that over. 'I didn't see that in the press about the case.'

'Ah, well, you wouldn't, would you? That was exactly what they wanted to keep under wraps, the tactics used by undercover police officers back in the day. Michael, bless him, didn't want Emma's name dragged through the mud so let it drop.'

We paused by a fallen tree. The river was looking very full, swollen by winter rain. It was dark already but the path was well trodden and there was just enough light from the college across the Cherwell to see our way. Wolfson was a modern building, a concrete and glass construction that reminded me of the kind of flats that would be built in some canalside regeneration, nice but nothing too notable. The grounds were lovely though and I often came here to walk Flossie, as the parks closed at dusk and these stayed open.

'What were you going to tell me, before we left?' I asked.

'What I learned from the headmaster at St Bede's?'

I nodded.

'It's about the grudge held by Mr Gulom – I discovered that it is deep and very serious. Alexei Chernov, the oldest child of Anatoly Chernov, was driving the car in which Fatima died.'

The poor girl's smiling face flashed before my eyes – those few awful tiny seconds between life and death. 'But it wasn't his fault, right?'

'No, not his fault. But that might not matter to a grieving father.'

'I guess not.'

Flossie bounded up with a stick in her mouth – not the one I'd thrown. That had been comprehensively rejected. She dropped her pick at Leo's feet. He plucked it up and threw it. The spaniel bounded after it with exuberant happiness.

'Fickle,' I muttered.

'She's playing you,' said Leo. 'It's you she really loves.'

We watched Flossie cavort for a few moments as she picked up the stick, dropped it, attacked it, then dropped it again.

'Jess, I really am sorry for not following through with the drink I promised you.' He leant against the stile we'd just crossed over. We'd have to turn back soon.

'That's OK.' Why was I letting him off so easily?

'No, it's not. You deserve an apology at the very least. When I got home that evening I found my mother on the doorstep.'

'Oh.' I immediately imagined my own mother in the same position: that would be a complete buzzkill to any romantic plans I might've had.

'It's more complicated than you might imagine.' He closed his eyes for a moment. 'This is hard to say. I don't tell people this stuff.'

It was on the tip of my tongue to tell him he didn't have to say anything if it were too painful, but maybe he needed to confide in someone? And maybe that someone could be me? So I waited.

'I have a toxic relationship with her. She's exhausting.'

His words stopped again. An owl hooted somewhere to

the east of us, hidden in a copse. The main road hummed in the distance, a low bass note to the owl's tenor like they were cooking up some Russian Orthodox chant between them.

'It's fine, Leo. You of all people know that I have a terrible relationship with my own father. You arrested him, after all. It can't be as bad as that.'

He gave a hollow laugh.

'Maybe it can?' I suggested.

'As a child, she dragged me from pillar to post in her quest for happiness. Happiness meant either to be cast in a role in some TV film or other, or to be cast as the girlfriend of a man who would look after her. To me they all seemed variations on her acting life, though she'd claim she actually felt something for the men she lived with.'

This didn't sound like it was going to end well. But now he'd started, I had to know the rest. 'That must've been hard on you.'

'Mostly people were nice. I was a cute, quiet kid, didn't make waves.' I could imagine that: a little dark-haired boy with big sad eyes. 'It only got more difficult when I became a teenager. We were living on a canal boat by then, at first with a decent guy called Bradley, then with a not so nice guy called Pat. They were friends and Bradley had seemed to pass her along once he tired of her.'

'You know, that Bradley doesn't sound such a great guy.'

'He wasn't the worst. Problem was that Pat had no one to hand her on to and got stuck with her. And me.'

I blew on my fingers and rubbed them together. 'Did you go to school? I mean, living on a canal boat must be a bit like being a gipsy?'

'Yes, I made sure of that. I'd catch a bus, hitchhike, do what it took to get to school. In fact, it wasn't that far from here, up in Banbury. We used to travel up and down the Oxford Canal in that stretch, avoiding paying for moorings if we could. I liked school. I liked how it made me feel.'

'Like you mattered. Like you were good at something?' I could remember thinking something very similar when I escaped my father in my school lessons.

He met my eyes. 'Yes, like that.'

I took his hands. They were very cold. 'You're not wearing gloves.'

'Neither are you.'

'Oh, I always lose them.'

He pulled a pair out of his pocket and handed me one. 'We'll share.'

I stuffed both of my hands in the big leather glove. He put one on and put his other hand in his pocket.

'Do you want me to go on?' he asked.

'Of course I want you to go on, but only if *you* want to.'

'I thought I might be boring you.'

'Leo! You are very far from boring me; frustrating me with delays, yes, but boring? No!'

He smiled. 'OK then. Here's the rest. My mother got cast in a small role in a TV drama and was away quite a lot. Pat turned his attention on me – and his attention was not welcome.'

'You mean . . .?'

'He was an any-available-body kind of guy, and didn't like it when I said, "No". I fled and went to school with a pair of black eyes, the school woke up to the fact something was wrong, and the authorities belatedly got involved. My mother was summoned back from her shoot, much to her annoyance. She never got another professional job after that, which she, of course, blames on me. Anyway, it was adios Pat.'

'That's good. I hope they put him away.'

'He was tried in a Magistrate's court and got a few months for GBH. The sexual aspect wasn't pursued as it was a "he said, he said" matter and the CPS hate those. The black eyes couldn't be argued away so they went with that. I hope it would be different now.'

'I'm surprised after what happened that you still became a policeman. You must've felt let down by the law?'

'It was exactly *why* I became a policeman. I never wanted to feel like that again, like no one would believe me.'

I slipped one hand from the glove and hugged him. 'That's for that boy whom the system should've protected much better.'

He gave me a quick squeeze back. 'Thanks. But this is all a very long way round to explaining just what the arrival of my mother means, and I'd better finish. You see, she found a way of making it all far worse. She is camera-hungry. She made friends with a guy on one of those morning shows – you know, the sort that do themed programmes along the lines "I married my mother-in-law" and so on?'

'Oh yeah. I never watch those.' I totally did. 'At least, only sometimes.'

He gave me a pained look. 'You might not again once I tell you the rest. She was talked into – or maybe talked her friend into – doing a programme on "my partner abused my kids and I didn't know". It was mainly girls as victims so she stood out as the mother with a teenage son who'd been abused, and she liked that. Got her the attention she craves.'

'You weren't made to appear, were you?' I knew how those programmes worked, and they usually had all parties present so they could film a huge bust up.

'I refused point blank. They were very disappointed as I think I'd been promised as the big crescendo for them.'

'You mean your mother had said you'd appear?'

He shrugged – and it was a far from shrugging matter. 'But I might as well have been there as she waived her anonymity.'

'Oh God, poor you.'

'Only child. Mother a minor, but known, actress. They didn't use my name but, of course, the kids in my school worked it out. I didn't go back, except to sit exams.'

'Why didn't someone do something?'

'What, Jess? Everyone was so very nice to me, but that just made it worse. I wanted them to not know, or un-know what they'd all seen. I almost preferred the kids who bullied me for it; at least I had a reason to hate them. I think I would've probably killed myself if I hadn't been in my last year, knowing there was only weeks to endure. I survived, moved on, never looked back.'

The pain of all that must have been nearly unendurable. I could sense that it still shook him, deep down. He'd seen school as his refuge and his mother had taken that from him too.

'But your mother still thinks she can move in after all she did to you?'

He gave a weary shake of his head. 'Ah, but you see, she's

the victim. She was betrayed by her partner, then cold-shouldered by her son. She doesn't deserve this.'

'Bullshit!'

He laughed, and this time it was a good sound. 'Exactly! But she is very difficult to get rid of – and I've tried, believe me.'

I slid my cold hand into his pocket to join the one he was warming in there. We laced fingers. 'And I've been mad at you for not going for a drink with me while you've been dealing with all this crap? I'm sorry. I should've guessed it was for a good reason.'

'She's the very worst of reasons.'

'Yeah, I get that. And we'll work this out. But for the moment, what about finding my dog and going home? I'll cook you supper and, while we wait, we can go for that swim.'

He took a deep breath. 'OK. Sounds like a lovely idea.'

Right on cue, Flossie bounded over, covered in mud from the river bank and looking very pleased with herself.

I sighed. 'Revised plan: Flossie and me, hose by the back door first, while you get the drinks; then swim and supper.'

'Deal.'

And of course I noticed that Leo didn't let go of my hand while we walked all the way back.

Chapter 12

Leo

Revealing so much of his past felt good, but Leo was now exhausted, like the land once the flood water receded. All was ugly, jumbled, confused, but with the hope that something would grow again in the brown-smudged space he'd cleared. It wasn't that what he'd said was even a secret. If Jess had ever done a search on him, she could've dug up the information. The only thing she would've needed was his mother's name. And now the drama only really meant something to him, as Haven Keene attracted no more interest from even the most gutter of the press. It was as much in the past as these things could be.

He lay on his back in the quiet swimming pool, watching the ripples on the ceiling. Blue silk. Mesmerising. Jess was upstairs cooking and dealing with Flossie so had told him to go ahead without her. She might even have sensed his need to be alone as she'd given him some astute looks when they got back from the walk. The search team was finished and there was no reason any longer not to take up her offer and borrow some trunks from the spares kept for guests. A swim would not compromise his objectivity. He relaxed, just doing enough to keep his legs from sinking. Let the burdens fall, he told himself. Just be.

A scuffing noise to his left caused him to turn. Jess was kicking off slippers and dropping her robe. He couldn't believe how beautiful she looked, lithe limbs and curves. His own Aphrodite.

'In deference to your newness to this, I even put on a costume,' she said, revealing a white bikini that did only a minimal job of concealing. She dived in and swam a quick length. He turned over and began a steady crawl, drawn to her by a sweet desire. The reflections now danced crazily on the ceiling, mirroring the wash of pleasure inside.

She bobbed up next to him like a seal – except seals weren't blessed with such exceptional breasts. He tried to keep his eyes above the neck. She shook water from her hair.

'This is the life! Come home from making your millions and slough off the day's stress in your own private pool. You can see why the gazillionaires want them. No kids with verruca socks, no fat old men ogling you, just you, the water and peace.'

He reached out and touched her cheek. 'Thank you.'

Tenderly she touched his face in exactly the same place. 'No need. I want you to feel safe with me.'

'I do.'

'Good.' With a smile, she kicked off for another length. He swam after her, enjoying the pure physical exertion. He'd not done much work in his garden recently and he missed it. He needed this.

A phone beeped from among her pile of clothes.

'That's our supper.' She got out and towelled off quickly. 'See you upstairs.'

He let her go and waited for the pool ripples to subside. The signals she was sending out were a little confusing. He knew they were attracted to each other but she was behaving more as a friend than lover. Was she waiting for him to make his own moves? Why was he always such an idiot when it came to women?

Drying off, he got dressed again, feeling less vulnerable once back in his suit. The trousers had got muddy on the walk so he brushed them off. Armour in place after the exposure, emotional and physical, of the last hour, he went upstairs, enticed by the smells coming from the kitchen.

'It's a quick veggie curry. I hope that's OK?' she asked, plating up his portion.

'Sounds great.' Say something, you fool! he berated himself. 'It looks great – and you're great. Wonderful.' He mentally face-palmed at his clumsy words. 'Jess, I just want to—'

She placed a finger on his lips. 'Leo, no need. Let's not rush this, OK? You've told me about you, but there're things you need to know about me too before we go any further. I'm not that great, really – pretty much a disaster zone. I'll tell you, but let's just have this evening. I want to enjoy what this could be.'

So it was right to read her signals as wary. That was OK: he wasn't an impulsive person; in fact, he tended to overthink things. More Hamlet than Hotspur. 'Right. No rush. So what shall we talk about?'

She led him to the breakfast table, which she'd set with wine glasses and a single candle. Cupping her hand around the wick, she lit it.

'Ordinary stuff. Work. Hobbies.' She offered him an Indian beer or white wine. He chose the beer and filled both their glasses on her nod.

'You know about my work,' he said. 'Tell me about yours.'

'The missing persons side is quiet at the moment. I need to do more marketing but there never seems to be a day when I feel like working out what that would mean.'

'I imagine there's not that many people offering what you do.'

'I agree but how to make myself visible? I probably need more help with my website. Anyway, I'm maternity cover at the moment at St Nicholas' college, in the development office. It would be a really good job if it wasn't for my dickish boss.' She went on to fill him in on the power struggle over the Christmas Eve service. 'And all he would give me was five hundred pounds!'

Leo cracked a poppadom. 'This is excellent, by the way.'

'One of my skills – jar opening.' She forked up a mound of basmati rice. 'Combined with chopping vegetables.'

'I've had bosses like yours. In fact, that's what modern policing is like under this Home Secretary: more with less. We're supposed to do everything: solve crimes, provide social services, protect people from terrorism, investigate allegations of sexual abuse, the list goes on. None of them are unimportant, apart from the paperwork maybe, but there's only so much anyone can do.'

'But you keep at it?'

'I do. I've backed myself into my corner in CID and so far have avoided most of the hassle by not climbing the tree any further. I'm not sure I want to. I'm not that good with people.'

She smiled. 'I hadn't noticed.'

'Most people. I hate managing them so to be a senior manager rather than an investigating officer would likely be a disaster. What's that thing about being promoted a rung above your ability?' It was freeing actually to admit it. He'd spent so long looking over his shoulder to see who would overtake him, and looking up to see the potential advancement in rank, that he hadn't stopped to ask himself if he cared. The part of the job he liked was getting justice for victims, finding a voice for the silenced, not the politics.

'What are you thinking?' she asked.

'Hmm? Oh, just that I might've been pursuing the wrong goal for the last decade.'

'Tell me about it. I've been more headless chicken than man with a plan – or woman with a plan in my case.'

He raised his glass. 'To clear sight.'

'And catching killers.' They chinked glasses together. 'I suppose my little dramas at work pale into insignificance compared to what you do.'

'You mustn't think like that. Is there anything I can do to help?'

She shook her head. 'Just listening to me griping about it helps.'

'I can do that. And I'm sure you'll find a way. Just be your usual imaginative self.'

When she cleared the plates and blew out the candle, he knew that he wouldn't be staying tonight. He got up and helped her stack the dishes in the dishwasher.

'Thank you, Jess, for a lovely evening. It was long overdue.'

She bit her lip and looked up at him. 'You know, this isn't like me. Normally I'd be jumping you and suggesting we have sex on the kitchen counter. Or in the pool – I had big trouble resisting you then. Had to just keep swimming. Like Dory.'

'Dory?'

'*Finding Nemo*. I take it you don't spend much time with kids?'

He laughed and shook his head. 'So why . . .?'

She shrugged. 'It's just an instinct. I want to be different with you. You may not have noticed' – she gave him a wry smile – 'but I'm a creature of impulse, yet this' – she gestured between them – 'is too important to treat as a fling. I don't want to sleep with you and have you regret it the next day.'

He really didn't believe that he would regret any second of it. The kitchen counter was looking more and more inviting with every second that passed. But it clearly mattered to her and he should be listening. 'OK. Slowly.' Taking the tea towel from her hands, he pulled her towards him. 'But not too slowly? I think that'd kill me.' Waiting for her to pull away if she wanted, he was rewarded as she stepped into him. He bent his head and kissed her. Her lips felt soft and sweet beneath his, parting gently as he deepened his own kiss. He didn't want to stop, and neither did she by the matching enthusiasm she summoned to meet his. She felt perfect, responsive, warm, careful of him but also letting him know with every touch, every brush, that she wanted him as much as he wanted her.

Then Flossie shoved her nose in between their knees, not wanting to be left out. They parted, and laughed – and that might well have been the best part, the shared amusement.

'Yeah, that was probably enough for a first kiss,' said Leo, exhilarated but also wanting to keep the fragile beauty hovering just a little longer. The carefulness, the delicacy of how they were treating each other: he'd not known that with anyone else.

'Will I see you again soon?' she asked, a little shyly for Jess.

Work came rushing back in, after the oasis she had provided. 'I've got to go to London tomorrow on the trail of Chernov's first wife. I also want to check out Glass Tower's main office, to see if there's any sign they're still in existence.'

'Oh.' Her eyes lit up. 'Maybe I could help you with that? They owe me, after all. Could we meet up in town, maybe go for drinks or do a little wandering? I love London and know it well.'

He tucked a strand of her blonde hair behind her ear. 'That sounds perfect. I could give my sergeant a break and you can be my partner. We've worked together in the past, after all.'

'We have?'

'You were my source inside the Children of the White Horse, remember?'

'Oh yes! Wow, me a police source. I totally missed that. I need to add it to my CV.'

'The interview tomorrow – it's not a contentious thing, just information gathering, hopefully some confirmation that the items we found really did belong to Chernov. I don't really need to drag my sergeant away from her day off.' He leaned closer. 'Plus it would be much more fun with you.'

'Then it's agreed. Meet at the station?'

'Yes. I'll get your ticket. Ten o'clock?'

'Fine.' She went up on tiptoes and pecked him on the cheek. 'Evening, Inspector.'

'Goodnight, Jess.'

As Leo drove away, he reflected that even the prospect of finding his mother at home would not spoil the last few hours for him. A door had opened in the prison he'd made for himself and he was determined to walk out into the sunshine.

Chapter 13

Jess

Had I been a monumental idiot, letting Leo go like that? He would've stayed if I'd asked.

I lay in bed, staring up at the sloping ceiling of my turret. It was a bedroom I would've fantasised about as a child and wasn't half bad now. When I closed the door at the bottom of the stairs, I did feel cut off from everything. I could've been sharing it with someone tonight if only I'd dared.

But Leo didn't know the sins of my past yet. He might not want to be with me once he heard the worst of my self-destructive behaviours. I'd been on a more even keel for the last year, but there had been very rocky times in the spiralling-to-crash-land relationship that had been my time with Michael. Fortunately we had both struggled free of the wreckage and managed to salvage a friendship, but I was ashamed of many things I had done during those years.

And then there were the teenage experiences of living on the street. The alcohol. The desperate phase where I would sell sex for money or drink. God, I'd have to tell him about those too, wouldn't I? And would he understand? If he didn't, then I suppose he wasn't the one for me.

Maybe nobody was?

Enough moping! I thumped my pillow, determined to put this all behind me. I'd managed one grown-up, impulse-free evening; I would just have to build on that.

I almost missed the train.

I had overslept and then, halfway through my wake-up cuppa, realised I had to give Flossie her walk early if I was going to be out all day. That was why the neighbours saw me jogging in my pyjamas just after nine, vacuum mug of tea in hand, Flossie bounding along with approval at my heels. I was probably lowering the tone of this coiffured neighbourhood, but I always found it a little too sleek-bob pleased with itself; a few split ends like me were humanising.

Dragging on a tunic dress, leggings, and knee-length boots, I hoped I looked the part of a police inspector's partner. It didn't help that drinking tea while running had given me hiccups. These were the painful sort but I didn't have time to attempt to get rid of them with any of the standard cures. Cutting it very fine, I shut Flossie in the kitchen with a bone bribe I'd saved for just such an occasion, and pedalled off to the station at my top speed. Abandoning my bike secured only to itself as there was no free space at the racks, I dashed into the station. Leo was standing at the barrier, face set in a worried frown.

'Sorry, sorry!' I grabbed the little ticket from him and fed it to the machine. It beeped. Wrong way round. The train just beyond the doors looked like it was preparing to leave. I finally got through thanks to the station guard opening the gate and I managed to get on board because Leo was holding the doors for me. 'Thanks!' I collapsed into a seat next to him. We'd earned ourselves glares from the other passengers.

Silently, Leo put a paper bag down on our table and took out a takeaway coffee in front of me. Then a croissant. I think that might have been the moment I fell in love with him.

'Aw, thanks. I don't deserve this.' Normally I would lie, blame traffic or Flossie, but I'd decided not to start my relationship with Leo like that. 'Overslept. So sorry.'

'There were other trains after this one we could've caught,' he said, sounding unflustered. 'I guessed already that you might live life on the edge of punctuality.'

'Oh no. Not on the edge. Well over into being late, I'm afraid.' I took the lid off my coffee. 'And you even got me chocolate sprinkles.' I licked the lid where they had stuck. 'Design fault with takeaway cups, don't you think?'

'Completely.' He had his in a reusable cup and took a cautious sip. 'Good morning.'

I leaned over and kissed him. 'Good morning.'

We grinned at each other as the train took us out through the flooded meadows of the Thames. Steel-grey and pale green, like a print by Eric Ravilious.

Content just to sit beside him, I leaned my head against his arm and watched the fields go by. This was lovely.

'What do you want me to do when we're seeing Mrs Chernov?' I asked after a time.

'Maybe you could take notice of anything that seems an

off-note in what she says. She's not a suspect, not yet, but if it is her ex-husband we've found, we always have to consider the spouse.'

'There another one, isn't there?'

'Yes, wife number two. That was a short-lived marriage – only lasted four years. She's in Cyprus now, living off the proceeds of her divorce settlement, and we have no record of her returning to the UK in the last two years. She's down the bottom of the suspect list. The lady we're seeing today is the mother of Chernov's children so that makes their relationship ongoing, even if they're no longer married.'

'You think they might've fought about the children? Or money?'

'Money is always a good motive but I've no idea. Let's see if we can find out, take a gauge on what she felt about him.'

I sat up to eat my croissant. At least the hiccups had gone somewhere in the sprint from bike to train. 'Thank you for this.'

'You gave me supper; the least I could do was provide breakfast.' He started on his own pastry, spreading a napkin out to catch crumbs. I'd already scattered my lap with them. That probably summed up the difference between us. But opposites attract, right?

Mrs Chernov had a flat in an apartment block in Knightsbridge, not far from Hyde Park. It was exactly the kind of place I would imagine the wealthy ex-wife of a Russian oligarch would live in, not far from Harrods and a short taxi ride from the most exclusive shops and restaurants of the West End. She had already decorated for the season and we were greeted by tasteful swags of fake greenery and enough lights to solve the problem I had back in the chapel.

A maid from some Far Eastern country – the Philippines? – showed us through to the lounge and invited us to wait while she told her mistress we were here. This was all an unsubtle power play as Leo had an appointment and, though the flat was spacious, it wasn't so big that anyone could be ignorant of the arrival of guests. That gave me ample time to appreciate that the lounge would've done Trump Tower proud with its white and gold approach to decor.

'It's like being inside a Fabergé egg,' I whispered to Leo.

'I was thinking more Cinderella's carriage,' he replied.

He was right! 'Do you think it's going to turn into a pumpkin?'

'When the money runs out.'

I bit my tongue, knowing it would be unprofessional to snigger on assignment.

Mrs Chernov swept into the room, fetchingly attired in a matching silk blouse and satin skirt in a shade of deep red. As a bleach bottle blond with a pale complexion, she could carry off the colour. Her nails were painted crimson. I imagined she was aiming for Confident Society Lady but I couldn't help think of Matriarch Vampire. Too much reading of *Twilight* in my misspent youth.

Leo clicked into his official mode, something that I have to admit gave me a little thrill.

'Mrs Chernov, thank you so much for making the time to meet us. I'm Inspector George, and this is my associate, Jess Bridges. She runs an agency that looks for missing people.'

That sounded good. I held out my hand and received the cool shake that Mrs Chernov deigned to give me. Seeing Leo put his card on the coffee table, I set mine next to it, pleased I'd done a good job on these on a do-it-yourself design website. She didn't take them up but did glance at them.

'Please do take a seat. Would you like some coffee?' She asked. Her accent was soft, just a few rolling Russian vowel sounds. It didn't seem as though she went to the ancestral home often to top it up.

As if on cue, the maid returned with a tray already prepared.

'Thank you. I take mine with a splash of milk,' said Leo.

'Miss Bridges?' She didn't risk chipping her varnish but let the maid serve us.

'Same please, but a little more generous on the milk.'

I was pleased that I'd asked for more as the coffee was punishingly strong. Mrs Chernov drank hers black. Brave woman.

'As my colleague explained on the phone, we're trying to locate your ex-husband, Anatoly Chernov,' said Leo, putting down the cup after a sip.

Mrs Chernov's gaze went to me, making the wrong, if flattering, connections. 'Miss Bridges looks for men like my former husband? I hope she has good links worldwide because Anatoly, in my experience, doesn't stay anywhere very long.'

I tried to project the air of someone with a contact in every city of note.

'Have you heard from him?' asked Leo.

'We only communicate through solicitors. It is better so.' She relented and added some sugar to her coffee.

'And your children? When did they last see their father?'

I raised a brow but I don't think either of the others caught the painterly echo.

'I haven't asked them.' She shifted, knees pressed together. 'They know to avoid the subject with me.'

'Because . . .?' probed Leo.

'Because Anatoly cheated on me with that *blyad* secretary of his. Well, that didn't last long, did it? They trade in the old car for the new and find they miss the classic lines and style after a few months of taking the new toy for a spin.' She was looking me as she stated this, so I felt I had to say something for the sisterhood.

'I'm sure he regretted it while the ink was still wet on the divorce papers,' I managed.

She gave me an approving nod. 'Never be someone's toy, Miss Bridges. Be the first wife, the one who makes the man. And get a good prenup.'

'That's . . . er . . . words to live by.' I glanced at Leo, looking for guidance as to what else he wanted. She clearly wasn't going to tell him anything, either because she didn't know where Anatoly was or it suited her to pretend otherwise.

'Mrs Chernov, you must be wondering why we are asking you about your ex,' said Leo.

She turned her face to the window, the soft light revealing the light dusting of her face powder. 'Not really. I only agreed because I understand you have a job to do, no matter how distasteful.'

'And I appreciate your cooperation. We found a body in the house Anatoly owns in Oxford.'

'He's still got that Victorian place? I thought he would've got rid of that once Anastasia left school.'

It was odd that she commented on the house rather than the body.

'The body was in the garden and had been there for over a year,' Leo continued. 'The pathologist puts it at thirteen months, so late last autumn. It is of a male of the size and age of Mr Chernov.'

She looked down at her hands then back up at him. 'Inspector, Anatoly is many things, but one of them isn't the kind of person who would end up buried in their own garden in Oxford.'

I added for her silently, 'Somewhere else maybe,' but not staid old Oxford. I didn't know if she intended me to make that inference.

Leo poured some more milk into his coffee. 'I'm pleased to hear that, but we're still trying to identify who it is. Mr Chernov's DNA is not on file and we don't have a sample to match the body to because no relative has come forward to offer one. We do, however, have some jewellery found with the victim and I wondered if you would be able to identify it for me. We can use that to establish whether the body is definitely Anatoly or not. The message on the back of the watch is in Cyrillic. We've had it translated. It's from Tolstoy.'

'Oh yes?' She had a very good poker expression, but that fact that she was using it made me suspicious.

'It's a quote from *War and Peace*: "Everything that I understand, I understand only because I love".' He didn't need to refer to his notes; he'd memorised it.

'Very pretty sentiment.' She smiled without humour. 'Tolstoy was a romantic at heart.'

'Clearly it is from a lover. Perhaps a former lover?'

'That would follow. Inspector, are you asking me if I know whether my husband had a watch with this engraved upon it? I'm afraid I cannot help you. As my divorce proves, Anatoly had many lovers. I cannot confirm or deny that it is his – and I still believe it is highly unlikely to be him. Could the body have been put there by an associate who knew the property was empty? Yes, that I can believe. Such a one might have seized his opportunity to disappear a rival. There are many Russians in London with foolish vendettas.'

'Why take a body all the way to Oxford to dispose of it?' I asked.

She turned back to me. 'To implicate Anatoly, of course! How better to hit at two enemies than to kill one and frame the other for it?'

As a theory it was interesting, but I was still not convinced she didn't recognise the engraving. I stood up.

'Excuse me, Mrs Chernov, but may I use your bathroom?'

Her eyes flickered with annoyance. 'Along the hall. Margareta can show you if you get lost.'

'Thank you.' I had no intention of asking the maid for directions – or of using the bathroom. Leaving Leo to run interference with his questions about Mr Gulom (not that Leo knew what I had planned), I went out into the corridor and, oh silly me, couldn't find the bathroom. I found several but not the one I wanted. The last door at the end of the corridor proved to be the one I was seeking: the master bedroom with en suite. Quickly checking I wasn't being watched and there were no internal cameras that I could see, I slipped inside and hurried over to the dressing table. This was a still life arrangement typifying the super-rich: exclusive scents, a tiered box of top brand make-up, an engraved hair-brush and hand mirror, and a locked jewellery box. I didn't think it would go well for Leo if I broke into that, so I contented myself with rummaging through the drawers. A sex aid. Good for you, girl. Some brochures for plastic surgeons. Nothing very interesting. Then I opened the drawer on the left and found what I wanted. A Rolex watch for ladies, decorated with little diamonds. I turned it over and used my phone camera to snap the reverse side with its Cyrillic inscription. Thinking quickly, I also photographed the family frames that she had displayed beside her bed on a teak dresser. Pretend to hate her ex-husband though she did, there were several pictures of him and the children that must date post-divorce.

I'd lingered too long. I darted out of the room, saw the maid at the far end of the hallway with a duster, so ducked into the nearest guest bathroom. I flushed the loo, washed my hands and came out brazenly.

'Oh, excuse me, which is the door back to the lounge? I've got myself a little confused,' I said loudly, hoping that any traces I'd not noticed that I'd left, like footprints in the deep pile carpets, would be put down to me getting lost.

'This way, Miss,' she said, opening the door back into the lounge.

I arrived in time to catch the tail-end of Mrs Chernov's account of Alexei's complete innocence in the fatal road traffic accident. He'd been in a new powder-blue Mini with an up-to-date service history – an eighteenth-birthday gift from her. He had been driving safely, his boy passenger and the girls in the back all wearing seatbelts. All this protesting was giving me an irrational suspicion that maybe he wasn't so blameless as everyone kept saying. How hard would it be for a super-rich man to buy off the poor sap of a lorry driver and get him to take the fall? I was going to suggest as much to Leo, and encourage him to do some digging, because maybe Mr Gulom's grudge wasn't without foundation?

Leo stood up when he saw me re-enter. 'Thank you for your time, Mrs Chernov. I'll let you know if there are any developments.'

She smoothed down her skirt, though the wrinkles wouldn't completely go. Natural fibres were a bitch for that; she'd be better off with some cheaper polyester mix if she wanted sleek.

'Good luck with your enquiries, Inspector. I hope my children are helpful. I'll tell them to be so.'

'Most appreciated.' Leo shook her hand and we retreated back to the lift.

Once inside, I opened my mouth but he pressed my hand slightly. I revised what I had been about to blurt out. Cameras: of course, there would be cameras in the lift to warn the inhabitants who was coming to the door: pizza delivery boy, call girl or bailiff.

'What a lovely flat,' I said instead. 'She seemed very nice.' I was getting better at lying.

'Very helpful,' Leo agreed, totally on the same page as me from the expression in his eyes. 'She gave me the current contact numbers for her children. I'll see if they know anything about their father's whereabouts.'

We both thought those 'whereabouts' were the mortuary, but for some reason the family were stonewalling the investigation. We exited past the concierge onto the street. I took some breaths to clear my lungs: the flat had felt airless with too many closed windows and cleaning spray.

'Underground to Oxford Circus?' Leo suggested.

'Or we could walk through the park?' Though it was December, it was one of those crisp, clear days.

He took my hand. 'I like your idea better. Maybe we could have lunch at the café on the Serpentine?'

Once we passed through the park gate, I felt it was safe to speak.

'Leo, I did a little wandering while looking for the loo.'

'Jess . . .' He looked pained, as if I gave him a headache.

'Totally by accident. I mean, she gave me permission to find it, didn't she?'

He groaned. 'You are going to get me into trouble.'

'Didn't you already know that?'

A cyclist zipped by on a pink bike ringing her bell. As she was only around six, I didn't mind. Her father jogged after her with a harried look and a quick 'sorry'.

'So are you going to tell me what you found?' Leo was better staying on programme than me with my butterfly brain.

I pulled out the phone and showed him the two pictures: one of the back of the watch, the other of the dresser top. Leo stopped and pulled out the enlarged photo he had of the blackened Rolex and the message that had been transcribed.

'It matches,' he said.

'Someone bought them, or maybe they bought each other, matching Rolexes with the same cute phrase. I'm thinking wedding or engagement present.'

'So she did know it belonged to him.'

I slapped my cheeks. 'Oh, shock horror, the woman lied to you!'

'She did give me her children's numbers.'

'And what's the betting that Vampire Mother is ringing ahead to tell them all to keep, well, Mum about what they may know?'

Leo looked annoyed with himself. 'You're right. She is a stone-cold . . .'

'I think the word you might be looking for is *blyad*. So she goes to the top of the list?'

Leo gazed back to the neat apartment block with its privileged, gold-plated divorcee. 'For doing it herself? No. For ordering it done, absolutely.'

Chapter 14

Jess

After a sandwich lunch at the café overlooking the Serpentine, followed by feeding crusts to ecstatic ducks, we cut through the park to Conduit Street, supposed home to the headquarters of Glass Tower. We were in the heart of Mayfair and I can tell you, the high price on the Monopoly board was justified if the amounts charged in the designer shops were anything to go by – not that they had tags, but you just knew you couldn't possibly afford anything in the window displays. One pair of shoes, one bag, one coat – less here was definitely more.

'Odd name, isn't it?' I mused. 'Glass Tower. Because there are no glass towers around here. If they were in the Shard or the City, yeah, I'd totally get it. But here, in low-rise London, just seems odd.'

Leo pulled me away from another impossible window where I'd been ogling some shoes with see-through heels. 'Suyin did a little more digging through the company records. One of the directors was a man called Jed Tower.'

'And that doesn't sound a made-up name, no, not at all.'

'What do you mean?'

'Well, if you were thinking up a name to impress, wouldn't you go, "Hey, Jed, that sounds strong; Tower, sounds manly"?' Poor Leo still looked blank. 'It's the kind of name you see in Superhero stories.'

He smiled at that. 'For the bad guy or the good guy?'

I swung his hand where it was linked to mine. 'Hmm, I'd say good guy gone bad. He's built himself the biggest skyscraper in No Hope City and has probably fallen into a vat of poisonous gunk that's given him special powers. I mean, where do they get that stuff? And don't they know about lids? Health and safety nightmare, those illegal laboratories brewing up disaster.'

'You should write to the mayor.'

'Ah yes, but he'd be in on Jed Tower's conspiracy. They always are. Boris would've been; not so sure about the current guy.' We stopped outside the building that claimed to be the last known address for my agent. There was a full run of brass plaques but none of them for Glass Tower.

Leo tapped the top one. 'Look, the stone is paler at the top and bottom edge. This has been replaced recently with a slightly smaller nameplate.'

'Woodbridge Consultants. Do you see the same pattern I'm seeing?'

'Glass Tower. Wood Bridge. Yeah, I think we might have a reincarnated company.'

'Walk away from your mess and start again – oldest play in the corrupt company book. You would've thought they'd try a bit harder not to be traced, moved office or something?'

'You would.' Leo took a photo of the nameplate and sent it back to his team. 'We'll follow that up on Monday.'

'Why don't we follow it up now?' I grinned at him and pressed the bell.

'Jess!'

'Just follow my lead.'

'Hello?' came a female voice.

'Gut afternoon,' I said in what I hoped sounded a vaguely Eastern European voice. 'We are here about let of our apartment in Knightes-bridge.' I grimaced. Crap, I was bad at this.

These, however, proved adequate magic words. 'Please come up.'

The door buzzed and Leo pushed it open.

'Are we really doing this?' he asked. 'I'm way outside my jurisdiction.'

'Hey, pal, you're just riding on my coattails for this. I'm chasing my pay, remember? That's a totally legitimate reason for tracking these bastards down. Just shut up and look expensive.'

I think that made him smile. We went up in the silent lift. There was nothing on the walls apart from a discreet number to call in the event of a technical hitch. That wouldn't be so bad, being stuck in an elevator, with Leo, for hours. As long as we could cover the cameras.

OK, enough lascivious thoughts. Time to rock and roll.

The door opened onto a small but plush foyer. A fern arched in one corner behind the frosted glass reception desk. A blond girl with very red lipstick and big thick framed glasses smiled up at us. She did well at the 'professional but wait until after hours and I remove my glasses' sexy vibe.

'You're the couple with the apartment in Knightsbridge?' she asked perkily.

'*Da*,' said Leo.

'*Tak, owszem*,' I added, nodding furiously. We had to hope she hadn't noticed that we were mixing Russian and Polish. But my exotic languages only stretched to ordering coffee from Polish baristas so what do you expect?

'I'll just see who's free to see you.' She ran her finger down a list and I spotted a very familiar name.

'We see Heather,' I said bluntly.

'You know Miss Westborne? Oh, sorry, I didn't realise you were already clients. I'll just give her a call. What name is it?'

I wilfully misunderstood her and instead gave her Mrs Chernov's address.

'Lovely,' she said, recognising the prime location. 'Heather? I've got a couple from Knightsbridge to see you. Do you have a moment? Good. Yes, I'll send them through.' She put the phone down and beamed up at me. 'First door down the hall. Go right in.'

Peeking through the glass, I could see that Heather was standing up to greet us. And, yes, it was the same Heather: reassuringly helpful smile, nut-brown bob cut to her shoulders, neat suit from an upmarket high street brand. I sent Leo in first as she wouldn't know his face. I slipped in behind and closed the door behind me.

Leo took out his badge. 'Miss Heather Westbourne? My name is Inspector George, Thames Valley CID. You're a difficult woman to track down.'

She took one look at me, placed my face, then looked back at Leo. 'Oh God,' she said and sat down.

'Not God,' I said brightly, 'though I admit he is a bit of an Adonis, isn't he? Also me, one cash-strapped house-sitter still expecting her November payment. Imagine my surprise when the police tell me you've gone out of business – this was after they dug up a body at one of the properties you manage.' I sat down on the desk and flicked through the papers in her in-tray. 'Looks to me that you're still very much in business.'

'I . . . I'm just an employee, Miss Bridges. I don't understand the ins and outs of our arrangements. Mr Tower liquidated the old business and started this one a few weeks ago. He offered me a new position. I'm sure he'd be able to explain.'

'That's Jed Tower, I take it?' I said pleasantly. 'I'm sure his clients will be very interested to know that he's been pocketing the money they pay for staff in their second homes and not passing it on. They are dangerous people he's crossing. My guy? Uzbek boss. Mr Chernov? Best friends with the people in the Kremlin. Jed really should think very carefully about his business strategy. It is going to see him in great distress if this all catches up with him.'

'We don't represent those properties anymore,' said Heather quickly.

'Do you really think that'll matter to the Chernovs or the Gulom family? We've got their numbers now. That's all it will take. One little call.'

Leo stepped forward, perhaps sensing I was enjoying myself a bit too much with my fanciful evocation of a mafia threat. Hell, I believed it, even if he didn't!

'Miss Westbourne, aside from what my associate is saying, I'm sure you are aware that there are laws against closing companies purely to avoid honouring debts. It isn't legal just to open up again under another name.'

'But Jed said . . .' Heather had to have known. The 'poor me, I know nothing' act was infuriating. She hadn't wanted to know.

'Do you see Jed here?' I cut across her. I looked under a file and in the biscuit barrel on the sideboard. 'Nope. No Jed. It seems to me as if the buck is stopping with you, Heather.'

Heather gave Leo an uneasy glance. 'Look, Jess, about your pay? I'll write you a cheque, if you'll just go away.'

'I'll only accept cash from you,' I said, folding my arms.

'I'll just run down to a bank machine then.'

Leo stood in the doorway. 'No one is leaving. I'm not through with you, Miss Westbourne. I have some questions that urgently need answering. The fraud I'll pass on to my colleagues in the Met to pursue, but what concerns me today is murder.'

She returned reluctantly to her desk. 'All right. I'll answer your questions if I can. I want you to note that I am doing everything in my power to cooperate with your enquiries.'

'When did you last hear from Mr Chernov?' asked Leo.

'Chernov senior?' It was interesting she made that distinction. 'That would be in the summer last year. He held a party at the house for his daughter's graduation from school. We organised the caterers and the extra staff.'

'And that's the last time the family contacted you?'

'No. Alexei Chernov called twice this year to check all was

running smoothly.' She swallowed. 'I believe Mr Tower contacted him last month to explain that Glass Tower had had to wind up and offered him very good terms to continue under Woodbridge management. Alexei is yet to reply.'

'But not his father?'

'Alexei implied that the house now belonged to him. He mentioned wanting to sell when the market improved.'

'I see. And what about the Guloms? You manage their house too?'

'I don't hear from them very often. Mr Gulom made it very plain to me last time we spoke that he didn't want to be reminded of the existence of the house. He wanted us to keep it ticking over and, again, like the Chernovs, he had plans to sell it. We sent him the same enquiry and also haven't heard back.' She saw our exchange of looks. 'That isn't unusual. Many of our clients have large property portfolios. The time-scale is usually months for things to change, rather than days. The houses aren't going anywhere, after all.'

Leo did a magnificent glower. 'I'll need a copy of every exchange you've had with Gulom and Chernov.'

'But . . .!'

'Or I won't wait until Monday to call the Fraud Squad. I imagine Mr Tower will appreciate the extra day to get his ducks in a row, won't he?'

She still hesitated.

'This is a one-time offer: five, four, three, two . . .' Go Leo: turning the screws like that! I wanted to jump him right there!

Heather folded. 'All right! I'll copy the files onto a memory stick for you.'

'That is appreciated.' He stood over her while she did so, then pocketed the stick.

We left immediately after that. Heather was already on the phone.

'What about my money?' I whispered as we breezed past the oblivious sexy receptionist. She probably wouldn't get paid either, poor sucker.

'Jess, I'm sorry.'

Yeah, I could see it would look bad if I extorted money from Heather with threats about mafia payback with Leo in the room. 'OK. But you can buy dinner.'

He flashed a smile. 'My pleasure.'

Once out on the street, we paused in the shelter of a shop doorway.

'Give me a moment: I've just got a call to make,' he said.

I looked from the London number he was putting in back to the offices of Woodbridge Consultants. 'But you promised . . . Leo, are you being a bad boy?'

'Oh no. I'm being a very good one. I promised I wouldn't call the Fraud Squad until Monday; I said nothing about putting in a call to my old friend who works in the National Crime Agency. He deals with organised crime. With any luck, he can get the wheels moving to seize the books before they vanish again.'

'He'll have to move fast,' I said. 'Heather? She might wear four-inch heels but, boy, I bet she can leg it at top speed in them.'

I decided Leo's devious side deserved a reward so I bought him a chai latte from a café while he was outlining the case to his friend. He'd bagged a table at the back so he could speak in relative privacy.

'Did that go OK?' I asked, putting the drinks down.

'Very well. Dennis said Woodbridge Consultants were already on their radar. He's very grateful for the tip-off.'

'But will he catch them in time?'

'It is a Saturday but he sounded pretty motivated. If he can persuade his bosses, they might well support the warrant, a raid and the overtime. But that's not our problem.' He took a sniff of the drink. 'What's this?'

'Spicy chai latte. Time to live dangerously.'

'Looks like hot milk to me.'

'Go on: try it!'

He took a cautious sip. Then another. Still he didn't comment.

'Do you hate it?' I asked anxiously. 'I could get you something else?'

'No. It's great. I was just seeing how long it took you to get worried.'

'Not long apparently.' I thought about it a bit more. 'Hey, you were teasing me! I like it.'

He smiled. 'So do I.'

'Where do you want to eat?' Leo asked as we walked down Regent Street towards Piccadilly Circus. 'Chinatown?' The crowds were out to enjoy the Christmas lights and themed window displays in the big stores. Red buses and black cabs streamed by, joyfully joining in the cliché of London at its shiny best.

'I was getting carried away earlier. I need to get back,' I confessed.

'Oh, I see.'

He really didn't. His tone suggested he believed I'd had second thoughts about what followed dinner. 'It's not that I don't want to stay up in town with you, but I have a spaniel who has probably eaten a hole in the carpet by now.'

His face brightened. 'Of course. Flossie. I should've realised. Great detective I am, not to even think about her.'

I bumped shoulders with him. 'You can still buy me supper. There's a good Chinese takeaway in Summertown I have on speed dial. Not quite Chinatown, I know, but near enough. Or we can take Flossie with us to the local pub: they welcome dogs there.'

'Agreed. Dinner in Oxford it is.'

That was when a young girl shuffled past us, the hurt look of the homeless in her eyes as she hugged her duffel coat around her skinny shoulders. I was catapulted back in time to my own months spent in this very same area, the roads between the Strand and Oxford Street. They'd felt safer because they were relatively affluent but that was an illusion.

'Jess, are you all right?' Leo's worried face swam into view.

'Yeah, sorry. I suppose now is as good a time as any.' I nodded to the girl, who was fast being swallowed up by the people milling around the statue of Eros. 'This is one of the things I wanted to tell you about myself. You know I said I knew London? Well, one reason is that I ran away when I was fifteen and lived on the streets round here for a while.' I didn't dare meet his eyes. Condemnation from him would break something in me. 'It wasn't pretty. Drink mainly. And scrounging. Some sleeping with people for money and a warm bed for the night, so I guess I'd better call it what it was, a kind of casual prostitution.'

I waited.

'I'm sorry that happened to you,' he said, putting an arm around me and drawing me into the warmth of his coat and the body beneath.

'I did things I'm not proud of.'

'No doubt.'

'You don't blame me?'

He tipped my chin so I could see that his expression held no scorn or disapproval, only concern. 'Jess, I met your father, remember? I know what you were running from.'

'Oh.' Put it like that, then maybe he could forgive me for those indiscretions? 'Thanks.'

'I just wish I'd been there to help you.'

I shrugged. 'You're here now. That's what matters.' I looked about and realised that we were standing in front of one of my favourite shops: the big Waterstones. 'Wait here a moment. I want to get you a present.'

'Wha—?'

With a grin I was through the doors and zipping up to the children's department. They had what I wanted – of course they did. They couldn't call themselves a decent bookshop if they didn't stock this title. The transaction was over in three minutes and I was back outside passing him the little paper bag that contained his present.

Puzzled, he felt the outline of the small hardback. 'Do I open this now or is it a Christmas present?'

'Now! Don't you realise I run on impulse engines? Waiting is not my strong suit.'

He looked inside and pulled out Beatrix Potter's *The Tale of Mrs Tittlemouse*. Poor handsome policeman still looked foxed. 'Cute but . . .?'

I pushed it towards his chest and patted it. 'Read it on the train. It's the best advice I know for getting rid of unwanted visitors.'

That made him laugh. He swooped down and swung me in a circle. 'Thank you. I will study it with great interest.'

Chapter 15

Leo

On his way out to the car, Leo paused for a moment, surveying the red house he was leaving. He'd had another wonderful evening with Jess but she was still holding him off. No invitations up to the turret, or even heavy hints by the kitchen counter. Content just to kiss and cuddle, she said it wouldn't be fair to take their relationship to another level until full disclosure on her part had happened. He was beginning to wonder if it were something wrong with him. He'd never got the message from previous lovers that there was anything lacking in his desirability and Jess had never struck him as the cautious type. Or was she paying him back for his stop-start treatment in the autumn? No, that didn't feel right. Unless he totally misunderstood her, Jess would just tell him how she felt, not play some complicated mind game.

He started the engine to head for home.

Perhaps he should just believe her that there was something more to tell, something worse than a life on the streets as a teenager? He felt nothing but pity for that time in her life, certainly no revulsion or condemnation as she seemed to expect. He'd lived close enough to the edge at that age to know how easy it was to tumble over. What was so bad that she still felt she couldn't green-light their relationship without him knowing? He was tempted to do a search on her, deeper than the one he did when they first met on the wild swimming case. But that wouldn't be fair. She was clearly circling slowly round to tell him herself, banking on these good times together to help steady the ship when she revealed her secret.

That worried him. If it had been really bad – like a conviction for a serious crime – he would've already known when he ran her on their first meeting in University Parks. He hoped to God it wasn't a crime she was going to confess to and ask him to cover up. It was even more worrying that he didn't know how he'd respond.

Surely it was nothing so extreme?

He pulled over short of his house, not wanting his mother of all people to interrupt his thoughts. He couldn't be dealing with her emotional dramas right now. And, really, there was no point trying to second-guess what Jess was going to tell him. He just had to trust that it was nothing too bad. He just had to trust her.

Locking the car, he walked the final few metres to his house and studied it from the outside. His mother's light was off. It might be safe to go in. Entering quietly, he kicked off his shoes and crept upstairs, switching off lights as he went. Sweet as Jess's present had been, he didn't think Mrs Tittlemouse's solution of reducing the size of his doors was a runner but the thought made him smile, relieving some of the dread that settled in his chest every time he came home. He put the book on his nightstand, an oddly childish note in his grownup house.

The door across the hallway from his opened.

'Leo? Where've you been all day?'

His tension ramped, like an F1 car screaming off the starting grid. 'Out.' He suddenly had a memory of himself as a teenager managing the same level of conversation with his mother on the barge where they were shacked up with Pat.

'But what if they come for me when you're not here?' She took a step towards him but he quickly closed his door on her and slid the bolt he'd installed since her arrival.

She thumped on the door. 'You can't just turn your back on me!'

He knew better than to respond. Going to his window, he drew the curtains and went about his usual evening routine, getting changed, folding up his clothes.

'They're watching the house!'

Unlikely, he thought.

She scratched at the door, like a cat asking to come in. 'I daren't go out with them around.'

He wasn't even sure she knew who she meant. He suspected 'they' were just an excuse.

'I know you don't believe me, but I know what I saw. Two men in a black car watching the house. They're still there, Leo. Still there! You can check them out for yourself and see that I'm not imagining things!'

Just in case, Leo went back to the window and looked out. Giving his eyes a chance to adjust to the darkness, he examined the street. There were streetlights but these were widely spaced, leaving pools of darkness between the orange glare. Parked in one of these darker spots by the wall that marked the boundary of a small hotel was a black BMW with tinted windows, probably darkened above code because he wouldn't have been able to see inside even in daylight. At this angle, it was hard to read the number plate.

'Go to sleep, Mother. I'll check it out,' he said finally, deciding this was the quickest route to achieving peace.

There was a huff and her door closed. She knew when he said he'd do something, then he would go through with it. He wasn't her.

Pulling on a pair of jeans and a black hoodie, Leo went out the back door. He needed to get one garden along to obtain a view of the number plate without being seen and he happened to know a good route. His neighbour, Moira, kept her garden low-maintenance, thanks to football-playing children. Many a ball he'd thrown back and many a child had climbed over without his permission, not willing to wait until he returned from work. He'd picked his shrubbery accordingly so as not to damage small people. He was about to benefit from the consideration.

Vaulting over, he moved slowly. He didn't think Moira had any movement-triggered lights – too many foxes round here to make that a good idea – but he didn't want to wake and scare her either. He crossed her lawn and made his way down the passage between house and garage, negotiating his way between the jumble of bikes and scooters. Standing on her green wheelie bin, he got a good view of the number plate. Taking a photo, he reversed course and returned to his own garden without incident.

By his back door, he asked himself what on earth he was doing. He was a policeman. He could just go up to the car, tap on the window and ask why they were parked on the street so late. That was if there was anyone inside.

The sound of a car engine disturbed the night. When he got back upstairs to his vantage point at the window, the black BMW had gone.

Just a coincidence. That was what Leo tried to tell himself as he slept fitfully that night. At first light, he was up and on his computer. He'd asked a colleague on nights to run the plates and had the results back. Current registered owner ZOB Security. Was that private security? He searched the name and got a very unforthcoming website – not much more than a contact email. It appeared to suggest only those who knew what they wanted would approach them that way; they weren't trawling for customers on the open market. What was a car registered to a security firm doing parked outside his house? None of his neighbours were of the income or profession that would attract such attention. If they were looking after someone in the hotel, they'd be parked inside the grounds surely? That left his mother. Were they there for her?

Hearing her stirring, he banged on the door.

'Mother, we need to talk.'

She came out, looking fragile in her dressing gown. 'It's not me who's been avoiding a conversation.'

'What kind of trouble are you in? I suppose I really mean, with whom?'

'Really, Leo. I can't talk without coffee.' She wafted past him and down the stairs. He dug deep for his control.

'You asked me to deal with the car. I've traced it. What I need to know now is what dealing ZOB Security could possibly have with you?'

She put the kettle on the heating pad. 'ZOB? I've never heard of them. I don't think that's one of Alan's companies.'

'And who is Alan?'

'He's the man I'm hiding from, of course!' She pulled a packet of porridge oats out of the box and tipped it into a bowl.

Leo steeled himself not to lose it while she painstakingly measured out the right amount of milk and stirred it into the oatmeal. He was used to this. With his mother it had always been 'hurry, hurry, hurry, then wait'. It was her own little way of controlling the world she had long since had any real influence over.

'He's a nasty man, Leo. You wouldn't like him.' She put the bowl into the microwave and set the timer. The kettle clicked off so she turned her attention next to making coffee. 'He says he's French but I don't believe it. I think he's Belgian. Do you want coffee?'

Leo nodded curtly.

'Manners, Leo?'

He wasn't going to respond to these attempts to mother him. Far too late for that. Not only had that horse bolted, but it had spent the intervening years in other pastures and been put down in old age.

She sighed, ever the victim with her Holly Golightly air of high-class dependency. 'He's got a nightclub in Birmingham. That's where we met. I caught his eye when I was with my previous friend.' This was code for the last man who had paid her bills for a short while. 'But Alan turned out not to be as nice as he seemed.' Leo would've thought she could have learned that by now. 'He ran with a rough crowd. I had to leave.'

So there it was. 'How did you leave, Mother?'

She shrugged, a little roll of her bony shoulders. 'I got the train here. I thought I told you that?'

'Let me rephrase: what did you take?'

'Only what I was owed. It was hard work being his hostess.'

'And let me guess, he wants to get his money back or punish you for stealing from him?'

'It wasn't stealing! We'd been living together for four months.' Her fine-boned features quivered with outrage.

Longer than he'd expected, he had to give her credit for that. 'And is he the kind of man to send a couple of men to intimidate you?'

She nodded emphatically. 'Oh yes. That is very much his way.'

And she'd stayed with him while knowing this? But hiring people to sit on a target, even for the payback of revenge, was an expensive business. It suggested a very motivated person. 'How much did you take?'

'Just ten thousand – maybe a little less.' Nice of her to dismiss many months of police pay like that. 'But how would he even know where to look for me? He didn't know about you.'

But a simple search online would've made the connection for him, thanks to her exploits in Leo's teens. 'Are you really that naive?'

She glowered as she poured coffee into two mugs. 'I didn't think he'd care. Ten grand is nothing to Alan.'

'Apparently it is. I imagine there's the little matter of hurt pride too. Do you still have it? Maybe if you sent it back, he'd call them off?'

She winced as she took a sip of too-hot coffee. 'I had

other debts to some not very nice people. I paid those off.'

Robbing Peter to pay Paul: how like his mother.

'You're unbelievable.' The exhaustion he always felt around her crashed back over him, undoing any of the good a day with Jess had done.

'You won't let them hurt me, will you, Leo?' She tried to look up at him appealingly but the time for such looks had long since passed.

'I won't boot you out of the door as I should, if that's what you mean. But this isn't my problem to solve.'

She opened her mouth but he held up his hand to interrupt her.

'You can stay here for three more days. They are very unlikely to break in. Being parked outside is probably to intimidate you – which it has. Job done. If you don't go out, you should be fine. They have no way of knowing you're still here if you don't show yourself. During the next three days, though, you must make alternative arrangements for yourself. I'll take you where you need to go and make sure you're not followed. You can disappear again and if Alan is still hunting for you, then it becomes entirely on you to stay hidden. I certainly don't recommend coming back here as this bolthole has been busted.'

'But I have nowhere to go!' she wailed.

'Then make plans and sort it out. I'll give you two hundred pounds: that can get you a ticket somewhere and a night or two in a cheap hotel. After that, over to you. Now, if you'll excuse me, I have some jobs outside to do.'

He slipped on his gardening shoes and retreated outside with his coffee before she could complain further.

Chapter 16

Jess

Sunday lunch with Cory and her kids: it was such a settled, grown-up thing to do that I felt a little surprised to find myself joining in. My Sunday meals tended to be just the same as the weekday ones, pasta and a jar of sauce with grated cheese usually involved; Cory, on the other hand, liked to have a roast, followed by a homemade dessert with custard. Her philosophy was that the children needed traditions. She wanted them to say, when she was old and crumbly, hunched in her chair in the care home, 'Do you remember Mum's roast dinners?' She was probably right; families needed these shared moments to knit together. More cynically, there was also the knowledge that the weekends they spent with their father, Brendan, usually ended up at the gastropub or kid-friendly restaurant, so there was a passive-aggressive one-upmanship in play. Whatever the cause behind the lunch, she reminded me of my own lack of these happy memories. Family dinners, when my mother still lived with my father, had been a hushed exercise in terror as each dish had to pass his approval or there would be consequences. Maybe that was why I'd never seriously considered having a family of my own to pass on my traditions?

I knocked on the door, noticing that the decorations had already gone up even though we were in single-digit December. A snowman made from cotton wool stuck on a kitchen roll tube grinned lopsidedly from the narrow window by the entrance. I missed Cory and the kids but after the events of the autumn we had agreed they would be safer if I took myself off to live independently. One home invasion was one invasion too many.

'Jess!' shouted Benji as he threw open the door and instantly skewered me with a death blow from his sword. That was OK, and to be expected.

I grabbed him up, plastic sword and all and hugged him tight. 'Aargh, Captain Blood, for that, it's over the side with you to feed the sharks!' I pretended to swing him out onto the street. He giggled explosively.

'Are you making Benji laugh-fart?' called Cory from the kitchen.

Benji and I shared a shamefaced look.

'No?' I said uncertainly.

Benji snickered.

'Race you to the kitchen!' I challenged him, dumping him back on his feet. We headed up the hallway. I lagged behind so as not to shatter the bottle of wine in my tote bag against the wall – otherwise I totally would have beaten him to it. I plonked the Pinot Noir down on the counter. 'Smells delicious.'

Leah, Cory's three-year-old, unglued herself from the craft table (this was not a metaphor) to come and greet me. She had glitter all over her hands and face.

'I'm making Christmas cards,' she told me solemnly, 'but you're not to know because it's a surprise.'

'Understood, munchkin. I absolutely do not know anything about that.'

She went back to the table where an outline of Father Christmas was being dowsed in red glitter paint.

Cory was checking the pans like a witch her potions. 'You know where the bottle opener is.'

Taking my cue, I opened the red and poured us both a glass. 'Cheers. So what's new in the world of Cory?'

Was it my imagination or did Cory actually go a little pink? 'Not much. Nothing compared to you. Bodies next door!'

'Only one.'

'And spending a lot of time with a certain policeman?'

I grinned. 'That has been an unexpected benefit to the aforesaid grisly garden feature. We went up to London together yesterday and he came back to the red house for dinner.'

'Just dinner?'

I shot a look at the children who were both now deep into their card project. 'Just dinner.'

'Why?' Cory wailed. 'What a waste! The man is gorgeous.'

'Even better without his clothes on,' I agreed.

'But you said . . .?'

'*Swimming*, Cory, we went swimming the other day, you know, in my private pool?'

'Your pool?' She snorted.

'As good as.'

'So why haven't you' – she glanced over at the children, who hearing her hushed tone had naturally tuned into what we were saying – 'done the deed?'

I sipped my wine. 'Because he needs to know first.'

'Know what?'

'About all my personal C R A P.'

'That spells "crap",' said Benji brightly. He was an advanced child.

'Yes, but that's not a nice word,' said his mother, 'which is why Jess didn't say it. You shouldn't either.'

'But she spelt it. Is it OK to use bad words if you spell them out?' His brow was furrowed as he looked for the logic; Benji had the brain of a scientist. 'So if I said F . . .?'

I could see where this was going. 'Nope, not cool to spell or say. I'm sorry. Do you have a swear jar?'

Cory shook her head. 'Daren't. I'd be overdrawn in a week. Right, change of subject. Kids, wash your hands. Lunch is ready.'

Father Christmas abandoned half dressed in his sparkles, the children raced each other to the bathroom. I went to the sink in the kitchen to follow the same advice.

'Have you thought that you needn't drag all that out again?' said Cory. I'd brought out all my skeletons during some drunken girls' nights in, let them dance and take a bow before her non-judgemental eyes. I was lucky in my friend.

'You think there's a danger that he might not want to be with me if I tell him everything?'

'Some of it is strong stuff, Jess. Before you've made a real relationship with him, he might find it too much. He might need to know you better – know that you've changed.'

I dried hands on a towel decorated with a sad-eyed puppy. 'But have I? I sometimes wonder if my good behaviour is more to do with circumstance than impulse control. I do bad stuff when the fences are down and I'm allowed to wander.'

'But a strong relationship would give you those fences so you don't stray again.'

Leah bopped back into the kitchen. 'Who's gone stray? Is Flossie losted?'

'Flossie is fine, Lee-Lee,' I assured her. 'Your mum and I were just talking about the fence at the bottom of my garden.'

'Can we walk her again?' Her eyes were expectant and as hard to turn down as the puppy on the towel.

'Maybe after lunch if your mum agrees?'

'Oh, actually, Jess, that would be a great help. I mean, if you could look after the children for a few hours. I maybe have . . . er . . . things to do.' Cory was blushing again. She was hiding something from me, but what?

'Cory? Have you got something to confess to me?' I tried to fix her with my best death-ray gaze but the battery must've been flat. She spun away to the oven.

'Excellent – the beef is ready. Who wants a Yorkshire pudding?'

The squeals of the children deafened me and got her off the hook. For now.

During the meal, I told them all about my week at work – not the home stuff, though Benji and Leah would probably have enjoyed that more as they didn't have a squeamish bone in their small bodies.

'Jess is going to be on telly!' exclaimed Leah when I told

her about the Christmas Eve service. 'What are you going to wear?'

I gave her a serious look. 'I thought I'd go with clothes.'

She rolled her eyes at me, showing the budding teenager who would not be impressed by any of my jokes.

'Maybe reindeer antlers or angel wings?' I suggested.

She perked up. 'I have some Rudolf antels. Do you want to borrow them?' She began to get down from the table.

'You haven't finished your broccoli,' warned Cory.

'Good try, munchkin.' I saluted Leah with my wine glass. 'My big problem though is that I have to decorate the chapel with only five hundred pounds to spend. My boss wants big impact so that we impress the BBC.'

Cory shook her head. 'That's not enough.'

'I know. I've been looking online at Christmas illumination specialist sites and all I can get for that is some tacky reindeer with teeth like sharks, a clearance item as no one else wanted them.'

'That would certainly make an impact.'

'But not in a good way,' I finished. 'Besides it's hardly the right message for a chapel – Killer Reindeer R Us.'

After lunch, I cleaned the pans while Cory stacked the dishwasher.

'You know, I've been thinking,' she said. 'You want to do something different with the chapel? For five hundred, I could get you some refugee artworks if you like? You could use it to raise awareness of the issue, seeing how the nativity story ends up with a refugee flight from danger.'

I stared at her, hands wrist-deep in suds. 'That is brilliant.

What kind?' It was exactly the kind of diversity-aware message I hadn't known I needed.

'Ones themed to the Christmas story? I know a really good artist in a camp in Jordan who does amazing work – she works in cloth so they should be big enough to hang.'

I threw my arms around her and hugged her tight. 'My friends are just the best!'

She hugged me back. 'Jess, actually, there's something—'

Something pronged my thighs. Leah was back, reindeer antlers on head. She'd just butted me.

'Oh wow, Lee-Lee, those are so great. But don't you want to wear them at playgroup?'

Cory cleared her throat. 'Unfortunately, Leah has been asked not to wear them at the toddler time again as she spent all morning as a reindeer.'

'That sounds nice.'

'Head-butting people.' Cory was trying hard not to laugh. Sometimes the stern parent act is hard to pull off.

Not so the antlers. 'Hmm.' I whisked them from Leah's head, saving Cory many mornings of argument. 'Thanks, honeybunch, I'll add these to my Christmas costume. Let's go find Flossie. Get your shoes on.'

Returning from a muddy walk by the river, Benji, Leah and I came across one of our neighbours from a street away. Mr Price was often to be seen patrolling the streets, a little dachshund in tow, part of the tribe of the Dog Walker. I wondered if I should suggest we all got a tattoo? A dog paw on our ankle?

Flossie went into a volley of barks that managed to sound

both a threat and a greeting, tail wagging. I took that as a sign that her intentions were peaceful and let her go nose to butt with the little dog.

Mr Price smiled at my two charges. 'These belong to you?'

'My friend's children. Benji, Leah, this is Mr Price.' They didn't look very impressed, more interested in his dachshund. 'He used to fly planes for the Royal Airforce.' That did it.

'Still do, as a hobby,' Mr Price said proudly. 'Only little ones now, not fighter planes.'

'Did you shoot anyone down like in *Top Gun*?' asked Benji, staring up in wonder at the smartly dressed man. You could see the military training in his stance.

The question took Mr Price by surprise. 'Not that I recall. I'm too young to have served in any of the major wars. Not much shooting down in peacetime.'

Benji didn't look very pleased so Mr Price had to up his game.

'I did serve in the Falklands though. Helped protect the Task Force.'

'That's right,' I said, thinking what Cory would want me to say at this point. 'It's better to deter the bad guys and never have to shoot them down, Benji. Sometimes the threat is just enough.'

'What's your dog's name?' asked Leah, happily bringing a change of subject.

'Amelia, after the brave female pilot, first lady to fly across the Atlantic. Until she disappeared.' His smile died as he realised that probably wasn't a tale for such young children. 'Sorry,' he said to me, 'it's a while since I've been around little ones.'

Too late. They were on to him.

'How did she disappear?' asked Benji.

'Magic?' said Leah.

'I'm afraid not. She disappeared over the Pacific while trying to fly around the globe,' Mr Price explained reluctantly.

'Cool!' said Benji.

'You mean, she died?' asked Leah, a quiver in her voice.

I needed to rescue poor Mr Price – and quickly before Benji asked for more details and Leah decided to take it personally. 'Right, OK, who wants to put stinky Flossie under the hose?' I asked brightly.

'Me!' screeched the children.

Mr Price gave me a grateful look. 'I'd better head off. Amelia is waiting for her walk.' Waving goodbye, he hurried off towards the park, the dachshund jigging alongside him.

Cory wasn't back when I returned the children to their home. Wondering what was keeping her, I set about the evening routine, checking homework was done for Benji (his reading book), kids bathed, teeth brushed. I'd done this enough times when I was a lodger that neither of them questioned why I was doing it tonight.

Finally I heard the key in the door and Cory breezed in at eight. Her eyes were sparkling and she had a flushed complexion. Either she had just taken up membership at a gym or my friend was getting some action elsewhere.

'So sorry I'm late. I got held up.' She kissed the tops of the children's heads. They were in their most adorable state: just washed and in clean PJs. If you could bottle that scent, you'd make a fortune.

'Held up?' I let the innuendo saturate my tone. 'Or held down? Or both?' I put up my hand. 'I'm hoping both.'

Her blush deepened. She deserved the teasing though: she'd used me as babysitting for her booty call and not even told me, the rat. I was sure there were all sorts of mates-before-dates rules about that.

'I . . . er . . . Benji, let me hear your reading.' She picked up the book bag I'd left by the door.

'I already read to Jess,' said Benji.

'Yes, because Mummy wasn't here,' I added. 'Mummy was playing with her friend.'

'Did you have a go on his electric chair?' asked Benji.

What? My head swivelled round so fast I almost gave myself whiplash. I knew only one man with such a chair.

'It works by electrickery,' said Leah, as if that was what interested me. 'It goes up and down, backwards and forwards.'

'I'm sure Mummy explored all those functions,' I said, scowling at Cory. Cory and Michael? How on earth . . .?

'Um, Jess . . .' said Cory. 'I can explain.'

'Mummy, you've gone really red.'

'Thank you, Benji.'

'I'll be very interested to hear your explanation.' I crossed my arms, refusing to move until I'd heard the whole story. 'Kids, I think it's time for bed. Mummy and I need to talk.'

Chapter 17

Jess

Flossie woke me in the middle of the night, head up, growling. My spaniel sometimes sounded like she was channelling Godzilla.

'What's up, girl?' I reached for my phone. 3am. Thanks, Flossie, I thought grimly. Probably just the urban fox coming to taunt her, as it did frequently. If you were quick, you could sometimes see it streaking across the lawn, the 'who, me?' expression on its face when it saw you staring, the client sneaking out without paying.

Then came a sound just outside – or did it come from downstairs? My anxiety surged from hiding. Flossie stood up on the end of my bed and barked. I grabbed a dressing gown. Not a fox. An intruder? My job was to be in occupation to prevent that kind of thing. I'm not a shotgun-on-the-porch kinda gal, but I could at least turn on some lights and try to scare them away?

Launching herself towards the door, Flossie continued sharp barks as if to ask why I wasn't letting her loose.

Could I risk her? I thought of burglars with coshes, or guns even. But I'd not heard anything inside for sure yet. It could be a chancer breaking in the shed or searching the garden.

That was bad enough though: I'd be blowed if I'd let them get my bike, crappy though it was.

'Shush, Flossie! I need to listen!'

She continued to bark and scratch at the door. Perhaps I didn't need to wait for more sounds: she was convinced her territory had been invaded and anyone in the house would know exactly where we were with all the noise she was making. I couldn't just stay up here waiting for them to come get me. The staircase was too easy to block.

Glass shattered. My heart accelerated from trot into flat-race mode. Flossie was beside herself. Someone *was* inside! I could picture them moving through the darkened rooms, snatching valuables, ransacking drawers . . .

Grabbing a hairdryer, the handiest object I could find until a better presented itself, I opened the door. Flossie shot out and raced downstairs, barking with a cutting edge that said she meant business. I rushed after her, holding the hairdryer like a gun, gripping the cord and plug with the intention of whipping it at any interloper. Maybe it would fool someone for a split second that I was capable of driving them off?

The timbre of Flossie's barks changed. She was outside, broadcasting her anger to the street. Outside? How on earth did she get out there?

I stepped into the drawing room with its unfortunate portraits. One of the double glass doors to the garden was shattered and Flossie had jumped through. Bare feet told me it would be a terrible idea to follow. But, oh God, broken glass meant . . .

I retreated so I could grab the house phone – and came

face to face with the intruder. He loomed in the doorway to the basement. My impression in the half-light was of a tall man, bulky, dressed in black, including a freaking ski-mask. Not to mention the little pickaxe over his shoulder, the kind you see in mountaineering programmes.

An axe! Crap!

He looked at me, looked at the hairdryer. Eyes narrowed. Speechless with fright, I whacked the plug towards him. He gave a guttural grunt, caught it and lurched forward, pulling the hairdryer away from me. Shit, miscalculation! Letting go, I finally managed to force a scream past a locked throat. This startled us both and he barged past me, pioneering a route across the broken glass in his boots and out the way he had come.

A totally inept fight on my part. I shuddered.

Flossie was still barking but she quickly went silent.

If he'd done anything to my dog . . .!

Finding a jolt of renewed courage, I grabbed a spray bottle of bleach from the kitchen counter and went out the backdoor. Flossie was standing by the wonky panel at the end of the garden. She looked confused rather than alarmed. Netting had been put up to stop her trespassing next door again but this had been ripped aside. Fortunately, she'd not followed the burglar through.

I knelt down and hugged her. 'Good girl. Good girl for staying put.'

I was shaking far more than her as I tugged on her collar to get her to follow me back into the house.

'Scary, hey?' I asked her when we arrived back in the kitchen. 'Let's tell the police, all right?'

* * *

The police, who arrived ten minutes later, agreed that there had been a break-in and that I wasn't a party animal hiding vandalism after a wild rave in my employer's house. That was nice of them. I made them tea while they checked the premises, but I think we were all fairly certain that the intruder had fled for good. Flossy rested her head on my knee, looking satisfied that she had won that battle. Indeed she had: I doubted the burglar would have retreated so fast without her quick intervention and ear-splitting barks. I didn't think my hairdryer brandishing antics tipped the balance.

'Miss Bridges, can you tell us if anything has been taken?' The officer was a man of my age, kind grey eyes and a mouth that looked like it preferred a smile to a frown – the kind of face they hired for *The One Show* TV presenters.

'Nothing that I can see. I'll have to have a proper look round tomorrow in the daylight but everything appears to be in the usual places.' There were several easily pocketable items on the side tables and mantelpiece of the drawing room – antique silver snuffboxes, an expensive carriage clock, some small figurines of dubious taste but immense value. Nothing had been taken from the home office either, if our burglar's taste had stretched rather to the easily fenced items of electrical goods. 'I don't think the intruder had time to do more than look around. He entered, I confronted, he fled – end of story.'

'What rooms did he enter, other than the entry point?'

'The door to the swimming pool in the basement was open – that's where I bumped into him – as was the shed in the garden. But there is nothing in either of those places, especially not since all the tools were taken by your lot last week.'

The policeman raised a brow. 'My lot?'

'Because of the body over the garden fence?' I prompted.

'That's near here?' He went to the window. 'Interesting. I hadn't made the connection. I'll tell the investigators tomorrow morning, in case it's relevant.'

I bit my tongue to stop myself saying I'd tell them myself. 'Relevant? In what way?'

'Criminal gangs follow news reports and, if they think a property is empty, they take advantage.'

That made sense: someone's tragedy is another's opportunity. 'This house hasn't been empty at any point, but maybe you'd better check over there then in Hay Road?'

He nodded. 'We'll drive by when we're finished here.' He put down his mug. 'You'll want to get that entrance boarded up.'

That was when I remembered the non-functioning agent. Who was going to foot the bill? I had no idea who insured the house.

'Yeah, I'll make a call.' I thought there were probably twenty-four-hour services for this kind of thing. Would they accept payment in snuffboxes?

The radio on the policeman's shoulder buzzed, reminding me of a pirate's parrot demanding a peanut. He tapped it to silence it. 'I'll send someone round to take fingerprints in the morning.'

He didn't sound very enthused by the idea. We both knew that the police didn't have the resources to investigate this kind of crime, especially when nothing but a little damage had been done and the intruder hadn't hurt me.

'Thanks. Appreciate it.'

His colleague joined us. He was an older officer who had a face that looked like it was well acquainted with the bottom of the whiskey tumbler, nose flushed with capillaries. 'All clear. Massive place you've got here, Miss.'

'Yeah, my employer likes his space.' So much so that he'd been keeping his distance for over a year. I'd need to knuckle down and find him so I could sort out urgent matters, like paying for things, including his sleep-deprived house-sitter.

'You'll be all right?' asked the younger officer.

'I'll be fine. Not going back to bed though.' I walked them to the door.

'I can imagine. Thanks for the tea,' said the other.

They returned to their patrol car and pulled away, the older man driving and the younger talking on his radio, giving details of the incident to the control room.

I really should stop getting myself mentioned in police despatches. It was becoming a habit.

Taking up a rug from a basket in the utility room, I curled up on the sofa near the kitchen table. Flossie nestled with me, head down, body relaxed. She'd recovered from the shock much more quickly than I had. I took out my phone and caressed the screen. I really should be calling a glazier but the mental energy required to summon one early on a Monday morning was beyond me. I'd do it in daylight. No one was going to come in again now, not with all the lights on.

Instead, I composed a message to the one person I really wanted to tell.

Hey. Thought you should know. I've just survived an encounter with a masked intruder armed only with a hairdryer – me not the intruder. He had a pickaxe.

I pressed send.

Chapter 18

Leo

Leo hadn't been sleeping well, dipping in and out of sleep like a sculler's oar. He must've been surfacing again when the whirr of his phone woke him. A message popped up on the screen from Jess. Sprawled on his back, he read it blearily, wondering what possessed her to contact him so early.

'Christ!' He was up and out of bed before he could form a coherent plan. Halfway through dressing, hopping into a trouser leg, he made himself slow. *Calm down, Leo.* His colleagues would have already been round to deal with the break-in. There was really no need for him to go off half-cocked. He had time to shave and call in on Jess on his way to work.

Taking a couple of deep breaths, he made his movements more deliberate. Plugging in the electric shaver, he ran it over his stubble, using the time forced to stand still to think. He knew that criminals often targeted empty houses that they heard about through the grapevine, homes left empty by death or recently robbed, giving just enough time so that new stuff would've been ordered to replace the stolen items. To his knowledge, the red house hadn't been mentioned on the news reports but anyone with eyes on that road would've seen his officers doing their search and drawn their own conclusions.

That was a stretch. Who had the manpower to keep watch round there? It could just be coincidence.

He splashed his face with cold water to drive away the last sleep. He didn't like that idea either. Coincidences did happen, but more often than not what appeared on the surface to be one had some deeper link. He'd already established that Gulom and the Chernov family were at odds. Had one of the Chernovs decided to look for their own evidence that Gulom had something to do with the murder next door? And what kind of proof could there be after the police had already removed the tools?

No, that didn't make much sense – too risky for little reward.

He needed to see what had happened for himself. Leo crept downstairs in his socks, carrying his shoes, not wanting his mother to hear his exit. This situation had to stop, he thought. He couldn't be this teenager in a thirty-something body.

That brought to mind the other scary mother he'd met recently. Backing out of the drive, something Mrs Chernov had said on Saturday came to him. She had thought that a rival might've killed someone and literally planted the evidence in the garden to implicate Anatoly. He didn't agree, being ninety per cent certain the body was Anatoly, but perhaps that could work around the other way? Now that the police had found the body, was someone taking action to point them at Gulom to disguise their own culpability? If that were the case, it wasn't about what had been taken, but what had been left behind.

* * *

Having messaged ahead that he was coming, Leo pulled into the gravel drive of the red house. Jess opened the door to him still wearing her pyjamas, hair rumpled, Flossie dancing at her heels. She winced when a door slammed somewhere in the house behind her.

'Come in quickly,' she said, stepping back. 'It's like a wind tunnel in here now someone so kindly made me a new entrance.'

He entered and the door clicked closed. Ignoring the spaniel's attempts to gain his attention, he bent down to kiss Jess, his hand tucked under the fall of hair on one side, cradling her cheek, as he searched her eyes.

'Are you OK?' he asked softly.

With a sigh, she put her arms around him. He hugged her tightly. He hated to think of her alone in the house with an intruder. There wasn't that much to her, standing no more than five feet and a few debatable inches.

'Thank you for this.' Her voice was muffled in his chest.

'For what?'

'For coming over, for caring, for asking how I am . . . so many things.' She pushed back, mood bouncing back. 'Wow, you look smart. And I look' – she glanced down at her Scottie-dog pjs – 'a mess.'

'A vision in canine print.' His lips quirked.

She gave a huff at that. 'Don't mock the dogs. Will you make me a coffee while I nip upstairs to get changed? I've got work at nine.' She slapped her forehead. 'Crap: the busted door! I can't leave the house like this. I'm going to have to tell my Grinch of a boss that I'm delayed again. He's going to love me.'

Leo grinned at her as she scooted off up the stairs. Of

course Jess would have novelty slippers – hers were snowmen, ready to walk in the air for Christmas.

Not only did he make the coffee but he also rang up a glazing firm he knew from previous crime scenes so that when she came down, he could present her with his triumph on her behalf.

'Karl the glazier will be here in thirty minutes, traffic allowing,' he said, handing her a mug.

Her mouth fell open. He enjoyed her reaction very much. 'What?'

She just shook her head.

'Drink your coffee. You might not be so late for work after all.'

She put the mug down and launched herself at him. 'Oh, this deserves a ravishing on the kitchen floor at the very least!' She began peppering him with kisses. 'You are . . . without doubt . . . the perfect man!'

He felt absurdly close to blushing. 'Nowhere near – don't get any illusions about me.' But he'd accept her playful ravishing.

She tugged his tie. 'Come here, gorgeous.'

On that signal, the kissing grew more intense. He carried her over to the kitchen table and sat her on the edge, moving between her legs. She'd put on a silky shirt for work, some turquoise number with infuriatingly stiff buttons. Giving up on the front, he slipped his hands underneath and cupped her breast. It was soft and full, a delicious weight in his palm. He lifted her shirt up and bent down to nuzzle her cleavage.

'Take it off – take it off,' Jess said urgently, writhing on the table edge.

'We are both going to be so late.' Not that he was stopping.

'Don't care – I really . . . do not . . . care . . . right now.' Her words were coming in breathy gasps.

The doorbell rang. Leo swore against her warm skin and stilled.

'We could just ignore it?' Jess said hopefully.

Emerging with disarranged hair, Leo smoothed her shirt down, then ran his hand over his fringe. Karl was doing him a favour. Their first time shouldn't be a hurried fumble in the kitchen. 'Better not.'

'Humph.' Jess wriggled off the table and hurried to the answer.

Leo concentrated on regaining his cool. He listened to her voice as it came from the hall.

'Oh, Mrs Price. I didn't expect to see you.'

So not the glazier. Leo checked that all his clothing was restored to tidiness, tie straightened, then picked up his coffee and waited. He hoped he looked innocent, but he guessed he wouldn't fool a trained observer. Jess returned to the kitchen with the lady who lived across the road from the murder scene, Meredith Price.

'Leo, this is Mrs Price. She and her husband run the North Oxford Protection Society.'

'Yes, we've met. Hello.'

Mrs Price brought into the kitchen her usual sunny presence. That impression was boosted by her choice of bright orange tunic with baggy green trousers, a turban-style head wrap. Her hand glittered with rings. Even this early in the day, she had found time to deck herself with some serious bling.

Very festive. 'Inspector George, lovely to see you again.' Her attempt to shake his hand was interrupted by Flossie demanding attention.

'Sorry!' Jess wrestled her dog down from ecstatic to merely overjoyed.

'I hope I'm not interrupting official business?' Mrs Price asked. Was that an arch tone he caught?

'Jess and I are friends,' Leo said hurriedly. Why was he feeling so guilty? 'I came to check that she was OK.'

'That's nice of you. But how horrible for you, Jess, to be here – with an intruder! What is the world coming to?'

'How do you know about that?' asked Jess, putting the kettle on again.

'The neighbourhood group. We get an alert from the community police officer whenever there's an incident. They don't give the address, of course, but we saw the flashing lights from our bedroom windows. Al would've come with me, but he's got a breakfast meeting at the town hall. He sends his regards.'

'Thanks.' Jess held up a teapot and the jar of instant coffee.

Mrs Price took a seat at the table that had so recently been the scene of other activities. Leo tried not to think about that. 'Tea, please. I only drink real coffee. I'm spoiled: my family grows it.'

Jess laughed. 'That would be nice. 'Fraid I'm living on a budget.'

Leo resolved to get her some coffee as a gift next time they met.

'As well as checking you're OK, I wanted to tell you that

we're calling a neighbourhood meeting tonight,' said Mrs Price. 'St Bede's will lend us their hall to hold it. The headmaster is very supportive of community ventures. We hope you'll be there.'

'Oh, er, didn't we have plans?' Jess appealed to Leo rather desperately.

'Yes, we did,' Leo said. 'We've a dinner reservation.'

Mrs Price's expression perked with interest as she deduced Leo's definition of 'friend' might go a little further than he let on. She then demonstrated that she was as dogged as her husband in getting her way. 'It won't be a long meeting – and we'd love you to come, Inspector, in fact, we were going to ask you as well. My husband knows the Chief Super, but this is so much better.' She smiled up at him, the threat plain that if he didn't agree this way, they'd go over his head. 'So two birds, one stone. Lovely.'

Resigned to the inevitable, Leo folded. 'We'll call in, briefly. I won't be able to tell you much about an ongoing investigation.'

'We don't expect that. It is just good to see our public servants face to face and be assured that they are working hard on our behalf. Seven pm?'

Leo made a note to steer very clear of the North Oxford Protection Society in future. 'Seven it is, but I'd better go. Us public servants have a lot to do. May I have a quick word, Jess?'

Her eyes sparkled. 'Or a long, slow word?' she murmured. She was going to kill him with her ability to make everything sound lascivious.

Leo towed Jess out of the kitchen into the hall.

'Dinner?' she said with a smile as she adjusted his tie.

'In my defence, I was going to ask you.'

She laughed.

'I'm sorry I can't stay, but I wanted to ask you if you noticed anything different after the intruder left?'

She adopted a mock-thinking pose. 'Er, like the great big hole in the wall where a glass door used to be?'

He shook his head, smiling. 'No, not that. I mean has anything new arrived in the house that you don't recognise?'

Her brow wrinkled. 'Like what?'

'A tool, like a spade, or just anything really, that wasn't here before?'

She wasn't slow to catch on. 'You think it might've been a set-up?'

He shrugged. 'It's a scenario I'm considering. We know Gulom and Chernov were enemies. If you wanted to deflect attention away from yourself, wouldn't you try to implicate someone with a good motive to kill our victim?'

'Oh yeah, totally. Us killers think like that all the time.' She went up on tiptoe and kissed him. 'I'll have a good look round and let you know. When shall we meet up? At the restaurant?'

'You're not abandoning me to that lot alone are you?'

She grinned, then shook her head. 'Tempting, but no.'

'Then I'll call in here first this evening, if that's OK with you? Ten to seven?'

'Very OK.'

A toot outside signalled the arrival of the glazier.

'You'd better see to your guests.' He snatched a quick kiss

and held onto her hand for as long as possible as they went to the door. 'Message me if you find something.'

'You'll be the first, I promise,' she confirmed, grinning broadly at some joke only she knew.

As he started the car, he laughed, realising that he'd just left her a very broad definition of what she might find. He looked forward to watching his message stream develop over the day.

Chapter 19

Michael

Nothing could put a dent in his day, Michael decided, not even a call to an emergency meeting at the AI institute in Hay Road. The day was chill and bright, frost on the bushes, holly trees posing for Christmas cards, and he was still reliving the time he spent with Cory on Sunday. His anxiety that he might not be able to cope with the physical side of a relationship had been allayed by the kindest and most patient partner he could imagine. She didn't expect too much from him, asked him not to expect too much from her, and that had freed him to exceed what he thought possible. He was fairly certain she left satisfied and eager to repeat the experience; he couldn't wait.

Pulling up outside the institute, Michael glanced behind him at the tape still fluttering outside the door of the neighbouring house. Of course, the body in the garden. The house belonged to the chief sponsor of the institute, a Russian loaded with funny money, Anatoly Chernov. In his younger days, Michael might've objected to holding his fellowship under such dubious conditions, but now there was no such thing as clean money in higher education. Universities had joined football clubs in holding their noses when taking generous donations from oligarchs wishing to rehabilitate their reputation.

The institute had been refitted last year, turning a large North Oxford house into an accessible building, most interior walls removed with just the facade remaining. That had infuriated the nimbies in the area, but Michael had no time for them. He would've been unable to get around his place of work so easily if they'd stuck to narrow staircases and corridors. As it was, this was ideal, spacious and reminiscent of the Tardis, feeling much bigger on the inside than it looked from outside.

A colleague from Keble College met him as he entered the foyer, Dr Fuller, a medical researcher with a growing international reputation. Of Jamaican parentage, she proved that the Oxford senior common room was slowly diversifying.

'Michael, any idea what this is about?' she asked.

'No idea, Claire, but I was wondering if the events next door had a connection?'

'Lord, I hope that doesn't mean they're pulling our funding?'

That thought took Michael by surprise. 'What?'

'As I see it, Chernov is only doing this to shine up his reputation. He might want to cut all ties with Oxford if the body in his garden gets a lot of play on the international news. I wouldn't blame him. In his shoes, I'd want to forget I ever knew us.'

Michael pressed the button to open the glass doors. 'I hope you're wrong. I've already got the Digital Brain grant application in with funding bodies.'

'Oh really? Who are you working with on that?'

Filling in the short walk to the room with academic news swap, they arrived in the meeting to find they were the last. The head of the institute, Professor Greening, was already standing in front of twenty research fellows to say a few introductory words. He looked nervous as he clutched the brochure for the centre that had been expensively produced to trumpet their existence. Liveried in dark blue, the leaflet was full of fresh-faced graduates in white coats writing on interactive boards or walking through parks with robots – all of which bore little resemblance to the actual work they did. A dark-haired young man with a sober expression sat beside the professor. Odd to find a junior in the position of an honoured guest. Greening's DPhil student to take notes? wondered Michael.

'Please, ladies and gentlemen, if you'd settle down. I don't wish to keep you long.' Greening, one of the pioneers in computer programming, was in his lap of honour at Oxford, setting up this institute as his final contribution to the field before retirement. Apart from lank grey hair and thick-rimmed black spectacles, he didn't look that different from the photos of him in the 70s working on computer technology in his parents' garage. He would always be geeky and boyish until he was uploaded into the great computer programme in the sky. 'I've called this meeting so I could introduce you to Alexei Chernov, the son of Anatoly Chernov, who, as you will all know, provided the seed from which this institute has grown.' Ah, so not a graduate; their paymaster. Michael gave closer attention to the young man. Expensive but casual clothes. A watch that probably cost more than a nurse earned in a year. Broad shoulders and muscled arms. 'Alexei has recently taken over the running of the Chernov Foundation from his father and wishes to familiarise himself with the major projects they are funding.'

Subtext, thought Michael, show him you're worth his time and money or we're all destined for the delete button.

'I'll ask each of you to say a sentence to introduce yourself and the headlines of your project area.'

So maybe not a death sentence to the institute but an invitation to do the tap-dance for a new funder. Michael quickly thought through how best to introduce his research for a millennial. His colleagues would no doubt bore the young man; he'd find a better way and entertain.

'Michael? If you'd like to start.' Greening turned to him.

Michael swore under his breath. He had been hoping for five minutes to compose his pitch.

'Imagine the world run by psychopathic computers, Mr Chernov.' Alexei looked up, interest in his eyes. 'We don't have to try hard because from *2001: A Space Odyssey* to *Westworld*, gifted scriptwriters have been doing just that. How are we going to prevent AI developing into the worst visions of our sci-fi dystopias?'

Alexei smiled and shrugged.

'One answer: by making sane algorithms that take the best from the human brain, not the worst. I'm Dr Michael Harrison, a psychologist. It's my job, with my programming colleagues, to develop systems to achieve this.'

Less is more, Michael reminded himself, so he shut up.

'That is' – Alexei tapped a finger on the table – 'extremely interesting, Dr Harrison.' His Russian accent had an American twang.

'And that is only the first of our many projects,' said Greening, giving Michael a pleased nod. 'Maybe Claire, you'd like to go next?'

'Thanks, Michael,' Claire muttered under her breath as she got to her feet, not sounding the least bit grateful. 'Can AI do the job of screening for cancer better than a doctor? We think that maybe it can.'

Michael had set the bar high and most of his colleagues responded with an upbeat pitch, hitting more TED talk than snooze button, though the mathematician from New College did lose everyone by the third sentence. Alexei managed to look engaged and Greening appeared to be shedding stress with every successful speech. Then the meeting broke up for coffee and a more informal time. Michael was flattered to find Alexei making a beeline for him.

'Dr Harrison, good to meet you.' Alexei held out a sun-tanned hand, calloused from rugged outdoor pursuits, or so Michael guessed. Hunting with the president; kayaking with a crown prince: the ordinary life of the super-rich.

'Mr Chernov.'

'Please, call me Alex. Mr Chernov sounds like my father.'

'Alex then. I understand that you're a graduate from Harvard Business School?' Michael had discreetly googled him while pretending to listen to the other pitches.

'Yes. Now I'm investing in some tech start-ups, which is why this part of the Chernov Foundation work is of great interest to me. I think we can cut through so much lab time on drugs and vaccines, make factories more efficient, run our houses in a green-friendly fashion, by the application of more AI to our lives.'

'Which means you see artificial intelligence as our ally and not our enemy?'

'If we make the right choices now. Like you, I don't want a post-human future where crazed machines are running things for their own benefit.' He sat on the edge of the table and folded his arms. Michael was aware they were the centre of attention despite everyone pretending not to look.

'Oh, I don't think they could completely do away with us.'

'Not yet at least. Who would change the batteries?'

They shared a smile and Michael found himself warming to the young Russian. He wasn't to blame from how his father earned the family money.

Professor Greening approached with a glass of some soft drink, possibly Coca Cola, for their guest and coffee for himself. He'd probably had to run to the kitchen to get that as academic meetings didn't usually consider the tastes of the under-thirties.

'We were sorry to hear that your father has stepped back from taking an active role in his foundation,' said Greening in his senior common room stuffy manner, quite spoiling the friendly tone Michael and Alexei had achieved. 'I hope that it isn't due to poor health?'

Alexei sipped his drink. 'No.'

Greening was flustered by the short answer and began twittering. 'Oh, well then, please do send our greetings to him when you next speak. Wonderful man. A visionary. And we're delighted to have you on board instead, of course.'

Clearly the topic of the father was a difficult one for the son. Michael needed to get Greening off the subject of families before he undid all the good work of the morning. He swooped in when Greening paused to drink his coffee.

'Neil, do tell Alex here how you got into computing. He won't believe the primitive conditions you and Bill Gates and the others started out in.'

Greening, flattered to find his name bracketed with Gates, began to describe the first forays into creating motherboards with early versions of the microchip, hand-soldered from odds and ends sourced from the toolbox. He made quite a good story of it and Michael was able to relax. Alexei too seemed to be enjoying what for him must have felt like ancient history.

'And I went to the Science Museum for a seminar the other day and saw one of the machines we all thought so advanced in its day in a glass case. My fridge has more processing power. We're becoming relics, my generation,' Greening concluded with a droll smile.

'Hardly,' said Michael. 'Don't believe him, Alex. AI is where the cutting edge has reached in our mad dash to the future. You're putting your money exactly where it can do the most good.'

Alex gave him a sideways look, a little smirk in his expression. 'I should hope so, or I'd have to reconsider, wouldn't I?'

Michael was reminded that this young man wasn't a friendly colleague or student. What a Chernov gave, a Chernov could easily take away. He gave Alexei a hard smile, showing he had the balls to take him on. 'Oh, we'll make it well worth your while, Alex. The best brains coupled with the best resources: nothing can hold us back.'

Chapter 20

Jess

Sanyu had decided that today would be a good day for a rehearsal of the readings. I thought it the worst possible for three reasons: one, the BBC were back to film Errol; two, it gave Paul more reasons to hate me; three, I'd discovered that the sixth lesson included the unpronounceable (to me) name 'Quirinius'. Who is he? Governor of Syria apparently. No matter how many times I said it, I kept stumbling over the syllables.

Oh, and I'd just thought of a fourth (and a possible reason why the name was giving me so much trouble): I still hadn't recovered from my night-time adventure with the intruder. Thanks to Karl the glazier, the door was now fetchingly boarded up in plywood, bringing an inner city riot vibe to the drawing room. But my castle had been breached and I didn't like it. I very much did not want to sleep alone tonight.

To cheer myself up, I sent Leo a picture of the offending Biblical name, saying how I 'found' it difficult. That joined the photo of the chocolate biscuit 'found' in my desk drawer, the spiderweb 'found' on my filing cabinet, and my colleague 'found' doing a wordsearch when she should be working. He was the first to know, as I'd promised.

His silence in response made me wonder if I were the only one enjoying the joke?

He's busy, I told myself, *get a grip, Jess.*

Paul hovered at my shoulder as he caught me going over the lesson in my lunch break.

'Humph,' he said.

'Nope, Queer-inny-e-us,' I said.

'You're saying it wrong,' offered Jennifer from the safe distance of her desk.

'I'm saying it the only way I know how.' I was tempted to throw a college prospectus at her but Paul didn't leave so I couldn't. *Play nicely, Jess.* 'Do you want something, Paul?'

'I just wanted to check you were coming to the meeting tonight.'

I quickly scanned my memory for some college event I was down to attend. 'Erm, no?'

'But Meredith is counting on you. After your break-in.'

'Break-in?' squawked Jennifer.

I did a quick one-eighty. 'You mean the North Oxford Protection Society meeting? Oh yes, I'll be there. How do you know about that?'

'I'm a member as I'm in a flat on Hay Road – a college house. I keep an eye on the graduate accommodation.'

I did know this, I recalled. I imagined that he kept his graduates on their toes with strict rules for recycling bins and where to park their bikes.

'The Prices are old friends,' Paul continued. 'They're not keen on your sort moving into the area.'

'Pardon?' That was rude, even for Paul.

'Not you – the owners of your house and that one where they found the body. Disgraceful! Russian problems imported into Oxford – it shouldn't be allowed.'

I stuffed an envelope with feeling. 'My people are Uzbeks.' That wasn't a sentence I ever thought I'd say.

He waved that – and a thousand years of history – away. 'What do they care for our heritage? Your house is particularly notable, from an architectural point of view. But I suppose you know that already?'

I kept a pleasant but neutral expression as I added to the pile of brochures I was mailing to inner city schools. 'Hmm?'

'Al Price's book on the area? Haven't you even bothered to read it?' He sounded like a teacher discovering I'd not done my homework.

'Sorry, not sure what you're talking about.'

With a put-upon sigh, he went into his office and returned with a slim paperback of local history. He opened it to Howell Road and put a Post-it in the place where the details about my house could be found. In case I didn't know how to use an index?

'I suggest you read this. It might give you a better appreciation of what we're fighting for.'

With that ominous pronouncement, he stalked out.

Jennifer rolled her eyes. 'And I live in a really notable semi in Cowley, if you're wondering. Built in the 1930s by the council, it combines a front garden with a back, and an indoor toilet these days.'

'Glad to hear it.' I grinned at her. I was in fact eager to read about the red house. It had character enough to be bigger than any single owner. All who lived under its roof were only passing through; it gave the impression of staying put for the long haul. Its chances were good, seeing that it was in a conservation area.

'What about your break-in?' asked Jennifer. 'I can't believe you didn't say anything to me all morning.'

'Flossie and I disturbed an intruder. Not much more to say than that,' I said lightly, downplaying the incident. Jennifer was likely to fuss over me, which is why I'd not told her.

'Oh, poor you. Don't you have an alarm system in a fancy house like that?'

There was, but I hated setting it while inside because I'd triggered it wandering out of my designated zone on several occasions. The alarm company were not pleased with me. It would definitely be going on tonight though. 'Well, you see . . .'

Jennifer nodded, understanding without me having to complete my sentence. 'It's "quee" to rhyme with bee, rin-ee-us,' she said. 'That's how I learned it.'

I was still muttering that under my breath when I made it to rehearsal. Errol was playing a piece on the organ, penned in by his camera crew. Sanyu, dressed down in jeans and shirt to show he was one of the people, approached me, hands outstretched.

'Jess, just the person I wanted to see. How are plans going for the decorations?'

I told him of the refugee artworks I'd sourced from Cory. 'Lovely, splendid, super, but will that be enough, do you think?' He frowned at the empty space around the Christmas tree. The nativity scene did look very small now I came to look at it from the other side of the chapel. 'The Master is anxious that we do our utmost.'

I seemed to be the only one utmosting, if that was even a word. 'I've not been given much money, Sanyu.'

He sighed. 'Oh well, we mustn't expect miracles. Or maybe we should?' He went into a peal of priestly laughter.

One of the BBC team approached: a stick insect of a woman with highlighted hair cut in a 90s Rachel style and a chin that came to a definite point. She carried a clipboard with the febrile air of a newsreader about to do a live broadcast.

'Jess Bridges?'

'That's me.'

'Errol told us all about you – how you have a side business looking for missing people and how you helped solve a couple of murders for Thames Valley Police?'

I was going to murder Errol and bury him in a garden. I happened to know a spot that had recently become vacant. 'I'm not sure the police would say I helped, but I tried not to hinder.'

'Still, it's an interesting angle – the young woman who consults for the police in unusual ways.'

I had a flashback of being in unusual ways in the kitchen with Leo. 'I suppose so.'

'You're reading the sixth lesson?'

'I am, if I can get my tongue around it.' Why did everything I said come loaded with innuendo today?

'We like to do a little segment on each of the readers, you

181

know, bring them alive for those watching? We'll drop in a little video interview while the audience—'

'Congregation!' boomed Sanyu.

The woman gave a pained smile. 'Sorry, *congregation* takes their seat. No more than a minute.'

'Oh, I'm not sure—'

'They've already filmed my family at the homeless shelter,' said Sanyu. 'We had to pretend it was Christmas already which confused some of the more challenged among the inhabitants.' He meant the ones who were out of touch with the normal passage of time due to their problems with drugs, alcohol or mental illness.

'Well, I . . .'

'We could film you here or in your home environment,' the woman persisted.

'I'm a house-sitter. I can't invite anyone into where I live.'

She scented another angle in my story. 'Oh? Interesting. Who do you house-sit for?'

'I'm afraid I can't say.' I probably could but there was enough going on at the red house without adding a BBC film crew into the mix.

'Then here it is.' She made a note, tapping her clipboard. 'Let's find a quiet corner.'

'But I'm not dressed for an interview.'

'You look fine. Follow me.'

I could see how she had made it to the lofty height of programme editor: she did not take no for an answer, or even consider it a possibility. I found myself herded into a corner to record a few lines. Oh well. I'd been wondering how to gain publicity for my business; I decided to recast this as an opportunity. Someone might be watching for whom I was an answer to prayer.

Leo and I were running ten minutes late for the meeting at St Bede's. That wasn't entirely my fault. I blamed Flossie, who had insisted on a walk, and then I'd got sidetracked by reading the book Paul had lent me, while lying in a bubble bath. My house had been designed by Frederick Codd, it told me, one of the leading designers of the Victorian gothic that had turned this area into something of a theme park for upper-middle-class fantasy houses. Turrets, quirky towers and stained glass proliferated. Fittingly for a property speculator, Codd had gone out of business because he overextended – too many unique houses, not enough imaginative buyers – and he'd been unable to repay his debts. He scuttled off to become City Surveyor, a safer bet financially. He would be amazed at the prices his houses now commanded, known worldwide as one of the UK's property hot spots for those attracted by the combination of top-flight education and congenial surroundings.

My house, the book opined, had been one of Codd's masterpieces. Commissioned by a man of the cloth, it included a secret passage to the parish church so that the prelate in question didn't have to mix with his parishioners or get his cassock wet. (That sounded rude too – what was it with innuendos today?) The priest was a neurotic man and had insisted the passage was left off the architectural plans, apart from the master set he owned, all traces of which had been lost. The parish church had gone, replaced by a larger building a few streets to the north. Utility companies sometimes came across hollows under the road but no one had done a proper survey to discover how much was left.

A secret passage? That was cool – but so was the bathwater. I got out and decided to investigate later – much later, if the date with Leo went well.

Deciding that an emerald wrap-around dress and knee-high boots would work at a public meeting and then a dinner, I was ready at seven. Leo had only had to wait a little while, but that gave him time to bond some more with Flossie.

'So how was your day?' I asked as we set out for St Bede's on foot.

'It didn't go as expected. Sorry I didn't reply to your messages; I got swept up.' He walked with the steady pace that hinted at a past life on the beat.

'Oh?'

'Alexei Chernov is in town. We had no idea he'd returned to the UK until he told the constable on the door of the property in Howell Street to leave.'

'He can do that?'

'We decided not to challenge the decision, seeing that we'd been inside the house in his absence. Grey area legally. And we've got everything we can from the garden.'

'Have you interviewed him?'

'Not yet but he'd said he'd fit me in tomorrow. That suits me as I'm expecting the DNA results.'

'Why don't you have them already? I thought you could get results in twenty-four hours these days?'

'The labs are backed up. Even priority cases get this kind

of turnaround time. That's what happens when you reorganise the forensic service and put it in private hands.'

'Ri-ight. Touched a nerve?'

He shook his head at himself. 'Don't get me started. Anyway, we took a sample from a man's hairbrush in the master bedroom and are using that for the match. It should give us more certainty as to the body's identity.'

'But you're sure?'

Leo put an arm around my shoulder. I loved him like this, striding out in his wide-lapelled Sherlock coat: so capable and handsome against the frosty dark sky. That made me his Dr Watson, didn't it, though I wasn't wearing a Martin Freeman pea coat but a mid-length red Puffa jacket. 'Yes. I'm convinced it's his father. I just don't understand why the family are behaving as they are.'

'Maybe they want to "take care" of it themselves?' I air-quoted the words. 'Isn't that what mafia bosses do? Keep it in the family? Most police forces aren't to be trusted in the kind of places they are used to.'

He gave me an appreciative look that made my tummy flutter. 'But I'm also looking at them as suspects. Family often has the chief motive to kill one of their number – feuds, inheritance issues, revenge.'

'I can see that.'

Lights were on in the newly built glazed building that was the St Bede centrepiece. We walked into the school hall and were embarrassed to find that all those gathered turned to look. It was only a small audience for such a large space, but it was plenty to daunt me.

'There they are now,' said Mr Price, standing up in his place at the centre of the speakers' table. 'Inspector, Miss Bridges, please come up the front.'

We were shepherded through the ranks of seats to the stage. There had to be about thirty neighbours gathered, not exactly a lynch mob but neither did they look very friendly. Leo was given the seat next to the chairman, and I was seated separately beside Paul. Great. Just what I needed for my evening off. I noticed he was taking minutes which clued me in on the fact that he was the secretary for this organisation.

'You're late,' Paul hissed, not looking at me as he scribbled the offending late arrival down on his A4 notepad.

He wasn't going to rule my personal time like he did the office.

I unbuttoned my coat and shed it like a salamander, a wriggle to reveal new skin. 'Like a wizard, I am never late. I arrive precisely when I mean to.'

He didn't get the Gandalf reference. 'That won't wash in the workplace.'

'Well, I'm not at work now, am I?' I gave him a sweet smile.

'Don't you ever take anything seriously?' And he had to have the last word, didn't he?

I settled for a broader smile which was all the answer he deserved.

Our little spat was interrupted by a disturbance at the back of the room. We weren't the last to arrive after all: a young man had come in, flanked by two square-jawed, square-bodied individuals who had to have been picked out of the Moscow edition of the catalogue of heavies-for-hire. I glanced at Leo down the table from me. He gave me a slight nod. Chernov. Interesting.

I don't think Mr Price had anticipated that. From the tightening of his expression and the look of disapproval on Meredith's face, I saw that they had to recalibrate their meeting. Their planned xenophobic attack on foreigners importing their problems into Oxford suddenly seemed exactly what it was: tacky.

Mr Price dealt with the new problem as he probably had been taught in his career in the RAF: head-on with machine guns rattling out the words.

'And, of course, I'd like to extend a special welcome to Alex Chernov, who has just come in. Back in Oxford after a long absence. As this matter concerns him very closely, I am encouraged to see that he has chosen to come and support the neighbourhood.'

From the look of Alexei's faintly amused expression, I wasn't sure that was his intention at all.

A woman shot up her hand like the faithful at Nuremberg.

'Yes, Sally?'

'I want to know who it is they found in Chernov's garden. We can't know if we are safe unless we understand what kind of person this killer is targeting.'

Mr Price turned to Leo.

'No, not him,' Sally interrupted. 'I know the police haven't a clue – fat lot of use they are. I want to ask Alex. I'm sure he and his family know full well.' She turned a scorching look on the young man who was seated only two rows behind her.

Mr Price contained his smile in a sombre expression. She was doing his job for him, which I supposed was rather the point of these groups where everyone agreed with each other. Alex had joined Leo and me as the equivalent of Christians before the lions. 'Alex, would you like to take that?'

Alexei stood up. 'Mr Price, thank you for your words of welcome. Mrs Houseman, I regret to say I have no idea who the person is. I leave such matters to the experts.'

Sally, or Mrs Houseman – I was impressed that Alexei remembered the name of an obscure woman in a place where he no longer lived – scowled at him. 'You're very good at playing innocent but we all know what you're really like.'

There was a muttering of agreement that went round the room. Alexei's expression chilled.

'It was made very clear at the time that I did nothing wrong. Your daughter was the victim of the lorry driver, not my driving.'

Daughter? The second girl in the accident along with Fatima. No wonder he remembered her. I'd have the bereaved family's surname engraved on my heart for all time if I had been the unwitting cause of a child's death.

'As I said at the time, I miss Patricia – and Fatima – more than you know.'

Meredith stood up. 'Please, Sally, there's nothing to be gained for raising that tragic accident here tonight. Of course, you're upset to see Alex unexpectedly, but he did a good thing by coming to be with us. Let's respect that.'

Her intervention took the tension down a notch or two. Sally Houseman sat and gripped the hand of the grey-looking man in a tweed suit beside her, whom I took to be her husband.

'To sum up, Alex,' said Mr Price with the air of someone determined to keep the stricken aircraft of a meeting flying, 'you are unaware of the identity and doubtless wish to have the matter cleared up as quickly as possible. Have you spoken to your father about it?'

Alexei's expression was unreadable. Was it anger, irritation or pure ice in his dark eyes? 'My father and I haven't spoken for over a year.'

I glanced at Leo. He was listening with a hawkish intensity to everything said.

'Oh, I'm sorry to hear that.' Mr Price kept hoping the engine would restart from its stall. 'I hope he's all right?'

'As I said, we haven't spoken.' Then Alexei glanced back at Mrs Houseman, not intentionally I thought. Father and son had clearly fallen out. Did that mean the accident was the matter over which they had had their disagreement? A Romeo and Juliet story where Romeo had survived to bear a grudge against the elders of the Chernov and Gulom families? Alexei with his dangerous brooding edge looked like he would carry a grudge very well indeed.

'In that case, let's turn to the events of last night,' Mr Price said like a pilot spotting a soft landing where he could bring the meeting to ground in one piece. 'Jess Bridges is the caretaker for the red house in Howell Street. I'll let her tell us what happened last night.'

I'd prefer to be back tangling with Quirinius in front of a snooty BBC editor. As it was, I got to my feet and told my story.

Chapter 21

Jess

Leo and I escaped with all limbs attached and only mildly scratched by the lions of the North Oxford Protection Society. They'd made me feel like I didn't care enough about the seriousness of the threat facing our area when I made a joke about driving the intruder off with a hairdryer. Apparently, according to Paul, it showed a levity that didn't do justice to the gravity of the crisis. It was people like me who gave the authorities an excuse not to take their concerns seriously.

I wasn't the only one criticised. Leo was told he and his colleagues were too busy catching innocent motorists exceeding twenty miles per hour on St Giles to care about murder. I took it that the white-haired gentleman who had that particular accusation had been caught out by the regular speed-trap on that local main road.

Alexei was asked no more questions but when he got up to leave no one approached him. They did corner Leo and me so we couldn't catch a word before he left. Didn't these people realise that they'd snubbed the T-Rex in their midst?

And my motto is that there is no point being a lion if you're in Jurassic Park.

'Why did we put ourselves through that?' I asked Leo as we walked through the frosted leaves that had gathered in drifts on the pavements of Park Town. This area just north of my house was worth the detour we had made: a little spot that looked like a mini-Bath dropped into Oxford, a circus and parades of houses with garden squares. It made me want to dance a quadrille with a dashing man in uniform.

'I came because I'm a public servant who knows my place.' Leo grinned at those words. 'You, because you're a mug.'

'*I'm just a girl who can't say no*,' I sang.

His smile dimmed. 'That's not very PC.'

'Don't blame me, blame Rodgers and Hammerstein.'

'Sorry?'

'*Oklahoma*?' He still looked blank. 'Now I'm certain you're not gay: you don't know your show tunes.'

'Is that the only thing that told you that?'

And right there we were back on track with romance. His wicked smile could melt the clothes right off me – and we were in the middle of a residential street. Could we . . .? No, he was a public servant. He couldn't get caught climbing a fence for a tumble in the garden square. 'So where are we eating?' I asked, narrowly resisting the urge to suggest a misdemeanour.

'Right here.' Emerging from Park Town, he pointed to a restaurant in a conservatory that filled the courtyard of one of the houses on the Banbury Road. It had a Kew Gardens hothouse feel, thanks to the plants and flowers that filled every spare inch. Right now it was wearing a Christmas costume of twinkly lights, fir trees and poinsettias. From the outside in the dark, diners were fish in a very upmarket aquarium. I'd always wanted to try it out but had been afraid of the prices.

'Oh, wow.'

'You like?'

'I like.'

Mulling the meeting over not with mull (though that was on the menu) but a cocktail, I wondered about Alexei Chernov's decision to attend.

'Why do you think he came?' I asked Leo.

Leo gazed at his spiced apple daiquiri. I'd chosen the cocktail called the Garden Toad. 'Not sure but I learned a couple of things and have a theory.'

'Go on.'

'He's taken over from his father and he is using the feud as a reason not to answer queries about his father's absence from public life.'

I stirred my drink with a sparkly cocktail stick. 'And he came because he guessed that the reason for the argument – the accident – would come up tonight?'

'In my presence, which the organisers advertised beforehand, so it looks like he didn't engineer the revelation.'

'Ah, canny.' I sipped the gin and vermouth combo that squatted toadishly in the glass. It tasted better than it looked, but wasn't that the rep of kissing an amphibian? 'Which means he's clever?'

Leo nodded. 'That's my take. I did a deeper run on him

today. His results from Harvard were excellent and there was no suggestion he didn't earn them himself. His grades at St Bede's were also good. He was head boy in his last year and they only give that commendation to those who excel both at academic work and on the sports field.'

'I think I hate him already.' I pulled a piece of ciabatta off the slice in the breadbasket and dipped it into the balsamic vinegar and olive oil. 'But if I'd been at school with him, I'd've probably had a crush. Like Fatima.'

I ate the bread, thinking of star-crossed lovers.

'Is it him? Is he the one who planted his father in some weird homage to the family tree?'

'It could be.' Leo resisted filling up on the bread, paying more attention to savouring his drink.

'Tell me your suspects.'

He rolled his shoulders. 'Assuming that it is Chernov senior, we've got Akmal Gulom, vengeful father . . .'

I bowed, taking the honour on myself as his representative.

'Alexei, son who wants to take over, Mrs Chernov the first, who bears a grudge at being thrown over for the younger woman, and I suppose after tonight, the Housemans, another set of grieved parents. I'll have to add them.'

The Housemans? I could see that. They could've thought that the father was to blame for the son having access to a car. Hell, they could've blamed him for Alexei's existence. Grief is a wild beast when it gets its teeth in your heart.

'Then there are the unknown business rivals, which we'll need to investigate, and anyone else that he crossed. I can't rule out an assassination paid for by someone who will never come into our jurisdiction. The only person who's had a good word for him is Mr Price and even that was mixed with the shading of local planning battles.'

I smiled and waved the sparkle stick. 'Ah, then it has to be him. He's the odd one out.' A funny thought struck me. 'I know: it was all the members of the North Oxford Protection Society together like in, you know, the Orient Express? They each took a turn with the knife for his sin against gardening.'

Leo smiled at my fantasy. 'It was a single bullet, I'm afraid. Execution style.'

I touched the back of my head. 'Ouch.'

'Do you think we can leave all that behind for a while?' Leo asked, taking my hand. 'I'd prefer to talk about us.'

My pulse went into overdrive. It hadn't been his intention but he'd reminded me of my promise to myself that I would give him full disclosure of my sins so he could decide whether he stayed in a relationship with me. I couldn't do it. I couldn't spoil this wonderful meal by dragging out the rotting bones of my skeleton onto this white marble tabletop and watch the maggots squirm out of the eye sockets.

The waiter, with impeccable timing, delivered my courgette soup and Leo's bruschetta.

The bowl of soup glared up at me accusingly, quail's egg bobbing like a white pupil in a green eyeball.

I'm a reckless creature and I can't keep a secret – at least not for long.

'What's the matter?' asked Leo. 'You shut down. Sorry, maybe you'd prefer to keep talking about murder?' He said it with a wry twist to his tone.

'No, it's not that.' I dug in my purse and handed over £20. 'Take this. I might need to walk out when I've finished, and I don't want to land you with the bill.'

He pushed the note back. 'Don't be silly.'

'I'm not being silly. In fact I'm being serious. For once.' I looked up at him, wondering how I could risk losing all this gorgeousness. But if I didn't tell him, then I'd risk losing him in a far more hurtful fashion a few weeks, maybe days, away. 'Remember I told you about my time on the street?'

'Yes?' He was wary, as well he should be.

'That's not the worst. I can give myself a pass for that as I was young and stupid.'

'You were young and damaged – vulnerable,' Leo corrected.

I shrugged. 'Maybe. But you won't be able to find excuses for the next bit.' Was I really going to do this? 'Right, here goes. When I was in a relationship with Michael, I wasn't well. Our time together was getting very weird, and I was abusing my medication, he was grieving his wife; it was a stupid relationship to start in the first place. Neither of us could help the other.' I paused. Did this sound too much like self-justification? I didn't deserve that.

'You'd better just tell me. Your soup is getting cold.'

I pushed the soup away. 'Please understand I hate myself for this and I apologise in advance. I was bad – very bad. I got hung up on one of my pupils in the school I was teaching in at the time. He'd turned eighteen, so don't shoot me, but still I was the teacher and he the pupil. It started as stupid flirting but then we had an affair, carried out on school premises.' In the stationery cupboard but I couldn't quite bring myself to admit to that detail and the thrill I got from rule-breaking. 'I came to my senses and tried to end it. He took offence and reported me to the school, making it sound like I'd come on to him when it had been the other way round. I had a complete breakdown and lost my job, as I deserved.'

Leo's expression was lifeless. My heart sank, feeling limp like a discarded condom.

'At first I blamed the young man – the boy – in question. But then I saw it was entirely my fault. I might've been in an emotionally fragile state, but that was no excuse. I should've walked away at the first risqué comment.' I took a deep breath. 'Anyway, this all happened a few years ago now, and there's been nothing like it since. I'm sorry that I'm a bad person. If you want me to go, just nod and I'll slip away and you won't have to see me again.'

He didn't move. That wasn't exactly a good thing, but it wasn't a disaster.

Then the waiter – please, someone strangle the waiter! – came over with his smarmy smile. 'Is everything all right with your meal?'

'Go away,' said Leo tersely.

The man backed off with an offended look.

'Leo?' Tears trembled on my lids. Shit, I was going to embarrass myself. I had to go. Leaving the twenty on the table, I got up and hurried to fetch my Puffa jacket from the waitress on the door. She didn't say anything when she saw my face, just handed it over with a commiserating smile.

Back on the street, I strode determinedly away and across

the road, risking being flattened by a bus as it pulled out of the stop. The driver hooted but I ignored him.

He opened his window. 'Stupid cow!'

Fair enough verdict.

It wasn't far to my home, but I had to resist the urge to run all the way to dive under my duvet.

But I didn't even deserve that comfort.

Chapter 22

Leo

Having to deal with the bill, Leo couldn't leap up and follow as he wished. He watched the door, hoping Jess would come back, but he then spotted her heading out to the main road and crossing in a crazily careless fashion, coat a siren red warning. Stuffing her £20 in his pocket, he left a fiver tip and headed out. The waitress had his coat waiting. Should he tip her too? In a panic that Jess would've disappeared entirely, he shoved the twenty in her hand and put on his coat while running.

So unfair not to give him a moment to gather his thoughts! She'd unloaded something huge on him and then been surprised that he staggered for a moment getting used to the weight. It was a horrible and damaging admission – he would take a while to come to terms with it – but for the moment he was convinced that the person she described was no longer the Jess he knew. She was worth running after.

Spotting a gap in the traffic, he darted across the road and caught up with her as she turned by the park into Norham Gardens.

'Jess, hold up!'

She hunched her shoulders in deeper misery and scuttled forwards.

'Stop, for God's sake!'

She took him literally, stopping but not turning.

'You shouldn't have walked out like that. You didn't wait to hear what I had to say.'

'What is there to say?' Her voice was flat, ironed thin by the hot humiliation of the confession.

'I want to talk this out.' He'd reached her now and stepped in front of her. If she was going to continue her scurry home, she'd now have to go through him.

'You can't possibly hate me more than I hate myself.'

That was enough of that! He took her firmly by the arms. 'I don't hate you. I was just lost for words for a moment. I didn't expect that your secret was like that.'

'Oh, what did you expect?' She reached for sarcasm. 'A love child with Hugh Grant or an affair with a Catholic priest?'

He had to laugh at that. 'That's so *Fleabag*. God, can't you see why I like you?'

'You're laughing at me?' But her own lips were betraying her, curving slightly despite the fact that her eyes were shining with tears.

'Yeah, you idiotic pigeon.'

'Idiotic pigeon!'

He'd hoped that would rile her. 'Look, I'm not saying I'm OK with teachers having sex with pupils . . .'

'I should hope not!'

'But I am saying that, if you regret what you did and have

no intention of crossing that line again, we should work on leaving it in the past.'

She started walking again and he kept pace. 'It's not that easy. It's always there.'

He stopped her. She needed to see his face for this conversation. 'Look, I know what it's like to carry baggage from things you regret and can't change; I want you to have a way forward, not get stuck in the events of a few months of your life.' He lifted her chin gently. 'Do you think that time defines you, that's there's nothing more to Jess than that?'

She closed her eyes briefly and whispered: 'I don't know. I hope not. But I have to be honest with you, I'm still that person in many ways. I take stupid risks and my moral compass sometimes goes awry. I try, I really do, but I'm basically deeply, deeply flawed.'

He bent down and kissed her. 'Welcome to the human race.'

Leo was relieved that Jess invited him inside when they reached the red house. He must've found the right thing to say to her. They still had issues that needed working through, but this was enough for tonight.

'You hungry?' she asked.

'Yes.'

'I'm sorry I spoiled dinner.' She gazed gloomily into the cupboard. 'Pasta and red sauce OK?'

'That'll be fine.' It wasn't the right moment for them to go to bed for the first time. Her confession had tainted that, but they needed to move on so another night . . . Murder it was then.

'Jess, have you got anywhere with finding out where Akmal

Gulom can be contacted?' He'd left her this morning promising the glazier that the house owner or insurance company would foot the bill.

'I sent a message to Heather at Woodbridge Consultants but she's not got back to me.'

And probably wouldn't if his mate from the National Crime Agency had raided the office over the weekend.

'What about insurers?'

'About that' – she tipped the pasta into the pan – 'I found a file in the home office and made a call. The problem is they won't accept a claim from anyone but the policy holder.'

'Which takes us back to Gulom. I'll get one of my best people on to it tomorrow. They can go back to the school and try that route. It seemed to have worked for Alexei Chernov.'

'Did it?'

'He turned up after we left messages at the apartment in New York. I guess that must be where he's living now. Or else he came when his mother told him.'

'I reckon Mother Vampire called him back. Head of the family now, isn't he? She would've told him he needs to sort this out. And I think the Guloms are in Tashkent and there's no ex-wife and other kids as far as I know. Just the son who was at school with Fatima. He must be about eighteen now.'

Leo set the table, finding his way around the kitchen by trial and error. 'I wonder if they moved him to another boarding school in the UK? He might still be here.'

'I'm not sure how you'd find out. St Bede's might know, I suppose.' Jess frowned as she stirred in the boiled water from the kettle. 'Unless maybe he gets himself mentioned, you know like in maths competitions or sporting fixtures? He might appear in a Google search.'

Leo got out his phone. 'Rashid Gulom.' He entered the search and waited. There were a few people around the world of that name but the entries were mainly in Cyrillic. He then found many pages down a mention of a Rashid Gulom in a sports report for a school in Kent. A cup in target shooting – interesting. The article was a year old but it would be worth checking out tomorrow.

'Thanks, that was a good thought.'

She placed the pasta and red sauce in front of him. 'Grated cheese?'

'Don't bother.' He felt like they were treading on eggshells of words which she wished she'd not said, fearful words of rejection and self-hatred that she'd probably heard so many times. 'Changed my mind: let's bother. But I'll get the cheese and do the grating.'

She watched him warily as he moved about the kitchen finding the necessary implements. 'You're taking this very well.'

'But you're not?'

She gave a sad laugh. 'You're right. I'm a disaster at handling my own disasters. Remind me: why are you still here?'

'Because I want to be.' He held the parmesan over her plate. 'Would madam care for a little?'

'Go for it.'

They ate in silence for a while, both alone with their own thoughts.

'Oh,' she said suddenly. 'I forgot to tell you.'

His heart lurched. He thought he'd done quite well with

one shocking revelation; he wasn't sure he could cope with another. 'What?'

'This house has a secret too – but a nice one: a secret passage. That book on the history of this part of North Oxford had a section on it. Do you want to go and look for it after supper?'

That solved the question of how to negotiate the jagged feelings of the evening: a distraction. 'How could I refuse?'

They began out in the garden, mainly because Flossie needed a late-night outing. Bundled up in their coats and clutching torches, it did feel exciting, looking for a hidden entrance under the shrubs and in the outhouses.

'Can we narrow it down? What do you think was here back then?' asked Jess, her breath forming a mist in the cold damp air.

Leo surveyed the garden, something he'd been wanting to do and was pleased to have the excuse. His torchlight caught on the slim figure of a girl standing at the side of the steps down to the grass. A stone Alice.

'Wonderland?'

'Odd, isn't it?' Jess patted the girl. 'It's not just her – the garden is littered with references. I suppose it does go with the house but not the current owner, unless there's a craze in Tashkent for Lewis Carroll?'

'Maybe they were already here and Gulom decided to keep them? They look old to me, not modern reproductions.'

There was a terrace immediately behind the house. The stones were new, having been re-laid when the swimming pool had been excavated, Jess explained.

'There's nothing in the pool area inside?' Leo asked.

'Our own pool of tears. Nope. Nothing like that.'

'They would've found it when excavating if it started in the house.' Then where? The circular lawn looked like an original layout. The espaliered apple and pear trees that surrounded it were old, at least fifty years he would guess from the amount of lichen that had grown on the gnarled branches. Beyond that lay a kitchen garden which had been divided into box-edged quarters. A toadstool birdbath sat in the centre, water like a cataract-covered eye gazing at the stars. Past that was what the Victorian liked to call their shrubbery or wilderness, a tangle of trees and rhododendrons.

'The Mad Hatter is in there somewhere,' Jess said.

'And the Queen of Hearts?'

'I've not found her yet. No doubt she's lurking angrily under a bush.'

It was only quarter of an acre, but it felt like a whole world in this little space. 'And what about the entrance: somewhere in the shrubbery?'

'But my priestly predecessor would've got wet going that far to find it. The book made a great fuss of his fastidious shower-dodging habits.'

'Then let's look at the outhouses. What've you got here?'

She led him to the buildings to the eastern side of the house. 'I think this might once have been some kind of store-room they repurposed for the car age. The part at the back seems very old. A coal store or brewhouse?'

Leo tugged on the door but it was locked. The Cheshire Cat smirked down on his efforts.

'One moment.' Jess knelt and lifted a flowerpot.

'Really?'

'Some clichés are clichés because people really do use them.' She brandished a big iron key and unlocked the door.

'Is there a light?'

She groped to the left and turned on the bare bulb that hung in the centre from a wire.

'I see the Guloms' passion for refitting didn't reach out here.' He stepped inside and prodded the plastic sheeting that protected the garden furniture, retired here for the winter. The floor was brick, with no sign that any of them had been moved since being laid over a century and a half ago. 'No secret entrance as far as I can see. We should be doing this in the daylight really.'

'Where would be the fun in that?'

'You know, if the statues are original, and the Alice theme was the choice of the first owner, then maybe we should think along a Wonderland theme to find the entrance?'

Jess lit up with excitement. 'Like a rabbit hole?'

'Do you know where the White Rabbit is?'

Frowning, Jess shook her head. 'Now you come to mention it, he's missing.'

'My guess is, find the rabbit, find the entrance. You're the missing persons expert: that should be easy.'

'Ha, ha.'

'Let's have a look in the garage.' He went to the door that connected internally. The key was in the lock here.

'There's just an old car under a tarpaulin . . .'

'Still, no self-respecting hunter of tunnels gives up without checking every possible place.'

'We won't be able to move the car. It's been parked there years so the battery must be pancake flat.'

Jess hit the light by the door and a strip light that stuttered on. As she said, there was just a small car huddled lumpily under a blue sheet. Leo lifted a corner to glance at the rear numberplate but there wasn't one.

'I think it's a Mini,' he said.

'That's a Mini in the same way a shark is a fish.'

'No, really, it is. The big model.'

'So hardly mini at all.' Jess completed the unveiling by tugging the sheet right off. 'Five doors and . . . oh, crap.'

The front of the powder-blue Mini was completely smashed, wheels askew like the chassis had been twisted by a giant in a tantrum. There was a huge dent in the side, windows shattered. In fact, the car was a wreck.

Leo shone his torch into the interior. There were black stains on the white leather upholstery, front and back seats. He'd lay money on them having been caused by blood.

'Are you thinking what I'm thinking?' asked Jess, stepping back as if the tragedy could still infect anyone standing too close.

'Yeah. The car in which his daughter died. But how did it get here?'

'What do you mean?'

'It would've been used as evidence in the criminal prosecution. My colleagues at the police pound would've stored it as evidence. You can't just buy cars that have been used in prosecutions on the open market.'

'But, Leo, have you noticed? The rear is untouched. There was no shunt.'

'I can see that. Which means this wasn't the car used in the case.' Leo shook his head in disbelief, wondering how the switch could've been made. 'This shows Alexei wasn't the innocent driver he claimed to be. This collided with something at high speed.' He pieced it together, imagining the accident. 'As the only conscious survivor, he staggered out and did what?'

'Phoned Daddy. "Hey, I've just by mistake killed my mates and I'm in big trouble?"' Jess's tone was sour. '"Don't let it spoil my life. I haven't got time to serve a stretch in an English prison."'

Leo nodded. 'Yeah, that fits. He would be used to falling back on his family influence. Dad swoops in, finds an identical model of car, puts the old number plates on that, has some fixer make the right kind of damage to indicate a rear collision followed by frontal impact and then . . .'

Jess looked over at him. 'Then what?'

'Then he must've bribed someone in traffic to make the switch.' Leo's tone was flatter than the battery. 'There would've been so much to tidy up – witness statements, photos to be doctored. A fatal crash like this is documented in huge detail.'

'But if you have enough money you could make all that inconvenient efficiency go away?'

'That would appear to be the case. And with the confession, it was never tested in court. They got away with it.' Leo got out his phone. 'I'll have to call this in. I'm kicking myself. My team should've spotted it when we were here for the tools.'

'But you weren't looking for cars and didn't know the history. Even if your guys did lift off the cover and check the boot, there was no reason to bring it to your attention. Don't beat yourself up.' She peered inside and wrinkled her nose at the marks on the leather. 'But why keep this – and how did Mr Gulom get hold of it in the first place? If I were Chernov I would've had it destroyed.'

'Both are excellent questions – and I'll be putting them to Alexei Chernov.'

Chapter 23

Leo

The following morning, Alexei Chernov agreed to meet Leo at the house on Hay Road, but only with his lawyer in tow and for a limited amount of time. Leo weighed up the advantages and disadvantages of his sergeants: Suyin would be a precision tool, Harry a sledgehammer. Though he rather liked the idea of taking a solid blow at the lies with which Alexei had surrounded himself, this was a task for someone who knew how to keep their cool. There were some hard things to say to Chernov and he wasn't sure what the young man's reaction would be.

'Mr Chernov, thank you for making time.' Leo introduced himself and DS Wong. They took the two guest chairs.

With his lawyer standing a little to one side, Alexei sat behind what had been his father's desk, sunlight falling over his shoulder from the window and onto the blotter that sat in the desk's centre. The surface was kept uncluttered. The leather in-tray was empty and the 'out' held a single envelope, address face down. From his angle in the chair across from Alexei, Leo noticed a faint suggestion of fingermarks on the polished wood of the desk as if cleaners hadn't been in and dust had begun to gather. Which they hadn't, he reminded himself, as Glass Tower had stopped paying them.

'I believe we were both at the community meeting last night?' he said affably.

Chernov's lawyer, boxer-bulky, pale skin and a greying goatee, the Jeff Bridges of the legal world, scowled, looking for some point of law to which he could legitimately object.

'Yes,' said Alexei.

Leo remembered from the night before the disarming preference for one-word answers. 'I'm sorry I didn't get a chance to introduce myself. The locals are worried, as you might expect. Break-ins, bodies . . .' He'd wondered last night, watching the forensic team examine the car, if Alexei had had anything to do with the incident at the red house. Did Chernov even know what was in the garage at that property? He can't have or he would've sent someone round to dispose of the evidence, not broken into the main house and put everyone on high alert. There were better ways to handle it if you wanted to get rid of something that incriminated you: for example, take it out of the garage while Jess was at work. No one would question a wrecked car being towed away. It might've been days before Jess even noticed the car had gone. Leo had concluded that the break-in, though linked, wasn't about this. But what had it been about? 'It's been a distressing few days.'

'So I gathered.' Alexei glanced at his lawyer.

'Inspector George, my client is a busy man. We agreed to this interview but we only have thirty minutes for it so I suggest you don't waste time.'

'Mr Smirnov, I have no intention of wasting anyone's time. As you know, Mr Chernov, a body was found in the garden of this house. I regret to inform you that the result of DNA tests I received this morning confirms that it is your father, Anatoly Chernov.'

Silent, Alexei looked at Leo, dead-eyed.

'That is not possible,' said the lawyer.

'How is it not possible?' asked Leo.

'You have no DNA to match.'

Leo decided it would be unproductive to raise the frustration of his attempts to get DNA from the family. 'Fortunately we did not require a DNA sample from a member of the family in the end. We were able to match it to a sample left in this house by Mr Chernov senior.'

'What sample?' asked Alexei, coming out of his frozen state. 'How do you know it is his?'

'From a personal item. That, coupled with the jewellery and clothes that have been traced to your father in photographs, means we have enough evidence to be confident in our identification. I'm sorry that I am the bearer of bad news.'

Leo watched as the young man said nothing. He was recalibrating his response. He had just been told his father was dead but he was treating it like another unexpected hurdle to overcome in a protracted business negotiation. What kind of upbringing made that your go-to response?

The lawyer waited for his client to indicate which way they were going to go on this.

'That is terrible news. I will have to inform my family,' Alexei said tersely. The words fitted the occasion but there was no hint of the emotion driving them: grief, pleasure, fear?

'I understand. But I still have some questions, so if you would answer those first.' What Leo really wanted to ask was why the son was acting this way, like it happened to a stranger. If he had killed his father, Leo would expect him to make a greater show of grief to hide what he had done. This coldness was next to impossible to read. 'Why, when we first raised this possibility, did you claim your father was still alive?'

'Because I thought he was.' Alexei tapped his pen on the blotter, the only sign of agitation.

'Why? Had there been any communication between you?'

Alexei stilled his fingers, perhaps realising he was giving too much away. 'You don't understand much about the kind of world I live in, do you, Inspector George?'

'Clearly not.'

'There was a gas pipeline deal that went sour.'

'Alex . . .' said Smirnov.

Alexei waved the lawyer to stand down. 'My father had fallen foul of powerful people in high places. He said that it would be a good time for me to step up and take on the business – a member of the family who did not carry the same baggage as he did. Then he disappeared – deliberately cut himself off for a while. We were expecting him to get back in touch once the anger of the individuals he had upset was past.'

'Anger? What kind? Business? Personal?' asked Leo.

'In Russia, business is personal.'

And that answered precisely nothing.

'Who were these people?' Leo doubted he had any chance getting an international arrest warrant for them.

'He didn't say.'

'But it is safe to assume we are talking very powerful people?'

'That is a safe assumption.'

'But to recap, your father willingly handed over the leadership of the family business? When was this?'

'Last autumn.'

Around the time that body was planted in an Oxford garden. 'And you have proof?'

Mr Smirnov swelled with indignation. 'We have filed all the paperwork with the necessary authorities. Anatoly signed away his share before he went on furlough.'

'Not furlough. Died,' said Suyin with disarming softness.

The lawyer stumbled. 'N—not until we see the scientific proof ourselves. I will be making an approach to ensure that there's no mistake.'

'There's no mistake. But I'm wondering, as you are still struggling to believe the evidence, who do you think it is, if not Mr Chernov?' she asked.

'Some rival, buried to make trouble.'

The Mrs Chernov theory. Interesting to hear it repeated. Clearly they'd been intending to run with that but did any of them really think it true?

'Joe, that's enough. I believe them,' Alexei said to Mr Smirnov. 'It is my father. You were wrong. They're not doing this to bring my father out of hiding.'

So that was what they thought was motivating the police suggestion that it was the householder who had ended up in the garden. Some plot to expose a man who had gone into hiding?

215

'I am only interested in the truth, Mr Chernov,' said Leo. 'I have no other motive.'

Alexei gave Leo a sour glance. 'You'd be the first policeman I've ever met to have such purity of mission. How did my father die, Inspector?'

At last: the first normal question from the family, rather the run-around he'd got so far. 'A bullet to the back of the head.'

'A single shot?'

'Yes. Death would have been instantaneous.'

'My father was not the kind of man to wait patiently for someone to shoot him. There were no other injuries?'

'No.'

Alexei pressed his fingertips together. 'Which means he let someone get behind him. Either he trusted this person or was caught out.'

'I agree.'

'Do you have a suspect?'

'Who do you think would want your father dead? Who do you think were the people he was hiding from? You said he didn't give you names, but maybe you knew them anyway?'

'That's a dangerous question, Inspector, and I suspect far above your pay grade.'

'Does it go all the way to the Kremlin?'

'I am on good terms with the President. I would like it to stay that way.'

So that was a 'yes' but Alexei would not be making any public accusations and certainly not to British police.

'And what about closer to home: how would you characterise your own relationship with your father, and that of your sisters?'

Alexei didn't bristle with offended feelings as many would've done; he took the question in the same stone-cold way he had the revelation that his father was dead. 'We got on but we were not close. Each of us are – were – busy with our own lives. We all accepted that Dad wouldn't be in touch for a while. We would be watched in case we led his enemies to his location and he didn't want to risk us or himself.'

'That seems . . . unusual.'

'We're not a close family, Inspector. That's all there is to it. I spent my life in a series of boarding schools and foreign universities. When did I have the chance to form that kind of emotional bond you are looking for with my father? I'm sure your own kicked a ball about with you at the weekend, turned up at your school matches, but we didn't have that chance.'

'Then you would be wrong.'

'Sorry?'

'I never knew my father – and I have evidence that your father would go a very long way to help you.' Hoping he'd unbalanced the unflappable Alexei, Leo pressed on. 'Mr Chernov, why did you and your father cover up that you were responsible for the accident that killed Fatima Gulom and Patricia Houseman?'

'What?' Alexei sat up.

'That is out of order, Inspector George,' snapped Smirnov. 'My client was cleared of responsibility. This interview is at an end.'

Leo held up a hand. 'It is, if you wish me to arrest your

client and continue this at a police station. Let's be accurate. Mr Chernov was not tried and cleared of responsibility; another man pleaded guilty to causing death by dangerous driving. Your client can still stand trial. We now have reason to believe that evidence presented in the original prosecution was tampered with.'

Alexei cast a quelling look at his lawyer, his emotions battened down again. 'What evidence?'

'Were you aware that Fatima's father found the Mini you had been driving?'

'That's not possible.'

'Like it wasn't possible your father was the body in the garden? I'm afraid you'll find that it is entirely possible. Nothing like the loss of a child to drive a man to find out the truth.'

Alexei opened his mouth, then closed it again.

'Were you going to say that your father got rid of the car for you? Not well enough, it appears. And money talks on both sides of this – what he paid to get rid of, I assume Mr Gulom paid to resurrect.'

Smirnov put a hand on Alexei's shoulder. 'Don't say anything, Alex.'

'I had my team check the chassis number: it matches the one registered to you at the time of the accident. Why are there two cars with the same supposedly unique chassis number – this one and the one used as evidence in the case? I'm sure you know the answer. The person employed to fix this did a very good job but not a perfect one. You used a very efficient dealership when you purchased the car. They logged the serial numbers on numerous extras you had fitted, including the sound system, which weren't checked because they had nothing to do with the causes of the accident. The dealership had copies of the sales invoice so we know that we have located the car you were driving and it is not the one presented as evidence in the prosecution's case.'

'I have no knowledge of any of this,' Alexei hissed.

'I'm sure you were kept out of the details, but it still remains that you let an innocent man go to prison for you. The case will be reopened and I have been instructed by my superiors to tell you not to try to leave the country or you will be stopped at the border and arrested. My colleagues dealing with the case now will be here after me to conduct a formal interview under caution. Mr Smirnov, I hope you will tell your client that he will have to make time for them?' The lawyer glowered but didn't contradict Leo. 'However, my business is not the accident but murder. Mr Chernov, do you have any idea where Mr Gulom might be now?'

Alexei was still reeling from the revelation that his secret was out and didn't seem to connect the name. 'What?'

'Mr Gulom had the car in his garage – it's no longer there, by the way, we removed it last night.' That should save Jess another night-time prowler looking to tamper with or destroy evidence. 'He knew the true condition of the Mini that you had been driving on the night his daughter died. He knew that the fatalities were caused by a collision with an object in front of you, not from the rear. He would, I think it safe to assume, blame you for her death and be infuriated by the fact that you got away scot-free. I see that as motive for murder.

Perhaps your father fell out with people in the Kremlin, but he also had a far deadlier feud with Mr Gulom, did he not?'

'I don't know.' Alexei for the first time looked shaken.

'He lived across the fence at the end of the garden. It would be a simple matter to take a neighbour unawares – plenty of time to lie in wait in the thick shrubbery his side of the boundary. Maybe he has an alibi but I haven't been able to locate him to ask. He, like your father, has been radio silent for some time now.'

Alexei nodded, acknowledging that.

'Don't tell me that he also has fallen out with people at the top and gone into hiding?'

'I don't know anything about his business dealings. I just l–loved his daughter.' The hitch in his voice was the first hint that there was something human beating underneath the hard shell. Leo felt a twinge of compassion for a young man raised in the most merciless of environments.

'Did you break into his house the night before last?'

Alexei looked up from the blotter. 'Why the hell would I do that?'

'Answer the question, please.'

'No, I did not. I did not break into Fatima's house.'

Leo noted that he didn't think of it as Akmal Gulom's house but the daughter's.

'Did you pull down the fence between the two houses?' asked Leo, following his gut.

Alexei gave him a brief bitter smile. 'Yes, we did. Did it for the first time when we were sixteen. Kept doing it so that they stopped repairing it after a while.' He swallowed.

'It was an accident, Inspector. I wish I'd been the one to die. I should've died.'

'Accidents are not always criminal; cover-ups are.' Leo stood, Suyin only a beat behind. 'Thank you for your time, Mr Chernov. I'm sure I'll be in touch with more questions. Do not try to leave Oxford until we contact you and say that you are free to go.'

They walked out, passing the team the superintendent had put on the reopening of the accident investigation. Inspector Jim Riley, a colleague who worked largely out of Abingdon, nodded towards the house. 'What's he like?' Riley had the square-jawed look of one who ploughed doggedly on through all conditions.

'He's got his lawyer, Jim. He'll make a run for it if he can.'

'Then I'd better arrest him and see to getting bail conditions.'

'Good luck with that. Expect the lawyer to make you do the dance.'

Riley grinned. 'No worries. I'm great at the wily fox trot.'

In the car, Suyin started the engine. 'I think he'll make a dash today.'

Leo reached behind for the buckle of the seatbelt. 'I think he'll stick.'

'Really? Want to bet, sir?'

'Ten quid.'

'Done.' She pulled out onto the main road. 'Why so sure he'll stay?'

'He'll trust to his fancy lawyer to get him out of it. He didn't arrange for the car swap – or we can't prove that he did. His father is dead so can't implicate him. There's enough reasonable doubt. He's not going down for the evidence tampering.'

'What about the accident?'

'First, the CPS have to release the man currently in prison. It is going to take a while to untangle the events, and time has passed. If the man was paid off, he's committed perjury – good luck to them sorting out the rights and wrongs of that. When Chernov's lawyers throw enough spanners in the creaky works of criminal justice, Alexei will probably not be charged with dangerous driving either. Too many loopholes to exploit. And the chance of getting clean forensic evidence after all this time with the car sitting in the garage? Nil.'

'But he was driving. Surely it's straightforward?' Suyin slowed for a red set of lights.

'Was he? Don't you remember the car? Concertinaed at the front, back relatively unharmed. The girls died; the boys, one was injured, the other walked away.'

'Ah.' She was seeing what he'd realised last night in the quiet of the garage, waiting for the forensic team to arrive.

'I think Alexei feels guilty because he let Fatima drive. I checked: Fatima only had a provisional licence. She hadn't passed her test.'

'Fatima caused the accident that killed her?'

Leo nodded. 'And I think Akmal Gulom knew that and it was that that broke him.'

Chapter 24

Jess

With high hopes, I unpacked the hangings from Cory's refugee craftswoman. They were wonderful creations of quilted felt, verging on abstract but with just enough detail to link them to the story – a star, a camel, a stable, one suggestive of a mother cradling a baby. I suppose I'd been expecting something more literal and naive, forgetting in my arrogance that refugees can be artists too. Paul wasn't going to like their modern take on the story, but I could predict Sanyu would love them.

My problem was, though, that they were only bath-towel sized. Pegging them up in the chapel, they were swamped.

Jennifer came in to give her verdict.

'Hmm.'

'I know.' I put my hands on my hips and stared up at the ceiling, my notional place for God to reside. 'Hey, God, need some help here.'

God didn't appear but I still had Jennifer. 'They are big, but just don't look it.'

'I'm aware.'

'I'll send a snap to my son and get his advice.'

'The designer?'

'Yes. He works in fabric. He must deal with presentation problems all the time.'

We sat in the back pew while the message winged its way to his London studio.

'How was last night?' asked Jennifer. 'Did the lovely policeman take you out as promised?'

'The lovely policeman did. We ended the evening with a treasure hunt and turned up a very odd find.' I proceeded to tell her about the car in the garage.

'I find it all very sad.' Jennifer buttoned her cardigan across her chest. It was no old-lady piece but a multicoloured creation with scalloped edges hand-knitted by Geoff, the designer son.

'My lovely policeman is wondering if there's a connection between it and the body. The story feels almost operatic – two young lovers from feuding families, one dies tragically, the fathers fight.'

'You think your employer did it?'

'I've never met him. Would you, in his shoes?'

'If someone caused the death of one of my kids?'

'Yes.'

'Oh, absolutely. I'd string them up and pierce them with knitting needles.'

'That's a little too specific.'

'You did ask. Every mother – every parent – has the instinct: you go after anything that would harm your kids like a mother lioness after a gazelle.' She glanced towards the altar. 'Sorry, Lord.'

Her phone pinged. 'Geoff says you need to change the backdrop. The problem is that it is too busy.'

'He does realise we are in a Tudor chapel and I can't change that?'

'He adds you should put in something neutral, white sheeting for example.'

'The BBC is really going to love the homemade touch of my bedsheets dangling like I've forgotten to take in the washing.'

'That's not very Oxford college. All that stuff is hidden away or sent to laundries.'

'So what is Oxford?'

'Close your eyes and tell me what you see.'

I did and the answer came quickly. 'My house.'

'The red house?'

'Yes, with its garden. It's what Ribena is to blackcurrants, concentrated Oxford.' I opened my eyes again and reconsidered the space. An idea grew, then sprouted. 'I think I've got it.'

'*By George, she's got it, I think she's got it,*' sang Jennifer, demonstrating that she did know her show tunes.

'It's obvious, really, when you think about it.'

'Obvious? Not to me. What's the answer?'

I grinned. 'I think I'll let it be a surprise.'

She looked doubtful – extremely doubtful. 'Jess, I'm your friend as well as a colleague so I do have to mention that not all your impulses work out for the best.'

I patted her knee. 'Don't worry. Tell Geoff thanks. I've got this.'

* * *

Arriving home, I walked around the garden for added inspiration. The Mad Hatter had been half-swallowed by a holly bush. Deciding that he needed freeing, like Han Solo from his icicle state, I clipped some of the branches with a pair of secateurs I'd found in a kitchen drawer. They could only manage the smaller branches but I soon had him free.

'Seen the White Rabbit?' I asked him.

He looked past me at a pair of ears poking out of a hazel. Pushing the twigs aside, I found the March Hare. Naturally. The Dormouse would be somewhere close by, but I'd look for him on another evening. It was getting cold and I fancied the idea of curling up with a book in bed as Leo was busy. I looked down at the branches I'd snipped off and decided to break my 'no decorating' rule. Some of them had lovely sprays of red berries. I gathered them up and took them back into the house. I amused myself poking them into niches and weaving through bannisters. Not exactly *Homes and Gardens*, but it was festive.

Sticking the last two sprays into a vase, I took them down into the swimming pool. There was a ledge at the end where you could sit to towel off and that would provide a perfect display spot.

The water was undisturbed. What had I called it last night? Alice's pool of tears. That had always been one of my favourite parts of the story, the idea of crying so hard that you could then shrink and swim in your own tears. The psychologist in me had a field day with it – the whole book in fact.

I sat for a while, admiring the dark-green-on-cream tiled backdrop. The White Rabbit was the first creature that Alice met. The placements in the garden roughly followed the introduction of each character in the story. In fact, I was sure you could follow a trail that would lead you past each in turn if you so wished, the Mad Hatter farthest out before you looped back towards the house. That was a sweet concept. I hope my Victorian predecessor had children and grandchildren to make it cute rather than creepy. So following that logic, the White Rabbit wouldn't be hidden somewhere out in the shrubbery but would be close to Alice on the terrace. And I knew that had been dug up when they excavated the underground extension. What if they disturbed the White Rabbit, broke him or moved him? Wouldn't you want to cover that up? Builders weren't exactly known for their respect of gardens when doing their works.

I looked down at the tiles. The ones that shifted when you trod on them had always bothered me, like that little patch of brown in a back tooth that you know you should get checked out by the dentist.

Oh God, I was going to do it, wasn't I? Ruin a perfect floor, risking cracked tiles and grouting? Mad Jess was in control, stuffing my more sensible self in my inner teapot. I knelt down, took the secateurs from my pocket and slid the blade under the loosest tile. It came up easily. Yes! I took that as a sign the gods of swimming-pool tiles approved. That made it simple to take up and stack the others. I was left looking down at a metal inspection plate. I was getting all worked up and I'd just uncovered the pool filtration system or something. I'd come this far: I had to check, of course.

I lifted the cover and suddenly found myself in much older territory. A set of steps sank away in a brick-lined tunnel.

I'd found the entrance. I was Oxford's answer to Indiana Jones!

What now? Phone Leo and go exploring with him? That meant delaying gratification and that just wasn't in my nature. This was the cream cake and I the spoon. I lit the cavity with my phone torch. It looked safe enough. I'd check it out and then invite him round to explore it with me later.

There was a handrail of old rope at the side which had survived remarkably well. I edged my way down, gripping tightly. My light caught on an eye and I almost dropped the phone. Forcing myself to calm, I took another look. The ears and face of a rabbit sat on the bottom stair like a horse's head in a mafia movie.

Poor old White Rabbit. A builder had done for you and left you here as a hidden admission of his sins.

I lifted the phone beam to see if I could locate the torso.

And got far more than that.

Chapter 25

Leo

Jess had found a second body. She sounded incredulous on the phone.

'What are the chances, hey?'

Pretty good, Leo decided, now that the shape of a larger set of linked crimes was beginning to form. Something had gone seriously awry between the inhabitants of Hay Road and the red house. He should've considered that possibility when he first heard that both rivals, Chernov and Gulom, were missing. Blood feuds never ended with a single strike.

After giving Jess a brief hug, Leo left her with Suyin in the kitchen while he covered up and went to look for himself at the body in the tunnel. Perhaps if they hadn't got sidetracked by the car yesterday, they would've thought to look down here and discover it then. That would've been far preferable. If he'd been first down the stairs, he could've spared her the grisly discovery. As it was, she'd gone hunting solo and racked up another dead body to her tally.

The body lay in a state of partial mummification, wrapped inside a covering of bin bags. Something – a rat or, as Jess preferred, when she reported it, a rabbit – had made inroads at one corner and exposed a hand. It was not much more than bones now. The odour was musty rather than foul, which put this back months or even years, most of the decomposition having already taken place. Leo predicted that it would not be pretty inside once the covering was removed in the lab. The rat would not have stopped at fingers.

At this point, what he could tell without disturbing the body was that it was large – an adult, probably male – and that he'd worn a gold signet ring. Leo knelt to take a closer look. Arabic lettering.

As he stripped off his coveralls he reflected that the householder has been the kind of man to wear jewellery. On his way back to the kitchen, Leo checked the photo he'd taken of the ring against the portrait and got a match.

He sat down next to Jess on the sofa and took her hand. Suyin moved to the other side of the room to give them some privacy while she made calls to continue the task of tracking down the Gulom family.

'Are you OK?'

Jess nodded. 'Do you ever get used to this?'

'I'm not usually the one finding the body. I tend to know what I'm going to see before I arrive. That helps.'

'I can tell you that it feels like something out of a horror film. All I needed was for the trapdoor to slam shut and the phone battery to die to complete the sequence.'

'Fortunately, it's not a film. You're safe and we'll take it from here. You saw the statue?'

She nodded.

'I'm thinking that the rabbit statue was put there first?' he suggested.

She leant her head against his arm. He shifted so he could support her comfortably. 'Unless you're dealing with a homicidal builder, it's hardly something you'd step over when constructing a pool.' She laced her fingers with his.

'How about this? Builders break an antique statue and, rather than own up, hide the damage in the passage they had uncovered.'

She tilted her head to look up at him. 'I'm thinking that the entrance might not even have been hidden, just an old door in the cellar that they had to work round. It doesn't fit with the clean lines and tiles so they cover it – and the statue – and walk away after presenting an eyewatering bill.'

Leo nodded. 'And they think they can get away with it as the client is rarely here.'

'"That old thing? Not seen it, mate". Plausible deniability.'

He liked the way they could reason this out together, both on the same page. 'Exactly. Then someone comes along who is familiar with the house and who has a body to dispose of. I think we'll find the victim is your missing employer, Jess.'

She groaned. 'I was worried it might be. Like the man next door, he was too busy, too important just to drop off the radar completely.'

'I wonder what the timing on his death will turn out to be? Before or after Chernov?'

'Or same time?'

'Then why not dump them together? You double the chance of someone finding a body by using two separate sites.'

'True.'

'My guess is that something happened here which ended up with Gulom dead. So the killer thinks, "How to dispose of the evidence?" What better place than the passage that is more crypt than anything as it no longer leads anywhere? No digging – just lift up a few tiles, raise the cover, and you're done.'

'Which makes it likely that the killer is someone very close to the family. Someone who was in and out, familiar with the house. Someone like Alexei?'

Leo had been wondering the same thing. The young man had judged his performance very well today. He'd been hard to read but had shown just enough emotion to suggest he really hadn't believed his father to be dead. But what if that had been another act?

'It also makes sense of the burglary,' continued Jess. 'It struck me as odd at the time that he'd opened the door to the basement when there was so much else to steal in more obvious rooms.'

'And the pickaxe now makes sense too. He might've expected the tiles to be grouted down and he was going to smash his way through as quickly as possible.'

'I'm thinking that the intruder was here to remove the body, if he could, in case we got suspicious when we couldn't find Gulom alive and well? It was obvious once he was identified that his arch rival would be a suspect and you'd be searching for him.'

'And Alexei wouldn't have necessarily known that you were in residence and could've thought he'd have a clear run at removal.'

She squeezed his hand. 'Looks like you've got your prime suspect.'

He kissed the top of her head. 'Will you be OK?'

'Go do your thing, Leo. I'll be fine.'

It was only a minute by car to Hay Road. Leo parked outside and stood looking at the house for a moment. Lights were on so Alexei was home.

'Everything all right, Inspector?' asked Mr Price from his garden gate. Meredith was peering out from an upper-floor window.

Of course the neighbourhood watch would be out in full force seeing the blue lights in the next road flickering on the windows and roofs. 'Yes, thank you. Just dealing with an incident. Your community liaison officer will fill you in tomorrow.'

'It's the red house again, isn't it? Is there anything we can do to help?' He was clearly fishing for an explanation, wanting an inside track and not to be palmed off with the general briefing. 'Meredith would happily sit with the young lady if she needs someone.'

'Miss Bridges is fine.'

'I suppose you have that covered?' Price left just enough of a pause to let Leo know he meant the policeman's relationship with Jess. 'Trained officers and whatnot?'

'Indeed. Jess is looked after. If you'll excuse me, Mr Price?'

But the man didn't retreat so Leo had to approach the front door with an unwelcome spectator. He rang the bell, which had a cheerful chime – off-putting, considering the purpose for which he was here.

Alexei opened the door. 'Inspector George.' The young man had on a shirt and smart trousers, though he was wearing slip-on house shoes, indicating he wasn't expecting to go out.

'May I have a word?' He glanced over his shoulder, directing Alexei's attention to Price. 'In private?'

Alexei met his neighbour's gaze with defiance. 'OK.'

Even with Mr Price to defy, Leo was surprised he was allowed in; he was expecting to be given the usual spiel about saying nothing without a lawyer being present. The reason for the cooperation became apparent when Leo found Mr Smirnov sitting with a bottle of wine at the kitchen table. A photograph of Anatoly Chernov with a candle was set in the centre. Leo was interrupting an impromptu wake.

'Joe, you remember the inspector,' said Alexei.

Smirnov nodded.

'I apologise if I'm intruding,' said Leo.

'Joe is a friend of the family as well as our lawyer,' said Alexei. 'That's why he is so defensive of us: he's known my sisters and me since we were children.'

That meant the lawyer *really* wasn't going to like what Leo had to say.

'It's good that you're here, Mr Smirnov, because I'd like to conduct this interview under caution. Would that be agreeable or would you prefer to arrange a time so you and your client can attend an interview at a police station?'

Smirnov frowned. 'I hardly think it appropriate to drag him to a police station. Have some compassion, Inspector. Alex has just learned he has lost his father.'

'The matter I wish to talk to him is urgent and not to do

with the events that took place on this property or the death of his father.'

'Joe, I'd prefer to get this out of the way.' Alexei sounded tired. 'And I have a few questions for the inspector of my own. Maybe we can ask them once he's had a chance to do his job?'

Smirnov nodded. 'All right, if you think so. But I'll be recording this.'

'As will I.' Leo got out his phone and recited the time, place and those in attendance. 'First the caution. Alexei Chernov, you do not have to say anything, but it may harm your defence if you do not mention something which you later rely on in court. Anything you do say may be given in evidence. Do you understand?'

'Yes,' said Alexei.

'Where were you on Sunday night?'

'Sunday night?' Whatever he'd been expecting Leo to ask, it hadn't been that apparently. 'Flying back from New York.'

'What time did you land?'

'Late. About eleven. Heathrow.'

It didn't rule him out. Heathrow was about eighty or ninety minutes away by car. He could have gone straight home and out the backdoor to retrieve the body if he was sufficiently worried it would be found.

'I picked him up at the airport, Inspector. I can verify those movements,' offered Smirnov.

Leo considered the lawyer. Friend of the family. The right build from Jess's description of the man looming in the doorway. 'Mr Smirnov, are you staying here?'

'I can't see that it is any business of yours.'

'Murder makes it my business, Mr Smirnov. Please answer the question.'

'Alexei had nothing to do with his father's death.'

'I'm not asking about his father.' He let them absorb that for a moment. 'Sunday night and early Monday morning, where were you?'

'Here. With Alex. I was in one of the guest rooms.'

Not a good alibi for either of them. Either one could have gone out without the other knowing.

'Mr Chernov, when was the last time you recall seeing Mr Gulom?'

Alexei made a face like he'd tasted something bitter. 'At Fatima's funeral. He hadn't wanted me to come. I kept to the back but he spotted me.'

'Did you talk?'

'I didn't say anything to him.'

'Did he say something to you?'

'Just that he wished me to rot in hell for what I'd done to his daughter. But it was her funeral and he was upset. I left when he said that. I didn't want Fatima's family to suffer any more than they already were. I'd said my goodbyes.'

'You didn't see him in Oxford after that? Not at the school, or in his garden over the fence.'

He shook his head. 'I know my father tried to talk to him but it didn't go well. My sisters messaged Rashid to say how sorry they were but he didn't answer.'

'Do you know where Rashid is now?'

Alexei squeezed his knuckles together. His hands gave more away than the rest of his body. 'He must've left school in the summer so I guess he's at university somewhere. Years back, when we last spoke, I know he wanted to do PPE at Oxford.'

So Rashid could be in the city, but if that was the case . . .

'If he is here, why isn't he living at the red house?'

Alexei shrugged. 'Probably hates the place. Wouldn't you? Depressing pile of red bricks with a stupid garden and just memories of his sister and how she died. Anyway, I don't know. My information on him is out of date. Maybe he went somewhere else for college? That's what I would do in his shoes.'

And had done in his own case, heading off to Harvard. 'I'll check. Mr Chernov, are you telling me that you've not been inside the red house since Fatima's death.'

'Yeah.' He forced himself to spread his fingers flat on the table. He too wore a signet ring, his on his little finger on the right hand.

'So there will be no DNA traces of more recent visits?'

'No.'

'Would you volunteer a sample now so we can verify that?'

Alexei glanced at the lawyer.

'We do have your father's profile on record. It wouldn't take much to use that as a reference.'

'I'll volunteer a sample,' he conceded.

'Inspector, why are you asking these questions about the Gulom house?' enquired Smirnov.

Leo stood up, signalling the interview was drawing to a close. 'Another body has been found.'

'Is it Mr Gulom?' Alexei's expression was perplexed but not fearful. 'When did he die? Recently? Was it suicide?'

'I cannot confirm the identity of the victim until the family has been notified. But I will say that the victim has been dead for some time.'

'Not another garden burial!' exclaimed Smirnov. 'Why's it taken so long to find it? You've had a whole week, haven't you?'

'Not a garden burial. That's all for the moment. Interview end.' Leo checked the recording had been saved then pocketed his phone. 'Stay available, Mr Chernov.'

Chapter 26

Jess

Do I still have a home?

I had to ask myself that question after I'd watched my employer being carried out in a body bag. No one was suggesting I leave too so I decided to stick for the night. As the police vacated, stationing a squad car on watch out front, I knew one thing: I really didn't want to be alone inside the red house. Intruders and now skeletal remains – this was a creepy place at night.

My mother would have conniptions if I told her and demand I drive into the Cotswolds to stay with her and my sister, oblivious to the fact that I didn't have a car and couldn't afford to abandon my job. Leo might come back later but for the moment he was busy with the little matter of hunting down a killer. So I rang Cory.

When I'd finished my story, she said:

'Oh, Jess, I really wish I could come over but I have no babysitter. Do you want to come here?'

'I told the police I'd stay. I shouldn't leave it empty.'

'I know what: I'll ask Michael. He's good in a crisis.'

I'd forgotten that they were now a two-for-one deal: tell one and the other would find out. 'Don't worry him; I'll be fine.'

'No, no, he'd be angry if I didn't tell him. You know how irritated he gets if he thinks people are handling him with kid gloves?'

She was right: Michael liked to feel he was treated exactly the same as before his accident.

'Well then, I don't want to sour that sweet romance of yours. Tell my ex, why don't you?'

Sarcasm didn't put her off. 'Thank you. Expect him to come round shortly.' And she put the phone down on me.

Fifteen minutes later I heard Michael's car pull in. Shutting Flossie in the kitchen, I went to greet him. Cory was right: it was a comfort to see him.

'Michael, you needn't have bothered.' He was on crutches tonight so I had to go up on tiptoe to kiss his cheek. I liked the fact he was using them. I hoped Cory was the one putting the confidence back in his stride.

'No bother. I'm intrigued.'

'Want to join me in a drink? I need something after my evening.'

He hopped over the threshold. 'That's why I came. If you go to the boot for me, you'll see I brought my own supply.'

'You're an angel.' I rescued the wine and the Scotch in their hessian carrier bag from the Covered Market. 'Like old times?'

'Oddly, it is for us – our tradition: drinks over murder. How many is it now?' He was referring to bodies.

'A gentleman never remembers a lady's body count.' I held Flossie's collar so she didn't knock him over with her greeting.

Once he was established at the kitchen table, I released the beast and she danced with joy to see her old friend.

'Want to tell me what's been happening?' Michael ruffled Flossie's neck. 'Why has this respectable little corner of Oxford suddenly developed a murder rate higher than Bogotá since you moved in?'

I mock-scowled. 'I'll have you know both victims were long dead before I took this job.' I handed him a Scotch topped up with ice, the way he liked it. 'But I would appreciate your take. Leo is looking at members of the families involved.'

'Leo?'

My cheeks went pink. 'Inspector George.'

He smiled. 'Cory did mention something to me.'

'Is nothing sacred in the sisterhood anymore?' I sat next to him with my long-stemmed glass of white.

'You're OK with it, I hope?'

'What? You and Cory? I think it's brilliant – unexpected but one of those things that make perfect sense once you try them, like a cheese and Marmite sandwich.'

He chuckled at that description, but also looked very pleased with the suggestion that it was a natural pairing. 'Back to your murders.'

'Not my murders.'

He grinned.

'Oh all right, if it makes you happy: my murders.'

'The inspector is looking at the family as suspects? That makes sense. You always start with those closest to the victims.'

'He's interviewing the son, Alexei Chernov.'

'He is? Alex didn't strike me as the murdering kind.'

'You know him?'

'Met him yesterday. He's taken over the funding of the AI institute I work for, the one next door to the house on Hay Road.'

'Oh, the brain computer thing?' Michael had explained it to me earlier in the autumn. I confess my grasp of what it actually meant was like cupping water in my hands. 'He goes in for that stuff?'

'I believe so. He was knowledgeable and engaged intelligently with the subject.'

More than could be said for me. 'Would he be good at the practical side, do you think? Sneaking into computers and doctoring records and such.' I was thinking of the changed evidence. Had he hacked the police system to mess with the files on the collision?

'I can't say. I do know that if he didn't have the skills, he would know many people who did. He employs them.'

And wasn't that interesting? 'You said you didn't think he was a killer?'

Michael swirled his drink. 'Perhaps I'm saying that because I liked him. He's tough but he has a sense of humour. If he killed, I'd expect it would be efficient and with logical reasons.'

'He sounds sociopathic.'

'I don't mean it like that. I think he's not on that scale. He struck me as tough, someone who will make the difficult decisions but with a cool head.'

'His father died with a bullet to the back of his skull.'

Michael considered this. 'That could be Alex – or someone he sent – if he thought he had cause. What about the other body?'

'Too early to say. Leo thinks it is Akmal Gulom, Anatoly Chernov's arch rival. The body was wrapped in bin bags and hidden in a secret passage in the basement. And there's more. We think someone broke in on Sunday night to retrieve the evidence. They didn't get far because Flossie woke me up and we scared them off.'

'Now that doesn't sound like Alex. He'd send one of his heavies to do the job but they'd simply shoot Flossie – sorry, dog – and dispose of you too.'

'Kill me? I thought you were here to cheer me up?'

'Maybe not kill you. Knock you out, most like. Tie you up. You don't exactly offer much of a threat to the kind of men who do the dirty work for rich oligarchs.'

'And yet you liked him?' I refilled my glass and waved the Scotch in his direction.

He put his hand over his glass. 'I'd better not. I'm not saying he did any of it. I was just imagining how he would go about it. More efficiently and get the job done, is how I read him.'

'I'll tell Leo to keep looking then.'

Michael nodded. 'But the inspector already strikes me as the kind of detective who would be doing that in any case. He's got a good brain and sound instincts.'

I warmed to hear my guy complimented. 'That's high praise from you.'

'He's one of the best I've met. He did good work on the White Horse case. Now where do you want me to bunk down tonight?'

I made up a bed for Michael in the ground-floor guest

room. His presence meant I could sleep in my turret without nightmares about who might be prowling on the ground floor. For added protection, I left him Flossie, who adapted to the change quickly once I dragged her dog bed beside him.

When I got to my own bed, I discovered my phone had been bombarded with messages from the neighbours, led by Paul, who must've handed out my details because I didn't remember giving them away. Meredith offered to make up a bed for me at theirs. Al said he and other men from the society would be 'patrolling the streets' so I could sleep easy. That sounded very *Dad's Army*. Sally Houseman advised me to stay with friends as the area had got so dangerous. Paul managed a 'hope you are all right' before ordering my presence at his Christmas drinks party for locals on Friday. His do was 'an important fixture in the community calendar' apparently. I tried to be charitable and imagine the invitation was phrased as a request but his 'I expect to see you' did sound suspiciously like an order. And why ask me so late? Not because he thought me worthy of the local community clearly. I guessed it was so I could be grilled again by my gossipy neighbours.

Taking a chance he was free for a moment, I called Leo.

'Jess?'

'Hey.'

'Hey.' We lingered in that sentimental couple thing of just enjoying hearing the other's voice.

'Where are you?' I asked.

'Still at work, I'm afraid. How are you doing?'

'Cory sent Michael around to babysit me. I'm fine.'

'Ah, that's good. I was worried you were alone. I won't come over then.'

I could've kicked myself. 'The more the merrier.'

'Thanks, but I've still got things to do tonight – and an early start – so I'll just dash home, crash for a few hours and call tomorrow. Is that OK?'

'Sure.' I looked at my phone. It was almost tomorrow already. 'Isn't today your mother's deadline for getting out? Maybe she'll be gone when you get home.'

He groaned at the reminder. 'I've not seen her since we argued. I very much doubt she's made any progress without my boot applied to her rear.'

'Wonders will never cease.'

'Yeah, well.'

'And if she hasn't slung her hook by Friday, I'll stage an intervention.'

'I'd like to see that.' He sounded brighter.

'Michael told me something interesting. He knows Alexei from that place next door. Apparently, Alexei is very engaged with the AI institute. Michael thinks if he doesn't have the skills to tamper with files, then he definitely knows someone who will.'

'Thanks. I'll add that into the mix. At the moment, I'm having difficulty finding anything to pin on him. His alibi for Sunday night is provided by his lawyer no less. They swear they've been together since Alexei returned.'

'I didn't see a lawyer type at the public meeting.'

'You're right. He wasn't there. And I just remembered something else about the Prices and Alexei. They seemed very polite to each other at the meeting but the Prices said that they had trouble with him when he was younger – racial abuse about their marriage. They even took it to the school. How could Alexei still have ended up head boy with that accusation involving a member of staff?'

'Maybe the Prices overreacted? Maybe it was a normal mouthing off of a teenage boy testing the limits with annoying neighbours?'

'But would you make that student head boy if you were Laurence Buckingham? Wouldn't Meredith had said something?'

'I guess you'll need to ask him. Actually, you might get a chance on Friday.'

'Oh? Why?'

'Paul, my Manager of the Year, has ordered me to attend his Christmas party. All the locals come, apparently. Want to be my plus one?'

There was a long pause.

'You want to come that much, huh?'

'I guess it is in the boyfriend small print, isn't it?'

Boyfriend? I hugged myself with glee. 'Absolutely. Next to "holding back hair while partner is being sick from the hangover that follows from drinking too much at terrible Christmas bashes".'

'That's a lot of small print.' But I could hear the smile in his voice.

'And maybe then you could stay over? And not in the guest room currently occupied by Michael?'

'You know how to give a guy an incentive.' There was a

burst of noise in the background. 'Sorry, Jess, got to go.'

'Love you.'

There was the briefest of hesitations. Then he said, 'Love you too.'

Chapter 27

Leo

His mother wasn't gone but she was avoiding him. Leo didn't see her for the rest of that week. Even banging on her door, demanding she tell him her plans for departure, got no more response than a faint claim to have a migraine. What cruel son would turf her out when she was sick?

Me, thought Leo.

He didn't have time to test how far he would push it. He decided, as she had ceded the downstairs to him and he was very busy with his enquiry, to leave her to her languishing.

'You're to be gone by Sunday – and that's final,' he shouted through the door, aware he'd given ground. He simply didn't have the time to engage in the battle that would ensue if he dragged her out and dumped her on a train to somewhere else.

It was now Friday and he was doing his duty by Jess. Paul's party was exactly as Leo imagined. He must be earning himself lots of boyfriend points for putting up with the not so gentle grilling he was getting at what was supposed to be a social occasion. At least he got to admire Jess looking lovely in her slinky blue dress as she chatted with Meredith over by the drinks table. She was the only person wearing reindeer antlers, though there were a few crowns of tinsel, Christmas-themed earrings and jumpers. He'd retreated from her side when he saw Mr Price approaching and was fully expecting Jess to accuse him of abandoning her to the enemy. Still, he hoped he could make it up to her in bed. He swallowed awkwardly. Tonight was supposed to be their first night together. God, he couldn't think about that now. They were in public.

He cast around for somewhere to land. The headmaster of St Bede's was possibly the only person in the room who didn't have a bone to pick with him about the murder enquiry so he made his way through the crowd to him.

'Mr Buckingham, nice to see you again.'

'Inspector George, I've not seen you at one of these before.' Lawrence Buckingham gestured with his mulled wine to the decorated parlour of Paul's spacious ground-floor flat in the college property. A large mansion converted to make apartments, the rooms had the generous proportions of a Victorian residence. A Christmas tree dominated one corner, all the ornaments the sort featured in upmarket country living magazines – strings of popcorn, candied fruits, glazed biscuits. It hinted at a homemaking heart in their host, but Leo kept getting visions of the gingerbread cottage.

'On duty?' asked Buckingham.

'Not tonight.'

'Have you moved into the area?' The headmaster was probably pondering why anyone would voluntarily put themselves through an excruciating meet and greet like this.

'I'm here with my girlfriend.' It was the first time Leo had said the word and it felt strange. 'She works with Paul and lives nearby.' He thought it best to avoid mentioning the red house. He was here as an escape from gossipers, not to answer questions about the body found in the passageway under the pool.

'Small world.' Buckingham drained his mulled wine and reached for a refill from the tray of one of the circulating waiters – moonlighting graduates, guessed Leo.

'Indeed. And you? Do you live locally?' Leo switched to water, thinking he wanted to be clear-headed for later.

'No, but I come each year as part of our community engagement. Our host is very active in the North Oxford Protection Society. I try to keep on their good side as much as possible.'

'I can imagine.'

'You say that like someone who has experienced their attention?'

'A public meeting.'

Mr Buckingham smiled wryly. 'Oh yes. I've been put through that too. Scary people.'

Leo thought it better not to agree out loud. 'Actually, Mr Buckingham—'

'Lawrence, please, as we're off duty.'

'In that case, call me Leo. I was wondering what you remember about Alexei Chernov from the time when he was your head boy.'

'Ah. Alex. I heard he was back from Al.' Mr Buckingham flicked his eyes to Mr Price, who was now talking to Sally Houseman. There didn't look to be much Christmas cheer in that conversation.

'Mr Price does like to keep an eye on things.'

'Put it like this, if this area went independent from the rest of the country, Al would expect to be our king.'

That summed it up nicely. 'I realise there's no love lost between the Prices and Alexei, I was just wondering why that might be?'

Buckingham swirled his mulled wine. 'The smell of Christmas!' He sipped. 'I didn't know there was any particular animus.'

'You don't remember any problems between Meredith Price and Alex, nothing that was brought to your attention?'

The headmaster wrinkled his brow, giving the question some serious thought. 'Not on my turf. I don't think Alex spent much time in the library – he was a good pupil but he was doing computing, sciences and so on. Rarely cracked open a conventional book as I recall. But Meredith is zealous that this generation doesn't lose the habit of reading so I suppose they might've bumped up against each other over that.'

Hardly the stuff of a bitter dispute. 'There was nothing about racial insults?'

'That doesn't ring any bells. Not that everything comes up the chain to me. If it were dealt with lower down, then I wouldn't hear. Certainly by the time we came to choosing head boy, there was no hint of anything like that in his disciplinary record.'

But how easy would it be for a boy with his skills to hack the system and wipe his record clean? 'That's helpful. Thanks.'

'I always liked Alex.' Mr Buckingham settled down, leaning against the mantelpiece, clearly in a chatty mood. 'He knows what he wants and goes after it, but he's loyal to his friends and rewards those who stand by him.'

That sounded almost the perfect character description of a trainee mafia boss.

'We always got on well together. He knew what I wanted from him as head boy, and I knew what the school needed to give him: the best launch pad into tertiary education.'

'And Fatima Gulom?'

'Ah yes, poor Fatima. She was the odd thing out in his life, and his most endearing trait. Still, I suppose it's reassuring to find that even in men brought up like Alex the heart still has the power to upset the best laid plans. She made him more human, much more willing to smile and be his age. It was a tragedy that he lost her. I hope he remembers what she taught him and doesn't default to his family way of handing emotions.'

'Which is?'

'Ignoring them, I'd say. Chernov Senior had a very utilitarian view of his children. He was always interested in what they could give him, how they could build up the family.'

'How do you mean?' Seeing a server going by, Leo passed Mr Buckingham another glass. The warm wine was doing a grand job of loosening the headmaster's tongue. He might regret saying so much tomorrow, but for now he was a very good source.

'Well, normally when head boy and girl are announced, the parents are over the moon and make sure they attend the special assembly we hold at the beginning of their term in office. But not Mr Chernov. He didn't come but sent a photographer so Alex's picture could be taken for the company website. Alex showed me the article – all about how he was demonstrating the leadership qualities that would suit him to his future role. There was no personal congratulation between father and son, or not that Alex mentioned. It was taken in the spirit of Alex making a good step as an employee of the family firm.'

'But Alex's mother was there at the assembly?'

Buckingham gave a bark of laughter. 'Oh yes, she was there. You're right: maybe that was why Alex's father didn't dare show his face. I've had dealings with many mothers over the years and she is definitely one of the more formidable.'

And that must be saying something, coming from the head of the one of the elite private schools.

The headmaster made his excuses shortly after this conversation, having shown willing by putting in an appearance. Leo felt a similar urge to leave but Jess looked absorbed in a conversation with the Prices so he didn't want to interrupt. He examined Paul's collection of photos on the mantlepiece. Unlike most people, he didn't have pictures of family members or friends, but architectural studies of famous buildings, many of them in Oxford. The Sheldonian in the snow. The fountain at St Nicholas. Wolfson College on Guy Fawkes Night, fireworks exploding behind the modernist building. He was very fond of his immediate locality, including an atmospheric shot of the red house against a night sky.

'Do you know much about photography, Inspector?' His host was at his elbow with a tray of hors d'oeuvres.

'Only in a professional context, I'm afraid. But these are very nice. Are they yours?'

'A little hobby of mine. I find it fascinating to see the details that the eye otherwise misses.'

'That's how we use it at work too.'

'I can see that – looking for evidence to catch your killer. But you move on once each case is solved; I like to circle back, take shots of the same place over time.'

That gave Leo an idea. He tapped the red house. 'I don't suppose you have more pictures of this, do you, going back – and Thirteen Hay Road?'

Paul looked proud to be asked. 'Indeed I do. I keep a local record for the Society, partly so people can't get away with pulling down fences or other features that don't suit modern taste. We are a conservation area, you know.'

'I did know. May I see those images?'

'Any particular time period?'

Leo thought back to beginning of this when Gulom and Chernov moved into the area. 'Last ten years?'

'Oh, good. That's easy as I've got all those digitally.'

'Did you ever visit the red house before it passed into the ownership of the Gulom family?'

'Indeed I did.' Paul tried one of his hors d'oeuvres, a Brie and date combination. 'It was owned by a delightful widow, Mrs Parkhurst. Her husband was a codebreaker at Bletchley during the war. Mathematician at St Nicholas afterwards until his death.' Paul paused. 'Is there anything in particular you want to see.'

Leo smiled. 'I don't know yet.'

'Ah, a hunch of the little grey cells. I understand.'

'Here's my card.' He put it on the mantlepiece. 'If you could send me the images?'

'First thing tomorrow.' Paul looked over towards Jess, drawing Leo's attention back to her. She was still with the Prices – an exceptionally long conversation for a party. What on earth could they be discussing? Leo wondered. 'You came with Jessica?'

'I did.'

'Is she worried about speaking live on national television, do you know? It's a lot to ask of a young woman.'

'She seems fine with it.' Leo hid his smile in his drink. Jess had warned him that Paul resented her taking what he saw as his gig.

'Well, if it gets too much, I'd be happy to step in. I'm an old pro at the reading from the lectern.'

'I'll let her know.'

With a nod, Paul moved off, convinced they'd made friends.

Finally Jess broke free from the Prices and joined him. Leo's thoughts immediately went from photographs to bedrooms.

'Ready to leave?' she asked.

'Half an hour ago,' he growled.

'Oh, Inspector George, are you having naughty thoughts?'

'Not naughty enough.' He found their coats in the pile on the spare room bed.

'Here's me hoping you've brought your handcuffs.'

An attendant came in before he had a chance to reply to that provocative comment.

'Got everything you need?' the cloakroom attendant asked.

'No, but I very soon will have,' Leo assured her.

Chapter 28

Jess

I had a fizzing feeling in my stomach that was nothing to do with the party bubbly I'd consumed but everything to do with walking home with Leo to what I hoped was a long night together. We'd put this off with a heroic effort on my part, creature of rash impulse that I am, and I was very ready for what was to come. I laid my head briefly on Leo's arm and he covered my hand with his where it rested on his arm.

'I brought my toothbrush,' he said.

'Good. I'm glad you remembered.' He looked so beautiful. Was I allowed to call a guy that? But he did: face to make a Renaissance artist weep for joy, defined cheekbones, dark eyes that shone with intelligence, and he knew how to dress to kill. Well, not kill obviously, as he was by instinct a peaceful man, but he certainly slayed me every time he turned up at a crime scene looking like he'd just come from a fitting in Saville Row.

'Jess, I've not thought of much else this week. You've been a huge distraction.'

'In a bad way?'

He sighed. 'In all ways.'

Poor distracted Inspector George. 'Have you made progress with the case?'

'Do we really want to talk about that now?'

'I guess it's not the sexiest of subjects but I do care how your work is going.'

'Then I'll just say that we've confirmed it was Akmal you found and informed the family.'

'Cause of death? Another gunshot?'

'No, actually. It was a heavy sharp object like a claw hammer or—' He broke off.

'Or pickaxe?' I could imagine the scene: Ukrainian business man with a pickaxe in the billionaire's pool, red blood blooming in the water.

'Yes.'

I shuddered.

'You OK?'

'Just trying not to think too hard about might-have-beens.'

He rubbed my hand in comfort. 'What were you talking about with the Prices for so long?'

'Oh, that. It was really sweet. Meredith was telling me the story of how they met. She's from Sierra Leone in West Africa, did you know?' Leo shook his head. 'Al was there on a posting that time when the Blair government was helping stabilise the country during the civil war. Do you remember that?'

'Year 2000 wasn't it? There was a horrific civil war. Armies fighting over control of diamonds and other resources, lopping off hands and feet to terrorise the population. I believe they say it was a rare example of a successful military intervention.'

I was impressed that he kept up with overseas news from a couple of decades ago. I had to remember he was a clever man with a mind for retaining details, unlike my own that relied on Google. 'That's right. And she told me how her family was involved in the UN process to agree a certification scheme to stop the trade in conflict diamonds. They managed to get this in place in 2002 – lightning speed for the UN apparently. Meredith's family are well-to-do, educated internationally, cousins all over the globe – diplomats, businessmen, those kind of people. She was in her early twenties, just back from college in Edinburgh, and had a job as a locally engaged member of staff at the British embassy where Al worked. They fell in love and married out there. She's been all over the world with him, until he retired and they moved here. I think the house has been in Al's family for a while. He grew up in Oxford and always planned to retire to his old family home after a life on the road with the military.'

'Didn't she say the other morning that her family was in coffee? That makes sense now.'

'They're a well-known family in Freetown apparently. Big merchants, handling the shipping of everything from coffee and sugar to gems. Hey, I wonder if they know my guy Gulom?'

'Uzbekistan and Sierra Leone aren't exactly next door to each other.'

'But how many people are in the diamond trade? That must cut down the odds.'

'You're right.' He squeezed my fingers. 'Next time I see her, I'll ask.'

'I could . . .'

'Best not to, not if it has any relevance to the enquiry.'

We turned into the short cut that led to Howell Street. It was a quiet stretch as there were riverside trees on one side and backs of gardens on the other. I moved a little closer. I never normally went this way when on my own as it gave me the creeps.

'I can tell you that Meredith knows her diamonds as well as her coffee,' I continued. 'She showed me her rings – so pretty. Al had them made for her in Sierra Leone by a second cousin of hers who studied in London. She dabbles in jewellery design herself and made the silver rings she was wearing. She said she'd show me a few simple techniques if I were interested.'

Leo brushed my bare fingers, drawing our joint attention to the fact that I didn't wear rings. 'I've always wondered about this world of the super-rich. Would you know your diamonds from your diamanté?'

'No!' I laughed at the idea. 'And I don't care. Can you imagine carrying so much money around on you, so easy to drop in a gutter or wash down the sink? I'd lose a precious stone within a week of being given it.'

'No rings for you then. OK, got it.' Leo glanced behind and gave a sudden intake of breath.

'What?' I whispered.

'Keep walking. Run if I tell you.'

I risked a quick look over my shoulder. A man dressed in black jacket and beanie last seen at the public meeting protecting Alexei Chernov was following and gaining on us. 'Shit: I'm wearing heels.'

'Kick them off if necessary.'

Then Thug #2 stepped out in front of us. Two of them, two of us. 'Leo?'

Leo got out his phone.

'I wouldn't do that if I were you, Inspector.' A tall man whom I recognised from Leo's description as Alexei's lawyer came out from the shadows to confront us. He was called something like Smirnoff, like the red label vodka I was partial to, if I recalled correctly. He held up both hands like we were holding him up and not the other way round. 'Don't be alarmed by my associates, they are just here to ensure we aren't interrupted. This is just a friendly chat to your own advantage. Nothing more.'

'Friendly chats don't involve cornering people in dark alleys, Smirnov,' said Leo, fingering the call button.

'By all means, let us walk to somewhere with better street lighting. But I'm afraid if you place that call you'll miss hearing something you really need to know. I give you my word we mean neither of you any harm.'

Thug #2 not so subtly moved closer, reinforcing the message we were not leaving until after this conversation was over.

Deciding not to escalate the situation, Leo lowered his handset. 'Say what you have to say then.'

The lawyer folded his arms. 'It's just for your ears, Inspector, not your lovely companion's.'

'I appreciate the "lovely", Red Label, but I'm not leaving.' I clung onto Leo's arm.

'I'm afraid that part is non-negotiable. Sergei, please escort Miss Bridges to wait in the car.' He nodded to Thug #1.

'Not. Leaving,' I repeated.

Then to everyone but the bodyguard's surprise, Thug #1 scooped me up and threw me over his shoulder in a fireman's lift.

'Unorthodox, but it gets the job done,' said the lawyer, as if this was an amusing episode we were all sharing.

'Leo!' I squawked. I tried to kick free but my captor had a firm grip on my knees.

'Put her down!' shouted Leo. I could hear a shoving match with the other bodyguard who was blocking his pursuit, but all I could see was the legs of my abductor and the pavement. Bucking did not good.

'She'll be perfectly safe,' said the lawyer. 'Sergei, as the inspector says, please put Miss Bridges down and wait in the car.' This instruction was addressed to my carrier, who started walking swiftly the opposite way to the one in which we'd been heading. Should I scream?

'Leo?' I shouted. All the blood was rushing to my head.

'Just stay calm, Jess. Cooperate!' he called, sounding far from calm himself.

To hell with that! I hammered at the back of my thug, but he only grunted and squeezed my legs more tightly.

'Put me down!'

'Shut the fuck up!' he said gruffly. 'You'll go in the boot if you are bad girl.'

I took a breath to scream but he must've guessed what I was about because he shifted me in a dizzying move to his front and put a big hand over my mouth. I tried to bite but could gain no purchase on his leather glove.

'Fucking *blyad*.'

Behind me a car blinked its lights and I could hear the electronic click of a door opening.

'Get in!'

He shoved me inside and slammed the boot closed.

Chapter 29

Leo

It was the first time in Leo's career that he had faced anything quite like this: his companion abducted because some slick lawyer wanted to turn the screws. This was the kind of thing that happened in the backstreets of the East End of London, or Moscow, not Oxford. The other bodyguard had shown his training by effectively blocking Leo's exit.

'I apologise for Sergei's enthusiasm. But I repeat, he is not harming her, and we are not harming you. Just creating a space for us to talk,' said Smirnov. 'If you hear me out, I'm sure you will be grateful we had this private word.'

Leo swore and took a step to go after Jess.

'I really wouldn't go after her, Inspector, not just yet. You must've realised by now that we mean no harm or we would've done it by now.'

'You must be out of your mind to think you can get away with this!' spat Leo.

'I hope not. Just listen and I'll let you get back to your evening.'

'My evening has just disappeared on the back of your associate.'

265

'And my man will take very good care of her – she's in safe hands. Forget about her for the moment and listen.'

'No, you listen. I'm now going to be spending the rest of the evening locking you three up in a cell!'

'I doubt that very much. We are going to exchange information and part ways amicably. Do you really want to spin this out or shall I just tell you what I stopped you to say?'

Leo reached for his control. Anger was gaining him nothing. 'I'm listening.'

'I want you to drop the newly reopened investigation into the car accident.'

'Ha!' Leo's laugh was loaded with scorn. 'You're kidding me, right? You do act for British clients, take cases through English courts? If you do, you know that I don't have that power.'

'You have the influence if you choose to use it. You can make it go away.'

'Just because you had bent coppers on your payroll last time, doesn't mean we all roll over when you wave a wad of cash.'

He didn't deny it. 'You know there's nothing there – it's a waste of police time and money to reinvestigate something that happened years ago.'

'If I thought that, I'd've changed my mind as soon as you took it upon yourself to persuade me there's nothing to find.'

Smirnov's eyes glinted with anger. 'Perhaps I should put this another way. Drop the case on Alexei or I'll tell your current girlfriend about the woman you're secretly living with.'

Leo's jaw dropped.

'That's right, Inspector. The first thing you learn in my business of protecting my clients is to know your client's adversary. So I looked into you. I don't think you'd want Miss Bridges to know about that, how you have the little woman tucked away in your house in Iffley while you play the field in Oxford.'

Leo's brain did a quick catch-up. 'You've been watching my house?'

'I make it a habit to know everything I can about those who might cause problems for my clients.'

'You're a fucking shark.'

Smirnov actually smiled. 'Thank you. That's how I win.'

'Not in this case. That's my mother you saw.' It was almost worth the weeks of misery she'd put him through to see the lawyer's face change. 'She's staying temporarily with me while she sorts her life out.'

'You're joking?'

'I'm bloody serious.'

'She's too young – no, no, I've seen the surveillance photos. She looks no more than forty.'

'And you haven't done your homework. Look her up: Haven Keene. I think she's still on IMDb. Claims to be forty-five but she's at least sixty.' Leo took a step closer to the lawyer. 'And you are in deep shit.' He could see Smirnov shuffling through his options now his best card had been taken from him. Leo had a Royal Flush of his own now, thanks to this encounter. 'Tell me, Smirnov, does Alexei know you're here?'

'No, he doesn't. Keep him out of this. This is my mistake, not his.'

It was Leo's turn to fold his arms and gloat. 'Then let's renegotiate – and that's non-negotiable, by the way. First things first: bring Jess back. If she's unharmed—'

'She will be.'

'Then we can talk. If you've put the least scratch on her, then we're taking a trip to the cells.' He started walking. 'But don't worry, you get to call a lawyer.'

Chapter 30

Jess

The lid of the boot opened and I looked up to see Leo framed against the night sky.

'Fuck, Jess.'

'Yes, please.' I clambered out and realised we had an audience. The lawyer appeared to be berating the thug for putting me in the boot. 'But not immediately.' I went over to the thug who had manhandled me and kicked him in the shin. 'You're a prick, do you know that?'

He glared at me but didn't dare retaliate now.

'See, your companion is unharmed,' said the Red Label.

'Your definition of unharmed is way different from mine, buster. I had a nice buzz going and now I'm guessing our evening plans are cancelled?' I addressed this remark to Leo.

He gave me a regretful look. 'Sorry, Jess, I need to talk to these people.'

'You're not arresting them?'

'Hold that thought. If they don't give me the information I require, I'll be asking if you want to lay charges for kidnapping against them.'

'Kidnapping?' scoffed the lawyer, but looking a little panicked by the suggestion. 'There was no kidnapping!'

'Er, excuse me?' I crossed over to him, tempted to kick his shins too. 'Carried off against my will, bundled into the boot of your car?'

'He was just supposed to remove you so I could talk to the inspector.'

'Then you should have your henchmen under better control!'

'It was a prank – a joke!'

'Rasputin here is known for his sense of humour, is he? I bet he's a riot on the Moscow comedy circuit.' The guy I'd nicknamed after the Mad Monk had a particularly granite face.

Leo put an arm around me and drew me to one side. 'Jess, would you mind playing it my way for now?' He kept his voice down while the three conferred in whispers. The two heavies looked ready to thump us and flee but the lawyer appeared to be urging caution. 'I'm happy to arrest them if you want me to do so, but I'd prefer to see what I can learn and then decide if the arrest goes ahead after questioning.'

'Oh, OK. I'm mostly pissed off that our night is ruined.'

He brushed my cheek. 'Me too.'

'But what did they think they could gain from this stunt?'

He gave a bitter smile. 'I think it went a bit further than Smirnov intended but why don't you sit in on the questioning and find out?'

That made me feel a little better. 'Deal.'

He turned back to the lawyer and his two heavies. 'Where do you want to do this? At the house in Hay Road?'

Red Label shifted uneasily. 'I'd prefer not to involve Alex.'

Someone was in trouble with their employer.

I glanced up at Leo. 'Mine?'

He nodded. 'That would work. OK, let's take this to the red house. Give me the details of your men and send them away. I don't want them in there.'

Good call: I didn't want Rasputin and his sidekick anywhere near me behind four walls.

The lawyer frowned. 'I'd prefer not to give you that information.'

'That wasn't a request,' said Leo. 'It's either give me the correct details or spend the next twenty-four hours extricating yourself from police cells.'

'They work for an agency my firm uses,' Red Label said reluctantly.

'Is that ZOB by any chance?' asked Leo.

Red Label looked taken aback. 'Yes, it is.'

Well done, Inspector! I mentally high-fived him. You, my over-steroided friends, were not going to wriggle out of this anonymously.

'I've got the information on that company already.' Leo's expression was set in avenging angel mode. God, he was so sexy like that. 'I just need names and addresses. I suggest you strongly suggest to your men that you don't mess with me right now. I'm beginning to think a night in custody is just what all three of you need.'

The lawyer glanced at his operatives. They didn't look thrilled, but neither were they making any move to stop this. 'Got a pen, Inspector?'

Leo handed over a little notepad from his pocket, complete with pencil. How old school. Red Label scribbled down the information and handed it back. Leo read it, took a photo and sent it as an attachment to an email.

'This has gone to my team so if you're thinking of doing anything stupid—'

'Anything else stupid,' I corrected.

'True.' He took my hand. 'Then think again. Shall we go? It's a short walk from here. You won't need your vehicle. But you probably knew that, didn't you, seeing how you've been keeping a watch on us?'

The lawyer had a quick conversation with his men. They got into the car and drove off.

The three of us walked back to the red house.

'What's your name?' I asked the lawyer, thinking I had to stop comparing him to a favourite brand of vodka.

'Joseph Smirnov. I'm with the firm Smirnov and Baskin. We're a big firm based in London, but we have an office in Oxford too, all private client matters handled.'

He sounded as if he was trying to reel me in as a future customer. 'And is Baskin as big on the old abduction by side-kick routine?' I wasn't so great on the forgive and forget part of things as Leo.

'That was not my intention. Sergei misjudged the situation.'

'And, class, who brought Sergei with him to a quiet chat?' I aped looking around an expectant room of students. 'Hands up if it were you.'

'I apologise, Miss Bridges, for inconveniencing you this evening,' the lawyer said stiffly.

'*Inconveniencing* me?'

Leo squeezed my fingers. 'Jess.'

'I'm prepared to give you something to recompense you for the distress you've undergone,' Smirnov continued.

I laughed. 'Trying to buy my silence, Red Label? That's rich. There's nothing you can offer me that I could possibly want.' Then the thought dropped down on me like a piano in a Tom and Jerry cartoon. 'Hey, you're a local firm!'

'A national firm, with a local office,' he said curtly.

I grinned with fiendish glee. 'Oh wow, I've just realised what I want from you. Give me your card. You'll be hearing from me tomorrow if Leo doesn't decide to bang you up in a cell.'

He handed me a card by the corner like I was a hooker and he the fastidious client.

'Don't look at me like that, pal. I'm doing you a big favour. Kidnapping a woman off the street like that could lose you your licence to practice.'

'It wasn't a kidnapping,' he hissed.

'Wasn't it?' I almost danced on the spot. It was so much fun having his dangly bits in the vice. 'But don't worry; you're going to love the favour I want in return for my silence.'

'I doubt that,' he said in an undertone.

At the red house kitchen table, I made Leo and myself a cup of tea, then relented.

'Want something to drink?' I asked Smirnov.

'Just water, please.'

I filled up a glass from the tap, earning another sniff from the lawyer. 'We don't run to Evian at this establishment,' I said, plonking it down in front of him. 'Here's the Thames's finest.'

He wisely didn't comment. 'Thank you.'

'OK, let's start the interrogation.' I took the teabags out of our mugs. 'You're up, Inspector George.' I sat down. 'He's the good cop, by the way, in this scenario.'

Leo rolled his eyes at me behind the lawyer's back.

'You're not a cop.' Smirnov couldn't help himself, could he?

'Are you always so literal? Forget it. I don't care. Leo, the floor is yours.' I splashed some milk into my tea and pushed the bottle over to Leo.

'Thanks, Jess. Mr Smirnov, did you order your associates from ZOB Security to break into this house on the night of the 8th of December?'

Smirnov seemed at ease with this line of enquiry. 'No, I did not.'

'Did Alexei Chernov?'

'No. As we told you in the interview under caution, I collected him from the airport that night. Neither of us left the house after we returned, nor did we order other people to break in here on our behalf. Why would we? What is there here that could possibly have anything to do with us?'

'Body in the basement, anyone?' I offered brightly.

Leo hid his smile behind his mug. 'What she said.'

'Alexei Chernov had nothing to do with the death of Akmal Gulom. He had nothing but respect for the man and understood the hard feelings Mr Gulom had towards him were motivated by grief. He kept his distance.'

'Someone didn't. Someone thought it a very good idea to

take a blunt object to the side of Mr Gulom's head about the same time as your client's father also met his end.' Leo got up to return the milk to the fridge. 'Now, you see, Mr Smirnov, a murder in Oxford is a relatively rare event; to have two next door to each other in the same time period can't be a coincidence.' He sat down again.

'I agree,' said Smirnov, 'I just don't have an explanation for you. I'd like to know as much as you do – maybe even more – because the answer to that will catch Anatoly's killer.'

'You want his killer caught?' Leo let the disbelief into his tone.

'I do.'

'Then why have you been doing everything you can to impede my investigation?'

'I wasn't impeding, I was protecting my client. Anatoly has enemies in high places. We thought you were complicit with those trying to bring Anatoly out into the open so they could get him. We had no idea he was dead – in fact, believed the opposite until you persuaded us otherwise.'

'They got to him anyway so your caution was too late. And why do you still not give me the names of these people who you say wished him ill?'

Smirnov's lips thinned. 'I want to keep breathing, Inspector George. Don't you?'

'More than spending a night in the cells and possibly losing your licence?' I asked.

He contemplated his glass of water. 'Yes. Have you seen what happens to those who displease the Kremlin? If I'm dead, my career choice is moot.'

Leo sighed. 'OK, let's move on. Who in the force did Anatoly persuade to doctor the evidence concerning the crash in the first place?'

'I forget the person's name.' He sipped the tap water and grimaced. 'It was a single contact who arranged the rest.'

'Then I suggest you remember the name. If you send me that tomorrow, I'll forget my complaint for tonight's little hold-up.'

I noticed Leo didn't volunteer my forgetfulness. 'He's got to do much better than that to satisfy me. I want to know what he knows about the background to this Romeo and Juliet story the two families were running between them. Why did two such mortal enemies end up living side by side? It seems incredibly stupid.' I leaned forward.' Oh, I know: maybe your firm was in charge of running the searches for the property purchase? The would explain it.'

'We were not!' said Smirnov indignantly. That was his Achilles heel, his pride.

'Didn't you do a land registry run on who was who in the area before your main man settled here?'

'That wasn't how it happened at all!'

'Tell me then how it did happen, because at the moment I'm thinking you must be the most incompetent private client firm in the country. It's like allowing Taylor Swift to move in next to Kanye and Kim.'

Leo smiled at the comparison; Smirnov didn't.

'Anatoly didn't move here by chance,' the lawyer protested. 'He moved here because once upon a time he and Akmal Gulom were friends and business associates. It only soured later when Akmal accused Anatoly of double-crossing him on a deal.'

I gave myself a mental tick in the result column for getting this new detail out of him.

'Interesting. You hadn't mentioned this before. And did he double-cross his friend?' asked Leo.

'Anatoly was under pressure from a very important person in Moscow who wanted the shipment in question for his wife. Insisted on it. It was a rare yellow diamond. Akmal and Anatoly were working together to ship the gem to a customer in Central Asia. Anatoly had to divert it or lose his standing in Russia.'

'So the president or someone close to him wanted some bling for their main squeeze and Anatoly folded, letting down his old friend,' I summarised.

'He hated doing it,' said Smirnov.

'I bet. Must suck being in the pay of powerful men.'

'It wasn't about money but survival.'

'And how did that work out for him?'

'Jess.' Leo was right, I might've gone too far with the flippancy.

'Sorry.' I caught the lawyer's eye. 'He was your friend and he's dead. That was uncalled for.'

'Mr Smirnov,' said Leo, 'it's clear that Akmal Gulom had two strong motives for murder: a business betrayal and the death of his daughter.'

Smirnov scowled. 'Alexei didn't kill Fatima!'

'But he allowed her to drive the car, didn't he?'

The lawyer couldn't hide his surprise. 'How do you know that?'

277

'I'm a detective. I do my job.'

'Then if you know that, why are you still re-opening the investigation?'

'The cover-up is often worse than the original crime. And he let his girlfriend drive when she wasn't able to handle a car. I'm guessing he'd been drinking?'

'That was never proven.' Smirnov looked truly miserable now. 'Fatima was definitely sober. She didn't drink. She chose to be behind the wheel. No one forced her.'

'I don't doubt that. But I think Akmal Gulom knew that too and blamed Alexei for letting his little girl do something for which she wasn't qualified. Young people can make bad decisions but Alexei still bears some responsibility for that.' Leo let the silence stretch. 'Do you think it possible that Gulom would shoot his one-time friend in retaliation?'

Smirnov twisted the glass in his fingers. 'I think it possible.'

'Would Alexei have thought it possible?'

'Alexei didn't know his father was dead until you told him. He couldn't have killed Akmal over a year ago in revenge if that's what you're suggesting.'

'But what if Alexei did know and hid it from you?'

Smirnov was keeping his temper with difficulty, his words clipped. 'I realise you don't know Alexei like I do but he's not the kind of son who would leave his father buried in a shallow grave for a year!'

'What kind of son is he?'

'He's a fine boy who thinks with a cool head. Remember, we did not know about the body in the garden. But if he even suspected Akmal Gulom then, yes, he might have sought revenge, but it would have been through legal means. He would've wanted to take down Gulom's empire first so the man suffered disgrace. He would've thought a quick death, the kind you are investigating, one hidden from public view, was too little to weigh the balance against his own father's murder. The family honour would demand more. That is why you can be sure it wasn't him.'

'Then who do you think killed Akmal Gulom?'

Mr Smirnov looked up and met Leo's gaze directly. 'I really don't know and I will swear whatever oath you think acceptable to prove that to you.'

Chapter 31

Leo

The evening wasn't salvageable for romance. He couldn't go from the interview with Smirnov into bed with Jess – there were too many details that needed checking, and frankly too many thoughts whirling around in his head that would spoil the moment. Once Smirnov had left, Leo kissed Jess regretfully goodbye, explaining that he was heading for home to do a few more hours work before turning in.

'What do you make of the lawyer?' she asked. 'Do you believe him?'

'He is loyal to a fault to the family – I sense genuine attachment there and not just a paycheck. Smirnov's mistake was to bring Alexei's bodyguards with him when all he wanted was a quiet word. I think they aren't used to subtlety.'

'You can say that again. And what was that word?'

'He was trying to put pressure on me by threatening to reveal to you the woman I'm living with.'

She laughed. 'I bet that boomeranged.'

'It did – and helpfully so.'

'You can stay here to work,' suggested Jess, twisting her fingers in a buttonhole of his coat.

'Do you want someone here tonight?' he asked, very aware that she'd had more than one scare that week. 'You know that the squad car will be passing at regular intervals to keep an eye.'

'Flossie and I will be fine. I just meant you don't need to leave.' She tugged on the end of his scarf.

He framed her face and kissed her forehead, her chin, then her mouth tenderly. 'If I stay, I'll want to do this – and more.'

Her eyes were shining with an undeniable invitation. 'I wouldn't mind.'

'You're bad for my work ethic.'

'Yes, that does sound like me.'

'And I have to get this on record. Smirnov is usually sharper than we saw that tonight. Once he's recovered from the shock of having the tables turned on him, we'd be wise to expect every kind of legal trick in his arsenal. I've got to get this in the system first so that he doesn't try to turn the tables on me, claiming police harassment or something.'

'Oh God, yes, I was so harassing him from inside the boot of his car.'

He had to smile. 'True, he'd have a struggle explaining that away, but he still has the ability to make my life a misery for the next few weeks if he changes his mind about cooperation.'

She let go of the end of his scarf. 'Did you believe him? About not breaking in here, I mean?'

'I did. As I said before, if Alexei had sent a man to do the job, it would've gone down with more efficient violence.'

'Yeah, Rasputin would've tied me up and locked me in a cupboard is my guess.'

'Rasputin?'

'The one who carried me off, and not in a sexy way. So not what I was hoping for from tonight.' She walked her fingers up his chest, little electric points of contact. 'But if you want to play Russian bodyguard with me, and carry me off to bed, I'd like that.'

He was charmed by her tone. It was so very tempting. 'Jess, I wish I could.'

She sighed. 'Postponed but not cancelled then?'

'Let's pick this up tomorrow night, if you're free?'

'I'll have to consult my packed social diary.' She wrinkled her brow in pretend deep thought. 'Yep, I'm free.'

He kissed her, letting a little of his frustration show in the roughness of his hands shaping her body to his, the glide of his palm over her bottom. He must be mad turning this down for a night with his files and computer. 'Tomorrow then, *Da?*'

'I can't wait. Go!' Laughing, she pushed him way. 'Before I change my mind about changing your mind.'

On the drive back to his house, it sank in as he approached his house that his mother's fears that her former boyfriend was after her were misplaced. But if he told her, she'd be able to claim his home was still a safe place for her to hide away. It had almost been easier when he could use the car surveillance for scaring her off.

Should he tell her?

He decided to ignore the issue for now and keep with the plan to get her out by Sunday. Best thing he could hope for tonight was that she was still hiding in her room avoiding a confrontation with him. He really couldn't stomach her issues right now.

He made himself a strong coffee, sat down at his dining table and got out an A4 pad to capture his thoughts. He could hear footsteps in the room overhead, the slight creak of a floorboard, soft closing of a cupboard door. He tensed, but she didn't emerge. Turning his attention back to the table, he opened the pad. He'd use this to organise his thoughts for his report. He read through the case log which had been opened as soon as Marigold Green called in the body, looking for any details he'd missed. The next thing he did was draw the timeline again: two murders of prominent businessmen at around the same time thirteen months ago; neither family filed a missing person report. The Chernov family did so because they believed Anatoly was in hiding, but that still left the Guloms. He underlined his question mark. This was the first question he was going to follow up with them.

What else did he have?

Two murders but two different methods: gunshot and blunt instrument. It was not true to say that murderers were usually identifiable by their MO – that was the stuff of the rare serial killer. It was more often the case of using the nearest available weapon, be it gun, knife or heavy object. Violence was violence. Yet the shooting required some skill, and the second needed only the muscle power to strike down a man of just under six foot tall. A strong woman or most men could do that. Or an older teenager. He mustn't exclude the younger generation as suspects for these crimes.

Motives? So far there was love, revenge and money in the shape of Fatima and the broken business deal. Plenty to cause someone to lash out.

Means? The heavy sharp object, pickaxe or hammer, in the second murder was fairly easy to come by, but he must follow up where his team had got in tracing the weapon for the first.

Opportunity? This was where the imprecise date of death for both bodies made it hard to exclude any of his suspects. Further lab results he'd received on the state of decomposition, pollen traces and insect activity placed the corpses in advanced decay with a likely time of death in October or November of the previous year. Gulom's remains were slightly less decomposed, but the pathologist thought this due to the coolness of the place he was found. That fitted with the last reliable sightings of the men. All of his suspects could have been in Oxford in the autumn of the year before, either because they lived here or because they were internationally mobile. Still, it would be good to examine Alexei's known whereabouts. He'd chase up the check already put in to Immigration. The young man kept off social media, so that wouldn't help, but there might be other records of his movements. If Alexei wished to prove he didn't have the opportunity, he might even help.

There was another decision tree split on the mind map Leo was sketching: one killer or two? If one, someone had reason to kill both men. Why? What did they have in common? The only person whom Leo had considered for that was Alexei but he wasn't confident that was a good fit, the reasons not clear enough. There were several counterfactuals. Why, for example, return to the country if the crimes were coming out? Alexei had no need to put himself back in the orbit of British police.

So two killers? Then that opened the possibility that one of them had killed and was murdered for that crime. This fitted with the theme of a family feud. It also bumped the Housemans down, if not off, the list. They might've had cause to kill Chernov, blaming him for the death of their daughter, but they had no motive to harm Gulom. In fact, surely they would've cheered him on.

Unless it was the other way round and Gulom saw them do the killing?

Leo shook his head, and struck out that suggestion. No, not likely; they were at the bottom of his list.

Which meant he was left with a riddle. That was appropriate as the red house was central to the mystery with its Alice in Wonderland garden. It hadn't been a book he'd read as a child but he knew some of the most famous quotes. Wasn't there one about asking for directions out of a muddle? He looked it up: '*Would you tell me, please, which way I ought to go from here?*' asks Alice.

'*That depends a good deal on where you want to get to.*' That was the Cheshire Cat, a sinister figure if ever there was one.

Where did he want to get? He wanted to get to clearer answers. But maybe that was trying to get to the end before dealing with the middle. He felt the case was forming like a bridge being built from either bank. He was missing the link in the middle that would make it all fall into place.

So, to answer the Cheshire Cat, he needed to begin in the middle.

And what was that? After tonight, he believed that would be the collapse of the friendship over the yellow diamond.

Chapter 32

Jess

Prevented from sealing the deal with Leo, I put my frustrated energies into a search for Rashid Gulom. No doubt Leo's team was also looking for the Gulom family but I imagined they would concentrate on locating the wife as the senior surviving member. Besides I felt I'd already made some headway finding that old posting about Rashid's target shooting and I was invested in locating him first. I trawled the obvious sites with no results. Then, noting his age, I decided to check out TikTok, which had been growing exponentially over the year, though I wasn't a user and only had a vague idea what teenagers saw in it. It seemed like the karaoke club of social media sites. I signed up and found a guy calling himself Rash Gul popped up in a popular hashtag challenge to put a T-shirt on while standing on your hands. I clicked.

Wow. I could report that Rashid had grown up ripped. I had to watch it a couple of times. Bulging biceps, perfect control as he went from one arm to the other. The third time through I took more note of the background. On the shelf on the wall he was using to prop him up I could see some college books. Taking a screen shot, I expanded the image and tried to make out which subject he was studying.

Economics.

I felt a little disappointed. At least it killed off my inappropriate crush before it could root. I then took note of the T-shirt that he had been expertly pulling on – it had the initials OURC. I ran that through Google and came up with three contenders, all from Oxford University: the Rowing Club, Running Club and Rifle Club. But we already knew our guy was the target shooter so I was fairly confident we'd found him. I followed up with a search for a way of contacting the club. This was going to be harder as I knew from St Nick's most of the students had already left this weekend for their Christmas holidays. Maybe the club secretary would still be contactable? I jotted down the details and folded up all my brilliance in a single message to Leo.

Good work, Watson.

I grinned at his reply. *I'd prefer to be Irene Adler – The Woman. Sexier.*

There was a little pause, and then I got this.

You have no problem in that department. Isn't she a shady character who goes off with another guy in the original?

So my man knows how to Google too because I did not believe he had that knowledge at his fingertips. I did a search to check it out because my knowledge was taken from TV shows. He was right, damn him. *OK. I'll be Watson.*

Sleep well. See you tomorrow?

You bet!

And is it unprofessional to admit that I took my phone to bed with me so I could keep re-reading his messages?

Relieved to have reached Saturday in one piece, I slept in and was only dragged from my bed by Flossie demanding food and exercise. Dealing with her needs first, I forced myself under the shower and blasted myself awake with the full spray. Taking my cereal into the home office I sat at the desk chair and swung round until I had the good view down the garden. Before the plywood arrived in the living room, I would've been sitting in there, as they rooms shared a similar view, but I didn't like the half-light and reminder of the night-time encounter. Alice stood looking up at the house, hands held behind her back. A robin landed on her head and stared back at me. A few flakes of sleet hit the terrace, then transformed into an icing sugar dusting of snow. My garden now looked like a real winter wonderland.

I rang Cory.

'Jess! How was it?' Cory knew almost all my secrets, including my plans for last night.

'Not how you would expect.'

'Oh.' She sounded deflated for me.

'No, not like that! What I mean is, we didn't get to that part of the evening because I was abducted.' I then began a colourful account of our encounter with the thugs, which I enjoyed much more in the retelling than in the experience of being stuffed in a boot of a car.

'Oh God, Jess, that sounds terrible! Weren't you terrified?'

'To be frank I was so angry that I blasted through terror to red rage. I kicked Rasputin in the shins when I got out. I'm proud of that.'

'Then why didn't Leo sweep you off your feet and celebrate surviving in the time-honoured fashion?'

'Because we had a slimy lawyer to grill. We're trying again tonight and I refuse to let anything stop us.'

'But isn't this typical for a relationship with a policeman – calls away to duty at the most awkward times?' Cory was my designated voice of reason. Everyone should have one.

I huffed. She was correct; I would be sharing Leo with his job. 'I hate it that you're right. Anyway, that's not why I rang. I was phoning because I wondered if you and the kids wanted to come visit the red house today? The garden is looking spiffy in its snow covering and I can even take them on the Alice tour. We've not done that yet.'

'They'd like that, not that we've got to Alice yet. Still stuck on pirates and princesses. It's probably exactly what they both need. I'll just bundle them up then come over.'

The next person I rang was Leo.

'How's it going?' I could hear birdsong in the background so I guessed he was in his garden. I was longing to see that because I knew it was a huge part of his life.

'Good, thanks to you,' he said. 'I've got hold of the Rifle Club secretary and she's finding Rashid for me. He's a student at Oriel College, though he goes by Rash Gul these days.'

'Yeah, probably sick of the Gollum jokes.'

'She says he's still up in Oxford because there's a team competition next week against Cambridge.'

'I wonder why he's not living here in the family home then?' And booting me out – not that I wanted that.

'Maybe for the reason Alexei Chernov suggested – bad memories? Rashid might want just to be an ordinary student, not one with a multimillionaire house.'

'Especially if he knew his dad was in the basement.'

'That's something I'll have to ask him. But there's no hint yet that there was any grievance between father and son. I'm not looking at him for this. Not yet.'

That's my suspicious policeman. 'Have you got hold of the wife?'

'Yes, via her solicitor. She's coming back to the UK.'

'Where was she?'

'Uzbekistan, so it might take her a few days to find a flight at this time of year.'

'Is she telling the son?'

'The solicitor has messaged him, but not with the full story. If you hadn't found the information on the rifle club I was going to use the lawyer to contact Rashid, but your route is better. Might get me direct to the young man rather than having to cut my way through red tape.'

I remembered Smirnov and his overly involved behaviour with the Chernovs. He was more godfather than employee. 'Jesus, these families are weird. Would you leave it up to your legal guy to tell your kid his dad was dead?'

'The lawyer did mention something about Mrs Gulom being fragile. Maybe she's too cut up to do it herself?'

'Hmm. So what did your review of the material throw up last night?'

'Diamonds. More precisely the yellow diamond that caused their falling out. Trying to live up to my Holmes persona, I've been digging into where they come from and guess where the most famous ones with the fancy yellow colour are found?'

'Give me two guesses. In the Tower of London as part of the Crown Jewels or in Elizabeth Taylor's collection?'

He laughed. 'I meant in the ground.'

'No idea. Maybe South Africa?'

'Point to you. And DRC – that's the Congo.'

'I do know – it's a massive country in Central Africa.' I'd had a puzzle of the world when I was a child and had always thought it an oddly shaped country, with a little trunk of land stretching to the Atlantic to give it sea access.

'There's that international agreement on the prevention of the sale of conflict diamonds Meredith told you about. Unfortunately, it's not that hard to get round. Which led me to wonder, how would you ship a diamond out of a war-torn country like DRC for a customer in Russia?'

'You'd use a reputable merchant in a diamond-producing country like Sierra Leone who could make it look legitimate. Oh, my word, Leo, are you thinking that the relationship with the Prices, or at least Meredith's family, existed before Oxford?'

'We found out from Smirnov why Chernov and Gulom moved in next door to each other, but not why they chose Oxford in the first place. There are other schools in other cities and other countries.'

'*Of all the gin joints in all the towns in all of the world, she walks into mine.* You're right. We should've asked him that.'

'I've sent him the question already, just waiting for the answer.'

'But the Prices claimed not to be that familiar with Gulom.'

'I know. Al Price mentioned something about coinciding in Berlin with Chernov but gave no hint they became friends then. But let's assume they met then. It's possible the Prices did only know Anatoly and Anatoly knew Gulom – a simple chain.'

'Want to move your kids to a school in England so why not move in near your old pals from Oxford. They could keep an unofficial eye when you're away. Yes, I can see that. Mr Price likes keeping an eye on things – why not forbidden romances too? That would've been right up his street. Maybe he told on Alexei and that's the reason they fell out, not racism at all?'

'But doesn't it seems highly unlikely to you, if they were dealing in diamonds together, that Anatoly would fail to mention his best mate over the fence, Akmal the Uzbek diamond merchant?'

'So Chernov's like the middleman? Mrs Price is from a family of diamond exporters, hired to do the smuggling. And depending how big this rock is, Meredith could've carried it out on her finger among her existing rings. Who would notice? As you said, few of us know our diamonds from our diamanté.' I hugged the phone. 'Leo, that is so cool. It sounds like a James Bond plot.'

'Don't get too carried away, I might be spinning a few wisps of straw into gold here. I've no evidence, only surmises based on a dislike of coincidence.'

'And there's another question we didn't ask last night.'

'What's that?'

'If Anatoly was afraid to let down his highly placed Russian by not supplying the diamond, who did his business partner Gulom have gunning for him for not producing the goods?'

'A customer in Uzbekistan who might send someone to take him out with a pickaxe?'

'Exactly.'

Chapter 33

Leo

Leo would've preferred to spend his Saturday afternoon with Jess and join in her Alice tour of the garden. She was going to dress up for Cory's kids apparently and he would very much like to see what she came up with. Instead, he found himself heading back to St Bede's because the OURC secretary had come through for him and located Rashid. The club used the school shooting range for their practices. Leo could almost hear the headmaster's spiel about community engagement running as a soundtrack to that promotional video. But a shooting range in a school? Leo had not come across this before in his years of going into schools to give careers talks or when following up enquiries. A quick search of upper-tier private schools showed that St Bede's was by no means alone in having a facility. Maybe it was natural for the landowning classes to train their offspring so they didn't disgrace themselves on a grouse shoot, but it struck Leo as bizarre. In his view, schools and guns were not a winning combination.

Just as he arrived outside the shooting gallery door, a new email popped up on his phone. The images from Paul. He didn't have time to deal with these now so forwarded them to Jess.

If you have a moment between playing Alice, could you have a quick scan of these to see what they tell you about the gardens of 13 Hay Road and anything significant about the red house?

She replied with a thumbs up and *Who said I was playing Alice?* She sent a photo of Cory's little girl dressed as Alice, the boy as a caterpillar and Jess in a top hat.

Of course, she'd pick the hatter. He should've guessed.

Tucking the phone away, he pressed the buzzer. After a moment, the door opened and a young woman with ear defenders around her neck stood in the entrance.

'Laura? We spoke earlier.'

She stood back. 'Come in. Rash is in booth two. I told him you wanted to speak to him. I hope that was OK?'

'That's fine.'

'It's not bad news, is it? Rash looked really upset when I told him.'

'Not great, I'm afraid. Are you friends with Rashid?'

She flushed a little. 'Yeah, we are.'

'Then maybe hang around in case he needs you?'

'I'd do that anyway, but yes, of course.'

Leo and Laura walked to the viewing gallery that ran behind the booths of the range. All were occupied but as each was clearly labelled he had no trouble finding Rashid. A young man, short of stature, five-six maybe, slim with wispy dark hair in a ponytail, was standing at a bench, rifle held competently in his arms. At the end of a long lane, a little like a bowling alley, a circular target was displayed. At the end of each round, the target lifted up on a wire and travelled forward so the shooter could mark themselves.

'Is he any good?' Leo asked.

She smiled. 'Almost as good as me. Though to be fair, he's better at a moving target. Completely crushes me at clay pigeon shooting.'

Rashid finished his latest round and removed his ear defenders. Laura tapped on the glass partition and he looked round. He held up a finger to indicate he would be with them in a moment, took the target sheet off the wire and exited the gallery.

'How did you do?' Laura asked.

'Aargh, I've been better,' he said modestly, though from what Leo could see almost all the shots were in the centre.

'This is the policeman who rang me earlier,' she said, gesturing to Leo. 'Inspector George.'

Rashid nodded to him. 'This is about my father, isn't it?'

'Your father? Something's happened to your dad?' asked Laura in dismay.

'Got a message from a family friend last night telling me to expect bad news. I'd guessed it might happen, Laura. I can't say I was shocked.'

'Oh Rash!' She clutched his arm. 'I'm so sorry.'

'Is there somewhere we can go to speak?' Leo asked.

Laura gestured to some benches at the far end of the viewing gallery. 'I'll keep everyone away.'

'Thanks, Laura,' said Rashid.

She left and Rashid led Leo to the benches. 'OK, Inspector, when and how did he do it?'

Leo did a quick rethink of how much Rashid knew. 'Mr Gulom—'

'Please, call me Rash. Mr Gulom is – or was – my dad.' He pulled a face, but his stoic expression cracked and his lips quivered. He hid his eyes. 'Oh fuck, I thought I'd handle this better.'

'There's no one watching you and you don't have to pretend anything with me,' said Leo gently, actually relieved that here was a son who at least behaved naturally when he was given bad news. 'I'll lay it out to you straight as I think you might have some wrong ideas about this. Your father's body was found a couple of days ago in a passageway below the swimming pool in the red house.'

He raised his head, eyes glistening. 'What? Here – in Oxford?'

'Yes. He'd been there some time, over a year. The autopsy revealed that he was killed by a blow to the head.'

The young man looked bewildered. 'He hit his head?'

'No. I'm saying that we think he was attacked and died as a result of his wounds.'

'No, no that can't be right.' Rashid scrubbed a hand across his face, wiping his nose on a sleeve. 'No one would want to kill Dad.'

'I'm sorry but that's what we found. Did you know that your mother is coming to the UK?'

'Yeah, the same family friend who told me to expect bad news is handling that. She's coming to see me tomorrow, I guess to tell me. Shit . . . fuck . . . This is all too much to take in.' He gripped his knees.

'I'm really sorry, Rash. Would you prefer to pick this up again when you've had a chance to recover from what I've just told you? I've got some questions but they can wait until your mother gets here.'

Rash's head jerked up. 'No, I'd prefer you to ask me the questions – not my mother. She's not in a good place right now – hasn't been since Fatima died. This might kill her.'

That was what fragile meant, Leo realised. This poor family. They couldn't catch a break.

'OK then. First question is what you were expecting me to tell you about your father. You were expecting different news?'

Rash blew out a breath. 'I suppose it doesn't matter now. I thought Dad might've finally managed to kill himself.'

'Your father was suicidal?'

'Inspector, I don't know if you've had a death in your family, but when Fatima died in that accident, it was like the rest of us died for a while too. I came back from that thanks to some really good friends, but Mum and Dad, not so much. Fatima was Dad's favourite – his golden girl – and he became fixated on revenge. As the years passed, he didn't get better, he got worse. He kept saying he'd get his own back even if it was the last thing he did. He turned all his hatred on Alexei Chernov, though Alex didn't do it on purpose. Alex loved Fatima. I told Dad he was completely overreacting and should let it go and that was the last time he spoke to me. Told me I was no son of his if I took Alex's side. That wasn't what I meant at all but he cut me off.'

'When was this?'

'That conversation? Oh God, I don't know exactly, maybe

28th or 29th of October last year? I rang Dad to invite him to the national finals for target shooting and we got side-tracked into that argument. I thought it would blow over but he didn't return any of my calls. Mum said he'd cut her off too. She's been unwell, in a private sanatorium to help with her depression. We only began to get worried at New Year when he still blanked us and hadn't been heard from by any of his friends or business associates. He didn't renew Mum's deal with the sanatorium, which really wasn't like him. His firm was going belly up without him and still he didn't get back in touch. We started to fear that he'd done something to himself – something drastic. I told our people to start looking for him in Tashkent, where he was last known to be, but we came up with nothing. We sorted out the firm in his absence but that was when I wondered about suicide. I thought he'd gone out to our country place and just walked into the forest or something. I had no idea that he'd come back here though. I thought he hated the red house. It would've been the last place I'd search.' He paused. 'Though maybe I should've realised. He did always associate the house with Fatima. Left her room and all her belongings there like a shrine.'

Leo had seen that when Jess showed him the house. The wardrobe still full of clothes, and a dressing gown dropped on the bed like the owner had just stepped out for a moment.

'It's doubtful you would've found him if you had. Did you know about the void under the swimming pool?'

Rashid shook his head. 'No. I don't remember anything like that.'

'It used to be a passage but is now sealed off. It was only by chance it was opened up again when the current house-sitter got curious.'

'I guess I should thank him then.'

'It's a her. A woman called Jess Bridges. She took over in November from Ben Major. If you want I can put you in touch? She needs to know what you and your mother want to do with the house, but that's not a problem for today.'

'Yeah, please do that. I'd burn it to the ground if I could, but I guess the house isn't to blame.'

It didn't sound a serious threat of arson so Leo let it go. He waited while the young man gathered himself.

'Any more questions, Inspector?'

'Yes, if you can manage them?'

'I can.'

'Do you know of anyone who might have reason to kill your father? Hold a grudge? Or a bad deal, for example?'

Rashid shrugged. 'My dad kept me out of his business – said I should enjoy being young. If there was a particular deal that went sour, he didn't say. Apart from that one with Alexei's dad years ago. Dad hated Anatoly Chernov way before Alex and Fatima started dating.'

'Do you know why?'

'Not really. Dad just said that he'd once thought he could trust Anatoly's word but that had been an expensive mistake. He told me to trust nobody in that family, which is why he went postal when I said he should let the accident go.'

'Were there any other people in the area that your father knew?'

'Not really. He didn't spend that much time in Oxford. A few of the parents from school I suppose.'

'And what about the Prices?'

'Who?'

'Meredith Price works in the library at St Bede's. They're neighbours.'

'Oh, Mrs Price! Yeah, I know her. She loved Fatima – one of her star readers. Me, not so much. Lost cause. But she's cool.'

'And her husband? Al Price?'

Rashid looked blank. 'Don't know anyone . . .'

'You might've seen him walking his dog locally – a dachshund?'

'Oh yeah, I think I remember seeing someone like him. Gave Dad grief about the pool but Mrs Price said that that dispute had no place at St Bede's parents' evening.'

'They argued at the school?'

'No, that's what I'm saying: they *didn't* argue at the school. St Bede's was like Switzerland, neutral territory. They argued in the council planning meetings, but Dad got the go-ahead anyway. Fatima loved swimming. Dad wanted it for her.'

Leo stood up. 'Rashid, thanks for answering my questions. Would it be OK to get back in touch if any others come up? I'll be talking to your mother, of course.'

Rashid shook his head. 'Her English isn't great. Best if you talk to me.'

'I will need to see her.'

'That's OK, but I'll make sure I'm there. You'll need someone to interpret.'

'I'm going to be talking to the house-sitter again later today. Is there any message for her?'

'Just thanks and sit tight, I guess. I'll sort it all out eventually.'

It looked like all the responsibility for the family was landing on the young man's shoulders. His time off from business was over. Leo left him his card and walked away. Laura was poised by the door.

'Is it OK to go in?' she asked.

Leo looked over his shoulder at the young man sitting hunched forward on the bench. 'Yes, that would be a good idea.'

She rushed past him and knelt before Rashid, touching his knee in sympathy.

'Oh, Rashid, one more question,' called Leo. 'Who taught you to shoot so well? Laura says you're almost as good as her.'

Rashid raised his head, a weak smile for his friend. 'Almost?' He knuckled tears away. 'My dad taught me. It was the one interest we shared.'

Leo nodded. 'Thanks.' He closed the door on the pair.

Chapter 34

Jess

It had been nice to hear children's laughter in the garden again. I think it helped banish some of the ghosts that the place had accumulated over the years. Cory took Benji and Leah home and left me with my homework for Leo. I opened the zipped file on my laptop and started flicking through. I have to hand it to Paul: he was as efficient in his photography as he was at the office. Each subfolder was arranged by location and by date.

I went first to the red house. He had been very exercised by the building works because he'd returned often to photograph what he could of the excavations. Some of the shots looked like they'd been taken from an upper storey of a neighbouring house. Looking around the area to work out the angle from which they were taken, I decided it had to be the AI institute before it was renovated. Had Paul known someone who lived there? Very possibly. It had been owned by another educational organisation in the university so he was likely to have been on good terms with them. If you flicked through quick enough, it was like watching a time-lapse video. When the leaves were off the trees, you could see the 'before' of the garden, white statues dotted among the ornamental flower-beds and shrubbery. The White Rabbit had been on the opposite side of the terrace steps from Alice, looking down at his pocket watch. Time had been up for him about a month into the dig. Alice had been moved to one side and the late rabbit vanished. A massive hole with a mechanical digger took their place. That confirmed the theory that the rabbit had been a victim of clumsiness some time before Gulom was killed, placed first in the hidden passageway. I flagged up the photos for Leo because it would help him establish the time-line more firmly. There were no more photos once the building project was completed about five years ago. The Guloms hadn't had long to enjoy their pool before Fatima's death.

I turned next to 13 Hay Road, looking for any changes to the property to indicate activity by the Chernovs. There were fewer photos, probably because the planning application had been turned down. Paul had captured the alterations to the front of the property though. What had once been a slightly scruffy professor's house had been ruthlessly done up to its current sparkling state with topiary planters and immaculate gravel drive. I imagined that coincided with the excessive tidying of the garden. I made a note to check with Marigold to see if I was correct. That had happened eight years ago. Did that mean that the Chernovs were the first to move to the area and that the Guloms followed? That was the way it looked to me. I'd suggest to Leo that he ran a search on the land registry to confirm.

So Chernov moved in first, his best mate followed suit

when his kids started at St Bede's, and all was sweetness and light until they fell out, probably over the yellow diamond. Our Romeo and Juliet then fell in love despite the feud, literally breaking down the fence between the families. Juliet, aka Fatima, dies in a tragic accident. Juliet's dad swears revenge and takes out Romeo's dad. Rather than own up to the crime, Gulom buries his old friend Anatoly where he fell, using his own spade, which was conveniently at hand in his shed. It felt all very operatic and tragic so far but then what? What made sense at that point?

Leo said he believed that Alexei hadn't know his father was dead until he told him. Otherwise he'd be the most obvious tit-for-tat murderer.

Maybe the motive was nothing to do with Fatima's death? I went back to the meticulous record provided by the photos. There were two other sources of local tension that we knew about: planning disputes and soured business relations between neighbours. Paul had taken to photographing the red house again last year after a few years of leaving it alone. I typed in the address to the local council planning portal and turned up something I hadn't expected. There was a lapsed application for planning for my property. I clicked on the file and discovered a long chain of submissions: architectural plans to convert the house into a multi-occupancy dwelling, an application to give over some of the garden to parking spaces for the new tenants, a move that would kill off the caterpillar in his kitchen garden. The letter accompanying the application explained that the current owner wanted to sell the property with planning permission to an interested buyer.

The objections came thick and fast. Nearly all the neighbours complained, and, of course, the North Oxford Protection Society was up in arms at yet another family home being turned into student accommodation. The application was rejected but not appealed.

From the date, that was probably because the householder was dead.

Do people kill over planning disputes?

From what I'd read about criminal psychology, I knew that they killed for much stupider reasons.

Maybe my Orient Express suggestion wasn't so far off target as I'd assumed?

I wondered how much my predecessor knew about it. Working out what time it would be in New Zealand – very early morning – I decided on sending a text rather than waking him up.

Hey Ben, Jess Bridges here. Hope all going well with the vineyard. Keep up the good work – people like me rely on you.

I pressed send. Then went to the next text box.

Just a quick question. Weird stuff has been happening here – like very weird – and the British police will probably be trying to get hold of you to explain. (Don't worry, you're not in trouble!)

At least I hoped not. I sent that and finally got round to my question.

I just wanted to know what you knew about the most recent planning battle for the red house. It was last year. Does this ring bells?

As I was setting aside my phone, the Skype app on my phone started chiming. Ben getting back to me.

I accepted the call and got a picture of my predecessor, framed against a magnificent sunrise.

'What the fuck, Jess?'

'Ben! God, I didn't mean to wake you!'

'It's high summer here. I get up early to do the work when it's cool. But what's happening?'

'Oh crap.' I now realised I probably should've restrained my impulse to tell him before Leo cleared it, but too late now. The news would be in the press very soon once the family were informed. I'd already spotted a couple of local reporters doing pieces to the camera in front of the house.

'It's about Mr Gulom. He was found dead in the house – in the basement – well, actually, in a hidden passageway under the pool. He'd been there over a year.'

Ben swore again. 'I had nothing to do with that! No idea at all.'

'Of course you didn't. But I guess there are two questions you might be able to answer – and I can pass this to the police as I'm helping them with their enquiries.' That didn't sound good. 'I mean, helping investigate. In a small way.' Shut up, Jess. 'Right, what I wanted to know is do you remember any fuss over a new planning application to do with the house?'

'Christ, yes. As soon as Mr Gulom put one of those yellow planning notices up, the locals went crazy, leafleting the neighbourhood, telling me off for living in the house where such sacrilege was planned.'

'Who led the charge on that?'

'That man with the dachshund he drags everywhere with

him, and another guy who kept taking photos. I had to run him off a couple of times.'

Mr Price and Paul. I thought as much.

'And did you see them confront Mr Gulom in person?'

'I never crossed paths with him. He always messaged me to clear out before he arrived and I'd stay with friends in Oxford.'

'You don't still have those messages, do you?'

'I expect so. I'll just switch views and check.' He came back in only a few seconds. 'Yeah, still got the message chain.'

'When was the last time he asked you to move out?'

'November the 1st last year. I was out for a week and moved back in on the 8th. Never saw him. Wasn't even sure he'd stayed in the house. In fact, that was odd. Normally he would send a message to say he was gone. When it didn't come, I just moved back in as we agreed.'

'Did you notice any changes to the house? Particularly down in the basement?'

'Nothing obvious. Though there were those loose tiles. I reported them to Glass Tower but they didn't send anyone to fix them.'

Of course not, because they were conniving bastards skimming off the money for their own pockets. They wouldn't do anything unless the owner made a point of asking.

'It wasn't too bad so I left it. Is that . . .?'

'Yes. There's an old passageway – or was – built under the house for the first owner.'

'Cool – I mean not cool that someone hid a body down there but I always loved the quirky features to the house.'

'I guess a body in the basement is a quirky feature.'

He pulled a face. 'I didn't mean that.'

'Sorry, I have an unfortunate sense of humour. If it's OK, I'll pass this information on to the police. If you wouldn't mind sending a copy of the messages to the inspector in charge of the investigation?'

'Sure.'

I gave him Leo's details. 'They'll probably have loads more questions.'

'Well, I'm not going anywhere except the vines today and we have Wi-Fi coverage all over the farm, so tell them they are welcome to call.'

'Thanks. Stay safe. Don't get sunstroke.' And I was not jealous at all of the thought of high summer in New Zealand.

'I would've thought you were the one who needed to worry about safety, Jess. I'm in paradise.' He gave me a quick 180° scan of his hillside.

'Until you did that, there was I thinking we could've been friends.'

He grinned and ended the call.

I sent a quick message to Leo apologising if I'd jumped the gun and updating him on Ben's information. Leaving the news winging its way to the enquiry team, I turned back to the images and decided to run another search, not by property but by date. Any image between November the 1st and 8th. I had them displayed on the screen as thumbnails. Of course – Guy Fawkes Night had attracted the photographer to take some great shots of Wolfson College with rockets bursting overhead. That would've been a good night to shoot someone because no one would imagine they were hearing a gunshot. If I were a stone-cold killer, that would be my preferred day for assassination.

I ran a little fantasy of myself as a *Killing Eve* protagonist before wrenching my thoughts back to the images. Some featured groups of people rather than fireworks. I clicked on one and found a slew of shots taken of what looked like a North Oxford Protection Society social at the Prices' house. Nothing very interesting, just people doing that smile-for-the-camera-with-raised-glass pose. I was about to call the search a bust when I kept clicking past the party. The time stamp was now 8.30pm. The Prices, and Paul presumably, had gone round to the red house to confront Mr Gulom on his doorstep. Paul had taken a picture of them handing over a petition against his plans, probably signed at that same social.

Hadn't Leo said the Prices claimed to have only a vague knowledge of Gulom? Yet here they were delivering a letter some time shortly before his death. I hadn't seen anything like that in the home office and Gulom kept detailed files on the house. There were several folders devoted to the pool alone, from planning application to building completion. In fact, now I thought about it, correspondence on the last planning dispute was missing or I'd've seen it earlier. If Mr Gulom used his usual methods, a dated and labelled file should be sitting in the cabinet.

Sorry to disturb you again, Ben, but did you get rid of any paperwork from the home office? I'm not expecting that you did – just checking.

He texted back immediately. *Hell no.*

A smiley face felt the wrong response so I texted a thumbs up instead.

I went to the cabinet and opened the top drawer. Was I imagining a gap? This had been rummaged through by several people since the beginning of this murder enquiry. Did the police remove anything?

Surely they'd've taken all of it, not just one folder?

It seemed more likely that someone had been covering their tracks and I was beginning to think I could guess who.

Chapter 35

Leo

With a skeleton crew in the office this late on a Saturday, Leo updated his superintendent by phone, folding in the new information Jess had uncovered. The timeline was coming along well, with a more precise window identified for the murders. He was fairly confident he knew half of the story now.

'Do you have enough to make an arrest?' asked Claire Thaxted.

'To bring him in for questioning, yes,' said Leo, 'but the only firm thing we've got is the fact that he lied to me during our first interview.'

'Do you like him for both killings? A military man presumably has easier access to firearms than the general population?'

'He doesn't have a firearms licence.'

'But he's travelled. Who knows what he's picked up on the black market?'

'That's true.' Claire liked to feel she was still a detective even though her seniority set her apart from the day-to-day investigation. Leo had to be careful. 'I still think Akmal Gulom is the most likely for the first kill. He was an expert target shooter – that was confirmed by his son today – and he had the strongest motives. He also had the opportunity, being back in Oxford during the right time frame. Jess Bridges, who's been helping out with the research, suggested that Fireworks Night – and the few days either side of that when displays are held – would explain why no one heard the shot.'

'All right. I can follow that logic. What was the motive for the murder of Gulom? Was Price a better friend of Chernov than we thought? Was it revenge for the murder of his good friend across the road?'

'That has to remain on the table but I'm not getting that from my interviews. The Chernov family lawyer' – currently unusually cooperative – 'claims that he'd not heard Anatoly mention Al Price or known him to socialise with him. Not that I trust everything he's telling me. He is fiercely loyal to Alexei and will claim client confidentiality, if he thinks his answers will damage the Chernovs.'

He could hear Claire puffing a little at the other end and a rhythmic thump of trainers hitting the ground. Was she on a running machine? That would fit with his Triathlon-running boss.

'Not a personal grudge then. What's the motive?'

'This is where I'm cautious to go out on a limb. There was a new bitter planning dispute brewing – we've online records and photographic evidence of that. They lost the one over the pool and were throwing everything at stopping the house conversion. But would you really kill someone because you disapproved of their aspirations for their property, particularly when their application had already been turned down once?'

'You might, if you were a fanatic.'

'Mr Price is devoted to his area but he doesn't strike me as crossing the line to lunatic about it. It seems insufficient. Unless it was a heat-of-the-moment action – a shove that went wrong during an argument, something of that nature. That's what I need to ask.'

Claire dialled down her machine her end and could be heard slowing to a walk. 'OK, Leo, put in for a warrant. We need more evidence to build a case against him, ideally the murder weapon or items used to dispose of the body. Then on Monday ask him to come in for a voluntary interview. I'd like to avoid arresting him until we have more to show the CPS. But be careful. Men like him know how to throw their weight around.'

'Will do.'

'And Leo, be prepared for a news conference on Monday afternoon to update the press on what we've found so far.'

He couldn't quite suppress his groan.

'You don't have to worry.' He could hear her wry tone. 'This is good work. You've made a lot of progress on what might have easily been two cold cases on our hands.'

'We have the North Oxford Protection Society to thank for that, with its habit of documenting everything that goes on in the area.' And Jess, but he thought it best not to mention her to his boss again as she had got ahead of herself contacting the old house-sitter. Claire would not approve of that initiative.

'You think Al Price might be hoisted by his own petard?' she suggested.

'We'll have to see. Good night, ma'am.'

Leo checked the clock. It was getting late, past end of shift.

He'd been delayed longer than he expected as he'd followed up Jess's call to Ben Major with one of his own. He had to get an official statement for his files, and Jess's update, full of her own brand of humour and emojis, was not suitable. That had both irritated and amused him. He knew though that this would be the nature of their relationship so he'd just have to love the grit in the oyster.

Gathering his coat, he prepared to shut down for the night. Finally he could get back to Jess.

His phone rang – his home number. He almost sent it to voicemail but as he had no intention of going home, he decided to accept the call.

'Yes?'

'Oh Leo – they're so pretty!' His mother sounded her most gushy and girlish, a tone that he hated.

'What are?'

'The flowers!'

There was little in bloom in his garden, apart from some winter jasmine and an evergreen clematis, but he doubted she meant those. 'What flowers?'

'A nice delivery man from Interflora came with an enormous bouquet for me.'

'For you?'

'Well,' she corrected, 'the card said for Mrs George so I guessed they meant me.'

He wanted to bang his head on the desk. 'Anything else?'

'Just a note saying that he was sorry if I had been unnerved by his surveillance vehicle. He said it had been connected to a case you were working and wires had got crossed.'

Vivid swear words tumbled through his mind. 'Was the name of the sender supplied?'

'A Mr Joseph Smirnov. Do you know him?'

'I do.'

'Oh, so it is true! Alan didn't send those men – he hasn't found me. I'm safe where I am. Isn't that wonderful?'

'I'm glad you're safe, but it also means it's safe for you to move on without being followed. You still have to go by tomorrow at the latest.'

'Oh pish!'

Did she really say 'pish'? Who did she think she was? Julie Andrews about to burst into song about her favourite things, like bouquets of flowers and free rides from sons?

'You should be happy that you can protect me and you know why I have to hide.'

There was no point arguing with her. She only heard what she wanted and dismissed the rest. She was a narcissist and there was no reasoning with someone who sincerely thought the world revolved around them.

'Pack your bags, Mother. You're leaving.' He ended the call and switched the phone to silent.

Great. His mood was completely destroyed again. It was almost impossible to imagine a night with Jess with this splinter burrowing its way under his skin. If this carried on, Jess was going to give up on him.

In a foul temper, he started his car and headed south to the red house.

Chapter 36

Jess

You didn't need to be a weatherman to see the thundercloud hanging over Leo as he got out of his car.

I bundled Flossie into the kitchen and returned to the hallway to take his overcoat. 'What's up? Hit a wall in the case?'

He shook his head. 'No, thanks to my conversation with Rashid and your work today, we finally appear to be making progress.' He tugged on the ends of the scarf still looped around his neck as if contemplating hanging someone with it. Not me, I didn't think.

'So . . .?'

'You know how I thought that Smirnov might bounce back and find a way of making my life difficult?'

'Hmm-hmm.' I took the scarf and hung it up.

'He did, but not in the way I expected.' He heaved a sigh. 'He sent my mother flowers.'

'Your mother? Flowers?'

'And a helpful note telling her that anyone she'd seen watching the house hadn't been there for her.'

'Oh.'

'Here was I hoping that self-preservation might finally winkle her out of the house and he blew it for me. She's clinging on like a limpet.'

'The man has a talent for being annoying. Did he do it on purpose?'

'Did he think he was pissing me off? No idea. He would have to have a deeper understanding of the mother–son dynamic to get that on target. I'm guessing he thought it would smooth the way with me if he flattered her.'

'And instead he's left you feeling like you could gargle with razor blades.'

'Got any?'

I took his hand. 'You're too nice.'

'Not because I want to be! But I've tried booting her out. She always circles back round eventually. I'm afraid she'll make up claims of abuse or something if I don't give in.'

I could see the bitch mother doing that. 'OK, so we have to make it her choice to leave.'

'That's what I was hoping from her fears her ex had found her.'

An outline of an idea was beginning to take shape. 'Do you trust me?'

He took far longer than I'd hoped to answer. 'Yes. Yeah, I do.'

'Hmm, we'll have to work on that, but to be honest you're probably sensible to still have your doubts. But I have a plan for this that I think will work. Will you let me have a go?'

He gave a helpless shrug. 'Your way can't be any worse than

my efforts, but I suppose I should say I draw the line at physical force.'

I grinned. 'Trust me: I won't need it.'

This was why twenty minutes later we pulled up at his house with all my suitcases in the back and Flossie to add to the confusion.

'Ready?' I asked him, kissing his cheek.

'I am. Are you sure you know what you're doing?'

'I read Beatrix Potter properly – you only skimmed. This is Operation Make the Door Smaller: one hedgehog's solution to keeping out unwelcome guests.'

He got out and opened the boot to heft out a suitcase while I held Flossie. 'Fine, but I'd prefer it if Flossie didn't dig up the garden.'

'Don't worry, unless there are bones involved, she's pretty reliable.'

He opened the door and I unleashed Flossie – literally. She scampered around the house, ecstatic to have so many new smells to explore.

'Oh, babe, it's so cute!' I gushed in as grating a voice as I could summon. I'd watched *The Only Way Is Essex*. I knew how to make my voice carry over the squeals of other girls.

The door to the kitchen opened and Flossie shot inside. A woman shrieked.

'Oh, get down, Flossie,' I said limply. 'Don't jump up at the old lady!'

'Where do you want the bags?' Leo asked, grinning at my 'old lady' crack.

'The spare room will do. I'm sure your mother won't mind us being all girls together.' I turned to give her a saccharine smile. 'Hello, Mrs Keene. Nice to meet you. I'm Jessie, a friend of Leo's, and this is Junior.' I rested my hand lightly on the pillow-bump I had beneath my most voluminous tunic dress.

'You're expecting?' She shot a look at Leo.

'That's right. Though you won't be a grandmother just yet, don't worry.' I gave a little tinkle of laughter. 'Leo's not the baby daddy. That's Trev, but he's a bastard so I moved out.'

She was still fending off Flossie's interested nose. 'I see.'

She really didn't. 'Leo, being such a sweetie, stepped in to help as I have nowhere else to go. Without him I don't know what I would do. Tre—Trev would kill me!' I gave a sniff and buried my face in Leo's chest. He patted my back awkwardly.

'There, there, Jess.' I squeezed him. '*Jessie*. Why don't we put the kettle on and you can settle yourself? Getting upset isn't good for the baby.'

I lowered myself carefully into one of the kitchen chairs, remembering what my sister was like when she was expecting her children. I'd made jokes about providing her with a beep and a 'this vehicle is reversing' announcement. I patted the spot opposite me. 'Why don't you sit down, Mrs Keene. You look tired.' There! That was one of the worst insults to give a woman. 'Tell me all about yourself and then I'll tell you all about Trev and the baby.' I gave a pleased sigh. 'It's so nice to find another mother in the house. I feel so unprepared. I bet you felt that way when you had Leo,

326

didn't you?' She opened her mouth but I didn't give her the chance to reply. 'And your experience is going to be so helpful. I wouldn't know where to start with nappies, colic, breast feeding, and getting up in the night when the baby cries.' I leaned a little forward then realised that wasn't a good idea with the cushion in the way. 'I hope you sleep deeply because there's going to be some nights when I won't be able to get the little terror to sleep. All the baby books tell me so. Maybe earplugs would work? What did you do about night crying?'

'Yeah, what did you do, Mum?' asked Leo a little acerbically, throwing a teabag in a pot. He needed to chill or she might smell a rat.

'I just put up with it,' she said tersely. 'Leo was a difficult baby.'

I nodded sagely, though I wanted to scratch out her eyes. I had no doubt that this mother played the dependent in all her relationships, and probably had hated every moment of the early years before the child could do something for her. Everything Leo had told me about her made sense now I'd met her. 'They mostly are, especially first ones, according to the books. I think they pick up on your inexperience and run you ragged. I'm so pleased you'll be around to stop me making those kinds of mistakes. And babysitting! Oh, I've just realised! Leo said you didn't have a job. I can pay you to babysit so I can attend my rehearsals.'

'Rehearsals for what?' She was looking at me as if I were a maniac.

'I play in an orchestra. Didn't Leo mention me at all?'

'He doesn't tell me anything,' she spat.

'Oh you!' I gently nudged Leo. 'He might've been a bit embarrassed for me. People often are.'

'Because you're a single mother?' she asked with a bite.

'No! Lord, what century do you think we're in! Because I play the ukulele.' A detail too far?

Leo's snort that became a cough suggested it might be, but it was the only instrument I could play in a half-arsed way if I had to carry on with this disguise. No going back, I was committed now.

'In fact my orchestra is the biggest ukulele ensemble in the country. We've got YouTube recordings and everything. Do you want to see them?' I typed in a random ukulele post and let it start playing.

She got up abruptly. 'Leo, can I have a word?'

He put a cup of tea in front of me and then rested his hand on my bump. 'Hey, did I feel him move?'

I rested my hand over his. 'Little starfish. All prodding limbs at eight months. Getting himself head down ready for launch day.'

'Leo!' said Mrs Keene, going to the door.

'Be right back, beautiful.' He kissed the top of my head, mixing the signals so that if his mother thought he was just doing a favour without his emotions being involved then she would be wrong.

'Don't be long. I wanted to discuss redecorating the spare room as a nursery!' I called after him.

From the hushed but furious tones in the hallway I could tell that our plan was working wonderfully.

'Just a bit of babysitting. She won't expect much,' I heard Leo argue.

'I'm not changing fucking nappies! Or sharing a bedroom with a baby!' With me out of sight, the gloves were off.

'She's a friend; she's in trouble; there's an unborn life involved; I'm her only fallback.'

'But I'm your responsibility – I came before her!' whined the woman I hesitated to call a 'mother'. She was the one acting like a child.

'But as you told me yourself on the phone, the flowers prove it was a false alarm. You have no one hunting you down. You're free to leave.'

'Aargh!'

'Look, she's not my girlfriend and you are staying in my twin-bed spare room. You'll just have to make room for a few days until you can make other arrangements. But no one is asking you to leave now. In fact, Jessie said she was really happy you were here and looks forward to making friends.'

'I don't want to be friends with that slut!'

From Leo's silence I could tell he was finding it harder to deal with that insult. 'She is a much-loved friend, Mother. She is not a slut. And if you are implying that having a child out of wedlock makes her one, then have you looked in the mirror recently?'

The silence that fell was broken by sobs. That meant she was playing her last few cards. We were almost through this. I patted bump Junior in congratulations for playing his part so well.

'You never loved me – never cared for me. I'm your mother!' Her voice took on a fiercer tone. 'You owe me!'

'Owe you for giving birth? No, that's not how it works.' He stopped there but I could tell he was thinking that what he got landed with as his parent proved that.

Her tone was now injured pride. 'I can't stay here with her.'

Score. I hoped Leo would handle the next bit diplomatically. Looking too eager to get rid of her might well swing her the other way. Fortunately, he stuck to the script we'd planned.

'That's a pity. I thought it might make life at home work better with another woman around. You'd have someone to talk to, someone to help who needs you.'

'I'm not a nanny.'

'No one thinks you are. But families muck in, don't they? We can all take turns. It takes a village.'

There was another silence and Flossie whined. I gave her a neck rub so she didn't interrupt at a crucial moment.

'I can't put up with this. I'm going.' Haven was crumbling.

'If you feel you must then my offer still stands. I'll give you some money for a train ticket and a few nights in a hotel somewhere of your choice. I'll run you to the station tomorrow.'

Ah no, that would give her time to regroup. 'Hey, Leo honey,' I called, 'would you mind rubbing my back? These Braxton Hicks contractions are really painful.'

'Coming, Jessie.'

'You don't think it's early onset labour, do you?' I asked as they came back in, hoping I sounded spooked. 'Mrs Keene, do you know the signs?'

'No, I don't!' said the woman shortly. 'I would appreciate if you would drive me to the station tonight, Leo. I'll take the train to Reading.'

'OK. Good choice,' said Leo. 'It's only thirty minutes by train and there're lots of hotels near the station. I've got the cash.' We'd stopped at a cashpoint on the way over, hoping for this result.

'I'll just pack my bags then.' She sniffed, probably trying to turn on more waterworks to sway him to her side.

I gave a muffled groan. 'Ow! That hurts.'

'Yeah, OK,' said Leo. 'That's if you don't want to stay and see if Jessie is all right? You'd be very welcome to help us out tonight. It's scary doing this the first time and I have to admit I've not a clue what I'm doing. I mean, you get first-aid training as a police officer but that was a while ago for me. You all right, Jessie?'

I gave another groan. 'I think so. I hope so. Is it normal for a tummy to tighten like a drum?'

He led his mother to the bottom of the stairs. 'I'd better go and comfort her. You get your things together and give me a call when you're ready for me to carry them down.'

He re-entered the kitchen, closed the door and did a very unLeolike boogie. I shushed him. She could burst in any moment and the jig would be up. He grinned and came over to put his hands around me.

'How's baby?' he crooned.

'Feeling stuffed.'

He snorted into my neck, then whispered. 'I can't believe it's working.'

'I can. What is kryptonite for a narcissistic personality?

331

Having to help someone else. What's the most demanding person in the world? A tiny baby with no idea of the difference between day or night. They can't be talked out of their needs, or told to button it, they make their wants known. Even the most determined narcissist can't beat that.'

He huffed. 'Believe me, I wouldn't have said any of that about her staying if a real kid was involved. Fucking up one child is enough for her.'

'You're not fucked up,' I told him. 'You're a miracle of the powers of human survival.'

There was a shout from upstairs. 'Leo!'

'Hold that thought.' He kissed my neck. 'I believe I have someone to deliver to the station – and then I'll be right back.'

Once the car left the drive, I shimmied out of Junior and left him on the kitchen chair. Next I had a little wander around Leo's house. I told myself it was to check his mother had taken everything but it was really because it's a side of my nature I can't shake. I'm like the cat that circles before sitting on a lap. It was a nice cottage but Leo hadn't done much to stamp his own personality on it. The rooms were magnolia and beige, not many pictures on the walls but quite a few books on the shelves. He didn't even have the lad set-up of large-screen TV and gaming station, owning instead a medium-sized screen and set top box. I switched on and found it tuned to BBC News. I guessed he didn't watch much TV. I opened the back door, grabbing a torch from the ledge placed there for just this purpose. Everyone who knew Leo even a little realised that he was all about his garden. I could wait until he showed me but again . . .

I made my way down the path that snaked away from the door. I saw at once that this was no boring gravel or concrete paver construction. It was hard to see in the dark but kneeling I could feel the cold, riven surface of slate slabs, surrounded by dark blue pebbles. Water from the melting snow trickled down a little gulley that wove among the stones. He'd made his path a stream – so clever. When wet, they must shine almost navy blue in the daylight.

I was beginning to feel guilty that I was preempting Leo from giving me the tour so I only went as far as the first bench. This sat alongside a large pond, inky dark under the trees but catching the light from the stars and an occasional passing plane where it was open to the skies. A ripple-ring started at one end, then again nearer to me. Switching the light off, I let my eyes adjust. There was something in the pool – something big. A flash of a white fin confirmed it.

Leo's footsteps alerted me to his approach.

'Why have you got a baby shark in your pond?' I asked him.

He sat beside me and took my hand. 'It's a Koi carp. I call him Goldemort.'

I scooted round and straddled him. 'You called your carp Goldemort?'

He shrugged, looking a little sheepish. 'Seemed fitting because he kept killing off all his followers.'

I began unbuttoning his coat.

'What are you doing, Jess?'

'I'm having my way with you, Leo. I can't stand it any longer. A guy who has a fish called after one of my favourite baddies definitely gets shagged.'

'There's a nice warm bed inside.' His voice rose a little as my cold fingers reached his trousers.

'Shut up and kiss me.' I pressed my lips to his as my hands parted our clothing. I realised I'd been putting this off for the perfect moment but that wasn't me. I didn't do scented candles and rose petals on Egyptian cotton sheets. An exuberant quickie on a garden bench was absolutely my kind of first time. 'You'd better keep me warm.' I ripped off my outer layers until I was wearing only socks and underwear. Even I'm not so impulsive as to surrender socks on a December night.

'God, yes, I'll keep you warm.' He undid my bra strap and dropped it on the ground. 'I think I just fed your bra to Goldemort. Sorry.'

'Lucky fish. Say you're sorry by telling me you've got a condom somewhere.'

'Trouser pocket.'

I groped for it. 'There's a good Boy Scout.' I helpfully retrieved it from him and suited him up. 'Ready?'

'Oh yes.' He moved my panties aside and drove up inside me. I laughed. It felt so fantastic. This is what we both needed.

'Let's do this in every part . . . of your garden, Leo.' I got a nice rhythm going. All thoughts of being cold were banished, though the contrast between the furnace I was sitting on and the night air made for a sensational ride.

'Agreed.'

'And every garden we ever visit.'

'Anything – yes.'

I was going to make a joke about disgracing ourselves at National Trust Properties but words failed me. I was getting close, limbs going liquid. This was going to be fast and furious – every single film in the franchise in one orgasmic hit. Feeling me falter, he took over and gave a few last thrusts and we both came together. Yes, it had been quick, but it had also been one of the most beautiful sexual encounters I'd ever had.

I slumped forward, head resting on his neck. His skin had a smooth spot just below his ear which I kissed and nuzzled. 'I think I might love you, Leo. You know, like properly love you?'

He wrapped his coat around us both. 'I think I might love you properly too, Jess.'

'Now we've warmed up, what was that about a bed?'

Laughing, he scooped me up and carried me back into the house.

Chapter 37

Leo

The warrant came through on Monday morning. Leo stood in front of the whiteboard in the conference room, his team perched on desks or standing at the back. It was only seven, but they wanted to be knocking on doors before people were heading out for the day. It was good that he was feeling full of energy after one of the best weekends of his life. From the excited buzz in the room, he knew his biggest challenge was keeping his team under control as they were raring to go, thinking they were nearing the killer. Harry was already fuelled up with coffee and snacking on some Danish pastries with some of the older uniforms. They were liable to encourage each other negatively if Leo didn't set the tone.

'OK, everyone. Thank you for being prompt. As you will know as you've all worked with me before, we're doing this operation by dotting all i's and crossing all t's. No one wants to be the reason why a conviction fails.' He scanned the room for any signs of rebellion. Only Harry's group were shifting their gaze to each other. Normally you'd expect the younger officers to be unreliable; in this group the reverse was true.

'Our target is retired so we can expect both him and his wife to be at their residence this morning. Sergeant Boston, you're with me in interview; Sergeant Wong will lead the search.'

A hand was raised from a young female officer. 'What are we after, sir?'

At a nod from him, Suyin answered, looking down at the list they'd generated. 'We are looking in particular for firearms, garden tools and anything that connects Price to either of our victims. I'll give each of you a more detailed list.'

'Is that clear?' asked Leo.

There were murmurs of agreement.

'The period of time elapsed since the murders were committed poses particular difficulties for forensic evidence but we do have the unsolved break-in from just a week ago to follow up. Dark clothing, boots and axes are also to be bagged and tagged. Price is a person of interest to the enquiry at this stage, not charged with any crime, so please treat him and Mrs Price with utmost courtesy.'

'I'll show him fucking courtesy as I handcuff him,' said Harry in an undertone.

'That's exactly the attitude I don't want taken onto the scene this morning,' said Leo, steel in his voice. 'This isn't optional. Anyone unable to conform to the rules had better sit this out back here. I've plenty of paperwork to keep them occupied.'

Harry looked down.

'Understood, Sergeant?'

'Yes, Inspector,' Harry muttered.

Leo left it at that. He'd probably pay for it later, on some other case, but Harry was usually fine when in interview with him. He was playing to his crowd rather than fomenting a revolt. Leo had decided that taking him as his interview partner was safer than leaving him on site as he wasn't the best person to deal with someone from an ethnic minority like Mrs Price.

The team went in three unmarked police cars. No need to tip off the neighbourhood and cause undue embarrassment, Leo reasoned, if Price turned out to be innocent.

Pulling up out front, Leo led the charge up the garden path. He rang the bell and, after a moment, Mrs Price answered the door in a dressing gown which she was still tying around her waist.

'Inspector, it's a bit early for you, isn't it?' Her smile faltered when she saw the team gathering behind him. 'What's going on?'

'Mrs Price, I have here a warrant to search your property. Is Mr Price at home?'

She looked down at the paper he handed her, bewildered. 'No, he's walking Amelia. He'll be back shortly. But this is outrageous!' She was regaining her footing. 'You can't just waltz in here!'

'I understand this is upsetting but new evidence has come to light concerning the murders that we're investigating. The warrant gives us the right to carry out the search.'

She didn't step aside. 'If you'd just wait for Al. I don't know if you're allowed to do this. I've never been in this position before.'

'I've explained the situation, Mrs Price. If you have any

doubts, read the warrant. Now, please move aside, so we can do our job.'

She stepped back and tried to close the door, but Leo put his foot in the way.

'I'm just going to get dressed,' she said stiffly.

He noted that she already had her jewellery on and her make-up applied. Was the dressing gown a deliberate pose? If Price was already out walking, perhaps she was already dressed? It was easy to imagine the Prices as early risers. 'And my female colleague will accompany you.'

Suyin moved past him. 'Let's go upstairs, Mrs Price. The more you cooperate with this process, the quicker we can be.'

Content that vital evidence wasn't being disposed of by the householder, Leo turned to Harry.

'Take a tour of the local streets in the direction of University Parks, see if you can find Price. Amelia is their little sausage dog so they should be easy to spot.'

With a nod, Harry headed off in one of the cars with a uniformed colleague.

Leo joined the search team on the ground floor. He had not expected to have an opportunity to look himself, but he took it as a chance to piece together the Prices' travels with the RAF prior to moving to Oxford. If his theory was right, Al had come across Anatoly Chernov long before the Russian moved to Oxford. Helpfully, the mounted photos provided a good record of the man's career, many of them showing various cricket teams made up of expats including Al as wicket keeper. There was one of him climbing Everest on a posting to Nepal, and another standing by a light aircraft on some jungle airstrip, very much the explorer in his beige shorts and short-sleeved shirt. He had been an active man, and probably found life in Oxford far too staid if he thought Everest the kind of challenge he needed.

So which came first? Berlin, Leo thought. After Germany, there was Hong Kong in the 1990s at the same time as the handover from Britain to China. Then Sierra Leone in 2000 with several shots of what looked like an embassy wedding judging from the Union Jacks in the background. Brussels – that had probably been a NATO posting. South Africa. Price had had a fascinating career. No Russian posting, not that he had on his wall at any rate, but an international businessman like Chernov could easily have coincided at one of these points on the globe.

Leo took a few photos to build the career timeline in his head, then went back to the Prices' wedding photo. There were several of the happy couple with their close family, but his eye was caught by the group shot taken on the steps of the embassy. It was a huge group, possible almost two hundred guests from all nations. There was a splendid collection of African shirts and dresses from Meredith's side of the family. In contrast to them, the international businessmen looked very plain, foils to some glowing local jewels. He wanted to see the faces, though, and not the clothes. He didn't have a magnifying glass to hand but he had the next best thing. He took several shots of the line-up on his phone, then enlarged the image on the screen. He couldn't be a hundred percent certain but two of the faces standing together at the back could belong to his victims. This wasn't a good enough resolution to be sure, but he'd add wedding photos to the list of things they should check. There might be more images of the reception that would remove all doubt.

And again it was something to ask Al Price once he was in interview.

A slight wheeze announced Harry was just behind him. His sergeant needed urgently to look to his fitness. However, he must've been successful for he had the dog on a lead.

'I've got Price in the car, Inspector. He's not happy with you. Do you want me to take him to the station and start the paperwork?'

Leo nodded. 'What do you think of this?' He pointed to the two men in the second to back row. Chernov and Gulom about twenty years ago?' Both men bore more resemblance to their surviving sons now rather than their last passport photos.

'Could well be our vics. Interesting.' Harry handed over the lead. 'See you back at base.'

'I'll be right behind you.' Shooing the dog into the kitchen, Leo shut the door on her and took the photo from the wall. There might be better images, but this would do for now.

'Mr Price, would you like to engage the services of a solicitor at this stage?' Leo asked politely, placing the photo by his chair in the interview room.

The question unnerved Price. 'I'm not under arrest, am I? Your man said it was to answer questions.'

Leo poured them both a cup of water. 'He was correct. You're not under arrest at this time.'

'If that's the case then I won't be needing representation this morning. I have nothing to hide.'

A lawyer would have told him that everyone had plenty they should hide in interview, no matter how innocent, but he wasn't going to make his own life difficult by telling Price that. 'Excellent. And Sergeant Boston has read you your rights? Though you are not under arrest, this interview is being held under caution. Do you understand that?'

'Yes, Inspector. I'm not a stupid man.' Price clenched his jaw and a little muscle ticked in his cheek.

But he was a hot-tempered one, it would seem. Pride and arrogance could be used against him.

'Good. Then I'll proceed with my questions.'

'You do that, Inspector.' Al Price sat back in his chair and folded his arms, not liking to cede control. His greying brown hair was a little dishevelled, not having been combed since his dog walk, his blue-grey eyes arctic. 'You won't hear the last of this – hauling me in here like this. I know your superiors. I've friends in County Hall.'

'And Superintendent Thaxted is aware we are talking this morning.' Leo opened his file on the case. The top sheet showed the floor plan of the red house.

Price swallowed. 'Is this all the thanks I get for years of service to my country and local community? To be dragged through the mud because you can't solve the crimes?'

'Mr Price, it would help the smooth running of this interview if you waited for me to ask my questions rather than making statements of your own.' Leo waited.

Price gave a jerky nod. 'Fire away, Inspector.'

'The main reason we brought you in here this morning is that, at our first meeting just after Anatoly Chernov's body was discovered, you claimed to be on friendly terms with your neighbour, but just as nodding acquaintances. Is that correct?'

Price seemed fascinated by the diagram of the red house in the file. It was an effort for him to look away. What did he see when he looked at that? The house where he'd killed someone? 'I said we were friends, yes. But we didn't live in each other's pockets.'

'In the same interview you had difficulty recalling the name of the owner of the red house in Howell Street until your wife reminded you of the planning battle over his swimming pool. Is that correct?'

'Yes, it had momentarily slipped my mind.'

'You made no mention during that interview that only last year you had begun another local campaign against Akmal Gulom's attempt to change the use of his house from single occupancy to student accommodation.'

Price put one hand on the desk, the other dipped into his pocket. 'I'd forgotten. That was all.'

'That seems out of character for you to forget because you spent the night of Monday, the 5th of November last year gathering names for a petition to be delivered to Gulom in person. I would've thought that was pretty memorable. Your society secretary documented those few days when you started the petition, beginning with the local fireworks displays on the Sunday to your social event on Guy Fawkes Night itself.'

'Paul's always taking photos,' he said dismissively. 'He must have years of the things.'

344

'But he also carefully notes times and place. We have a photo of you doorstepping Gulom to present the petition with the time stamp of 8.30pm on the 5th of November.'

'That's probably correct then. The application didn't go any further so I'd forgotten it.' He touched the cup but didn't drink, turning it on the table. He looked up, not quite meeting Leo's eye. 'Inspector, do you know how many planning applications we are fighting right now? I'll tell you: thirty! Every cowboy developer wants to be part of the Oxford property boom. Even governments are getting in the act with the Chinese trying to turn one of the Banbury Road houses into their cultural centre. Cultural centre! They trying to spy on us under the pretence of serving tea. They'll probably use it to steal the university's intellectual property if given half a chance. Someone has to stop them! The council is spineless without us to force them to keep Oxford, Oxford.'

Leo let him fume for a few more Sinophobic utterances before intervening. Evidently Price's years in Hong Kong hadn't turned him into an admirer of the Chinese regime.

'If we can get back on track, Mr Price? So to sum up your relationship with the two men, is your earlier statement still accurate: that you barely knew Anatoly Chernov, and didn't remember Gulom?'

Price inspected his shirt cuffs. He had silver cufflinks with his initials engraved on them. 'That's about right.'

'When did you meet both men for the first time?'

'Oh, not sure really. Who remembers things like that?'

'Where did you meet them first?'

'As I think I told you, Anatoly and I possibly crossed paths in Berlin way back.'

He'd actually said they were on opposites sides of the Wall and implied they'd not met. 'And afterwards?'

'He may have coincided again a few times at the same parties and whatnot.' Price gave Leo a sour look. 'Stuck here in Thames Valley Police you probably don't realise that the international expat community is in practice relatively small – all of us moving around the same capital cities, going to the same drinks parties. Paths cross and re-cross. But the first time I remember having a proper conversation with Anatoly was here in Oxford when he moved in.'

'And Gulom?'

'Possibly ran across him at school events. One has to show willing, you know? The wife likes her job.'

'So you first met him through St Bede's?'

'Really, Inspector, I don't remember.'

Leo lifted the wedding picture out of the evidence bag. The fury in Price's expression was unmistakable. 'I removed this from your house this morning. Do you recognise it?'

'I do.'

'For the record, would you tell us what it shows.'

'Oh for God's sake, Inspector!'

'Mr Price?'

'It shows my wedding day in September 2000. My wife and I got married at the High Commission in Freetown.'

'How many guests were there at your wedding?'

'I forget exact numbers. You'd need my wife for that.'

'Roughly?'

'Around two hundred and twenty.'

'Friends and family? Everyone had to have an invitation?'

'What are you implying, Inspector?'

'Stuck here in Thames Valley, I would still find it highly unlikely that a member of the public could walk into a wedding reception held on the grounds of the British Embassy.'

'High Commission,' snarled Price. 'Get your terms right!'

'High Commission. That implies that you had to have invited everyone. There's probably even a record of the guest list if the Foreign Office dug back through its files for us.'

Price kept silent.

'I'd like you to look at the two men on the far left of the second row to the back of the crowd. Who are these men, Mr Price?'

He glanced down. 'You've got better eyesight than me if you can see their faces. Two men in suits.'

'We're bringing your photo collection in for a closer look, Mr Price. It would be better for you if you don't withhold information which will only come out later – today from your own photos, or in a few days once the FCO has looked back through security records.'

He didn't like that. He scowled at the photo as if he wanted to set light to it. 'I can't tell who they are. The picture isn't clear enough.'

He was sticking with that, was he?

'Is it possible that the two mystery men among the guests at your own wedding are Anatoly Chernov and Akmal Gulom?'

He shrugged. 'It's possible Meredith's family might've invited them if they were doing business in Freetown. I don't recall them being there. I only had eyes for my wife that day.'

'Oh, I think they were there – and I think you were better friends with both of them, certainly with Anatoly Chernov, than you have admitted. You were very good friends and that was one of the reasons why he moved to Oxford for his children's schooling, at the school your wife recommended. Now that makes me wonder: why aren't you telling us the full story?'

'What are you implying, Inspector?'

'I'm not implying; I'm asking you to confirm or deny. Were you friends with Anatoly Chernov in Freetown?'

'We possibly met. Once or twice. Our wedding was a big event. Almost the entire business community came. I don't know half of the people in that photo.'

'Were you in business with him?'

'I was in the RAF, Inspector. I've never been in business.'

'No? Not even as a sideline? Your wife's family had connections to diamond producers. Anatoly's business dealings remain opaque but we know he was at one time dealing in diamonds. Akmal Gulom was an expert diamond merchant. We've been told they were business partners for many years. Can you see how that sounds like a great team to do a little diamond trading? You and your wife had diplomatic immunity so were not subject to the same kind of checks as ordinary travellers. No one would fault you if you augmented your pension with a little buying and selling as long as the diamonds came from reputable sources.'

'I haven't bought or sold a single diamond in my life!'

'No? Not even for your wife?'

'Obviously for her wedding rings, but other than that, no! I never earned that kind of money, Inspector.'

'And yet you live in a large house in one of the most expensive parts of the country side-by-side with millionaires.'

'It's my family's home, Inspector. It's not a sin to inherit your wealth, though maybe people like you think it is?'

'People like me?' Leo turned to Harry. 'Do you know what he means?'

'I've got my own ideas,' Harry grinned.

'Left-leaning *Guardian* readers, of course!' scoffed Price. 'The kind who have let our country go to the dogs and think it fine to sell off the family silver to fund sex-change operations on the NHS! The country has gone mad.'

'*The Guardian*? I always had you down as a reader of the *Socialist Worker*, Inspector,' said Harry.

And that was why Leo still put up with Harry despite everything.

'You must've been incensed that the good friends you invited to live near you turned against you. You realised you'd brought the enemy within the gates, didn't you, when you found them trying to change the area you love to fit their own more flamboyant tastes?' said Leo. 'No wonder you fought the planning applications so bitterly. You were to blame.'

'I bear no responsibility for their ignorance,' said Price. 'I did my duty.'

'By killing them?'

'I won't dignify that with an answer.'

A constable entered and handed Leo an update on the

search. He gave it a quick scan. Suyin and team had found what he needed.

'Well, that certainly changes things.' He passed the note to Harry. 'Mr Price, my team have discovered an ice axe, ski mask and black boots with what appear to be minute pieces of glass embedded in the treads, in the attic at your home address. When we run our tests, will we find the glass matches that in the window of the red house – the same window broken by a masked intruder a week ago on Sunday?'

Price stared straight ahead, eyes fixed on the wall behind them. With this new evidence, Leo could see that he was going the full 'name, rank and service number' routine on them. 'I have nothing more to say without a solicitor present.'

Leo rose. 'In which case, interview end at 10.38. Alfred Price, I am arresting you on suspicion of breaking and entering 37 Howell Street, the property known as the red house. Other charges may follow.' He continued with the rest of the required wording to ensure there was no legal loophole for the man to crawl through. 'Sergeant Boston, please escort Mr Price to the cells. He can phone a solicitor from there.'

'Right you are, Inspector. Come along, sir. Let's get you sorted.' Harry took Price by his upper arm.

Price marched out, straight back, proud tilt of the chin, looking like he was the aggrieved party.

Leo glanced back down at the list of items the team had removed so far. They might have Price on the break-in, but they didn't have him yet on the murders. There was still much to be done.

Chapter 38

Jess

'Is this your doing?' Paul thrust his phone in front of my eyes, a message from Meredith on the screen.

'What?' I looked up from the schedule for the interview candidates who were currently loitering like lost souls in the college. Jennifer waggled her eyebrows at me in a 'what the heck?' gesture. I shrugged.

'Your lover' – he spat the word like it was an insult rather than a lovely fact – 'has arrested Al Price.'

Trying to banish memories of our pondside lovemaking, I focused on the distraught message from Meredith. There had been a search and her husband had disappeared with the police. Next thing she knew she was being told he was arrested and held for further questioning.

'Poor Meredith. No, I didn't know anything about it. I guess Leo is just doing his job.'

'He's barking up the wrong tree if he thinks Al would do anything like this.' Paul attacked the nearest thermos flask, trying to pump some coffee into his cup. We'd already served the contents to the pale-faced youngsters as they accepted their briefing pack for interview. Jennifer got up and removed the empty flask to start a new one.

'Here you are, Paul. Why don't you sit down for a moment? You've had a shock.' She offered him her desk chair.

'And I thought I was helping by sending the inspector my photos! Instead he's using them to frame an innocent man.'

Ah. Now was not the moment to mention my part in that. 'I'm sure no one is framing anyone for a crime, Paul. What's Mr Price been charged with?'

'Breaking and entering. Even they aren't so stupid as to charge him with killing anyone! But you can tell the police it wasn't Al, can't you? You were the only witness. They'll have to believe you.' So that was why he'd come storming in to see me. He thought I'd exonerate his friend if he browbeat me sufficiently.

'I've already made my statement, Paul. The intruder was masked and carrying some kind of little pickaxe. I gave them rough height and build but they must have more than my description to go on if they feel confident enough to make an arrest.'

'Do you think it could've been him, Jess?' Jennifer asked, intrigued.

'It could've been – I can't confirm either way. He's about the right height.' And I thought of the missing files and petition that would've linked Al to being to see Gulom around the time he was murdered. Why take the petition away if not to destroy the proof? Maybe that was the reason he'd broken in?

But no, the timing didn't work. I'd not seen the files even

before that and my habit of nosing through other people's things made it unlikely that I would've overlooked them in the home filing cabinet. Their disappearance predated my job.

'Maybe he did break in, Paul,' Jennifer said gently, 'but maybe there's a good explanation. Maybe he thought Jess was at risk in some way?' That was stretching it, Jennifer, but I had to remember that the intruder had completely bypassed any chance to hurt me. I could give Paul that comfort.

'Whoever the intruder was, he meant me no harm. I was standing there with no weapon of my own and he ran away rather than attack me.'

Paul tried to fold this new idea into his reasoning. 'Jennifer makes a good point. No violence. Al and some of the other men do patrol the area when they're worried for us. Yes, yes, I must tell her to pass this on to their solicitor. Maybe someone else broke in and Al saw it and came to help. He might've chased the real culprit away, then left when he saw how it would look to others to be found there. That's what must've happened.'

I rolled my eyes at Jennifer, who smiled serenely back at me. Her goal was to make the workday bearable, not solve crime.

'Are you feeling better now, Paul?' she asked.

'I am. Thank you. I'll just call Meredith. Jess, I want you to come with me this afternoon to tell her the same thing. We'll get her to bring the lawyer to the meeting.'

I held up my hands in a 'Whoa, boy' gesture. 'Hang on, Paul. This is a police investigation. I can't just go talking to the defence team.'

'But Meredith isn't charged with anything – nor is the solicitor. You would just be telling them what you already told the police.'

I looked to Jennifer for backup but she was pretending to be very busy by the filing cabinet.

'I really don't think . . .'

Sanyu chose that moment to breeze into the office. 'Ladies, Paul, how are you all today?' He swooped on the coffee. 'Errol told me where to come when I said I was gasping for a cup.'

Paul shot an angry look at me. Strictly speaking it wasn't supposed to be given to undergraduates like Errol.

'All ready for the big day?' Sanyu sat on my desk, breaking the eye-line between me and Paul. Either he sensed the tension or had impeccable instinctual timing. 'Got your tongue around a certain Governor of Syria yet?'

No, only a certain Inspector of Thames Valley. I might've quipped that if Paul hadn't been in the room. 'He's coming along,' I said instead.

Sanyu glanced between Paul and me like an umpire just catching up on a rally. 'Did I interrupt something?'

'A neighbour of ours is in a difficult place and I was asking Jess to help,' said Paul self-righteously.

'That's good: love thy neighbour. Excellent. That's what Christmas is all about.' He stirred sugar into his mug with a ringing sound. 'Anything I can do to help? I'm always happy to listen and offer what advice I can.'

Perhaps Meredith would like to be counselled by Sanyu? He had a warmth that was hard to ignore and could never be faulted for his good intentions. 'We could suggest it. She's not a member of the St Nick community.'

'But if she knows Paul and you then she's mine by extension.' Sanyu smiled at me. 'And the Good Samaritan never stopped to ask the man on the road if they were connected – in fact he knew that they weren't!'

If I didn't take action, Sanyu would treat us all to one of his little sermons on his favourite parable. 'I'll tell her to contact you if she needs to speak to a pastor.'

'See, Paul, I told you that Jess would help.' Sanyu turned to my boss and Jennifer, all right with his world.

How had that happened? I'd been backed into agreeing the very course of action I had said I would not do. It was how I ended up doing the reading all over again. Sanyu must have a super-power for gaining compliance. I gave Paul a grudging nod and went back to my work. Maybe there was silver lining. Meredith *had* come to visit me after the break-in to see I was all right. If Al was the burglar, of course, that wasn't such a nice gesture, likely calculated so that she could find out what I knew. But if they were innocent, then I had to assume she was being kind. I could reciprocate as far as calling round with Sanyu's name for her. That would satisfy Paul and my conscience. No interviews outside police procedures though. I'd put my foot down over that even if Paul did haul a solicitor over this afternoon. I'd just walk away.

Paul was waiting already in his winter coat as I switched off my computer at five.

'I'm not talking to a lawyer,' I stressed, wrapping my long scarf three times around my neck.

'But you'll at least talk to Meredith, set her mind at rest?'

I didn't know if I could do that. The intruder could've been her husband and I couldn't believe Jennifer's suggestion that he'd rushed in to save me. With a pickaxe and a mask? That was taking local vigilante to absurd extremes. 'I'll say a few words, but that's it. No interviews or statements.'

When we arrived at the Prices' house, we were both dismayed to see the news crews that had gathered on the pavement outside. The news of Al Price's arrest must be out.

'Vultures! Keep walking,' whispered Paul. 'There's a way in around the back.'

Gripping my arm, he hustled me to his own apartment building and took me through the garden. It was an oddly shaped piece of land that did a little bend round to some sheds at the back and ran down behind the properties, including the Prices'. Al's book on the area had told me that Paul's house had been the original big house in the area; as the family had faded in wealth and importance, it had sold off parcels of land for the homes to be developed by the Victorian speculators, which explained the irregular plot.

'We'll check the studio first,' Paul said. 'She rents it from us.'

I just let him lead, which was how he preferred to operate. I did rattle off a quick text to Leo though:

Fun fact, Leo. Did you know Meredith has a studio on St Nick's land? I'm going there with Paul to check she's OK.

We reached the sheds before Leo had had a chance to reply. I could hear the sound of a machine whirring inside and remembered Meredith's conversation about her hobby as a jewellery maker.

356

'She's here?'

'Wouldn't you be if you had the press camped on your door and the police tromping through your house? I know she comes here to escape.' He knocked on the door. 'Meredith, it's Paul. How are you bearing up?'

The door opened a crack. Looking past her I could see a workbench with a powerful angle poise lamp illuminating a little vice that held a silver pendant. Papers were piled on the bench standing next to a shredder. That was the machine I'd heard.

Then I had one of those moments when the pieces tumbled into place. It had been flashing in front of my eyes like her rings. Meredith was the one interested in diamonds. She was the one whose family dealt in the gems. This wasn't Al's scheme, it was hers.

'Paul?' Meredith sounded teary. 'Oh, and Jess?' The tears dried up when she saw me. She opened the door wide, revealing the gun in her hand. 'That is unfortunate.'

Chapter 39

Leo

At the press conference, the media were delighted to get the scoop that a fifty-nine-year-old man was helping them with their enquiries so they gave Leo a relatively friendly reception. He'd been at these before when they had made him feel that a lack of progress was entirely his fault rather than the consequence of the difficulty of a case.

'Do you think the person you have in custody killed those two men?' the *Oxford Mail* reporter asked.

'He is not charged with that at this time,' Leo said.

'Is his motive hatred of non-dom owners of Oxford houses as some have been speculating?' Though Price's identity had not been made public, it looked like the local rag had got its own sources and begun adding two and two to make fifty-five.

'No comment.'

But he could guess the direction the press was now going to take. Non-domestic owners of second homes in the UK had become a favourite target for national dislike. They'd probably end up making it sound like the victims' fault for daring to live here, inflating property prices for everyone. They needed reminding of the humans behind the labels.

'It is inappropriate to say any more and I would be grateful if you would be responsible in how your report this and stick with the facts we have given you. Our enquiries are ongoing. I reiterate, there have been no charges made in relation to the murder of either of the victims. Mr Gulom leaves behind a wife and son; Mr Chernov, a son and two daughters. Our intention is to get justice for them and find out who killed them.' Leo looked to his right where his superintendent was presiding in the central seat. 'I have nothing else to add at this stage.'

Fortunately, this was one of those cases where Superintendent Thaxted stepped up to protect him.

'Thank you, everyone. You can pick up a hard copy of our statement from the communications liaison officer but that's it for now. We must let Inspector George return to his duties.'

With the green light given, Leo escaped. Claire would stay behind to talk in the margins because she actually enjoyed playing politics. That was why it was her rather than him in the big chair and he had no regrets.

Back at his desk, he checked in with Price. The officer in charge of the cells said that he'd been with his solicitor for an hour now. Did Leo want him brought up for more questioning?

Leo stood up to get the attention of the officers still hard at work processing what they'd gleaned from the scene. 'Anyone got anything new from this morning to report?'

No one volunteered anything. He sat down. He had quite a few more hours to hold Price but he'd prefer to have some more physical evidence to confront him with before returning to interview. The lab was processing the ice axe and the clothing but that would still take at least until tomorrow before the results were known.

He checked his inbox. The medical examiner had got back already. He'd asked her to see if the dimensions of the axe worked as the murder weapon on Akmal Gulom. Opening the message, he found his hopes dashed. The ice axe had a serrated blade for cutting notches in snow. There was no trace of this on the skull. She preferred a conventional pickaxe or a tool like a cross pein hammer – the technical name for the kind with a pointed side.

Leo knew his garden tools but not his DIY kit. He ran a search for the hammer and found it came in many hobbyist sets and for carpenters. Nothing like it had come out of the tool box confiscated from the Prices' house. He went back into the room where they had laid out the evidence for registering by the officer in charge of storing them. No cross pein hammer there.

He stopped in front of the wedding photo again, lingering over the faces at the front. The best man looked familiar from one of the other photos he'd seen in the house, the one of the cricket team in Hong Kong, thanks to his shock of ginger hair. He swiped back through his photos and enlarged the shot. The names were included under the photos to identify team mates. Lieutenant Colonel A. E. Lees.

He put a call through to an old university friend who now worked in the MOD.

'Leo, to what do I owe the pleasure?' asked Freddie, picking up on the third ring.

'It's about a case I'm working on.'

'It's always about a case you're working on. When are we going to get you up in town for a night out with the gang? And we've not seen you at our reunions for a few years.'

Leo didn't think he'd ever been to the annual weekend away, not being the reunion type. But maybe, if he could bring Jess, he'd change that policy. 'When's the next one?'

'We're having a little house party in the Cotswolds in February. Not usually much happening then, but we might get lucky with an early spring. Significant others welcome. I'll send you the details.'

'Thanks.'

'How can I help you?'

'I'm trying to trace a lieutenant colonel called A.E. Lees. How would I go about locating him? He was in the diplomatic side of things in 2000 but I don't know if he's still in the service or retired.'

'Let me check.' Freddie tapped away at his computer. 'Yep, he's approaching retirement but still with us. On the RAF base Brize Norton in charge of training. Isn't that your patch?'

'Yes. That makes life a lot easier as they know us. Thanks, Freddie.'

Freddie cleared his throat. 'Oh, er, I thought you might like to know that Janice is single again. She'll be at the weekend.'

Janice and Leo had dated briefly in Durham. He'd liked her more than she'd liked him so match-making Freddie thought it possible Leo might still had a weakness for their glamorous friend.

'Thanks but I've just started seeing someone from Oxford.

If it's still going well in February, I'll think about risking introducing her to you all.'

Freddie chuckled. 'So glad to hear that. No man is an island – or so Lauren tells me. Though now we've got three kids, I sometimes wish I had a little bit of clear water around me. Roll on the reunion weekend when we get time away on our own.'

'Thanks for the information, Freddie. Speak soon.'

Next call went through to the police contact at Brize Norton. With over seven thousand people on the base, many of them young RAF recruits, it was only sensible to have a dedicated liaison officer to smooth over any difficulties that happened off base. That officer put Leo directly through to Andrew Lees. Having been promoted, he was now Colonel Lees.

'How can I help you, Inspector?' The man had a bluff manner, the sort that indicated he didn't want to hang around with pleasantries.

'I'm looking into the background of a man known to you in Sierra Leone.'

'Good God, that shower. Most of the business community were very dodgy geezers, but that was what we had to work with. Who has crossed the path of the Thames Valley Police?'

'I'm actually interested in a colleague of yours, Alfred Price.'

'Al? Gracious, I hope nothing bad has happened to him?'

'No, he's well. I can't say too much but I'm trying to untangle some relationships he might've struck up with a couple of Russian business men – well, a Russian and an Uzbek to be exact. Anatoly Chernov and . . .'

'. . . And Akmal Gulom. Oh yes, I remember them. They had an import-export business with an office in Freetown.

The spooks were very interested in their dealings, not that I know the details, I just remember them being given the evil eye by my SIS colleagues when they turned up to embassy functions. They were invited everywhere.'

'Would they have been at Al and Meredith's wedding?'

'Oh, very likely, if they were in country for that bash. Lovely day – sun shone, but then it pretty much always did in Freetown in my memory.'

'How well would you say Al knew the pair?'

'Al? Not at all by my reckoning. That was Meredith's side – the family business was growing, exporting local goods to the new markets in the former Soviet countries. The Chinese were also moving in at that time. Lots of dubious money washing around and some of the diamonds weren't all that legit if you ask me. Plenty of conflict-ridden countries in Central and West Africa funnelling their uncut stones through grey channels, especially after the certification scheme came in. Al kept well out of it. The less he knew the better was his philosophy.'

'But Meredith knew them?'

'Oh, undoubtedly. She had done Russian at college – strange choice, going to Edinburgh to study Russian of all things. Anyway, she ran that part of the business for her father. I think she gave it up when Al retired but I know she kept it up for a while from their other postings. Her family saw her as something of a roving ambassador making contacts for them.'

'And that was allowed?'

'Good God, Inspector, HMG doesn't *stop* diplomatic spouses – there'd be a riot in the ranks if we interfered in their lawful activities. We're in a new age of spousal equality, don't you know?'

'And if these activities were unlawful?'

'Then that would be up to the country in question and you people if it happened back here, wouldn't it? Just like other citizens. And there was never a sniff of suspicion about Meredith that I heard. So, tell me, what has happened to Al?'

Leo suspected now that Al Price had found himself stuck between a rock and a hard place. His philosophy of ignorance is bliss had run out on him when Meredith's business contacts turned up in Oxford. 'I'm afraid I can't say, but if you're his friend, perhaps now might be a good time to get back in touch.'

'Hmm, very cryptic, and it doesn't sound at all good. But I'll let you get on with your job. I hope I've been helpful?'

'Very. Thank you.'

Leo set the phone down and looked back at the equipment set out on the table. Meredith Price, the warm lady whom everyone instinctively liked (apart from Alexei, that was). A champion of reading, but unlike most librarians he'd met, she did this decked out in designer jewellery. Travelling salesperson for the school in Africa. He recalled her fondness for rings and Jess telling him Meredith had offered to show her some silversmithing techniques.

That was the missing element.

He went back out into the incident room. His phone buzzed. He gave it a quick glance. Message from Jess: *Fun Fact, Leo. Did you know . . .*

He gave an exasperated sigh. He usually enjoyed Jess's jokey messages but she obviously had missed the memo that he was in the crucial stage of his enquiry. Normally he'd open her messages immediately but he had to get this idea wrestled to the ground before he lost his train of thought. He pocketed the phone.

'Suyin, did you find any equipment for making silver jewellery at the house?'

The sergeant frowned and shook her head. 'No, but Mrs Price had lots of lovely pieces in her dressing table. I left them behind as I didn't think they were relevant.'

Which meant they'd missed something important. 'There was no workbench, no shed with supplies?'

'No.'

'Then we'd better get back there and ask her where she does her silversmithing.'

As he headed for the car, he began to see that his instinctive liking for Meredith Price had blinded him to her as a potential suspect. She, not Al, had known Chernov and Gulom best, she was the one who ran the diamond trade; she also was the one with access to a cross pein hammer. Leo suspected he might have arrested the wrong Price – or at least had only half the team sitting in the cells.

Chapter 40

Jess

'Meredith, what are you doing with a gun?' squawked Paul.

Meredith motioned us inside. 'Defending myself, of course. You'd both better come in.' I hesitated. 'That wasn't a suggestion.'

Paul shuffled forward, reluctantly crossing the threshold. I could see that he was struggling to compute such a strange departure from normal Oxford behaviour. 'You don't need to protect yourself from us. We came to see how you were and offer our help.'

Meredith waited for me to pass her then shut the door. 'Sit down, Paul.'

Meekly, Paul took a perch on the high stool that she used at the bench. I went to the right, drifting towards the window to look for another exit. The wall there had a large map of the world with different pins marking capitals and major cities. Threads ran between them, making a web of connections. Trade routes? Smuggling routes probably as some of the pins were in locations no normal person put on their holiday itinerary. Underneath the map, a pile of papers sat next to a shredder – that had been the machine we'd heard. Curls of paper had already gone through the blades, forming a heap in the waste collection.

Meredith noticed where my gaze was directed. 'It's a useless machine. Thought I'd be finished well before now. Gets too hot too quickly. I'll have to burn the rest.'

Paul still hadn't lifted his eyes from the gun, which was pointed at me. I didn't get the sense Meredith intended to shoot; she was just keeping us at bay while she took on board that her plans needed adjusting.

Did I play ignorant or try and get her to confess? No point in a confession if we didn't live to pass it on. Diversion and ignorance were my best gambit.

'Is that a real gun?' I said in my best 'I'm impressed' tone.

'It is. With real bullets too.' Meredith was patronising me but I could live with that if it meant I lived.

'You must need it with all the silver you've got in here – you must be worried thieves might try to steal it.' I offered her the benign explanation of why she felt it OK to hold us at gunpoint, hoping she'd take it.

'That's right!' Paul grasped at the excuse as he had at the Al-was-just-patrolling suggestion Jennifer had put forward. 'But we're here to help, Meredith. Why don't you put it away?'

'Put your phones on the bench first.' She gestured to the space by the vice.

There wasn't much choice. I put my crappy smart phone next to Paul's latest model. Meredith put the gun down, rather than away, and slipped the phones into a drawer. She locked it and pocketed the key.

'I'm so sorry about Al,' Paul said rather desperately. 'I'm sure it'll all be sorted out and he'll be back with you.'

'Really?' She swept the remaining papers into a holdall. 'I very much doubt that.'

'But Jess doesn't think he was the same person as broke into the red house.'

I hadn't said that – but I wasn't so stupid to mention that when the gun was still lying on the counter. 'I saw very little really.'

She unzipped the front pocket of a travel bag and I glimpsed a passport inside. She tucked her purse next to it. 'Do either of you helpful people drive?'

Paul shook his head. 'Never learned. Sorry. Are you going somewhere?'

She turned to me. 'What about you?'

'Sorry, no,' I lied.

She cursed – a very un-Meredith like action. But maybe this was the real woman? 'Then I'll take one of you with me. I need someone else in the car.' I didn't think this was because she wanted the company; she wanted a hostage. She looked between us. 'Jess, you'll come with me. And yes, we're leaving your phone behind. I don't want you calling your friend in the police.'

'But–'

'I'm not going to hurt you.' She picked up the gun again, her actions not giving me any confidence about that. But she just moved it further out of my reach so I couldn't make a grab for it. 'Paul, you'll have to stay here. Someone will come and find you sooner or later.'

'What?' Before Paul could object, she pulled out a long plastic cable tie, fastened it around his wrist, then fastened that to the work bench. She took a second tie and fastened his free hand to the stool. I have to admit: I was impressed by her efficiency at restraining him.

'Meredith!' Paul sounded scandalised. He really wasn't keeping up.

'She's making a run for it, Paul,' I told him, hoping he'd have enough braincells to tell the police this when Leo finally read my message. I was peeved he hadn't already been knocking on the door.

'No, she's not!'

'Jesus, this isn't pantomime, Paul. Meredith is cutting and running.'

'There's no more time to waste.' Meredith gestured to me. 'Carry my bags to the car. The gun will be under my coat but I promise you it will be aimed at your back all the way to the carpark.'

'OK, keep calm. I'm not going to do anything foolish.' Like make a dash for it and run screaming towards the gathered press outside her house. I hovered, tempted. But from the word 'carpark' I guessed she'd already moved her vehicle to Paul's house so she didn't have to run the gauntlet of the media at her gate.

I picked up the bags. They were incredibly heavy. 'What have you got in here? Rocks?'

Oh. Maybe that was exactly what a diamond smuggler would have?

'Get moving.' She nudged me out of the door, turned off the light, then closed and locked it behind me.

'That's a dick move, leaving him in the dark.' I struggled to carry the bags so I pulled up the little handles. 'You know they won't let you take this on as cabin baggage. Far too heavy.' I dragged the two bags along, making use of the roller wheels over the bumpy path. They kept veering out of alignment like Bambi's legs on the skating pond.

'You talk a lot.'

'My nicest characteristic. Cheerful and friendly. I'm the definition of upbeat.' If I were very annoying maybe she'd choose to dump me in the carpark? 'You know this is the second time I've been abducted this week. That has to be a record of some kind.'

She pressed a button and the boot opened on a Mercedes Benz parked in the shelter of the bin store. It was a shiny charcoal colour and looked brand new. I should've noticed the car before when it was parked outside their house. They may have had the house from Al Price's family, but a car like this showed they also had real money. Or at least Meredith did. How much had Al known about any of this, caught up as he was in his local battles? She probably encouraged his obsession to keep him busy while she got on with the real business.

'Put the bags inside.'

I hefted the bags up – no easy feat – not sorry that I scraped the paintwork at the back. She didn't seem to care – probably because she had already reconciled herself to the fact she was leaving the car – and her husband – behind.

'Now get in and sit facing away so that your hands are behind you.'

I didn't want to join the bags in the boot – having been

there, and done that . . . I sat on the rear seat and put my hands behind me. As I anticipated she got out another plastic tie and fastened them securely.

'Kick off your boots.'

She had to be kidding: my feet would freeze.

'Quickly!'

I toed off the boots. Come on, Leo. I was running out of time. At least she didn't make me take off my socks. Watching for any sudden movements from me, she lay the gun wrapped in the coat down on the ground and looped my ankles together. The plastic cut into the bony part of my ankle.

'That hurts!'

She was unimpressed. 'Now sit up.'

I did as commanded. She took seat belt across my chest and snapped it in. Then she pulled sharply on it so that it locked in place.

'You've abducted many people before?' I asked with cloying niceness.

'The diamond trade takes you to some rough places.'

I took that as a 'yes'.

I waited until she was in the driving seat. 'Killed anyone with that gun?'

'Not with this gun.'

I decided silence might be my best option.

'Here are the rules. You sit up and look straight ahead. You don't make any facial gestures or do anything to draw attention to yourself from other vehicles. I can see what you're doing in my mirror and I'll be watching you, OK?'

I said nothing.

'OK?'

'Not OK but I understand,' I hissed.

'Good. Now it's not far. This needn't turn into anything unpleasant if you just behave.'

Someone had told me something very similar in what now seemed like a very innocent abduction last Friday.

I comforted myself that Leo would eventually read my text and when I didn't respond, he'd at least come and check the workroom. He wouldn't want to leave it out of the search his team had made that morning. Paul would pass on the news that Meredith had taken me and we were heading for an airport. I could imagine squad cars racing us down the M40 and forcing her off the road before we reached Heathrow. I was thankful she'd put the belt on me in case this became a high-speed chase. I didn't want her to have too much time to regret keeping me alive, so I decided to keep her distracted.

Yeah, I know, silence. But I'm me: silence was never going to be a sustainable strategy.

'Is that gun Akmal Gulom's?'

She glanced at me in the mirror. 'It is. How did you know?'

'I think Mr Gulom shot Anatoly Chernov on the weekend of Fireworks Night. You had nothing to do with that.'

I could see from her expression that I'd finally impressed her. 'He did. Idiot.' She muttered the latter under her breath.

'Did you see him do it?'

'No, but I heard the shot. Gunfire is nothing like fireworks if you're used to hearing it.' And she grew up during Sierra Leone's civil war: of course, she knew what it would sound like.

'So you saw him burying the body from your upstairs

window?' I guessed. The same window that I'd noticed her peering down at the street from on many occasions.

'I did. Another stupid decision. The man was a fool. He spoiled everything with his feuds and his grudges. He wouldn't let anything go. Anatoly should never've invited him to live here.'

'He lost a daughter – and a business deal that mattered to him.'

She shrugged. 'People, unfortunately, die. Deals fall through.'

'When you saw him burying the body, did you tell Al?'

She glanced back at me. 'No, I didn't. I arranged to talk to Akmal directly at the studio – where we could be private and Al wouldn't interrupt us. I wanted to tell Akmal that he had to move the body. Ground burial is never reliable, especially in an urban garden. If it were found, questions would be asked.'

And their little cosy business dealings would be exposed.

'And did you tell him?'

'Yes, but he was planning to use the body to lure Alexei back to Oxford. He wanted it found. He didn't just want the father to die; he wanted to shoot the son. He'd quite lost it, I'm afraid, no sense of self-preservation.'

'You argued?'

'We did.'

'And then . . .?'

She sighed, slowing to join the bypass. She was taking an odd route for Heathrow. 'The argument became heated. He started waving the gun around, threatening me if I stopped him, so I hit him with one of my tools. Self-defence. Idiot even had a thin skull and went down like a fallen tree. He couldn't do anything right.'

'Leaving you with a dead body on your hands. So you put him where you thought Akmal should've put Anatoly, in the passageway, which your husband had told you was under the house.' It seemed unlikely she could've moved the body on her own. Al had probably got involved at this point but as she was probably telling me this is exonerate him, there was no need to anger her by suggesting it.

'It led to what had once been a chapel – like a crypt. I thought it would be respectful. He was a friend. I hadn't intended to kill him.'

Interesting definition of respectful – to be wrapped up in plastic and dumped with a headless White Rabbit.

'Why didn't you move the other body to join it?'

She shook her head slightly, either at the lorry that swung into her lane or at my suggestion. 'It was decided that it would be too risky.' In other words, Al had talked her out of it.

'But you sent your husband over to move the second body, didn't you, once Anatoly was found?'

'No.' A police car with flashing lights approached on the other side of the road – but carried on past us. She breathed a sigh of relief. 'That would only have drawn attention to it. I wanted Akmal to remain gone.'

'Then why did Al come into the house? He knew I was there.'

'He was going to move it further down the passageway and then collapse the ceiling to bury it.'

'Sounds bloody risky.'

She was a cool customer. 'Not really. He'd explored the passageway before with Akmal's blessing after he first moved in. Al knows everything about the buildings around there, even enjoys encouraging the mystery of the secret passage. The ceiling is just waiting to come down a little further on, thanks to all the digging up the utility companies have been doing putting in a new water main. It was propped up a few years ago to make it safe and all he needed to do was pull out the struts. He could do that with rope from the stairs.'

'But I disturbed him?'

'We thought you wouldn't hear up in the turret.'

'He broke a six-foot window.'

She huffed. 'He didn't know it would do that. He thought he could just cut out a circle by the handle to reach the lock. But it didn't go like that.'

Basically, he was an amateur who had watched too many heist films. I suspected that Meredith would've made a better job of it.

'Aren't you afraid I'll tell the police?'

'Oh, if you do, I'll deny that I told you anything. In fact, if the police ask, I'm telling you that the intruder was employed by the Chernovs – that Akmal died because Alexei killed him in revenge for his father.'

'The police don't think that.'

'It's not what anyone thinks, it is what can be proved. They have nothing on Al. I'm leaving because I'm scared of Alexei Chernov and the police are harassing my husband, exposing us to press intrusion. Once I'm gone – once there's no evidence that Al was involved in any of the deaths, they'll swing back to the most obvious suspect.'

'Alexei?'

She nodded. 'Akmal would be pleased. Alexei can pay secondhand for killing his daughter by being charged with killing him.'

'And everyone goes home happy,' I said sourly. I didn't think that would work while I was still breathing to bear witness to the true chain of events, which made me worry about my immediate future. 'Hey, we're not going to Heathrow.' I saw from a sign that we were heading north.

'I didn't say we were going to Heathrow.'

She took the filter lane leading to Oxford Airport, a small airstrip that was capable of taking private planes. I should have realised that she was too comfortable for someone about to go through high security at an international airport. Here she'd have the equivalent of a bloke in a hut munching on cheese sandwiches to check her documentation. She'd jump on board one of her family planes and be gone in ten minutes.

She pulled up at the far end of the public carpark then turned in her seat to look at me. The gun was in the cup holder between the seats. She picked it up.

'I've never killed anyone in cold blood,' she mused.

'No need to break that habit,' I said hurriedly.

She ejected the cartridge, checked the ammunition, then slotted it back in place. 'But you see, you know too much. We shouldn't have talked. Things haven't gone to plan.'

I opened my mouth, but couldn't think of anything appropriate to say. What came out was:

'But you're a librarian!'

Not what I had anticipated would be my last words before being shot in the back of a car belonging to a conflict diamond smuggler.

Chapter 41

Leo

The press were hovering outside the Prices' house. Suyin rang the bell but there was no answer.

'She's not in, mate,' called one of the newspaper reporters. 'Took off hours ago in the car with suitcases. Gone to stay with her mum probably.'

As her mother lived in Sierra Leone, Leo sincerely hoped not. 'Thanks.'

'What now?' asked his sergeant.

'Let's take this discussion somewhere else.' They returned to the car. 'You're sure there was no studio in the house – not in the attic or any of the outhouses?'

'Really sure, sir.'

Leo got out his phone. 'We need to talk to someone who knows them well. Head down the street and turn into that big house at the end.' He didn't have Paul Cook's contact number but he thought Jess might. Tapping on her last message to ask her, he finally read it. He swore.

'What's wrong, sir?'

'Meredith Price does have a studio – it's in the grounds of

this property. It sounds like Jess and Paul Cook were going to meet her in it. Pull up so that no one can get in or out of this parking area. Then follow me – but be careful. We don't want to spook Meredith. Let's keep it that we don't suspect her of anything.'

'Understood.'

They walked quietly but without trying to hide their approach.

'Which one is it?' asked Suyin as they passed four sheds.

'I'm guessing it is the one with the clean window.' Leo gestured to the one at the end of the row. 'She'd need good light to work.'

'But there's no light on inside.'

Leo checked his phone. Jess hadn't replied. She usually leapt on his texts and rattled off a message the instant she received one. This didn't feel good. He held up a hand to keep Suyin back.

'Let's call this in – put out an alert at all borders for Meredith Price and for the location of her car. I'll go as far as the window and see if I can see anything inside but it looks like we might be too late.'

Suyin backed off to get the alert activated. Leo crept forward, listening hard in case Meredith was waiting inside the shed with the lights off to surprise him. As he got closer, he heard a shout.

'Is anyone there? Help! I need help!'

Anticipating a trap, Leo went as far as the window and peered inside. Paul Cook sat on a stool, his arms at an awkward angle. He appeared to be the only one in the room.

The only part of the studio Leo couldn't see was directly below the window.

'Mr Cook, are you alone?'

'Yes, Inspector, but I'm tied up!'

Deciding he no longer needed caution, Leo tried the door. It was locked. He cast around and found a concrete cycle stand by one of the other sheds. Using that as a battering ram, he broke the door open and switched on the lights. Paul blinked owlishly at him.

'What happened?' asked Leo. 'Where's Jess?'

'With Meredith. I don't understand. She has a gun!'

'Meredith Price had a gun?' Leo knelt beside him and cut the ties with his pocketknife.

'Yes! She made me sit here and threatened me if I didn't let her tie me to the bench. Then she forced Jess to go with her to the airport. She said no one would get injured if we did what she said.'

'Which airport?'

'I don't know!' Paul wailed. 'She just said it wasn't far so I guess Heathrow?'

Leo stood up and made a quick survey of the studio. This had to be the real Meredith Price, the one who ran a little smuggling business on the side to keep herself amused. His eyes were drawn to the map. The threads leading the UK didn't appear to go to Gatwick or Heathrow. They landed a little to the left of centre.

Al Price, RAF, flying enthusiast. How had he met Meredith? What if she liked flying too?

'Does Meredith fly for a hobby?' Leo asked Paul.

'Both she and Al do. They have a little plane at Oxford Airport. I've even been up with them a couple of times. Oh, you think she's going there?'

'It would be a smart move on her part – get airborne before we even started looking for her. Mr Cook, stay here until my officers take your statement. I need to get to the airport.'

Paul stood up straight. 'Of course, Inspector. I'm shocked – shocked.'

Leo had the distinct impression that was going to be his refrain for a long time to come. He just had to hope and pray that Jess would be there to put up with it at work.

'Wait. Someone will be with you shortly.' He ran to the car.

Chapter 42

Jess

In the car, Meredith grimaced and lowered the gun. 'Change of plan, you're coming with me. The deal is that I tell the airport staff that you're a friend I'm taking to Portsmouth. It's your luggage. No border checks, no fuss. If you say a word, I'll shoot you. I can still get to the plane and get away before they realise what's happened so no tricks.'

Hunched in the backseat, I nodded. 'Got it. No tricks.' I was unspeakably relieved she couldn't quite make herself into someone who killed in cold blood.

She made some adjustments to her flight plan and submitted it electronically. 'That's done. Let's go.'

Leaning over, she cut the ties on my legs. I wriggled my feet back into my ankle-high wellies. She got out, went round to the rear and opened the boot to remove the two suitcases, stuffing the last few documents in the front pocket. Then she opened my door.

'Hands.'

I held them behind me and she sliced them free. I shook

them out to regain the feeling that had deadened thanks to the tight ties. She hesitated.

Please don't second-guess yourself, I prayed under my breath. Meredith liked to give the impression she was in control but obviously matters had slid off the downhill course and she was slaloming around random pine trees fearing a cliff edge ahead.

I had to get out of the car. It was much easier to shoot me discreetly while I was in the back. I slid across the seat and got out on the other side from her.

'Don't you dare run!' she warned.

'Wouldn't dream of it.' I walked around to the back of the car and pulled up the handles on the roller bags. 'I'm having so much fun.' Then louder. 'Ready when you are.'

Her face cleared of its scowl and she went back to non-killer librarian rather than the ruthless diamond dealer. 'All right then. Let's just take this calmly, like we're friends. You're going home for Christmas. I'm giving you a lift in the plane as my Christmas present to you as you've always wanted to fly.'

'I have always wanted to fly,' I agreed. Though not in these circumstances.

'If asked, say whatever you need to convince the staff of this story and I'll let you go when I reach my destination.'

'Understood.'

It was hot work wheeling both suitcases while bundled up in my red Puffa coat. Or maybe that was the brewing panic that could feel the barrel of the gun between my shoulder blades? I was acting calm but inside I was howling.

We arrived at a small terminal building. Meredith didn't

go in but handed her paperwork over to the man sitting in the glass cubicle.

'Nice to see you, Meredith,' he said cheerfully, checking what she'd written against the flight plan she'd submitted. 'Just a short hop then?'

'That's right. I'm taking my friend to Portsmouth. I'll be back tomorrow.'

He nodded and stamped a few pages. 'How's Al?'

She swallowed. 'He's good. I expect he'll be up here later in the week for the Friends of the Airport meeting.'

'Good, good. We rely on you both to keep us in business.' He passed the papers back. 'Have a safe flight.'

'Thank you,' said Meredith.

I managed a brief nod.

'The plane is in the hangar on the right,' she said loudly. 'Not far now.'

I set off trundling the suitcases. They seemed to make a hell of a lot of noise as they rumbled over the tarmac.

Meredith pressed a button on the wall and the hangar doors opened. A little white plane sat among much bigger corporate jets. It had been brought to the front though which suggested she'd already requested it to be prepped for the flight.

'You've got enough fuel?' I asked.

'Yes. The technicians checked it over for me. I have a few pre-flight checks to do, but don't worry, I know how to fly safely. Your job is to sit quietly and not distract me.'

I nodded. 'I understand.'

'Once we're underway, you realise your safety relies on me landing the plane?'

'A hundred per cent.'

'Then I won't need to tie you up again.'

'No, you won't,' I agreed.

She unlocked the cabin and activated the exterior stairs. I took one suitcase up, stowed it in the gap between one of the row of passenger seats and the next, then returned for the second while she kept watch. She followed me quickly once I had wrestled the final bag inside and closed the door.

'Sit there.' She gestured to the back row of seats, where I would be too far to reach her. 'Keep buckled in or I'll tie you up.'

Obediently I unzipped my coat and clicked the seatbelt closed. Meredith took the pilot chair, picked up a clipboard and ran through the flight checks, chatting with the tower as she did so. It was dark now but the runway was well lit. I couldn't see any other planes landing or taking off. There would be nothing to delay us.

Meredith started the plane taxiing. Then stopped. I couldn't hear the air traffic control end of the conversation, but her end was clear.

'But you'd cleared me for take-off!'

Blue lights flashed over beyond the terminal building. The police were massing. Meredith's scramble to get out of the country had been detected.

But we were on a plane – practically on the runway . . .

Meredith must've decided the same thing as she started the plane in motion again, turning it towards the head of the runway. Out of my cabin window I could see three cars – two squad cars and what I thought was Leo's BMW – splitting up as they tried to cut us off. Leo ignored the tarmac and drove straight across the grass, coming out on the runway. He spun the wheel and headed right at us. I wanted to scream at the idiot to get out of the way. He was going to hit us and in a plane versus car battle I couldn't imagine him getting the better of it. I could imagine a massive fireball as our fuel-filled plane exploded.

Just as I thought we were going to hit, Meredith wrenched the joystick to one side and took us off the runway. We bounced over rougher ground and came to a stop. One of the suitcases jiggled free and spilled papers over the floor. I leant forward and grabbed a handful, a plan forming. It wasn't much more refined than the hairdryer impulse but it might just help.

The emergency vehicles now surrounded us, leaving Meredith with little choice. She got up and pointed the gun at me. We were back at me being her hostage, were we?

'Up!'

I unfastened the seat belt and shuffled to the door, the clutch of papers hidden in the folds of my coat.

'You get out first.' She pressed the door release and the steps folded down. Her hand gripped my collar, the gun cold against the back of my head. 'Walk slowly forward and do as I say.'

I took a step.

Chapter 43

Leo

The comms were crackling with information as all the nearest squad cars headed for the airport. The airfield was close to the police HQ so it was likely others would get there before Leo.

'Do we have anyone at the airport yet?' he barked into the radio.

'Just pulling in now, sir. We can see a grey Mercedes matching the description parked in the visitors' carpark.'

'The suspect is armed and has a hostage. I repeat armed and possible hostage.' Adrenaline flooded his veins as he drove up the opposite carriageway on the Banbury Road, lights flashing, siren blaring. It was just past the peak of rush hour but many drivers weren't on the ball. He had to thread through the interchange at the Marston Ferry turn, undertaking some idiots who were still making their right despite his sirens. Buses pulled over for him as he screamed through Summertown. 'Can you see anyone inside the car?'

'The windows are dark, sir. The interior lights are off.'

He wanted to tell them to see if Jess was hurt but he had

to follow protocols. 'Hold your position. Wait for the armed officers to arrive.'

The radio fizzed again and another voice came on. 'Inspector George, I'm in touch with the air traffic controller at Oxford airport. He says that he'd given a small light aircraft permission to take off but when you sent out the message to hold all flights, he's got them on the taxiway. He's not sure if they're going to remain there as they've stopped talking to him.'

'What flight plan have they lodged?'

'Portsmouth.'

Where, no doubt, Meredith would fail to stop and continue across the channel to an airport where she had contacts. 'Get onto the Belgian and a French authorities and tell them who might be coming in if we can't stop her this end.'

'Yes, sir.'

He turned into the airport and saw a ring of squad cars surrounding the vehicle as ordered. On the airstrip there was only one plane on the taxiway, a white Cessna, or maybe a Beechcraft. Perfectly capable of making a short international flight. It began moving.

'Ask the airport to let me through the airfield gate. I'm coming in,' said Leo. If she'd hurt Jess, if Jess was onboard, he was not letting her get away if he could do anything to stop her.

The automatic gate hummed open on his approach. Two of the squad cars peeled off to follow him.

'We'll box her in,' said Leo. 'First car, go left. Second come in behind. I'm going to head right at her and try to get her to leave the taxiway.' In other words, play chicken with a desperate woman. He sped up, cutting corners by driving across the flat grass that she had been avoiding. The plane had almost reached the turn to the runway. She had to slow for that, giving Leo the fraction of a second he needed to cross to the runway and head straight towards her before she'd completed her turn. If she got enough momentum she could simply take off over him. This manoeuvre might end in an epic fail but maybe . . .

He could now see the pilot, staring wide-eyed through the cockpit window at him. That's right, lady, he wasn't going to stop. The plane sped up, and so did he. This wasn't going to be pretty.

Then at the last moment, she turned the plane and bumped onto the grass, losing momentum. She'd bottled it. Leo had to brake hard before he hit the fence at the end of the runway, but his colleagues had boxed her in by the time he'd done his one-eighty.

'Nice driving, sir,' said one of the patrolmen. 'You were leaving it very late to avoid a collision.'

He hadn't intended to avoid it, but they didn't need to know about that moment of recklessness.

'Any sign of the hostage?'

'No, sir.'

'But we know where the suspect is. Officers, move in and search the car.'

More vehicles arrived – a late showing by the airfield fire brigade, more police cars, including an armed response unit, and an ambulance. Leo stopped his car and got out. The white Cessna – he could now see the make – sat forlornly on the grass. What would Meredith do now? She had to know she was caught? It would all depend if she had any cards left to play?

The door opened and the stairs came down. Two women appeared in the exit, Jess in front, Meredith behind, holding a gun to her head.

Chapter 44

Jess

Leo was standing by his vehicle, facing us. Armed officers were hunkered down behind open car doors, using them for cover.

'Meredith, let Jess go and put down your weapon,' he shouted. 'You have to realise you can't escape now so it is in your interest not to escalate the situation.'

Meredith lifted the gun higher so it was more visible. It was now at a more awkward angle for her to hold. The breeze blew directly in our face, making my open coat flap and the papers rustle, but fortunately she didn't notice. 'No, you listen to me. You remove your vehicles and clear the runway. Jess will come to no harm if you let us leave.'

'But there's nowhere you can run to. Your plane can make it as far as continental Europe but you'd be tracked and arrested as soon as you touch down there. We have extradition agreements with every country you can reach in a plane of that size. What would you achieve except adding kidnapping to the existing charges?'

'You're not listening, Inspector. Back off – take your armed officers with you – let us leave.'

Stalemate. I had no desire to repeat this scene at some French airport as she demanded refuelling or whatever was her long-term aim for this escape. Time for Operation End of Alice. I threw up the handful of papers I'd grabbed, then slid out of my Puffa jacket, leaving her holding an empty coat. The pages fluttered right into her face, she reflexively pulled the trigger and I felt a hot pain on my right ear and deafened by the shot even as I threw myself down the stairs. Winded, I looked up to see shocked faces, Leo's in particular. Rather than run to him, I rolled under the stairs and under the fuselage, making me an impossible target.

I clapped my hand to my ringing ear. It was hot, wet and hurting and the top of my ear felt distinctly jagged.

'Officer Kent, move in with me!' Leo ordered. 'Get to the hostage!'

Above me, a door slammed and the plane began taxiing again. My brilliant hiding place now looked like a very good way to get run over. I was most worried about the propeller at the front, but fortunately Meredith was heading to the biggest of the gaps between vehicles immediately in front of her, rather than reversing to mince me up. The plane cleared me, leaving me beached on the grass. I was immediately scooped up and hugged by Leo. He hefted me from the ground.

'She's been hit,' he called, as he ran with me in his arms over to an ambulance. I wanted to blurt out that my ear did not affect my legs, but then decided I'd let him do this. He didn't seem that interested in what happened next to the plane now

I was safe, but I heard a scrape as the wing just passed over the top of one of the police cars taking the vehicle's radio antennae with it. She bumped back to the runway and accelerated.

I clung to Leo's neck as he lowered me to the stretcher. 'Aren't you going to shoot?'

'And risk that thing going up in flames? No. I wasn't lying when I said she'd not get far.'

I now saw some of the pages I'd used to distract Meredith with were blowing around the airfield. 'You might want to get your guys to collect those. They're evidence.'

He grinned at me and kissed me hard. 'You can't be hurt too bad if you're thinking so many steps ahead.'

I tilted my head where the paramedic was swabbing at the injury. 'Do I have an ear left or is one side gone elf?'

He shook his head. 'Just nicked.'

'Ears bleed like a bitch,' said the paramedic cheerfully.

'I think I'm deaf that side.'

'To be expected. That'll fade. Think of it like going to a heavy metal concert on one side of your head.'

I now noticed the man's tattoos of Iron Maiden so I could imagine he was speaking from experience. 'How long?'

'Couple of days. Your hearing should come back.'

The change in the engine noise alerted me to the plane lifting up and heading out west. She then banked and turned the plane south until it became just another blinking light in the busy night sky.

Leo returned from giving orders for the papers to be collected and tucked the blanket around me. 'You've knocked years off my life.'

'Did you like Operation End of Alice?' I accepted the plastic cup of tea a police officer passed me.

'What?' Leo looked puzzled.

'Well, earlier I was kicking myself that I'd not learned my Alice lessons well enough. I live in a house devoted to the book after all. I should've realised it wasn't about the men we suspected. It was always about the Queen of Hearts – or Diamonds in her case. She's the one everyone is terrified of, the one pulling the strings behind the events. Alice escapes by throwing the cards in her face, so I thought I'd do something similar. Then jump out of range before she could see me.' I warmed to my theme as I sipped the tea.

Leo sat beside me and stole a sip from my cup. 'Do you always decide your course of action from classic children's books?'

I mock-scowled at his impertinence for taking my drink. 'Not normally. Must just be this season's theme.'

And we sat side by side for a moment, watching the policemen scurry like the soldiers from the Queen of Heart's court as they collected in the pages. It is harder than you think to capture an A4 paper as it whirls and twirls in the wind.

'Such a curious dream,' I murmured and rested against him.

Chapter 45

Leo

It was midnight and the Cessna hadn't arrived at any of the airports they'd alerted in France and Belgium within a reasonable timeframe. Leo began to wonder if Meredith had outwitted them all by not leaving the country and instead landing somewhere unexpected, a disused airfield on the south coast for example. The radar had tracked her as far as the Isle of Wight but then she'd got too low. Had she turned round?

He looked up as breaking news started to cross the bottom of the BBC News Channel.

'Reports are coming in of a small aircraft accident in the Channel,' announced the news anchor. 'The captain of the late night crossing from Portsmouth to Le Havre saw a white plane ditch into the sea and alerted the coastguard. There is as yet no word on whether there are any survivors. A search will resume at first light.'

His colleagues also still in the incident room turned to him.

'Do you think she went kamikaze on us?' said Harry with his usual sensitivity.

'I think that is very possible.' They'd been about to release Al Price as bail had been arranged. He now had to break this news to him. 'I'd better inform the husband. No one is to tell the press. I want this news locked down until we get confirmation. I don't want her slipping past us as we give up on looking prematurely.'

He turned to Suyin. 'Tell the custody officer to bring Al Price up to an interview room. Under the circumstances, I think we can arrange for him to have a lift home.'

While that was being done, Leo put in a call to Andrew Lees, hoping the man would not have his phone on silent.

'Who's calling?' Still on duty then.

'Colonel Lees, it's Inspector George. I think your friend will need you tonight if you are available to come to the station?' He passed him the address.

'You can't tell me what this is about?'

'No, sir.'

'But it's bad?'

'Yes, sir.'

'On my way.'

It was the worst aspect of his job, telling someone that their life was over because the person they cared about most in the world was gone. There was no sense of just deserts, no sense of vindication, as he informed Al Price that his wife had abducted an innocent bystander then fled in their plane. No happiness in saying that the same aircraft was feared to have been lost over the Channel.

'I don't believe you!' said Price, his officer's stiff upper lip still slammed in place.

'We're awaiting confirmation,' Leo told him. 'In the meantime, we're releasing you on bail. I've arranged for a friend to collect you.' Because his wife had abandoned him to face the music alone. 'Colonel Lees?'

On that signal, the colonel came in and held out his hands. 'Good God, Al, this is a terrible mess!' Al swayed and collapsed forward. Lees moved quickly and clasped the man to his chest and let him sag there. 'I'll take it from here, Inspector.'

Nothing more painful than seeing a proud man crack and cry. Leo left the two friends to the difficult business of shoring up a collapse.

Leo didn't have time to see much of Jess over the next few days as sorting out the tangled crimes took up all his time. He didn't even go to interview her at the red house as he thought his personal relationship with her might prejudice that statement. Reading over the transcript, Jess had provided many of the missing pieces. From Meredith's confession to Jess, Gulom had shot Chernov, and Meredith killed Gulom. Whether it had been self-defence or she had struck out in anger would now never be tested in court. Al Price had admitted to the break-in but not to knowing there was a body in the basement. It was up to the CPS to decide if they wanted to charge him with secondary liability for the murder or manslaughter in assisting his wife to cover it up. He'd also claimed that she was the one who removed the documents on the petition from the home office on the same night she hid the body there. There was no trace of these papers and no forensic evidence that he'd been the one to do that deed so again that would be up to the CPS to pursue. Leo's impression was that they'd go for the low hanging fruit of breaking and entering and not try to prove a crime where the main perpetrator was likely dead. Perhaps the scales of justice had been balanced? The man's reputation was destroyed, he was putting his house up for sale and leaving the area. That was a cruel punishment for a man who'd devoted himself to his small world of North Oxford.

As for Alexei Chernov and the accident, when Leo chased up the investigation on this, he found his colleagues had been warned off. The charges had been reduced to being too young to act as a qualified driver in a car in which a learner is practising. In other words, a slap on the wrist. Mutterings about 'university funding' and 'important donor' had been heard in government circles, filtered down to the Thames Valley top brass and ended up with this damp squib of a resolution.

Again, Leo couldn't find it in his heart to protest. The young man had been punished by losing the girl he loved – and later his father. There was no prison sentence that could match that.

To pay his respects to the families involved, Leo attended the funeral of Anatoly Chernov. His body had already been cremated, but there was a remembrance service at the Russian Orthodox Church on Canterbury Road, not far from Chernov's house. A small circular modern building, it was packed with the Russian community He stood at the back as the impressive patriarch read the funeral service. Alexei sat with his mother and sisters at the front, Smirnov in the row behind.

It took Leo a moment to realise that between the two girls was a young man. Rashid Gulom was sitting with the family, his hand clenched tightly in the fist of the youngest daughter. Leo took it as a sign that the feuds of the older generation had not been passed down to the younger. That love can outlast hate.

As the mourners filed out past the family at the door, Leo joined them.

'Inspector, thank you for coming,' said Alexei, his face as hard to read as ever. Jess had claimed he was the Cheshire Cat in the little drama which had played out, creepy in how cryptic he appeared. 'We appreciate the work you've done to solve our father's murder.'

'I would like to have done more.'

'But that was taken out of your hands. The family isn't dissatisfied with the outcome.'

True. Meredith brought a severe penalty on herself. Had she done it on purpose, knowing there was no escape? He rather thought she had. 'Will you be staying in Oxford much longer?'

'A few more weeks. Rashid and we have decided to set up a graduate scheme in honour of our fathers – to get something good out of something terrible. The Chernov Centre is buying our house and the red house to use as accommodation. I've been told that a new college devoted to artificial intelligence would be looked on favourably by the council and the university.'

And the North Oxford Protection Society had been gutted so there was no local opposition to be expected.

'That's a good way to remember what had once been a friendship,' Leo said diplomatically. 'By the way, Alexei, I do have one question. What did you say to Meredith Price that upset her so much? They told me you made racist remarks.'

Alexei shook his head. 'I'm not a racist but I hated her. I knew she was leading my father into bad business decisions, her and her family. Our main business was never in that kind of dealing – conflict diamonds are small beer and not worth the risks. I think he got sucked in by the romance of it. People lose their heads over gemstones. I told him this – and I told her this. She got her own back by claiming I was attacking her family because I was prejudiced.' He shrugged. 'It blew over as my tutor thought it a matter for my father to handle as the argument happened off school grounds. She couldn't afford to keep protesting as I knew what she was doing.'

'And yet you didn't tell us?'

Alexei gave Leo one of his Cheshire Cat smiles. 'If you'd excuse me, Inspector, I have to speak to the holy father.'

Leo moved on. He had the distinct impression that the UK authorities would never manage to land a blow on Alexei after today. His sponsorship of one of the elite research institutes had guaranteed a lot of looking in another direction. But it wouldn't stop Leo keeping a close eye on the development of the new Chernov College of Artificial Intelligence. Or was he the only one wondering, post the Russian hacking of elections in 2016, if it were a good idea to give a Russian citizen the keys to such an influential kingdom?

Chapter 46

Jess

Christmas Eve arrived and my scheme to decorate the college chapel was about to face the judgement of my colleagues, and the nation thanks to the BBC. The technicians had set up the day before and said they were pleased with it even before I'd put the finishing touches, so I was feeling fairly confident. At least thirty per cent confident. My nails were a chewed mess. I'd insisted Leo only see it when I'd got the last sprig in place. I know he was worried I'd misjudged my audience and I'd been stoking his fears by leaving the most garish catalogues of illuminations lying around on my kitchen table. He didn't have much faith in me as a result – and I was beginning to wonder if maybe I'd been a little too fanciful . . .?

We were cutting it fine to finish up and the congregation were already arriving. Errol's home church choir, dressed in blue and gold, billowed in with a wonderful ripple of 'Alleluia' and 'Praise the Lord' when they saw the decorations. His mother swamped me in her embrace. They were happy. Let's hope the Master of the college shared their taste.

I helped Marigold sweep up the needles that had fallen from the last delivery of Christmas trees. She'd been my chief co-conspirator.

'What do you think, Marigold?'

She gave me a nod. 'I don't think you could do anything more without spoiling it.'

'Don't forget, I've reserved you a seat.'

'I'll just get rid of this last load then and I'll be back.' She walked off with her wheelbarrow.

Two arms squeezed me from behind. I gave a squeal and turned. 'Leo! You came early!'

'No, Jess, you're running late,' he said with a grin.

Whatever. I was finished now. I swivelled so my back was to him and looked at the view he was taking in for the first time.

'Do you like it?'

'I'm . . . speechless.'

Between Marigold and me, we'd transformed the ante-chapel into a winter wonderland, a slice of Narnia or any children's fantasy of magical snowy landscapes and pine trees. There were two focal points at either end of the display: a much larger Christmas tree than originally ordered, festooned with lights and handmade fabric ornaments. These had been crafted by Jennifer's designer son and depicted characters from all of the children's classics that had come out of Oxford. In addition to the *Alice in Wonderland* cast, there were hobbits and dragons, lions and fauns, witches and wardrobes, moving castles, subtle knives and amber spyglasses. My suggestion of a dog with a garden fork through it had been vetoed on the grounds of distressing the children, but we did get a splendid dog *before* the curious incident instead.

At the other end, against a backdrop of evergreen trees, was the Victorian stable surrounded by the refugee artworks. The theme that connected the two was written in patchwork bunting: children in strange lands. All the great characters from Oxford children's fantasy were refugees, having to leave the Shire, or the professor's house, or their known world for another. The nativity story was also a series of flights – the journey to Bethlehem as a result of a decree a certain Governor of Syria oversaw, and then the flight to Egypt.

And how could I afford this handmade display of new ornaments, strings of lights and forest of trees supplied by Marigold Green? A little sign just in the entrance gave the answer:

St Nicholas' College would like to thank the local law firm of Smirnov and Baskin for their generous sponsorship of this year's Christmas display.

That had been the price of my silence, and I'd enjoyed every second of extracting it from Smirnov. I'd even set the BBC editor onto him so he had to go on record about how much he loved working with me to create this fantasy land.

Revenge is sweet, especially when served mulled-wine-hot with a sprig of holly on the top.

Paul came in with the Master, sign that the VIPs were

all arriving. Paul met my eyes and nodded. We'd had an odd relationship since our shared trauma and there were no more threats of having my job cut from under me. Indeed, he'd actually given me the last word on a number of occasions.

'Master, this is Jess Bridges. She is the staff member who came up with the display,' said Paul.

'Under Paul's management, of course.' I too could hold up my end of the olive branch.

The Master gave me a regal nod. 'Wonderful work. My grandchildren will be thrilled to see it when they come tomorrow.'

I squeezed Leo's hand. The stamp of approval! 'That was the idea: I wanted to give pleasure to the children at Christmas and remind us all of those who don't have a home at this time.'

He smiled and moved on.

Then Fresh arrived with his publicity team, the rap star who was sponsoring Errol. He started to take social media photos, arms crossed in a cool scowl by the tree and crib, which I think meant he loved it.

'Let's sit down before I fall down,' I admitted to Leo. 'Michael, Cory and the kids are saving seats for us in the choir.' I began leading the way. 'Not in *the* choir obviously – you don't have to sing – but in the bit called the choir.'

'That's good. My choirboy days are long over,' murmured Leo.

'Oh, do show me tonight – and tomorrow,' I whispered.

'Down, girl.'

'If you insist – but later.'

I think I made him blush but he was able to hide it by scooting along to his seat.

'You did a marvellous job,' said Cory. 'I knew you would.'

'It is amazing the number of people who discovered they just had to help out in the end,' I said with satisfaction. I turned to the kids. 'Excited for Santa?'

They grinned at me and began telling me at the same time just how excited they were, bouncing in their seats.

Cory rolled her eyes. 'Trust you to wind them up.'

Michael leaned over to the children. 'If you both keep very quiet now, I'll let you have first go in my chair tomorrow.'

They sat back, lips clamped closed.

Cory whispered to me. 'I bought him an Apollo 11 rocket launch video as a Christmas present and space suits for the kids as their present from him. I might've let them know as a bribe. They can't wait to try it out.'

'Good psychology,' I admitted. 'You're spending Christmas together?'

'I couldn't let him be alone, could I? Brendan is coming too with his girlfriend. Should be interesting.'

I patted her hand, but any comment was lost in the rumble of the congregation getting to their feet for the first hymn.

Everything was going beautifully – both choirs soul-wrenchingly wonderful, the readings well delivered. With Leo beside me, my friends around me, I felt even Quirinius could not defeat me. I was not going to mar the atmosphere by tripping over my words.

'And now for the sixth lesson,' announced Sanyu.

I slid off my jacket to reveal my reindeer Christmas jumper. Taking out my sparkling antlers and putting them on carefully around my ear bandage, I approached the lectern and smiled at the camera.

'In those days, Caesar Augustus issued a decree . . .'

THE END